Marching Home

by
Donald Honig

ST. MARTIN'S PRESS
NEW YORK

Acknowledgment

This book was written, in part, with the support of the Connecticut Commission on the Arts through the Connecticut Foundation for the Arts.

Library of Congress Cataloging in Publication Data

Honig, Donald.
  Marching home.

   1. United States—History—Civil War, 1861-1865—Fiction. I. Title.
PZ4.H773Mar   [PS3558.05]   813'.5'4   79-22771 ISBN 0-312-51443-3

Marching Home

By DONALD HONIG

FICTION

Sidewalk Caesar
Walk Like a Man
No Song to Sing
Divide the Night
Judgment Night
The Love Thief
The Severith Style
Illusions
I Should Have Sold Petunias
The Last Great Season
Marching Home

NONFICTION

Baseball When the Grass Was Real
Baseball Between the Lines
The Man in the Dugout
The October Heroes
The Image of Their Greatness (With Lawrence S. Ritter)

EDITOR

Blue and Gray: Great Writings of the Civil War
The Short Stories of Stephen Crane

For my mother

One

THIS TIME THE WOODS frightened Susan. It was frightening because this band of surly men had invaded her sylvan realm of gossamer memories and touchable sky, all of it cached with intimate and tender secrets. The men were splitting the brier and plunging through plumed gateways, their sizzling pine torches throwing baleful shadows high into the unleaved elms and maples, which had only lately shed their whited trimmings.

"You're out here too, are you?" one of the men said to her dispassionately. His torch, held aloft, cast a roseate blush upon her cheeks. "You ought to be home."

"I want to know what happened to him," she said.

The man grunted. He doesn't care, Susan thought. None of them did. They were thrashing about in the night-locked woodland because they were being paid to do it, to find Ben, declare him dead or alive and then return to their taverns, to their whiskey, to their talk of crops and stock and weather, and their rough-hewn opinions about what Southern shells falling on that fort in Charleston Harbor meant.

Then they broke free of the woods and headed across

the rock-strewn meadow, nearly twenty men, like a pagan procession with their torches burning the cool April night, the lurid glares weaving upon their stolid faces, their beards, their round-crowned hats. One, unknown to her, looked like death itself, shuffling at the fringes of the group, staying always just outside the torchlight; wearing a black coat with the collar raised and a black hat pulled forward so that his face was hidden, keeping to himself, lone, faceless, like a shaft of night given legs and motion.

She was out there because if they found Ben's body, someone had to care. They would not; they would simply haul it back to town, minds diverted by thoughts of ale and whiskey, and leave it somewhere on a table in a dark room. Desecration by callousness, by indifference. She could not tolerate the idea.

Only Hook, of them all, seemed detached from the grimly ceremonial aspects of the search. Only this strange man seemed a nonparticipant; he who was the youth's guardian, who had brought Ben here to Capstone fifteen years ago (at the same time ending his own unexplained ten-year absence from the Long Island community of his birth and rearing)—only he, whose heart was the most involved, moved through the night with aloofness, like a spectator of great sophistication. He was walking just ahead of her, wearing his customary derby, his customary suit of fine broadcloth, carrying his walking stick, moving with the same dignity and aplomb as though he were a meditating scholar crossing a common. Alone and impervious as ever.

She watched him morosely, then pulled her shawl more tightly around her head and shoulders, bit her underlip for a moment and then moved abreast of him.

"Mr. Hook," she said.

He made no acknowledgment.

She whispered, "Do you really think he's gone and done it?"

The man said nothing. Short but thickset, bull-necked,

with a brief V-shaped beard trimmed with utmost care, he remained fathoms deep in that reserve which was either profound or self-protective or simply perverse—no one could ever be quite sure—and which was virtually impenetrable when he so willed. It was he who had found the note pinned to Ben's pillow that afternoon: *Suicide is not confession but accusation,* written in the fine, almost feminine script that sometimes seemed so incongruous, as though there were mockery in it or in the hand that shaped it, or even some elaborate deception for the eye that read it; as if to say: Nothing is what it seems to be; as if to say, If the hand is a lie, what of the words themselves? Hook sat with the note in his hand for almost an hour, brooding. Then he went to the Dooley House, to the crowded bar there, and asked if any had seen Ben. None had. So he made a rare statement and told them. Word spread and at dusk the search began.

"I saw him only yesterday," Susan said, "and he gave no sign of . . . "

"It might be a prank," Hook said. "It would not be unlike him."

The men were heading for the swamp now, a place that Ben had always loathed. In the beginning, when they were children, he had been wary of this place. He had been afraid of the dead spongy expanse where ugly stalks grew through the stagnant water and snakes spun away like the ends of whips and thick green flies buzzed with enmity. But because he was afraid, because of the torpid pervasion of something corrupt and soul-sucking, he went there, to dare it; went there and brought Susan, as if to taste his fears in the presence of someone, pressing yielding ground with his foot, pushing down until the brownish water oozed forth and pooled under his bare foot. That was when he was seven or eight years old. When he grew older, his conquered fear changed to hatred and he would offer somber opinions about and judgments upon the place: because it would neither live nor die, the swamp was evil and malicious, its stagnation an indestructible threat and taunt and snare. Because it was the most repelling place he knew, she felt that if he had wanted to do something that was in violation of both Scripture and reason, he would have gone to this bled-out tract to do it, to defy the laws of man and God from a place already gone to damnation. So it was she who suggested they search the area of the swamp, and because they no longer knew where to look, the men were heading there now.

As they crossed the meadow, a horse came galloping toward them, sudden and imperious. The men stopped as the rider rode into the flaring torchlight and reined in so abruptly the huge black charger reared for a moment on its hind legs, white teeth snarling around its bit.

"Have you found anything?" Eva asked.

"No ma'am," she was told.

"You must keep looking," she said. She was wearing a long black cape, the hood thrown back from her loose, titian-colored hair. She sat still for a moment, panting, her eyes in the torchlight angry and impatient. The men watched her.

I should be grateful, Susan thought, looking up at the young woman who was her own age but whose voice possessed an arrogant authority beyond any she had ever heard, from man or woman.

"Keep looking," Eva said to the faces watching her expressionlessly through the torchlight. "There will be money waiting for you all at the Dooley House." Then she snapped at the reins and the horse wheeled—even the animal seemed possessed of that arrogance, that almost contemptuous brusqueness—and she galloped away, back into the night, jouncing lightly in the saddle, her hood tossing rhythmically against her shoulders.

The men waited deferentially, until she was out of sight, before they resumed walking. I should be grateful, Susan thought again, almost in self-reproach. No one else could have gotten the men out to search like this. But so what if Eva was standing the money? She had enough of it, or her father did anyway. I wonder what her father will think of her being out here like that with all the ragtag and bobtail, tearing around on her horse at night because some farm boy left a suicide note (and not just any farm boy, but *that* one, the one her father knew all about). But Eva would contrive a story. Girls like that, Susan thought sulkily, were skilled at contriving because otherwise how did they always manage to have their way? And she did have a talent for having her way, for having her wants and desires maintain a constant and undeviating inward course toward her. Everybody seems to have some sort of talent, she thought, pulling her shawl around her. Eva's was for getting what she wanted; Ben's was for writing those delicately beautiful lines of poetry, which he would only infrequently show to her (there were two levels to the mood, it seemed: the desire to write the poetry and then the impulse to show it). And what's my talent? she thought. Patience? Or was that a virtue? Maybe. But it seemed to her that too much of it could turn virtuous into foolish.

It's none of my doing, Ben said. She insinuates herself on me. Waits for me on the road, rides her horse across the fields when I'm working, finds me in the woods. It's like she's got her spyglass on me all the time. I know I can chase her off—you don't have to tell me that. No, I'm not being petulant about it; that's just the sound of my voice. No, I'm not playing her because she's rich. Listen, she may be rich but she's lonely and unhappy, too, living in that big house with just her father and the battalion of servants. You can laugh. But you can be rich and beautiful and unhappy, too, just like anybody else. What? Oh. I did? I said she was beautiful?

I know he's not tied to her, Susan was thinking. But she is so rich, and she dresses like nobody else, and she knows how to influence a man—isn't that what they teach them at those schools where the teachers wear lace cuffs and perfume their hair and talk with a little bit of Paris in their voices? It made a difference, to have had the benefit of that, of having infused into your education the suggestion that you were select, better. But all the same, she still didn't know her man.

There was proof positive of that only a few weeks ago, that she didn't know her man. Oh yes, she could be friendly enough when she was alone with him—maybe even friendly enough, as she had overheard a man say in her father's tavern one night, to slide down those frilly white bloomers for him. The remark made Susan furious, and that night she had been subjected to a dream of Ben looking at Eva's firm white backside, deep in the woods. Ben's smile was sly and ambiguous the next day when, after summoning her courage, Susan confronted him with the content of her dream, as though it were somehow aligned with fact. Describe everything to me in utter detail, he said, and had then been quick enough to stop her hand in midair before the blow could fall.

But Eva didn't know her man, and that gave Susan a measure of mordant satisfaction. Yes, she could be friendly enough when she was alone with him, but when she was walking with her father along the board sidewalks on Grant Avenue, she ignored him. Not just ignored him but did not even respond to his greeting. She should have known better. Any girl who had once looked into those dark, restive eyes with their implication of no soundable depth or temperate emotion, that seemed burdened by the outcries of ancestral torture—any girl, any person, once given that view, that caution, should have known thereafter that you made no sudden noises near the ground upon which this creature stood, that banal ploys or foolery were sparks falling near gunpowder.

I knew that without benefit of private tutors and lacy New England schools, Susan thought. Or maybe that kind of education made you insensitive to the feelings of other people, made you incapable of deemphasizing your own self-importance. Whatever it was, Eva had made a mistake, and not even the forbidding presence of her father was going to let her get away with it.

She ignored his greeting. He called out to her. But Eva and her father kept walking, like a pair of statues charged with mobile powers only and none of any sensory nature. He began to follow them, his boot heels sounding like blows on the boardwalk, and the loungers straightened up to watch, as they always watched this boy anyway. You don't want to say hello? he demanded. Are you afraid it will put a canker on your lips? Then LeGrange, Daniel LeGrange himself, stopped and spun his shoulders, whiskered face furious, eyes smoldering with indignation. How dare you address my daughter? And Ben: Ask her if she has never kissed me. (Dear God, but he wants sense, Susan thought when she heard about it later. Of all things to say, whether it was true or not. Dear God, the more I understand him, the further away he slips.) LeGrange erupted and struck with his stick, a heavy length of mahogany purchased across the river in Manhattan. But none of that—the carved stick or its impressive cost or the silk-lined box it had come packed in—did any good, because Ben was quicker and because LeGrange, money or not, manor house or not, servants and horses and Concord coach or not, was in this instance a fool. He was simply a man accustomed to utter deference and obeisance, to tongues on the insteps of his boots, waving his magic wand at something and having reality intervene with devastating logic. LeGrange missed. He had not really swung hard enough or fast enough, probably thinking that the magic electrifying the air at the lifting of the wand would be enough. But it was a day of misjudgments for the family, and he missed. He had swung hard enough, though, to leave himself off balance, and the next thing he knew the stick had been wrested from his hand and his high-crowned hat swatted from his head and his next aggressive move—an angry step forward—arrested by the tip of the stick pressed hard to his chest. The rest of it lay imminent in Ben's eyes; but it was canceled by LeGrange's common sense. So there was no rest of it, for the moment. LeGrange took his daughter's arm and, with exquisitely poised outrage, went away, leaving the hat lying upside down in the street 'and the stick in Ben's possession. Ben laid the stick down in the street next to the hat and went away. The objects lay there for hours—no one went near them—until around dusk, when one of LeGrange's men rode into town, picked them up and rode out again.

The rest of it occurred two nights later in the bar in the Dooley House. Ben was there drinking when three of LeGrange's men came in and went directly for him. No one dared move in on it because the men were who they were and everyone knew it had to happen anyway, it was inevitable; so let it happen in the light where at least they could prevent a murder. The three knew they were in a fight. But they were three and he was one. When Dooley finally came around from behind the bar to end it, Ben was slumped against the wall, blood running from his mouth and nose, his fists still clenched. He had knocked one of the three unconscious and when it was over the other two carried their comrade out, but not before one turned and said, Compliments of the young lady.

So she did it to you, Susan said. She was applying hot compresses to his face, tenderly, as a woman in love would. And nobody cared, nobody helped, she said. No, he said tonelessly, nobody cared.

Except Hook. When he heard what happened, Hook had moved with furious suddenness and taken his pistol and started for the door, but Ben stopped him. Who are you going to shoot? he asked. The girl? Both, Hook said. No, Ben said. His hand was on the older man's arm, his eyes were steady and entreating, and, oddly, a faint smile was on his lips. Dissuaded, Hook turned around, climbed the stairs to his room and disappeared behind a slammed door.

She did this to you, Susan said, dabbing with a damp

cloth at the cuts on his face. Your great admirer. Her dignity was offended, Ben said. She has no dignity, Susan said irritably. But she does, he said. Don't you see? He lapsed into quiet, a vague preoccupation in his eyes. Now you'll keep away from her, Susan said. Stop smiling, she said angrily. It isn't funny.

He disappeared the next day. She had expected it. It was not the first time. She never knew where he went or what he did when he was engulfed by these moods, though it was probably nowhere and nothing, in the sense that he merely mounted his horse at dawn and rode until tired and then slept wherever he was, on some quiet Long Island lane, or in someone's barn, with permission or not, or under the open boughs of trees or beneath the stars themselves, perhaps meditating his complex aloneness. She would think constantly of him, and in her mind he was always riding at great speed across a starkly dramatic landscape into threatening skies, in flight from that which was lodged in his own heart; and if it rained she would stand at her window and watch it pour into the ground, knowing that somewhere it was falling upon him who was riding alone through strange places.

He reappeared one evening three days later, with fresh cuts and bruises on his face. It happened in a tavern out on the Island, he said. Some farmers. Did you start it? she asked. Yes, he said. So she understood the reason for this particular disappearance: he had needed to release what the beating at the Dooley House had wrought in him. Not wanting to do it in Capstone, he had ridden off somewhere and found strangers and tangled with them; apparently he got the worst of it, but he seemed unbothered by it, because there had been a different quality to the blows he had taken. He was eased, relaxed. But she was frightened, because the teeth marks on his knuckles showed how hard he had hit someone. But now, she said, you'll keep away from her, won't you? I was riding with her this morning, he said.

The torch flared suddenly over her head and streaked through the air, its blazing wings of fire falling into the stagnant green slime, where it was sucked into extinction.

"Well, he's not here, either," said the man ' who had thrown it.

They gathered at the edge of the swamp. The burning torches cast a diabolic saffron gleam over the inert, sullen water.

"He might be underneath," one said.

"A body would rise."

"Not always."

"Why would he come here to do it anyway?"

The voices were petulant, impatient.

"She says to keep looking."

"Well, where?"

"He could have blown his damned brains anywhere."

"What's she so interested for anyway?"

"As long as she's paying out, she can be interested."

"Well, we've done all we can."

"He'll turn up somewhere. You can't hide something like that, not with summer coming. It'll smarten the air someplace and then we'll know."

They were turning back now. Susan watched more torches thrown, heard the swamp hissing like some submerged, pestilent beast.

She saw Hook drift off by himself, alone into the dark, like a flamen whose deity has vanished. She wanted to join him, talk to him. But she didn't, because she knew he would not allow it. He would return to the old, rather ramshackle house that stood at the edge of the modest farm he had taken over (but never worked with his own hands) after his sister's death, and he would sit in his upstairs room and that would be the only light in the house. There was something else that forbade her joining him, something that she admitted guardedly to herself: she was afraid of him. She would no more have walked through these black woods with him than she would with the devil.

She went alone, circumventing the woods. From the distance she could see the men going through the trees, a few torches still burning like huge fireflies. She drew the shawl more tightly around herself. It was dark, from the damp April earth to the chilly April sky, nothing but a loom of unbroken darkness hung from heaven to earth. She walked on a narrow cow path, past a low stone wall beyond which the cricketing fields spread back into the night.

Then she noted a curious silence. The crickets had stopped. It gave her an odd, chill feeling. She paused, looking up at the trees, squinting to distinguish their static tapering talons.

Then she knew she was not alone. Even before her eyes moved and picked the quietly standing figure from the night, she knew someone was there. He was standing a few yards ahead, next to the wall. I will have to pass him, she thought. She wondered where the men were now, how far. She gathered a deep breath and held it, as if trying to raise some sort of defense. Then she began walking again, moving with unnatural stiffness. Her eyes slid to their corners as she passed him. It was the person she had noted earlier, the one who had held back in the dark, the one with the hat-covered face and the dark coat.

When she had passed him by some ten feet, she heard him stir. She thought: What will he want? What will he do? And it was so strange when he spoke, so unexpected, so startling: she did not even think, How does he know my name? nor did she immediately recognize the voice: what startled her beyond all was the quiet familiarity with which he pronounced her name, his voice soft, practiced. Involuntarily she paused, letting him walk toward her, her back to him. Then, even as she knew she should be furiously angry, she felt tears starting to her eyes. She wheeled on him.

"Why did you do that?" she demanded. "I was sick with fright. I was . . . "

He pushed the hat back on his thick, tawny hair and stared at her, head cocked slightly to one side, smiling listlessly.

"And then to walk with them," she said. "To be part of it."

"I even said to one of them, 'Good riddance to him.' The son of a bitch snickered."

"So what did you prove? What did you want to do?"

"Stop crying."

"I'll cry if I want to. Don't tell me not to cry." She was trembling. "Oh, God, why is it never easy with you?"

"You had better go home. I'll take you."

"No you won't," she said heatedly. "I'm angry with you, Ben. Very angry. Why did you do a thing like that? You had me frightened to death. I know why you did it—you wanted to see what they would say. You thought it would be a fine joke. But all you did was hurt the hearts of the people who love you. All right. You did that. Now leave me alone. I can get home by myself."

He waited a moment. His eyes closed as he drew and then expelled a deep breath, then reopened, fixed upon her. The smile was gone. "Go home, Susan," he said.

"Don't tell me what to do. I'll go home if I want, or not, just as I please."

"Yes, of course. As you please."

"I don't need your advice."

"No."

"So . . . I'm going home. Don't follow me. I don't want to see you. I'm very angry, Ben." She knotted her fingers nervously in front of her. She waited. "So I'm going."

"Yes."

"And what was she doing there anyway?"

"Who?"

"You know who. She was riding around like a lunatic, paying them money to look for you. Why did she do that? She's in love with you, isn't she?"

"Do you want me to take you home?"

"No. Maybe I'm not going home. I don't know where I'm going. And anyway it's none of your business where I go. So leave me alone."

"All right, Susan."

"Now I'm going."

He stepped aside to let her pass. She did not move.

"What are you going to do now?" she asked.

"I'm going to be left here by you."

"I want you to go home," she said.

"I might do that."

"So go ahead then. But first let me tell you that I'm angry with you." She began to sob. "Very angry," she said in a voice made childlike by the sobbing. "Ben, Ben, I thought you were dead," she said and broke into a run. She ran fast, to leave him as far behind as quickly as she could.

When she had run a certain brief distance, she stopped. She was panting. She dabbed at her eyes with her shawl. There was a light breeze now, humming thinly high in the dark trees. She turned around. Where was he? She took a few steps back, peering into the darkness. Tentatively she spoke his name aloud, as if trying to evoke him. She was certain he had followed. Perhaps she had run too quickly, come further than she had realized. Even so, if he were following, his strides should have brought him at least close enough to hear her now. She felt despairing anger. He had let her run off, just like that.

"Ben!" she shouted into the darkness, as if remonstrating with him.

She heard the crickets again, all around her, beating with constant, indolent clarity. Now she whispered his name, inquiringly, plaintively. He was not there. She felt her tears coursing slowly along her cheeks. Why was it every time she cried, his name was on her lips?

"Ben. Oh."

She turned and began walking home. God, why do I love him? What sort of affliction was it? She could not remember when she had not loved him. Must she always be so imprisoned? I'll stop it, she thought. I'm going to stop loving him. Everything will be so much easier then. That's what I'm going to do—stop loving him.

He had no right to let me run away like that.

When she reached her house, she had a start. She thought she saw someone standing at the corner of the porch. She hurried there, a pleased smile on her lips. She was about to say, Why, I knew you wouldn't . . . But it was only the old rosebush, emergent from its long, flowerless winter in the shape of . . . someone. She fingered its cold leaves tenderly in her disappointment.

Two

RYLER WAS SIX YEARS old when it happened. He was standing in the cool shade at the stream, down the incline from the box-shaped one-room schoolhouse. The sounds of his schoolmates at recess were faint in his ears. His eyes were fixed intently upon the bluejay sitting on a lower bough in the sun-speckled foliage of the high oak on the other side of the stream, its small figure trim and aristocratic. Clenching a stone, Ryler's fist was raised to shoulder height, poised to fire, his face severely resolute, his mouth almost grim. He fancied himself at this moment the hunter, emulating his older brothers who shot rabbit in the Little Village woods north of Capstone. He would be like them, entering the house via the kitchen and dropping his slain on the table and waiting for his mother to say what she always said to them: Well, let's see what we can do with this.

His arm hurled forward and the stone sailed, far off its mark, striking a limb somewhere above the bird and alarming it into an abrupt arrow of flight. Empty hands at sides, he lifted his face and turned to watch the bird leave the trees and attain the blue sky with unerring grace.

He heard his name then, shouted urgently. Turning, he saw Susan running down the incline toward him, her long calico dress swirling around her legs, golden hair flying. Her face was animated with alarm. She ran up to him and took hold of his arm with both her hands, then turned around and began pulling him with her, her sob-trembling voice incoherent. Unwilling, but curious, he started to trot back up the incline with her, in tandem, trying to shake her loose but unable to.

They were hitting the new boy, she said when she was able to control her voice, running hard, pulling Ryler with her. So what? he thought. He hardly knew the new boy and what little he did know he did not like. The new boy was sullen and unfriendly, always on the periphery, watching impassively, almost critically, as if he did not approve of what he saw. Only this one thing about him impressed Ryler; the new boy did not cry or so much as wince when Mr. James caned him for inattentiveness (which seemed to be the only infraction he was ever guilty of); the only sign that anything was happening to him was a fierce dilation of his pupils as the teacher's cane hummed and whacked, and Ryler's eyes would move from the boy's face to the teacher's, aware of knowing something that the teacher did not. The new boy had appeared at the school one day that spring, held by the hand by a man with a beard, whom Ryler had never seen before either. The man had talked quietly but earnestly to Mr. James, about the boy evidently, giving advice, it appeared, or instructions, maybe even orders. Then the man went away and left the boy there, alone and shy, staring tight-mouthed at the strange, unabashedly curious faces. Mr. James called him Benjamin and sat him in a far seat and for all Benjamin took part he could have been deaf and dumb or invisible.

I was Benjamin McKinley's first teacher, Carson E. James wrote some fifty years later, an old man writing a memoir of his life as a country schoolteacher, a totally uneventful life which had left him obscure and anonymous except for the accidental fact that the future poet had been brought to his tiny schoolhouse in Capstone, Long Island, one day in 1845 and increased his class from nine to ten. *I shall never forget the day,* Mr. James's unsteady, arthritic hand wrote. *I shall never forget the boy's shining brow and alert, inquisitive eyes. Did I immediately recognize his qualities, the sum of his future achievement? Perhaps not. But I discerned at once in him a quality that was both sensitive and angelic, atypical of the average farm boys who attended my classes and sat until they were old enough or strong enough to be called by the family into the fields. His guardian, Mr. Henry Hook, who brought him to the school on that memorable day, advised me that he believed the boy to be somewhat special. He did not elaborate, but high marks for Mr. Hook's perception. He also informed me that the boy was an orphan whose parents had died tragically. Nor did he elaborate upon that either. (I sensed that this was a man one did not question, casually or otherwise.) He further advised me that the bulk of the boy's education would be administered by himself, but that I was to instruct him in the fundamentals, in what he described as—and I shall never forget his phrase—"The divine simplicities." I assured Mr. Hook, a taciturn creature whom I did not like, that I was quite capable of educating children. It soon became obvious that young Ben was the sort of jewel child that a teacher comes across but once in a lifetime. His intelligence was of an alert, inquiring nature, his curiosity insatiable, his capacity to absorb remarkable. His one drawback was a tendency to indulge his own reveries. I must admit, too, that Mr. Hook was probably not a totally detrimental influence, since the lad soon had knowledge of a curriculum which, because of the limitations of my pupils, I was unable to teach in my classroom. As soon as he had learned to write, he began to show indications of his unique talent and imagination, gifts which were later to be used to dazzling effect. He showed immediately a fertile mind as well as a highly independent and original way with language—all of this considering his tender age, of course. One composition which he wrote, and which remains vivid to my mind to this day (ah, if only I'd had*

*the foresight to preserve it), dealt with the consumption by fire of
a house, which was quite remarkable coming from the imagination
of an eight- or nine-year-old.*

Now, even though he did not like the new boy, Ryler
allowed himself to be hurried up the incline by Susan.
Perhaps it was the contagion of her excitement that pro-
pelled him, his six-year-old's inclination to find this sort
of thing irresistible. And besides, Susan was his friend, and
for all he knew he was going to avenge some hurt or insult
that had been perpetrated against her.

When they arrived at the crest, he saw them—the five
boys pushing Ben among themselves and Ben taking it
without protest or resistance, with the same controlled ferocity with which he accepted Mr. James's canings. If he,
Ryler, had been there when it started, he would doubtless
have been one of them. But he was being interjected into
the situation as savior, protector, and from a vantage point
where the bullying and cruelty were painfully obvious. A
vague sense of indignation implored the separation of
right from wrong. Through the school's single window he
could see Mr. James's head bent—to some book or paper,
no doubt—oblivious to the shouts and taunts outside.

He shook himself free of Susan's grip, pushed his curved
bangs still further aslant and moved toward the group,
watching Ben's sullenly angry face, Ben's eyes as they roved
from face to face with stolid, tearless calm. Ryler bent and
lifted a large rock that was almost too heavy to carry, much
less throw. He had to hold it with both hands. He advanced
with it. One of the boys, dancing back from a shove at
Ben, bumped into him. As the boy, with full-toothed glee,
spun around at him, Ryler drove the rock forward into
the boy's middle with what force he was able to muster,
then let it fall. The boy gasped and collapsed to one knee
and began to cry. Then Ryler stepped next to Ben and
stared menacingly at the others. He is my friend, he said.

They were four, and one more kneeling in breathless

sobbing on the grass, and he was one, but there was no move toward him because they knew Ryler Stevenson alone could whip any one of them (he had proven it), which in itself was worth considering; but they knew, too, that he had three older brothers who stood bare-chested in the fields and muscled the earth and who carried rifles when they hunted in the woods. So the others desisted, fell silent, were outmatched. They broke up and drifted away, with the brooding muteness of boys whose fun has been spoiled.

Ben talks to the squirrels, Susan said. That's a lot of ruck, Ryler said. Squirrels can't talk. But they can listen, can't they? she asked. She described in an awe-soft voice how she had sat with Ben in the woods—absolutely still and motionless, under his orders—and waited for the squirrel to appear. After a long while a quick-eyed, vigilant rodent face pried cautiously through the brush and began to advance with more trust than she had ever seen before. It might have come all the way up to them and nuzzled them, she said, if she had not involuntarily moved and frightened it away. What did he say to it? Ryler asked with grudging interest. I can't tell, she said. It's a secret. That's a lot of ruck, Ryler said. I've played in those woods more than he has and I've never seen it. That's because he can sit still for whole hours, Susan said. So can I, Ryler said pugnaciously. I can sit still for whole days if I want to. Not like him, she said. He told me once that a she-wolf came up and licked his ear and that another time a rabbit jumped into his hand. Oh, Ryler said with bored knowingness, that's . . . It isn't a lot of ruck, Susan said indignantly.

Ryler's people owned a modest-sized farm and Ben would go there and walk in the fields with his friend, setting his small leather boots carefully on the turned fur-rows, and they would watch Ryler's brothers plant and harvest, and Ryler would ask, Do you like farming? I don't. It's not for me. And Ben: But what else is there? We'll see,

Ryler would say. We'll see. They tied ropes to the high beams in the barn and swung back and forth over the straw-littered earthen floor, and they would run and shout and wave their arms and scatter the chickens around the barnyard and in turn find themselves being chased by the Stevensons' barking collie. There was here a warm, integral family life that Ben envied; he enjoyed the solidarity and unspoken intimacy that characterized this house. Frequently he slept there, and in the morning Mrs. Stevenson, a large, untidy, good-natured woman with enormous fleshy arms, would come upstairs and pull away the covers and get the boys out of the bed by tipping it until they spilled out, and then go downstairs laughing and prepare large breakfasts for them before springing them into the long yellow days that stretched languidly over the quiet farms and small, verdant hillsides. And Ryler would say upon occasion (it would be at day's end, when they were tired and sitting in the barn shade or perhaps in the woods stealing serious suffering smokes on the clay pipes Ryler had lifted from his father's hand-carved rack), God, it must be exciting to be an orphan. You might be a prince or anything else. Someday it'll all come out and you'll have bags of money. Then you won't know us. No, Ben said. I'll always be your friend. Sure, Ryler said with expansive skepticism. You'll live in a house like Eva LeGrange and hold your nose whenever you pass farm boys. Never, Ben said. Never.

He thought about it, of course. Susan knew he did. She was curious but she never put the question; she knew him well enough to know he did not brook intrusions, for one thing, and for another, that he was supplied with no answers. A detached, inquiring, strangely serene expression would come to his face. A prolonged, profound silence would ensue, ending with a vague half-smile, a kind of ironic self-amusement. There were long periods of time when the inner quest, the curiosity, was suppressed or ignored; but it always returned, like a slow-burning stick, with the ash gradually outgrowing the stick as his mind withdrew with soft melancholia into the bittersweet question of his origins.

Then, after assailing himself with this brooding, he would mount his horse and ride out and be gone for days (he began this when he was sixteen, soon after Charlotte—Aunt Charlotte, he called her—died, her death causing the only tears Susan ever saw him shed, and she remembered the strange envy she felt for the dead woman nailed into the pine coffin resting on the wooden horses in the living room, because Ben had cried for her). The first few times he went away she was not sure he would ever return, the departures were that furious, that precipitous. She would go each day to the farmhouse, where she would find Hook sitting on the porch, wearing his suit and his derby and smoking a cigar, looking always like a man waiting to have his daguerreotype taken, fixed and unapproachable. Is Ben about? she asked. No, the man said. You don't know where he's gone then? she asked. He would not even bother to say no a second time but ignored her, as if the first no had made her vanish, which to his mind she probably had, as he continued to stare with his small, sharp, sardonically amused eyes, preoccupied, self-contained, insulated by whatever it was he had experienced or survived during those ten years when he had left Capstone, the time of which he never deigned to elucidate to anyone. Not even to me, Ben told her. And perhaps the man's obdurate reticence was purposeful, part of his device, his invisible leash; for as long as the youth was dissatisfied with the story of his antecedents, he would always return. I know it's more than he tells me, Ben said. More than him just working for my parents in Virginia and then the house burning down one night and my father dying while trying to save my mother who was already dead in the upstairs smoke, and him carrying me out of the house and bringing me to Capstone after a journey that beat any you'll find in the Bible. He says that's all there is to it, Ben said. But I don't believe him.

In all the world, across the continent and then over the ocean to China and on around the world across other continents and over other oceans, it seemed that only Hook, only he, this twisted-named man laced and webbed with secrets, had knowledge, as if he had read forbidden books and watched the stars fall and spoken with the dead; knowledge which had made him raise and tutor Ben not like son but more like crown prince, who endured the boy's willfullness with tight-lipped stoicism, as if the horizons were Ben's natural corridor in which to surge. She had known (or rather seen) him for fifteen years and had heard him speak perhaps a hundred words. People had stated flatly that the man was crazy. She had heard that when she was seven or eight and it made its impression; it led her to watching him more closely, waiting—warily—for some manifestation of the alleged disorder. Whenever she came to the farm to see Ben, she would stare at Hook, who was invariably sitting on the porch, his eyes seeing a long way out, and it was peculiar, disconcerting, that she could stand so near and stare so intensely at him and not ever have him notice; he never so much as shifted his eyes toward her. He was there like a statue, merely to be gazed upon, contemplated. Then she decided one day that those people were wrong, that Hook was not crazy. It came to her sudden and unsought, like revelation. There was too much iron control in the man, almost as though he were obeying or carrying out some infrangible compact. For all his reticence and impassivity, she sensed some reason, a logic. *It's like he's standing guard,* she thought.

Ryler Stevenson and Susan Gibson, the little girl with the yellow hair and friendly brown eyes whose father owned a tavern in town, were his friends.

At ten years old the motherless Susan was keeping house for her father, washing and cleaning and cooking, and keeping her eyes sullenly averted from the faces of the women he occasionally brought home; as well as working in the tavern part of each afternoon, mopping the floor and rinsing out the beer pails. When the Reverend Mr. Lloyd came one day to remonstrate with Gibson for thus using the little girl, it was Susan, with incendiary loyalty, who came at the prim-lipped clergyman with a wet mop and swiped at him and told him not to criticize her father, in fact chased the minister into the street, where he gasped and pointed the Lord's finger at Gibson while the men at the bar covered their smiles with discreet hands.

The years conjoined the three children into a friendship of fierce mutual loyalty and devotion, and one day—they were eight or nine at the time—an amused drinker in Gibson's asked Susan which of the boys, Ryler or Ben, she would one day marry. Looking up from her work— she was sitting on a barrel doing some mending with slow, meticulous fingers—she answered, Both. Aha, but you can't do that, the man said. Her eyes burned and she glared at him and cried, I can, I will! And Gibson grunted from behind the bar and said, I know a man who has four daughters and each an old maid. I have one daughter and she wants to marry two boys at once.

One thing—something important to young boys—was settled when they were ten, settled then and for all time. To the day she died, Susan would never forget it; never did she feel such panic, such helpless anguish; never did she feel, simultaneously, such overwhelming love and hatred for them both. Ben and Ryler had a fight in the woods, over nothing, a trifle, something which was forgotten by evening. Or perhaps it was more than a trifle but the inevitable eruption of accumulated events and postures, the furious culmination of the drive toward ascendancy, so enigmatically natural to the species, so avidly striven after, so bitterly contested. Since the day at the schoolhouse, when he had intervened on Ben's behalf, Ryler had assumed the superior role; Ryler was the leader, the arbiter, to whose decisions and judgments they deferred, at whose house they gathered to begin their day, who led them into their adventures and their wandering. Ryler's pranks had left Ben sprawled in streams or tumbled in snowbanks, left him licking his pride and forcing his smiles, eyes shifting uneasily toward Susan, who never, never laughed at his predicament or his embarrassment. So the fight did not need a reason either visible or substantial, simply its moment of maturity.

They fought in front of Susan's horrified eyes, swinging their fists into each other's faces with a ferocity that shocked her who did not realize how primal it was nor how central she herself stood to its cause; bruising and bloodying themselves in their desperate struggle for privilege and position. She screamed and implored, and when she tried to separate them was flung violently aside. Then they wrestled into the underbrush and dislodged a nest of hornets. A moment later a cloud of black hornets rose with vengeful darting and swooping. Ryler yelped under the sudden stinging and tried to swat away his attackers, but Ben kept at him with ferocious single-minded purpose, oblivious to the sharp little pincer stings at his neck and face. Ryler tried to escape, but Ben kept him there and continued fighting even as both their faces began to raise welts. Finally Susan lunged between them and separated them long enough for Ryler to turn and run. Ben chased him all the way home, unmindful of the throbbing imbedded stingers in his flesh.

After that it was to Ben's house that they came in the mornings to begin their days; it was Ben who walked first and determined their direction. Ryler remained his friend, but with a certain subtle wariness now; it was almost as if he was afraid not to be Ben's friend.

I don't know why you say that, Susan, Charlotte said; I think Ben has a very nice disposition. A bit on the serious side maybe, but that's all right. You can't expect him to walk about all day grinning like a blithering idiot. Charlotte

was already dying then. It was fixed in her face, that In-
dian-like face with the high, taut cheekbones whose ridges
were becoming increasingly accented every day, and the
long, straight nose always so strong and proud but so un-
happily inartistic—a face that had apparently helped keep
the suitors from her door and condemned her to her cel-
ibate life, to live alone and oversee the farm that had been
left to her and her brother, the brother who appeared and
disappeared and reappeared as casually and unpredictably
as a moon behind traveling clouds. Finally he came back
that rainy night to stay—though he did not announce it
that way, but this time he had the boy with him and he
did not leave again. She heard the sounds in the yard, and
peering through the window into the dark driving night,
she was able to discern a man sitting head-bowed on a
horse, his stolid immobility in the drenching rain indicat-
ing a long and arduous journey and profound, soul-dull-
ing weariness. One hand held the reins while the other
clutched the boy in front of him on the saddle. Then he
finally dismounted and from the ground lifted the boy
free, and from the way the boy's arms and legs hung
limply, Charlotte could tell he was alseep, in spite of the
hard-driving rain. She had not seen her brother for ten
years, and his greeting as he came through the door was
a glance of stale and taciturn familiarity, as if he had been
in her company only an hour before, as if he had not been
away, silent and uncommunicating, all those years. But she
was not surprised. Always spare with words, secretive,
moodily eccentric even as a child, he had established his
pattern early and adhered to it thereafter, leaving some
morning without word, gone again, gone somewhere,
lonely and intimate, like some indefatigable visionary
whose tongue and whose feet defer blindly to a prayer in
recitation over the horizon. So she had learned through
the years to be prepared but not to hold him in prospect,
and even in the lengthiest of her lonely hours seldom
thought of him, for he had never released enough of him-

self even for idle contemplation. Now he was there again, brusquely bridging the gulf of years, sudden and inexplicable, emerging from the dark rainy night and yet somehow still inseparable from it, its gloom clinging to him. As Charlotte went to close the door, she saw something weird, uncanny. The horse was sinking, slowly, ponderously, from sheer exhaustion it seemed. She watched the depleted animal sink and like some ruined and ravaged vessel of the sea roll gently on its side and die. My God, she thought, how far have they traveled?

That was how they arrived, Charlotte said, staring intently upon her knitting, needles and fingers twitching ceaselessly. Already the numbed, wistful look of death was in her face, canceling all thoughts of hoping and planning, obliterating into resignation the pride of years that one saw in the faces of older people, her flaccid cheeks slashed with death shadows. Just like that, she told Susan. Out of the rain after ten years, with the horse dying in the yard. No, he's never told me any more about it than he has anyone else. It's been another ten years now and I don't suppose he ever will; if there is any more to be known I'll never be privy to it. If he doesn't talk of it, Susan said, then that must mean there's something behind it. Charlotte ceased her knitting for a moment, her eyes raising to Susan with an expression faintly appreciative. Does it, girl? she asked, then resumed the knitting. But listen, she said, don't tell me Ben is a sulky or morose person. He isn't. He's brightened my life, I can tell you. This was a mighty empty house before he came. Oh, it took him time to warm up; but remember, he was a stranger, a small, frightened stranger with no people, just barely old enough to remember what the faces of his dead father and mother looked like. He took his time, yes; maybe two years of it, but then he knew I was his friend and he's been, well, like a son. Oh, he's been willful and troublesome all right; but who would have a son that wasn't? That wouldn't be much of a boy, would it? It's made all the difference to me now in these times, knowing someone is concerned and will cry for me later. It helps, knowing somebody is going to cry for you. I know that sounds selfish, but sick people always are; old ones the worst. Henry is concerned, I know, but he just can't show it—he can't reach out when the pain gets bad—and he was born without tears in him, which is really more his sadness than mine. Maybe Ben just doesn't know how to show you tenderness yet, or what you call tenderness now anyway—he's only fourteen and a pretty girl is still God's strangest creature to them when they're at that age. They're too busy trying to be what they think are men. And anyway, child, once you've picked your man you have to take him the way he's made; so don't despair until you see what the finished job looks like. No, it isn't that he always wants his way; it's that he wants no one else's imposed upon him. It isn't so peculiar either, when you stop to think—if you know your Bible—that a lot of king-doms have been risen on the same principle. If you were only his real mother, Susan said. Charlotte smiled with her lips. Wouldn't that make a fine dish of gossip, she said.

Mischief, gaiety, laughter, imagination all marked the long, indolent, gossamer summer of childhood, of the hot blue and yellow days of childhood, the old, old days that swam one into the other like a blur of butterflies; days of incubation for memories that would throw warm shocks into the wizened and superannuated gaffers who would recall the sounds of golden laughter even as they sat in their chairs like relics. For Susan those soft summers were preserved like pressed flowers, memories bedded in satin, incused upon silver, framed with gold leaf. Long, long after pavement had been laid where bare calloused feet had raced, even after the heart of the woods had been blackened by a terrible fire, she could, with narrowed eye and half-smile, evoke the dead and respin hoary gossamer on a mystic loom.

The ponds, the fields, the treeful back lanes, and the woods—above all the woods—were loam and chrysalis for these expanding, spiraling times. Mild blue winds purred through the treetops in sweet and pious elegies. Here and there sunshafts appeared like altars in the woods. The way ahead dipped into a shady hollow and a stand of silver birch. A stream slipped in brown silence between spongy banks, occasionally throwing off a liquid jewel of sunlight. Further along they came to the place of the slain giants, where trees once strong and erect lay hurled across the woodland floor. The dead grandfathers were broken clean from implacable stumps as though victims of slashing axes; but the truth was they had been felled in the great hurricane of 1841, when all the winds and all the rains had torn and warred through this place; and one could still sense the awesome struggles waged here between wind and tree—the wind as if infuriated at having been snared in this place—the roar and the hiss of the final shuddering surrenders, the yielding and the cracking, the outraged titanic cries as one after the other the old, mighty trees toppled and crashed, clawing at everything that lay in the vast arcs of their shattering descents. The sense of herculean combat still brooded in the funereal silence, the mythic rage grim and static in the rotted moss-covered trunks.

There was one murdered tree in particular. It was the lord of all the heaven-struck dead. It had been perhaps the oldest tree in all Capstone, old even when the Mespatche and Mantinococ braves filed under its branches, old when the Dutch farmers rowed across the river from New Amsterdam in 1642 and began colonizing the northwest shores; had certainly been the tallest and the mightiest, and dead like a king too, with power and dignity and with an aura which drew pilgrims. They walked over carpets of purple leaves, past the royal blood of wild roses and small patches of star moss. Through openings in the woods they saw their dead lord, its great shattered body appearing behind its palladium of living timber. It had been struck by lightning in the time of the great storm, terribly and vengefully struck. The Jovian dagger had split it in three, exposing it to its very core as if with a furious, vertical thrust. Smudges like black paint along its dead flanks attested to the terrific scorching it had received. It lay hurled in three separate directions, perhaps a hundred feet in each. The jagged blast had left a crude gray throne at the stump, complete with splintered back. Pads of white and green fungus hung like bloated tongues to the sides of the gray stump, evilly parasitic upon the remains of the dead giant.

Like the Greeks of old, they regarded this lightning-struck place as sacred and fenced it around with their love and veneration. It became Susan's throne, and the first time the little girl sat upon it she wept as her boy-subjects knelt before her. With an elm switch she touched their shoulders in stately ceremony and named them her Cavaliers, and they in turned vowed their loyalty, their devotion, and their love. It was their secret place, solemn and revered, the sanctified throne of their kingdom, and all the trees and the birds and the creatures of the woodland were subjects of the queen and soldiers in the army of the Cavaliers.

They were fifteen when Susan realized the gossamer had begun to unravel. The blue and yellow days were beginning to set into memory, sinking into frames of rising margins, readying for the gloss and luster of the mind's burnisher.

She overheard the story in her father's tavern. She had come in through the rear entrance and was in the back room, unseen, when she heard the voices from the front, heard a man mentioning Ben's and Ryler's names and guffawing and another interjecting with a certain lewd curiosity, probing for details. Susan moved close to the wall, near the doorway, fingering her underlip as the laughter-provoking story unfolded from inside.

Ben and Ryler had been—it was the man's phrase—bare-assed swimming in the pond at the foot of Billy Goat Hill with Mamie Pollard, a farm girl some five years their senior who defied her father and never went to church and had a bad name in town. She was a large, foolish, amiable girl of great physical abundance who drank with the men at the Dooley House bar and was known to enjoy a roll in the hay with whoever took her fancy. She had a full head of incongruous tiny black curls and could sound waves of laughter loud enough, it was said, to fetch the pigs.

She was down there with them this morning, Susan heard the covert, salaciously toned voice say, swimming with them in the altogether. It was her idea, I would reckon, since both those boys, hellions or not, still had the innocence they were born with. Then, after they'd skinny-dipped and the water was still on them, she began making up to them and laughing and cupping her hands in private places until those boys started in to realizing there are better things in life than stealing watermelons. How'd you get this story? Gibson asked. From Blue Cashman, the salacious voice said. He was watching it all from the top of the hill, standing up in his wagon to see it full. And probably diddling himself at the same time, another said. But wait, the narrator said, the best ain't told yet. She took them on, both of them, right there at the edge of the water, right in God's own sunlight. Blue says it took them about thirty seconds each. Blue says those boys must be part rabbit. Which part? the other voice asked and giggled. He says Mamie just lay there in receiving position grinning up at the one who was watching and that when they were through the boys grabbed their duds and run away like deer, leaving Mamie there on her naked ass slapping the ground and laughing like a lunatic. And then Blue says he saw something white flashing through the trees in the slope. It was a palomino and it was moving like it had bees in its ass. It come up through the trees and right past where he was sitting. You know who it was? Tell us, Gibson said. It was the LeGrange girl. Blue says she must've been sitting there the whole time watching. He says when she shot past him she was crying and sniffling and that she was whipping that horse like it owed her money. But, a voice said, she made sure she'd seen it all before she rode out. Wouldn't you? Gibson asked.

Still unnoticed, Susan slipped out the back door. She wanted to cry but would not let herself—because Eva LeGrange had cried. I won't be like her, she thought. Her father has all that money and they live in that big house and she rides a palomino and doesn't talk to anyone, but she cried when she saw that. Oh, those boys. *Oh,* those boys! She resolved never to see them again. To have done such a thing, with such a girl, in broad daylight, where people could see. Where people *did* see. She was furious enough to have bitten off the top of the stone hitching post. She hated them. They were both of them probably in love with Mamie Pollard right now. And Eva LeGrange had seen them naked. *Oh!* It was too much to think about. There were other boys she could fall in love with. Decent boys, who worked hard in the fields, who attended church, who washed their faces, who were polite and mannered, who wouldn't even dream of continually pulling the trousers off Mr. James until the schoolteacher had finally uttered curses and left Capstone forever. No, by Jesus Christ, she said aloud, there are plenty of others. Plenty of others. And I'm a free soul.

She went home and tore into as many pieces as she could the poem Ben had written for her a few months before, the one in which he had addressed her as goddess and evoked her in images of spring, summer, autumn, and winter, and which she had loved and memorized. Then finally she did cry and hated herself for it. She wandered around the house rubbing the tears from her eyes with her fists. Oh, those boys just had no sense, no sense at all.

Later she washed her face and left the house. As she was heading back to her father's tavern, she heard her name sung out, loudly and playfully, the single lyric of a giddy, monotonous song. They were standing in the alley in the Dooley House shade, arms around each other's necks like a pair of drunks, grinning at her and singing. *Susan. Sooozann. Soooo Zannn.*

Do us a favor, Ben said. No, she said churlishly. Lift us a pail of beer from your father's. Go to hell, she said and ran away, the burning tears starting again to her eyes.

She stood outside her house fingering the cold leaves of the rosebush she had taken for Ben in the dark. If he had not followed her, where then had he gone? It seemed an old familiar refrain, part of the breaths and rhythms of her life: where had Ben gone? She gazed around, appealing, at the full, dominant night. The nearest house was down the dirt road and around the bend, so even if there was a light in it she couldn't have seen it. She could smell the heralds of spring, faint green scents which the mellowing breezes had been sharing the past few days. For a moment she thought she heard the sound of galloping hoofs, but then it stopped. If it had been, who was it?

Perhaps it had been *her*. Going where? To Ben, to his house, to see if . . . Susan walked quickly into the wagon-wheel-rutted road, a resolute pout on her lips. Suddenly she found herself hurrying. I had better get there, she thought. The idea of Eva LeGrange riding up to Ben's house and going inside, now, tonight, was a real and alarming vision. She wants him as her toy, her plaything, Susan thought. Just like those other boys she had toyed with, had enticed and led around by the nose until her father stepped forward and put a stop to it. She didn't love her men enough to fight for them. She didn't love her men at all; they were merely toys, toys like she must have rooms full of—expensive, stuffed and hand-carved and painted toys, on strings and rockers and wheels, and she had outgrown them now, so she was replacing them with new ones, real, live. Eva wanted Ben now, to pull him on a string and then leave him in the stale nursery with the others; even if she wanted him for only one week or one day, she meant to have him. She was even willing to pay money to those sons of bitches in the Dooley House to light pine torches and search the night for him: dead or alive, Eva meant to have him. It probably made no difference how they found him either: Give me the body, it's mine, I paid for it. At least it's good enough to throw darts at or else hang up in the fields to scare off the crows.

She thinks so, Susan thought sternly, moving faster now. *Well, so she thinks.*

She had to cross through the woods to get to Ben's house. It was pitch black but she wasn't afraid—not very much anyway. The men and their stinking pine torches were gone and it was hers again. All the same, she wished Ryler were with her, just so she didn't have to listen to the sound of her own footsteps. She had run straight to Ryler that afternoon when word of Ben's suicide note reached her. Look for him? Ryler asked. Where? Everywhere, she said, excited, agitated. He was lounging casually in the doorway of Mariah's general store—he had taken the clerking job just a week before, to avoid working in his father's fields. I can't leave anyway, he said. Get somebody to watch it for you, she said. Can't, he said. But Ben might be dead, she said. Hell, he said, he's probably just emptied a couple of jugs. But . . . And if he is, he interrupted, then what can we do? Will you come later, she asked, when you're through here? I'll try, he said. But he did not appear, at least he did not join the group of men with the torches. She did not understand it. Dear God, would she ever grow old enough or wise enough to understand either of those boys?

She found herself pausing for a moment at the path that led to the dead, triparted tree. Suddenly she felt a terrible lostness, a sudden fatal waywardness, as if her touch with life had become tenuous. It had not lasted, not lasted. The hand of notional whimsy, which had led them through childhood's summer, through these flower-col-

ored light-birded memory-clouded woods, had suddenly
vanished and left behind yearning, cheated souls. The
moppets' banquet had left in its cobwebbed wake a famine
of flown visions and slain enchantments; the heady-scented
bewitching purchases of imagination had flown away upon
some vagrant night breeze or melted into the secret snows
of spring, and all that remained was a stern, somber vacuum filled with silent, ingenuous laughter. The way behind was turned to water and the way ahead piled high
with fallen stone. Not one stroke of any of it remained on
any clock. They had effused themselves with an overin-
tensity of playacting, and now the stilled music of their
spirits was wandering lost in the vast world beyond the
woodland. Their physical bodies had transcended the
dreamed and artful fables, but their souls had never fully
disengaged and now obsolescence was beginning to turn
with decay.

What did they hear in it that a woman did not, could
not? Let it fill a man's ears and before your eyes he was
transfigured, he lost all resemblance to yesterday as he
swelled to dare the Lord's wrath. She had sat as dire pro-
phetress to the tongues of contention, pious to the pagan
drum, on her aunt's porch when the soldiers had come
marching down the road just a few days ago. Judd, her
cousin, only seventeen, was working in the pasture near
the rail fence, scything the weeds, his bare arms flashing
back and forth, the scythe catching and throwing the glint-
ing sun. First she thought it was the rumble of many wagons she was hearing, but she knew that that many wagons
never came along this road. So she turned to look and it
grew louder and it seemed to be bringing distance with it.
The noise was surging ahead of itself through the trees,
a proud sound now, proud and inexorable, like the her-
alding of a new, strong, confident age. She looked at Judd.
The scythe had fallen from his hands and he was walking
through the uncut weeds toward the fence, oddly, like the
blind man in town did when he had to walk somewhere

by himself. He walked to the rail fence and leaned on it with his hands and his head was turned toward the sound.

They came thumping down the road, led by a squad of flag bearers. A parade of men in blue uniforms and squashed blue caps, some of them beating with sticks on drums that hung from their waists, and it was as mysterious as if the trees had come to life and begun walking. Susan could see Judd's head turning with their passage, but it was as if the soldiers were blind, or had eyes like statues, that could look in only one place, the one place somewhere far where no one else could see. They never looked at the youth. They marched past, rapping on the drums and sending that low thunder that spelled the twilight of many summers rolling across the pasture and up into the trees, mysterious and untranslatable and compelling, and Judd's head had turned all the way from left to right to see after them, the marching carven-eyed soldiers whom she was watching too now and wishing they had not come. Then more soldiers came marching, though they did not look like soldiers yet, with neither drums nor uniforms nor rifles: they were youths and men from the next town, some carrying pieces of baggage, some not, but all quite sober of mien and erect, prepared to follow their beckoning of grief and malice over a cliff to hell. When they saw Judd, they became boys again and shouted to him and laughed and swung their arms and told him to come. Judd looked at them as if startled, and then he wheeled his head around toward the drums again, his shoulders hunching as if he might spring over the fence. She could see it, the sound filling him to the brim, the sound that had come loud and proud and sudden—it was dimming now, beginning to fade. Then the youth ran along the fence, trying to get within hearing again, a transfiguring excitement in his face, running until he struck the far fence and then standing there, his arms at his sides, looking as if the fading drumbeats were emptying him, depleting him.

What did they hear in it that a woman did not, could not?

And then the drums were beating urgently under the blue April sky and the high proud flags rippled and fluttered silkenly in the languid breeze in front of the Dooley House. She had followed them in, curious, resentful. A major, in a blue uniform and felt hat, with sword and scabbard leaning out from his trim flank, stood at the head of the stairs, arms akimbo, his grave, red-bearded face surveying the rapidly swelling crowd that was running to the summoning of the drums, filling the road before the high-porched front of the Dooley House. Two steps below stood his sergeant, a gaunt, slack-jawed jackal of an old soldier whose forage cap pressed upon a bristling nest of gray hairs, whose watery eyes were casting predatory looks upon the young men in the crowd, daring them to stare back at him. The major said something to the sergeant, who repeated it in an automaton's sudden and inflectionless voice to the drummers, and they ceased instantly to play. The abrupt silence froze the crowd and they stood still, expectant.

The major began to speak. The nation, he said in a slow, passionate, stentorian voice, was at war. The flag had been fired upon at Fort Sumter. He hooked his gloved thumbs into his belt and stood at his ease, glowering at the crowd as if anticipating some dissent. Then he spoke forcefully, rendering a Fourth of July oration; it was a talk flavored with the old pompous and flatulent phrases long since left bare and impotent by indiscriminate usage, phrases they had all heard before from the round mouths of frothy politicians and hired speakers at sunny picnics and patriotic occasions: but now they listened, because now the orotund phrases suddenly possessed a significance, and when there was meaning and exigency in them, they were uplifting and irresistible; uttered in the foreground of threat and danger, they could weave and conjure, could foam blood and constrict the heart and evoke shivering in the deep souls of reticent men.

The governor was asking for volunteer regiments. This unit was marching through various Long Island communities. There was a quota to be filled. The Union needed men, patriotic God-fearing intrepid men, to restore the outrageous and unlawful disjunction.

Who will be first? The major put the question and settled his eye upon a straw-haired youth in overalls near the front of the assemblage. The youth's eyes widened and his Adam's apple worked several times and suddenly he was moving forward as if inspired. A great cheer rose from the crowd and the drummers beat a flourish, brief, blood-moving, giving the sanction of Mars to the youth's action.

Chance for travel and promotion, the ravenous sergeant kept saying over and over in an arid, mechanical voice.

Many in the crowd were grave, standing silently, hands to face, in thought, in solitude; the older women in particular, watching somberly as the cubs began to slip from the lair. But there was excitement and exultation, too, and cheering for every youth who went forward to sign the long sheet of paper that draped a lone drum which stood under the high, silken flags. It was time, many were saying, and others nodding to it, it was time the thing was settled. Various rash and unflattering estimates of Southern fighting capacities were offered by some; others were not so sure; the South had been priming for this for a long time, they said cautiously. Still others saw in it the hand of God: a judgment from heaven had been made; this war would be like a great primal beast arching its back under the earth; the horns of mountaintops would crumble and all the natural affinities which kept the seas from surging upward and the stars from tumbling like a juggler's wares would come disjoined as the very Union itself had gone asunder—the phenomenon of Civil War would invoke these many things and more.

Susan stood at the fringe of the crowd and felt a loneliness unlike any she had ever felt before. Nothing so diminished a woman as the coming of war. The inscrutable beat of drums, all across the land now, in cities, towns, and villages, stuttering their irremediable blood cries under the suddenly frightening flags, clearing the opening arenas, was utter alienation.

There was pale candlelight in the downstairs window of the ramshackle farmhouse with the weathered, mouse-gray boards. Susan went toward it, stealthy, breath held. Coming close, she was greatly relieved not to see Eva's horse in the yard; the stable was closed. Everything looked very quiet and peaceful, and she was satisfied. She would have gone away then but for the voices. They were drifting out from behind the lighted window. She moved in closer then, wanting to see Ben; that was all she wanted, to see him for only a moment.

She saw them both, misty behind the frayed white lace curtain. Hook was sitting slumped in a chair at the dining room table, gazing abstractedly into the candlelight as if mesmerized by the small flower of fire. His vest was unbuttoned and hung like a parted curtain over his white shirt. One hand rose to the point of his short beard, posed there for a moment, then fell. Behind him, in and out of the shadows, Ben was pacing, restive, intense, his broad shoulders swinging aggressively each time he wheeled to redouble his steps.

"I'll tell you this." Hook's voice was quiet, detached, as if he himself were inattentive to what he was saying. "You gave me a very bad time today."

"Maybe it was not all prank either," Ben said, passing to and fro behind the man in the chair, a crispness in his voice, a petulance. "Maybe the weight of all these years of not knowing, of speculating, guessing . . . "

"I thought of it tonight." Hook said, "while I walked the roads not knowing whether you were dead or alive. I said to myself, perhaps he should be told, once and for all;

perhaps it would enable him to better cope with it. And then I felt that perhaps knowing would be worse."

"Worse? I think not. Either way, it's time." Ben had stopped pacing, was standing in a corner, shrouded in shadow, hands on hips, his voice quiet but severe, carefully modulated, encased in a thin membrane of tension.

They were misty behind the frayed curtain; they were like figments of dream, seen in a sleep. Hook rose and bent over the candle, cupped his hand around the flame and then gently blew it out. They were in darkness.

"Come upstairs," Hook said.

Susan heard them leaving the room, moving through the dark house. A moment later she saw a lamp flare in an upstairs window and she stepped back to look up at the pale yellow light, an expression of deep consternation in her eyes.

Ben, she whispered. *Ben, don't listen to it.*

Three

THERE SHOULD NEVER HAVE been any doubt in my mind about your father. If I say that some of it was my fault, I say it not out of nobility of soul or magnanimity of character (I lack those public virtues, with the evidence of a lifetime to prove it), nor with that impeccable vision known as hindsight, but simply because I refused to listen to a voice of truth that kept trying to shout over the fat, round syllables of rational self-deception. I say some of it was my fault because I was in a position to do something, to be a preventive, an interceptor. I am convinced that those critically situated people who act too late are the ones responsible for the perpetuation of the laws of inevitability. Or maybe I'm deluding myself in this notion; perhaps that cataclysm was as unavoidable as any power of nature's. I don't know. Of course, it was an old situation that I stepped into, one that had been riding back and forth on its rails for a long time, and it may be presumptive of me to think I could have brought any external influence to bear upon it. So it often is that people who do not act become not spectators but participants.

Never mind what I was doing in Richmond. The year

was 1844 and the time was summer. I was living in a small, not inelegant hotel on a rise on Washington Street near the James River. I spent my mornings reading books next to an open window, occasionally raising a wanderer's contemplative eye to watch the James send its pleasant tides out to sea. A friend of mine was a bookseller and he let me borrow what I could not afford to buy. All he asked in return was some conversation, and I was pleased to oblige; he was a rare and splendid man who had the blessed gift of knowing when to close his mouth and open his ears.

I spent my afternoons walking—Richmond was a pleasant place for that, more so than Charleston or Savannah; less bustling than Charleston, less somnolent than Savannah. At dusk I went to Mr. Boyd, the bookseller, and we drew chairs together in his back room and chose our topics from the width and breadth of the spinning globe. One evening a customer came in and began rapping the counter with his stick for attention. When Mr. Boyd went out, the customer proceeded to create a disturbance. I heard a cultured but intensely irate Southern voice spewing invective upon the bookseller, who, like most practitioners of his trade, was a gentle man, one who always held his face with one hand when listening to tales of violence or indelicacy. At fault, it soon developed, was a book the man had purchased in the shop, a translation of Pindar. It was terribly inadequate, the man shouted, berating Mr. Boyd for daring to sell such trash. Mr. Boyd, mild, as I have said, an unpretentious scholar of sorts, informed the customer that the translator was a Cambridge don, highly regarded in the field. His field? the customer said heatedly. He belonged in a cotton field, if this was a fair example of his learning. The customer's displeasure finally rose to such choleric heights that I felt obliged to step out of the rear room to present a show of support—physical, not intellectual—for my friend. The customer was a magnificent-looking specimen: tall, athletic, extremely well tailored. But he was foolishly excited, tempestuously irate;

I swear, but he was about to explode into violence in another moment. He was taller than I and at a glance it was apparent possessed of great physical strength; but his anger had made me angry and I came forward and placed myself between the two men.

You had better lower your voice, I said. Instantly he flashed upon me a pair of burning black eyes, eyes animated with a furious indignation. Who the devil are you? he demanded. You'll find out who I am, I said, if you continue this display. He held me in his lofty, contemptuous gaze for almost a full minute, or so it seemed anyway. Apparently he was unused to such defiance, for his eyes widened a fraction to express utter incredulity, the way you or I might regard some unnatural phenomenon. Then he became quite calm and his eyes turned ironic, sardonically amused, as if I were a child pressing against the leg of a behemoth. I could tear out your ribs one at a time if I so choose, he said. I said nothing, I was not entirely satisfied that he could not carry through his threat; as I said, he seemed to possess enormous physical strength. You would look a sight if I did that, he said. I remained mute. I did not want to antagonize him further, nor, on the other hand, did I intend showing him any fear. Then he said, I'm going to demand satisfaction. For what? I asked. For this insult, he said. I told him that was quite asinine, that I had not insulted him and anyway that where I came from we considered dueling childish and idiotic. Then how do you settle your disputes? he asked. We negotiate them with our wits, I said. He gazed at me for several moments with an expression of utmost despair, then said, you're either a very brave fellow or else an extremely foolish one. With that he turned and strode out of the place, throwing Pindar back over his shoulder.

Foolish, the bookseller said when the tension had left the air. Brave, too, he said; but mostly foolish. He was grateful for my intervention, he said, but it really had not been necessary. The man was a regular customer, a very good customer. He would be back in a day or two and this scene would be totally forgotten, as had been others he had created. He was undeniably irascible and maddening, I was told, but actually a gentleman and quite erudite. He came to Richmond every few months, bought many books, howled about some after he had read them, but always returned, never repentant, of course, but gracious. Then perhaps the translation is indeed a poor one, I said. If he said so, then undoubtedly, Mr. Boyd said. He reads the Greek, you know.

Yes, your father was an erudite man and a temperamental one, very difficult to know but once known impossible not to like. He had great personal charm, which he employed when he pleased, and it was irresistible. He had a deep, sonorous speaking voice that could hold one in enchantment for hours. He proclaimed himself and commanded attention wherever he went, commanding it perhaps because he seemed indifferent to it. He wore his virtues with great ease. But like many attractive men he was self-centered, with a keenly honed vanity. But it's also true that vanity is a sheath into which we place our doubts. He spoke perhaps a little too loudly now and then and perhaps showed a bit too much white in his eyes when flashing them around to see who was listening. But people always listened. His presence alerted every mind and stilled every corner of the room. He was a brilliant conversationalist, though his thoughts were sometimes difficult to follow: when your mind was but treetop high his was already bounding over the planets, and if you strained harder to climb to him, why, as you rose, so, perversely, would he descend to the level of grass blades just to mock your reaching.

He was, as I have indicated, an extremely cultured man, and quite conscious of it. He equated knowledge with immortality; it was the edifice upon which men built their continuity of existence and justified their right to breathe and procreate. He spoke often of immortality, of the intact soul striding onward through eternity: to walk on stone and leave a footprint, he put it. I remember him once telling me: My ancestors were from Warwickshire in England, Hook. From Snitterfield, not far from Stratford. Why, they might have walked along the River Avon with Shakespeare himself. They might even have implanted in him some of the seeds that were to shoot forth later. I like to think of some clever and somber McKinley embodying some characteristic of Hamlet which the sweep-eyed poet took in . . . which, in an oblique way, would make Hamlet a descendant of mine . . . the blood of a McKinley running through that story's teeming arteries. Why, who knows if the great man himself might not have climbed into a back window some night—he was not above that, you know—and I might have a drop of that divine blood in me. Yes, my ancestors discussed pigs and gloves and infinity with Shakespeare in Warwickshire. It is so because I believe it to be so.

Richmond 1844 is long ago and far away now, but that summer is pressed down in my mind like the corner of a favorite page in a cherished book. Only in memory can time be imprisoned; as man's incredulity dismisses the awesome significance of the cosmic, so can he make static time's incessant flow. Time wears the apparel of each man's recall; it can be grand or sordid, revolutionizing or stultifying, its tomb mildewed or marmoreal, to the extent of that man's experience and his perception of it. Let me tell you, there is a certain amount of fortuity in everything—this heightens the spirit somewhat, to the reduction of the intellect—and we never know when we are walking at the margins of fateful beginnings.

Finally, there remains the bemused wonderment of retrospect. We weave our filigreed arabesques around each other's lives; we're helpless puppets on other people's strings, as they are upon ours. I had made a studious career of minding my own business. I was militantly private. I kept leaving home because there were people there who knew me too well (or thought they did, which is even worse), and my mind had the constant feeling of being invaded, innocently invaded, so always had to be vigilant and unnecessarily distracted. But trespassers are everywhere, and as long as you pull breath, you will feel encroachment. Your father was the chief invader of all, my Mongol horde. Not only did he perceive what I thought were my most profound depths with offhand comments, but he did more: he unveiled and confided to me the dawn and eventide of his soul with what I, the private person, thought were shameless disquisitions. By compelling my attention he made me his prisoner.

"Fortuity, Ben," Hook said in the shadow-wreathed gloom of the upstairs room. He sat on the rocker, his arms in repose on the rests, his voice in slow monotone, in slow spiral from the ever-widening crypt. The youth sat across the room from him, straddling a reversed chair, hands and chin resting on the back, his intense, winkless eyes seeing the configurations being painted by the slow, mild monotone.

There were Negro servants standing at the front door, wearing silver-buckled frock coats and satin knee breeches and powdered wigs, holding burning torches, and the guests were filing in between them. Whenever I see something like that I become uncomfortable; I know I am a guest in the house of a supreme ass, an arch pretender. I went to the party as escort to a young woman named Olivia Pentwright. She was a petite thing with grand manners whom everyone thought was the perfect lady, but she smoked cigars in my room and begged to be told of my rougher experiences in the Cumberlands. She was a friend of this grandiose Porter family, whose house stood upon a rise above the James waters like an imbecile's dream of the Parthenon.

There was a little string orchestra trying to saw their way through Mozart and Haydn while the guests danced with elegantly mincing little steps. We all gathered in the ballroom after the serving of libations, under a ceiling of painfully detailed oval plaster medallions with rings of outfurling thistle leaves, with dimple-cheeked cherub heads smiling with angelic decadence around the borders. It was artwork execrable enough to make Michelangelo sigh in his grave. Good Havana smoke webbed through the French bronze chandeliers as lazy as the honey-thick voices around me. The patriarchs and the matriarchs sat on the apple green satin-covered sofas lining the walls, the men alternating puffs from their cigars with sips from brandy-filled Venetian glasses. The talk would be centering on tobacco and the affairs of the world soon enough, and the ladies would be gathering their skirts and trotting discreetly to the other side of the room, where they would bind themselves together with light, insipid conversation. Of course everybody was insufferably polite to the Yankee.

After a while I stepped outside to the terrace to get some cool air under my collar. That was when I saw the horseman sitting across the immaculate lawn carpetry, near the woods. I wondered about him. I accounted him as some local who had come as close as he dared to steal a glimpse of the self-esteemed aristocracy. There was a bright moon and I could see him plainly. He was like sculpture, utterly motionless. Then I went back inside and for some reason or other headed upstairs. I was halfway up the spiral staircase when I heard a cry from the ballroom. I had to bend just a little to get a full view. That was when I saw Allen Travis McKinley for the second time.

He was riding across the stone-floored terrace where a moment ago I had been standing, coming through the turned-back curtained doors, mounted upon an enormous black stallion, bareheaded, wearing a black flannel shirt open at the throat, his trousers tucked into leather boots. One hand was clutching the reins, the other held a large club that looked like oak or elm.

I sat down on the stairs and watched through the carved

cherrywood balustrade. It was a virtuoso performance. He drove the horse into the center of the room as the women shrieked and the men shouted and all scattered. The club snapped through the air and decapitated a porcelain griffin, smote in two an ivory-eyed bust of Caesar, shattered the row of candelabra on the harpsichord and finally came down viciously on the shoulder of a man who tried to unhorse him. The horse moved out of the chaotic ballroom and its hoofs clucked and clattered on the floor of the marble entranceway directly under my eyes, your father seething and furious in the saddle, burning with a self-righteousness that only he could muster. That was when I recognized him—the outraged Pindar scholar I had encountered a few days before. The club flashed again and smashed the ballroom's Regency doorhead and hammered notches into its lovely graduated shelving effect.

Everybody was yelling get him, get him. Mr. Porter had turned absolutely bilious, was screaming hysterically above the din of shrieking women and shouting men and crashing debris. The club poked out at a sculpted growling lion crouched on a pedestal at the ballroom doorway and sent it flying into fragments over the polished floor. Then the horse returned to the living room, driving through the darting guests—faces were peering out from behind furniture as though at play in a children's game. A brandy glass was hurled and struck harmlessly against the rider's chest. The horse wheeled again as your father clubbed at the chandelier—he couldn't quite reach it, which seemed only to infuriate him more. My pistols are upstairs, Mr. Porter wailed, his voice reproaching the gods for the inconvenience of his brace. Then I saw the fresh, malodorous pads of dung on the entranceway floor. Look at that, someone cried. (This was looked upon as the worst desecration of all.) My God, Mr. Porter cried and lost his Southern-gentlemen manners in front of the ladies and loosed the most sulphurous stream of profanity and went for your father, only to be driven back by a violent kick in the chest that sent him tumbling. Then your father hurled the club—with good aim—at a tableful of glasses and bottles and decanters, and galloped the horse through the terrace doors and outside, leaped over the low marble balustrade and rode off into the night, leaving behind the chaos, the shambles, the screaming women and the outraged men, and the clods of dung like festering sores on the marble floor.

There were other sides to his disposition, of course. He could be sunny and friendly and light-spirited, the most convivial of companions. His unpredictability, his variegated moods, altering with quicksilver suddenness, enlivened by a trenchant wit, kept one at all times alert in his company. But above all he was dominated by his faults, his weaknesses, his frailties. He spoke once of his pestilence, of how the craftsman who had shaped his soul must have worn black gloves. He was ruthlessly honest with himself because he had taken to heart the Apollonian *Know thyself.* He admitted to being a wastrel, going through an inheritance as destructively as he had gone through the Porter ballroom that night.

When next I saw him, it was at a table in one of Richmond's better barrooms. He was sitting alone, having a glass of wine. I came in and stood at the bar and sipped my whiskey for a time until I noticed him in the back-bar mirror. I stared at him in the mirror, curious and amused. This was about a week after he had wrecked the Porter ballroom and I was surprised to see him, on two counts—that he had had the bravado to remain in town, and, having done so, that he was still alive. Several times he caught me staring at him; he was quick. Finally I turned around and faced him. He looked at me with a rather wan smile. By this time my curiosity about the man was so overwhelming it was no longer containable.

Nothing had emerged from the gabble that followed his exhibition in the Porter place which had explained anything. Nor had I expected it to. If anyone there knew of a legitimate grievance Allen had for what he did, it was not spoken. Nor would it have been, I suppose, people being loath to make unflattering confessions about themselves. There had only been the general outcry, the normal fulminations—fiend, madman, son of a bitch, et cetera—and an effort made to go after him, though finally no one did anything but stand there and exercise thundering oratory.

Certainly I'll tell you why, Mr. Hook, he said after I had joined him at the table (the scene in the bookseller's was never alluded to; it was as if he had completely forgotten it or it had never occurred). We sat there for several hours. One thing I noticed: he drank no more than the single glass of wine he had with him when I sat down. Through the months that I knew him, I never once saw him drunk, in fact never saw him take more than two drinks in a single evening. Excessive drinking put a man at a great disadvantage, he said. It produced evil, he said with a sardonic smile. Were you—? I started to ask. That night? he said. No, I have not been drunk in years; not since college. No easy excuses, Mr. Hook. Sobriety produces evil too: man produces evil, as surely as he does blood, and values it no less.

He had been invited to the gathering by Mr. Porter, he said, but then it was learned that he planned to bring with him a certain young lady whose forebears had not landed in Jamestown in 1607, who was in fact a South Carolinian who had been requested to leave Charleston after being the pivotal figure in several scarlet affairs that had ended with cards being exchanged and men being ventilated. When it was learned that Allen planned to bring this notorious young lady, his invitation was rather brusquely withdrawn, lest all in attendance suffer infection. He took great offense, he said, and so did what he did, with a thundering sense of justice and retribution. He asked me what I thought of his action and I told him he had enlivened what had been for me a rather dull evening, and with that he announced that I was a man of uncommon sense and had to be his friend. I told him I would be delighted. You may find it interesting, he said, almost as an aside.

He was to remain in Richmond for another week, he said, and we were to make the most of it. At this point I still knew very little about him, but did not ask and was not informed. But the sun smiled upon that week and the moon too. Allen and his replanted Charleston trollop and myself and Miss Pentwright (who fell immediately in love with your father, worshipfully, reverently, fearfully) rode into the countryside in your father's rented carriage, stayed the night at roadside inns, picnicked and debauched in the woods, sailed on the James, laughed, frolicked, and generally drew disapproving frowns from the staid and the envious.

Then he came to my room one morning and told me he was returning to his home. He lived outside of a town called Laurelton, about seventy-five miles from Richmond. His business in Richmond (as far as I could tell, it had been limited to carousal and mayhem) was completed and now he was going. He told me I must come to visit him; that I must write. He was in one of his more ebullient moods; he grasped my hand and held it firmly while he fired salvos of good wishes, invitations and farewells. Then he left.

It had only been a week, a week in the summer of 1844, but Richmond seemed an empty place without him. It was a moody time for me. Miss Pentwright had become so hypnotized by your father that she became utterly useless to me and I had to salute her good-bye. I thought incessantly about your father during the weeks that followed. No, there should never have been any doubts about him, but I didn't listen to that voice of reason that kept trying to urge itself forward inside my head. Now, I had met a lot of colorful characters in my travels. I had worked on barges on the Erie Canal and cut timber in the Maine woods and been to other places and done other things. (He coaxed from me my entire history by sly, maieutic questions. He was amused by my passion for privacy and consequently kept trying to penetrate it. If he suspected I had been to a place, he would begin making deliberate misstatements about it, until I felt constrained to correct him, whereupon he would ask me how I knew that, and I would have to say I had been there. Why? he would ask, and it would go on. He called me a cultured vagrant, a deluded romantic, a one-man sect. I remember it all. He probed my mind and came out with the startling bit of information that I considered myself mankind's last beacon of independence and integrity and that I would be buried on the side of a mountain because I would die climbing, die on the skirts of a cloud. He would say, Hook, you are the most frustrated human being within the ken of the planets. Why do you say so? I would ask. Because you yearn for a secret. You are insanely reticent and private and lack honest justification for it. You need a secret. Perhaps one day I'll give you one, he said. He was to be true to his word.)

But I had never met anyone like him. And neither had anyone else, apparently. I rode out to the Porter mansion to ask, very innocently, what they had done about the violent invasion by "that stranger." I was hoping to get some unadulterated opinions about my friend Allen Travis McKinley. Porter invited me out to the terrace, where we sat and sipped whiskey while we talked. Oh, that, he said when I finally put it into the conversation. He scowled. That was Allen McKinley, he said. Do you know the man? Ah, no, I said. Well, Porter said, he's Virginia's most bizarre and flagrant scandal. As a matter of fact the whole family have been troublemakers. Brother committed suicide, in a most peculiar way. Had a nigger tie him to the mouth of a cannon and light the fuse. You can imagine what was left . . . a pair of boots and an ankle bone, I think. They hanged the nigger, of course, though some people said he'd only been doing what he was told . . . but never mind. And then the father, Jesse, well, he was hanged by his peers in King William County some years ago for taking the life of a woman. An *affaire de coeur,* if you understand, but sordid, and then ghoulish. He took another man's wife. She was going to go away with Jesse. I don't know about your part of the country, Mr. Hook, but down here that is one of the most mortifying things that can happen to a man. When you hear about a situation of that nature, you just sit back and wait for the violence to occur. Well, to everybody's surprise the husband, hopelessly distraught, put a bullet into his own brain, out of heartbreak or shame or disgrace or whatever it is hysterical men do things for. The consensus was that he had shot the wrong man. So the wife, the widow now, well, you might imagine her frame of mind. She was almost out of her mind with guilt and went back to her babies and told that crude pig McKinley she never wanted to see him again. So he killed her. Put a bullet in her heart one evening while she was standing in front of her house. Did it with a rifle from a hundred yards away—the son of a bitch was a dead shot. There was a trial and he was acquitted because of lack of an eyewitness. Had a lawyer from Roanoke named Mason who they say was too clever for measure. But everyone knew damned well what the truth was. So he got off free and clear. But then do you know what he went and did? You had better take a firm hold of your drink, sir. They caught him one night, digging up her grave. That's right. Desecration of the dead. And why? *I want my bullet back,* he said. *That bullet belongs to me.* So they had him good and tight this time. He walked to the gallows shouting military commands to his executioners—he'd been a captain with Jackson at New Orleans.

So, I said, you plan to do nothing to Mr. McKinley for having raised such hell in your home? I've decided to be magnanimous, Porter said. I'm a gentleman and a Christian, he said. If Allen McKinley stays away from Richmond, I won't molest him. But if ever my eyes apprehend him again in this city, I shall shoot him down like a dog. That was the purest nonsense, of course. He couldn't have

helped knowing that Allen had stayed on in
Richmond—flagrantly so—for a week after riding through
that elegant ballroom. But not a hand was raised against
him. They were afraid of him, that was the blunt truth of
it.

After Miss Pentwright had wandered off into the mists
heartsick over your father, a smiling irony saw me take up
with his Charleston trollop, Miss Blanton. She seemed always to have money, no visible means of support, but a
lovely face and figure. I did not allow myself so much as
to cross the merest thought over what she might be doing
to earn that money, particularly since my own funds were
running low and she was good enough to share with me.
So I stayed on in Richmond with Miss Blanton through
the dark end of autumn. She had little to impart about
your father. He had met her in Richmond only recently,
he had shown her a good time, and then he had gone
away. She was a rare female soul in that she was not
strongly taken with him; she thought him unpredictable,
a little bit strange, even cruel, and admitted to being always
uneasy in his company. This was, of course, spiced with
a certain sense of intrigue, which such men often cast into
women. One thing I learned from her was a story Allen
had told about his paternal grandfather. The old gentleman, it seemed, had walked around the last thirty years
of his life with a Bible tied to the top of his head, because,
he said, the human brain was the Lord's noblest work. She
had thought it very funny, but she said Allen frowned
when she laughed.

It was late November when the letter came. He had
assumed I was still living in the same place and he had
guessed right. My name was scrawled across the length of
the envelope in a fantastic hand that seemed to have swum
up and down with a pen in hand. The letter, in its entirety,
read: *For God's sake, man, come out here if you can. Immediately.
Allen.*

I said to myself, You owe this man nothing. He apparently has let his playful temper run out too much slack again and wants an ally to help him out of his trouble or a friend to whom to impart another confession. After all, I said to myself, what is he to me? An acquaintance of mere days. So I decided I wouldn't go. It was the very thing I had been sedulously avoiding all my life—personal involvement. Tact and discretion and no commitments had so far kept me content and unencumbered. So I decided not to go. I kept deciding it even as I rode up along the pebbled driveway under a ring of towering oaks to his house, riding a horse I had rented at the stagecoach terminus some ten miles away. It was not the grandest of houses, but nonetheless imposing. I saw it first at dusk and it had a mood about it, a sullenness almost, an alienation, as if it were some temple of ancient, repudiated philosophies. At dusk certain country houses have a way of imparting something about their inhabitants by the way the night spreads upon the walls and eaves and roof, by the way windows close up into darkness. It stood in the shadow of a heavy woodland and in the closer shade of oaks and the long combings of melancholy willows. The boxwood hedges were turning into wild growth, the front lawn was taking on a rather ragged quality; a statue in the middle of it—it was Homer, your father insisted—had only one arm, the driveway was beginning to show tiny knots of grass amid the scattered pebbles, and even some weeds along the curving margins. Time was on the place, you could feel it—more, you could see it, a heavy rendering of it, as if it had been vanquished once, repulsed by pride and determination, by a deadly belief in self and after-self; but now it was coming back, in layers, to reclaim what it had never truly relinquished in the first place. Its fist was on the wrought-iron fence that ran the length of the downstairs veranda, its sinister film was upon the grayish Doric columns that supported the upstairs porch, its breath was like a pernicious fog in the willow trailings that surrounded the place like a committee of praying arboreal nuns, and its pallor was on the walls and the double doorway, and its ghost was the centurion helmet that hung as knocker. Time the infinite, the container and bestower of all things known and unknown, is a horrific force to see in its finite shape as it comes to annihilate what is doomed to be mortal or perishable: upon this house time was not awful in its oldness, but in its design.

I was admitted by a Negro in a frock coat. He was very courtly. There were two: this gentleman and his wife. They lived in quarters behind the garden house. When your father saw me—he emerged from the library in his shirt, holding a quill in his hand—a look of great relief crossed his face. He took my hand and thanked me for coming, very genuinely. We went into the library and sat and talked. He was quite calm, relaxed, even serene. After a while I started feeling perturbed, put upon. Why did you ask me here? I demanded. Can you stay? he asked. You had better give me some explanation, I said. I want you to stay, he said. The rest will be self-explanatory. You don't have to do anything you don't want to do, but I would like you to stay. And do what? I wanted to know. We're not idle here, he said, relaxed in a deep chair. I can see him now, at his ease, a trifle pleased because he knew he had put me off balance; his smile enigmatic, but at the same time as stated as a promissory note. He had whetted my curiosity and he knew it. He was a subtle, involuted man, with a penchant for playing serious games mischievously; and although he did not take advantage of people, loved to have them at disadvantage—a thing he would make distinctions about. Yes, he was cussed, damn him. A keen appraiser of himself; he had so shrewdly mastered himself that all others were easy, were prey. He was either totally profligate or utterly niggardly with his personal charm, and often either swing of this pendulum seemed without rhyme or reason. Was it practiced or natural? I couldn't tell. And I was a cynic, the man of closed shutters and locked doors. I thought I knew something. But your father was not a man of one-dimensional secrets; rather he was a person of veils and layers, of partial revelations. Whatever he was, whatever he knew—all would be offered in its proper time and place, and often with an almost esthetic structure, as though certain things were too significant to be haphazardly disclosed. Perhaps he had a melodramatic quirk in him; yes, I think that might be true—he was too self-conscious for it not to be true.

So he said we would not be idle there. We would ride, he said, and hunt, and read (he had a well-stocked library), and talk, and work when we wanted (he owned a patch of unworked land not far away, but we ignored it), and when I felt like catering to my baser instincts (he said), he knew women in Laurelton who would be amused by a man of my sensibilities. So I said, Yes, I'll stay, though not because of anything you've told me but because of what you haven't.

The first great shock came soon after. Just before dinner he introduced me to his wife—your mother (you were then somewhere close to your fourth year and truly your parents' pride: remember that: you were never less than fully and dearly loved by them both). She was an exquisitely beautiful woman. Jennifer Rawlin McKinley. She had a white, unblemished, oval face with wide, darkly luminous eyes—the dark that gives light, your father said of those eyes. She was a very proud woman, of admirable breeding and charm, with a strong, sober mind. Your father was most attentive to her. He once confessed to me (that was his word; why, I don't know. Perhaps he found my knowledge of his peccadillos inhibiting) his deep love for her. Nevertheless he was obviously uncomfortable in her presence. The voices they exchanged were polite rather than casual; they seemed wary of one another. Occasionally I noted an expression of poignant, nostalgic affection in her eyes when she looked at him: it was the expression of someone who had once been very proud of her man but who had suffered some crucial disappointment or sadness.

Your father's refulgent personality was substantially muted when he was around your mother. He was prompt and tender with her. He seemed happiest and most at his ease in her presence when he could do something for her, fetch her tea or raise the light or wheel her into another room. She was paralyzed from the waist down.

We took a long walk around the grounds that night. Allen was carrying an unsheathed saber and from time to time would angrily swipe at a weed or bush. He was in an extremely agitated state. We didn't exchange a word for a long time, until finally he said, All right. Give out with it. You're about to coronate me as the most infamous son of a bitch since Judas. You're about to ask how I can . . . how I could . . . painted whores . . . when I have. . . . I told him: I retain the right to think and speak as I please. If you want to lacerate yourself with my alleged thinking, go ahead. But remember, it's *your* thinking, not mine. All right, he said with some contrition. What do you think?

See me then: A stranger, a virtual stranger, who had answered a mysterious, almost hysterical invitation—an explanation for which I had yet to be given—to come to that house and spend time with these people. I was not an ignorant man, nor an insensitive one, nor was I easily led up paths; I was a man who had always treasured and cultivated his independence. And there I was, permitting this thing to happen. I was a stranger in that house, but already I knew too much, sensed much more, and was allowing myself to be drawn in further and further out of a sense of intrigue, compassion, and helplessness. See me, coming into that house where that beautiful sad-eyed cripple was living with her decaying memories, crushed into captivity by the falling tower of her broken spine, living with a pair of invisible Negroes and a husband who had flayed his morals until they were raw. See me, touching your mother's ivory white hand and hearing her say that Allen had told her all about me. All about what? I thought: About a week's roaring and whoring with ferociously healthy and lusty women in Richmond? I told her you were a scholarly friend I had met in Richmond, he said. With whom, I said, you have had scholarly discussions about the texture of Miss Blanton's breasts. He laughed. You're a good man, Hook, he said. But he had to know what I thought: Was I appalled? What was my judgment of him? It seemed very important to him, and I knew I would get no rest until I gave it. By the looks of it, I said, you're occupying ground midway between nobility and abomination, with good instincts for either direction. He laughed. I'm relieved, he said. I thought you might disapprove of me . . . That was your father.

Your mother knew her merchandise, however. I do not for a moment doubt your scholarship, Henry, she said. But I do know what Allen does in Richmond. Oh, I have no spies, no secret reports; but I do have an imagination and a knowledge of my husband. (I was truly embarrassed. But she was kindly; she was not a person who spoke to enhance herself or to discomfort you; she believed in candor above all, that without it friendship and respect were nothing.) She said she knew quite well that I had not been an unwholesome influence upon her husband, and she hoped that he had not been one upon me, as she prayed I was a man of my own mind, unsusceptible. The McKinley's were a headstrong family, she said, and she understood Allen. Occasionally, she said, he became rather impulsive. They had had a wonderful first few years of marriage, had hunted and ridden together—she had been a skillful equestrienne, had enjoyed jumping. I asked if that was how . . . She said no.

Curious things began to happen. The first occurred about two weeks after I arrived. It was late at night, a chilly, windy night with the clouds blowing across the face of a sinisterly bright moon. The sounds of a howling from deep in the woods penetrated my sleep. I lay awake in bed under a pile of quilts, listening. It was a dog, I decided. And then I thought it might be a wolf. I remembered a man in Kentucky who used to imitate wolf cries, who would come into a tavern and swell up his lips and issue the most authentically wild noises if you would buy him something to drink. I got out of bed and stood in the chill room at the window, staring out at the moon-webbed woods, listening to that lone, lost cry. I thought: A creature that should be either shot for being so unhappy or else sainted for it. The cry was so terrible, so primal, that it rooted me at the window for a long time after it had ceased. Then I was startled to see a moving shadow slip from the woods and head for the house. As it crossed toward the side of the house in the moonlight, I recognized your father. He was striding quickly, blindly it seemed, for one hand was holding his forehead and covering his eyes.

What he had been doing in the woods at that hour I could not even begin to surmise. A small graveyard, where his family was buried, lay on the other side of the woods and perhaps he had come from there. He had a peculiar affinity for the dead, particularly his own dead. He seemed very often to be responding to an argument that was never made—that all life existed as a mosaic of fragmented futility, that it was all random and irregular. He liked to see himself as part of a continuous linear cavalcade, a contributor to a densely interrelated perpetuity. I have never known a man so obsessed with his ancestral background. Unquestionably his ancestors had wondered what he would be like, he said, and undoubtedly his descendants unborn would wonder what he had been like. He alone knew the answers to those sacred questions. Who among us has not deeply dreamed upon the lineaments of our progenitors, he said. It is they who have given us our place in time—in history if you like; we are decidedly not accidental, nor of little consequence, any more so than the striving relay runner who clutches the baton for a short time. Are you familiar with the laws of origination, Hook? Hook was not. Hook knew enough: father a farmer, God-fearing and industrious; grandfather the same, and beyond that no one knew, or cared. Most men are as indistinguishable from one another as sands upon a beach anyway, I said, if you want to consider how much of interest finally comes out of them. I don't give a damn about it all, one way or the other. But: Ah, Hook, your ancestor did not link arms with the godhead in Warwickshire; you have not tumbled from a line that was always young, spirited and talented—that sun-fed trinity of virtues so deadly in their commingling. Pride of ancestry was sheer nonsense, I told him. Blood or no, at soul all men are strangers to one another, all are fleshed and blooded by chance. Father and son often the greatest defectors from consanguinity of all. But: Hook, only because you in your blasphemous solitude have never seen your father's skull, eyes, and beard as moon, stars, and comet; cannot feel that creak in your bones when your grandfather turns in his grave; do not feel a millenium's forebears tugging upon your fibers. I don't say we were all heroic, Hook—no discernible kings or earls on our tablet—but people always knew damned well when there was a McKinley about. The color of our eyes and the shape of our thumbs are evidence of life gone before, of intellect and disposition making genetic journeys through the ages. We inherit and we bestow, and because it is steady and ongoing does not reduce its importance. If I don't care, I told him impatiently, then it is not important. To me, I said, importance is all a matter of emphasis.

I said nothing to Allen about what he might have been doing in the woods with that howling going on. He looked at me peculiarly the next morning. I had the feeling that he was anticipating some queries. But I said nothing. Then a thing happened which broke the water once and for all.

It was the dead of winter and I had to return to Richmond to retrieve the rest of my belongings, for I had decided to ignore what better judgment was saying and stay the rest of the winter at your parents' house. My reasons were partially selfish. I had been tiring of Richmond but had not planned any moves. Your father was, of course, a devilishly fascinating companion; but the primary motive was your mother, that most rare and remarkable woman. Although she never said it in so many words, she was most anxious for me to stay on. She was afraid of your father. It was all by implication, but she had premonitions. A decompounding ardor raises these things, I suppose. Perhaps it was that house, that loneliness. I know I had a disquieting feeling as I rode away on a gray January morning, and as my horse galloped over the frozen road, I looked back with a sense of escape, not departure. As a restless traveler, I had often passed houses, by day and by night, and because of the very nature of what I was, could not suppress an occasional pinch of envy (or at least melancholy curiosity); and I thought about travelers—other ones—who must pass the McKinley house and about their envy at the thought of the tranquil people and warm fires within, and how sadly misplaced that envy. Sometimes that lonely wind over your head affords more comfort than might the soft yellow lights that glance from strange windows. I tell you, boy, it can be a solitary feeling, looking sideward when you're traveling; but it isn't always justified.

I returned five days later, on the horse I had borrowed from your father. The Negro man let me in and as I entered the house I met your mother. She was sitting in her wheelchair in the hallway, just as if she had been waiting there for me, a knitted red and blue afghan covering her inutile legs, a maroon shawl around her shoulders. She smiled wanly at me, a most wistful expression in those big, beautiful, dark eyes. She appeared to be studying me very carefully, almost shrewdly, as if taking stock of me, like a man who hires you for a job might appraise you. Allen is in the library, she said; not even hello, no greeting, no salutation; just that smile, and that piece of information, the disposal of which was to be left up to me: I could walk into the library, or not. We exchanged a long, intensely searching set of stares—I trying to divine what she was thinking, she trying to determine something of my mettle—and then I headed for the library.

The door wouldn't open all the way; it swung into some heavy object on the floor and I had to sidle my way in. Allen was across the room, kneeling at something. When he saw me he sprang to his feet and hurried toward me, his large, strong hand eagerly outstretched. He took possession of my hand and squeezed it. His voice rang out like a zealot's, did not sound like his voice at all, sounding artificially loud like a stage performer's in projection. He was delighted I was back, he said. I was in time to help. Look what he had begun. He stepped back and proudly swung out his hand to show me.

That was the saddening and embittering moment, when all doubts were confirmed, all hope nullified. Because I had been resisting the idea for weeks, when finally it broke upon me its horror had unspeakable clarity and impact. All of my self-deluding rationalizations disappeared like feathers in a hurricane. No, God help us, I said to myself, no sane man would be building a boat in his library—the keel was already laid and the frame beginning to rise—and stand there proclaiming with a zealot's ascending voice and inflamed eyes that he was going to take her across the Hellespont. Not mere insanity, but an inspired visionary madness, driven by its own cyclone, enchanted by its own declaiming voice: inspired by its own inspiration. He strode about the room, sleeves rolled to the elbow, his every gesture brisk and impetuous, and struck postures, and described our course (I was going to be mate on this voyage). His gift of rhetoric struck my brow with sea breezes, put a briny taste on my lips, filled my ears with the lurk and prowl of ocean waves, made me see vast lanes of water and feel the sway of mighty girth. He believed it, believed it all, with a passion that was soaring through his head like a covey of spangled comets: talking about a thing he would have to dismantle his house to move even one inch.

Hook paused and he laughed, a hollow-souled eremite's pitiful laugh, into his beard, and Ben said, "What? What is it?" By now dawn was at the window, a callow peeper out of the east, and Hook glanced at it and murmured, "Don't worry, Master Ben. You'll hear the whole of it. We'll leave no stone placed where it was before."

Because I helped him build it. I kneeled there like an imbecile and helped him raise the gunwales, lugged timber and drove nails; helped him raise a seaworthy vessel on the earth-colored carpet of his library, while he strode about as enchanted and soulfully ravished as must have been the young Phoenician mariners who first went down to the sea from Tyre and Sidon in their flimsy galleys. Yes, I helped him build the damned thing, what building of it he did.

It will soon pass, your mother said. The whole thing will pass and he'll awake from it like a child from a dream. She was used to it, of course, or at least familiar—I don't imagine there was any getting used to it. I had seen insanity before, God knows: in the faces of cackling old men, in the bewildered stupidity of young men who chewed their words, in all the hidden, secretive lines of pathetic jibbering faces that had been abandoned (or maybe never visited) by their God. But nothing like this, that so seductively embraced the lives of others. Believe me, I never hammered nails truer or laid boards with more care, because I was never absolutely certain that he couldn't dissolve his walls and bring a river rushing in to lift that horror into buoyancy.

She and I spoke about it at great length. I drift, she said, between a wife with one child and a widow with two. But he always comes back. What else has he done? I asked. Nothing really harmful, she said (that was a magnificent woman, Benjamin, mark me). He talks to his ancestors and lectures his descendants, bays in the woods, builds cabins and burns them down. His father and brother were similarly disquieted at times, and from what I understand, the grandfather too. But my son is not like that, she said. He simply has imagination. There is a difference. What do you mean? I asked. She was reluctant to tell me, but I coaxed it from her. Her little boy would awake screaming in the night, insisting that God's face had appeared to him, God's face ripped with a bloody laugh. Merely a nightmare, I said. Of course, she said quietly.

It lasted for about a week. And then one morning I came downstairs and Allen was in the library, dismantling the thing. The Negro was carrying the planks out. Your father looked at me—he was sitting on the floor ripping out nails with the claw of a hammer. He smirked (perhaps it was an attempt at bravado, but not very persuasive if it was). Were you frightened, Henry? he asked.

We walked through the woods for hours. It was a bright, cold day. The woods were dead, the leaves fallen, the tree-tops like so many ragged spires against an ice blue winter's sky. We pulled on our pipes and walked with our heads down, for the most part silent. We came to a stream coated with ice. He knelt there and with a stone broke the ice and made the waters run again. It's like that, he said, looking up at me. Like a freezing. The waters are always running clearly underneath, but something quite gripping and ty-rannical overlays it for a time. Have you done anything about it? I asked. No, he said. I fight through it. A particle of me knows what's happening; but it's like I'm a thousand miles away; I can see it but there's nothing I can do about it. Something else, someone else, takes possession and I, the rightful tenant, am compelled to stand apart helplessly. And then there's the brutal turnabout. Now, right now, Henry, I can feel *it* standing a thousand miles off watching *me,* right at this instant; its little eyes, cracked with streaks of blood, watching me. My ancestor's friend in Warwick-shire had the same problem (he said this with a wry smile, as if embarrassed at making the reference when he was lucid), but the difference is Mr. Shakespeare had the power of mind and the disciplining strength to harness the force and make it pull a pen across paper when it had taken possession of him. He mastered utterly both the art of madness and the madness of art; he was able to tyrannize his demons. With me it's quite the opposite. If there is sufficient puissance in your creativity, well, then it's the Lord's madness in opposition to the Devil's. If you don't have that balancing power, well, then you had better not go lighting matches near gunpowder.

I asked him what he intended to do. We were walking again, following a curling little path through the woods. Nothing, he said. But some harm may occur, I said. It already has, he said somberly.

Two years before, it seemed, even the atom of vision that stood a thousand miles away must have been shuttered, because he did not even remember the scream and Jennifer had lain for two days at the foot of the stairs and the Negroes were afraid to come into the house. She always maintained to your father that she had slipped, but he knew better. If she had merely slipped, he said, why then did that precious flicker of love and trust leave her eyes? I mean that golden incandescence she always had for my face. It wasn't just pain and mourning for her tragedy that replaced it, but fear and distrust. Why then do her shoulders clutch in upon themselves when my hand comes even most tenderly to them? No, I did it, Hook. God almighty, Hook, think of it—think of a hurricane, think of the windy leaves in Aeolus's cavern, think of an electrical storm—and imagine it all inside your own head, your thoughts running amok, like rabbits under the gun. Think of your own body as a cage for diabolical spirits, your blood foaming like an idiot's lips; think of all the exquisite balance and precision that is the human mind falling inexplicably apart like rotted timber; think of yourself as deprived of all will, all restraint, all dignity, scuttling to the whims of creaking ogres. And above all, Hook, think of yourself as a living menace to those you love most dearly.

He stopped and looked into my eyes. He spoke very

quietly, evenly. Stop me, Hook, he said, if ever you see me attempting harm upon my family. If necessary, kill me. Give me your promise on it. I say this calmly, soberly, master of each word.

It was like making a covenant with a shadow. He made me swear it. Then suddenly, so characteristic of that mercurial spirit, he laughed. You have a great advantage on me now, he said. You have been given full dispensation to be my assassin.

Liken him to a bedeviled, bedazzled Herostratus at the end, stirred to strike for the sake of some distorted sense of immortality, driven by some final mad lust to unleash his spirit upon eternity. He had been speaking of the treasures of his library. There were thousands of beautifully bound volumes, some quite valuable. There was one with Doctor Johnson's scrawl in it, others supposedly owned by Donne and Pope. On the shelves were many statuettes, some with shards of emerald for eyes. It was his temple of Ephesus, he said. I should have been vigilant, from this talk. But I failed to recognize the signs.

That terrible miasma locked its toxic affinities for the last time one black night in February. I awoke to the smell of smoke and by my lamp saw it curling under my door like a poisonous gray wool. I pulled on boots and trousers and raced out and plunged into a compartment of hell. The smoke was swirling densely through the upstairs hall. I saw robes and wreaths of orange fire, and tongues and sheets of it. Your mother was screaming from behind her bedroom door. The fire was heaviest there and I could not get near it. I raced downstairs with the intention of getting an ax from the kitchen, hoping to somehow chop through to her. I got the thing and was heading back when I saw Allen running up the stairs ahead of me. His library was a raging inferno, brilliant, hot, lusty. I chased after him, calling his name. At the head of the stairs he suddenly halted and wheeled upon me. Give me Methuselah's span and I'll still never forget the look I saw in his eyes. They were, so help me, simmering, as though they were about to blister like boiling water. We fired questions at each other—I: What have you done? He: What are you trying to do? I: Where is Ben? As I tried to get past him, he seized me. We grappled for a moment at the head of the stairs. He was trying to throw me down. I broke free and retreated several steps, lifting the ax behind my shoulder and then hurling it around with all my might. I cut into the side of his neck and as he fell away— I never saw him again—I wasn't sure if I hadn't, am still not sure to this day, decapitated him altogether. He seemed to flee into the smoke, as if dissolving into it. I was unable to get near your mother's door; it was simply engulfed by a curtain of fire. Her voice rang out from within, clear and strong: *Henry, the boy!* I ran to your room and threw aside the door. You were crouched on your bed. I scooped you up and carried you like a loaf of bread under my arm. As I ran with you, I shouted out, *I have him! I have him!* And I pray to God that she heard that much at least before . . . I ran downstairs and outside, into the night air's cool reason. The Negroes were there, their eyes huge and terrorized, and we drew back and together, without words, watched the house raise high flames that burned away the skirts of the night, watched it finally shudder and collapse with a roar and a seething galaxy of sparks.

What happened after that, I don't know. I'm sure some drawling Christians came and gave the remains a decent burial, though there is not tomb deep enough nor field broad to sleep that tormented soul that was your father's. I took a horse from the stable and left. I had no intention of staying around to offer explanations, for it was I who had swung that ax. So I rode off, away from that smoldering heat and into the cold night, clutching you like an Israelite with his firstborn, and we came to Capstone.

Four

I'LL NEVER FORGET THE coming of that dawn, the brightening of the sun in that room, the final cessation of his voice. It was a tale told by night, and for night, and I believe he would have gone on and on in somber narrative as long as the dead side of the night hung. At dawn he stopped, weary and depleted; not just physically, but mentally and spiritually, too. Of course he had been there and seen it, been participant and witness. For me it had been mere narration; for him, reliving and reconstruction (and I knew better than most what could happen to mind and spirit when memory turned excessive).

"The rest you know," he said.

Yes, the rest I knew, beginning with that endless and (for a four-year-old) incomprehensible trip north, riding that horse through rain and snow and sleet, listening to its hoofs sucking up and down in the mud. Not remembering all of it, of course—when does memory begin subscribing utterly to experience?—but enough: riding that horse, the man's rapt and unchanging face, his arm around me like belt to the coarse blanket I was wrapped in, the occasional falling of his eyes to look at me; crossing rivers and streams, stretches of dirt road and of field and meadow and forest that had become portraits in memory; sleeping in roadside inns, sometimes in stale-smelling barns, sometimes even on the back of that swaying tireless animal; and then the startling sight of paved streets as far as the eye could see and countless people and the high formidable buildings, and then the passing of those amazing places as the paved street ran once again into the dirt road.

The old man (he had aged perceptibly to my eye from midnight to dawn) sighed. He was soul weary. He had made the journey once again and this time had relinquished something and was the emptier for it, in both body and spirit. He had needed a secret, had found it, nurtured it, and now he had been compelled to yield it. Soul weary, yes, with a patina of melancholy upon him. He had brought the dead back a long way and they were slow to die again, their hands loath to withdraw from him. It took some time before he reinterred them and resealed the crypts, some time before his eyes returned from their poignant inward vision. Then he seemed to remember I was there and those eyes were up and studying me.

"It's difficult for me to feel for people whom I never knew," I said.

He was astonished. His eyes dilated sternly for a moment. "That isn't—"

"You knew them," I said. "They were your friends. From your description of their lives, it seems it was all unavoidable. It was interesting to hear it all, finally, and I am saddened by what it was."

"But what I wanted to convey most importantly—"

"And now I understand the reason for your long silence," I said. "They probably want you for murder down there."

"That isn't it at all," he said with some heat. "That thought has never occurred to me."

"It wouldn't be unnatural if it had. But you could have

told me long before this. Your secret would have been safe with me."

He was furious. He leaned tautly forward in his chair and fixed his eyes on me. "*My* secret?" he asked in an incredulous whisper. "*My* secret?"

He should have let it be. He should have known I was not so obtuse. He had driven the nailhead below the wood and should have stopped there. I lost my temper. "I know what you wanted to tell me," I said angrily. "You said it all quite plainly: people wearing Bibles on their heads, blowing themselves up in the mouths of cannons, opening graves, building boats in their libraries . . . You were not very subtle."

No, he had not been subtle, and he saw it. "It does not necessarily follow one generation to the next," he said quietly. "But you should be aware of the history."

"History?" I asked. "And what were you doing—writing the preamble to the next chapter? If there is a seed, you have just planted it. Your implication was unmistakable; you knew when you rang your Sanctus bell upon your story."

"I told you this to feed your strength," he said, "not undermine your weakness."

"My weakness?"

"Call it what you will," he said coldly. "But one thing you must never doubt or question is my concern about you."

"I'm aware. You've always been there with your clinical eye, studying the evidence. And now that you know that I know, you'll be harder at your studies than ever. Except that I'm relieving you of them. You'll be able to sit peacefully. I'm going away."

"Away?"

"Yes," I said, "I signed a piece of paper. I'm going to war."

Five

"WHAT DOES HE WANT?" Ben asked. He was lying on his cot. The flap of the Sibley tent was open and Malloy was standing there, arms crossed, blocking the blue sky. Malloy shrugged.

Ben sighed. He hadn't even pulled off his mud-caked boots. He had thrown himself down on the cot and felt peace and comfort beginning to filter into his bones for the first time in a week, a week of tense, perilous, belly-crawling spying along the perimeters of the Confederate lines as part of a nine-man reconnoiter; a week of sleeping under the Virginia sky, in the spring rains, of counting tents by day and campfires by night.

"I can't move," he said.

"You'd better," Malloy said.

"I have to think. I have work to do."

"Work?" Malloy asked quizzically.

Of the most onerous kind, Ben thought. For instance: What did you do with the memory of a head bounding down the side of a ridge at South Mountain? Five men gathered around the thing and stared with reverence and horror upon the gaping dirt-clogged eyes and the thin

slack lips, just stared stupidly until one of them said, I ain'
feedin' it. What did you do with memory's etching of wild
dogs scratching at hastily dug graves outside of Mechan
icsville? It was all an imposition upon the sensibilities of
a poet.

"You'd better go in and see him," Malloy said.

"Doesn't he know I just got in?" Ben asked.

Malloy shrugged, then went away.

Of course, I've been properly outraged and horrified
at it all, Ben thought. He sat up on the cot and swung his
legs around and set his boots on the plank floor. I've had
two years of practice now. The cries of widows and orphans
have torn at my heart. The faces of the dead, their piled
husks (especially after Antietam), their stink—hasn't it all
properly assailed me? Did I really expect anything else?
It's quite normal, isn't it, to say of things that are awful
and terrible that they are awful and terrible? But what is
suspect, my boy, is to wait for normal reactions and then
be relieved to have them.

As he walked along one of the lanes created within the
vast encampment, he came upon an artist sitting cross-
legged on the ground sketching several soldiers who were
lounging in the grass nearby. The men were sitting quietly,
staring rather sullenly at the artist, obviously uncomfortable, but at the same time grudgingly cooperative. The
artist—he was from one of the weeklies—was profoundly
absorbed, and it was this total absorption that was holding
his subjects in place, as if perhaps they were scenting a
zephyr of immortality. Ben paused to study both artist and
group for a moment. Perfect, he thought, moving on. This
was the job of the artist—any artist: to give rank and honor
to the ordinary and the commonplace and then ship them
along the esthetic byways and let them achieve their own
levels of acceptance.

The colonel welcomed him into the large command-post
tent and told him to take a seat at the writing table.

"The captain tells me," the colonel said, "that you have

the finest penmanship in the company. I want to dictate to you some thoughts I have for the talk I'm going to give the company tomorrow. Will you please take them down?"

Ben lifted the quill and poised it over the topmost sheet of paper of the modest stack before him, pondering that clean white space. The colonel sounded like a stuttering engine as he cleared his throat. Then he began to pace, then he began to give voice to his thoughts. Soon his eyes turned eagle-keen as he drew inspiration from the air around him, his voice hit a certain level of pomposity and maintained it, his hand slid flatly into his tunic. For almost an hour he paced back and forth in the tent, knocking together fustian splendors of language into sentences that swayed in their frames and buckled at their centers. Occasionally he paused, rubbing together his lips as he considered his next thrust of verbal pageantry, priming his verbs and loading his adjectives, then plunging ahead into another botanical cluster of oratory, as Ben sat head-bent at the table, quill sailing in smooth, unbroken tides across one sheet of white foolscap after the other.

When the colonel had exhausted his supply of thoughts, he stood at the front of the tent and studied the blue spring sky and breathed with great satisfaction. Then he turned to Ben. "I'll read it over now, sergeant," he said, taking the sheaf of papers from the table as Ben looked up at him with a strange, mildly offended expression.

The colonel began reading. His eye ran down the top page, quickly, then he turned to the next, and to the next. Then he flung the papers to the floor and glared at Ben.

"What the goddamn hell do you think you've done?" the colonel demanded, face flushed with anger.

"I'll still call you sergeant, just from habit," Malloy said, glancing at the empty lines left on Ben's sleeve by the torn-away chevrons. "What the hell did you do anyway? Why won't you tell?"

"Don't you know, Eamon," Ben said, "that there are people in this world who need secrets?"

"I don't understand that," Malloy said.

"Neither do I. But it's true nevertheless."

They were moving through a north Virginia woodland, part of a twelve-man squad dispatched to try and locate where Confederate raiders were crossing the river. Ben was tired. His back hurt and his legs were weary. Because of the colonel's spite and anger, he had been sent out again, just one day after having returned from a similar mission. You damned ass, the captain said to him, it's just lucky you're not being court-martialed. He was all set for that, but I spoke out for you, you damned ass. The captain had referred to heroism at South Mountain and Fredericksburg. Such men could not be spared, he told the colonel (who himself recalled the sergeant's gallantry in rallying his men on the frozen terraces of Marye's Heights). All right, the colonel said. But I have been deeply insulted and something must be done about it. I'll have his stripes and I'll have his respite. Add him to tomorrow's reconnoiter.

There was a soft, exploratory spring breeze in the woods. He listened to the sounds of soldiers walking: boots on the sun-flecked woodland floor, the beat of a canteen against a thigh, an occasional metallic rattle. It would have been impossible to explain it to that self-important son of a bitch, he thought. I had not held a pen in my hand for more than a week and suddenly I had all that clean paper before me, not the backs of envelopes this time or cajoled bits of wrapping paper, but large white clean square sheets. Thank God I was wearing no sidearm, Ben thought, remembering the colonel tearing to shreds the long stanzas of poetry, or else I would have shot out one of his eyes. Now that poem was gone forever, like the one that had been shot away with his hat in the cornfield at Antietam. It was impossible to summon them a second time; it was as though they existed as part of a single impulse, a single irretrievable natal moment. The one in the lining of his hat was a lovely one and he liked to speculate upon its fate. It had been tucked so far inside the lining that someone picking up the hat might not notice it. So perhaps somewhere, someone, Union or Confederate, soldier or civilian, man or boy, was wearing the poem on his head; or maybe the hat was still lying on the battlefield, a doughty bit of culture amid the cornstalks. Add to the casualties of war one poem, and let's leave all conclusions to the romantics, the incurables.

It was past midday now and the spring sun was high and bone-warming in the blue sky. Shirts were beginning to darken with perspiration. The squad struck a dirt road carved out by generations of wagon wheels and hoofbeats. They passed under the branches of stately oaks beginning to load with acorns. Following their lieutenant, they passed an abandoned homestead and began moving through a field of yellow knee-high grass, across which the wind was blowing shadows. They were heading for a small, uncovered hill that commanded the area a half-mile away.

He began having strange retrograde feelings and without examination leaped to embrace them. He felt an acquiescence, more of body than of mind, an almost physical impaction upon what for two years had been laboring under bitter spiritual denial. *I've been here before.* And not as a soldier either—the memory was too mist-laden, too taunting in its familiarity. That road back there, the trees, the rock formations, the farmhouses—it was all becoming more and more sharply defined in gradually relinquishing memory. When the wind blew and those trees moved and this grass swayed, those old solemn portraits stirred. Yes, we came this way, the spurious self-styled Israelite and his tender charge. Now what had been coldly and skeptically suppressed began to come to life with palpitant urgency; curiosity surged into yearning, into a longing which now had him relentlessly in its hold. For the first time he found himself consciously, even willingly, lending credence to

Hook's night-long narration of concatenated blood and horror. He realized that he had been refusing to accept the story, been resisting its veracity with a carapace of self-defense. But now the might of its truth was upon him, with a vividness that seemed to be springing upward from out of two years of mindful suppression.

They were several hundred yards from the hill's lower slopes when the sight of something made each man stop and freeze in place. A lone horseman had suddenly risen from the rear slope and come still against the sky, fixed there as though that crest were its pedestal. The Union soldiers stood equally still in the soundless sunlight, each man with the suspended animation of a pendulum stopped in midstroke, gazing with alertly inquiring and unwinking eyes, and for the slimmest of moments it seemed as if it would be a contest of wills—the squad of men in the blowing grass against the lone horseman who was watching them with an almost feudal air from his eminence like an ancient symbol of claim and possession. And then something moved behind him, rising, elevating from the back slope, slowly and quietly spreading along the treeless crest with the ease of natural growth.

The half-dozen figures in gray sat their horses and gazed down the slope and across the grass at the arrested squad of Union soldiers, giving an impression of complete command from their position, and not just because they were mounted and held the heights, but because they seemed splendidly self-possessed, exuding a profound sense of being indigenous to the land, component, of having indwelled here for centuries, of being defenders, allied with the Southern earth and the Southern trees and the conspiring Southern sky. Ben would always remember it as having come rushing from out of that blue sky and into a foolish old sunshine meant for love's renewal: Confederate troopers leaning into their horses, speeding down the slopes, sabers high, emitting little yips.

The squad broke and were off in different directions

before their lieutenant could order them into a line. Some
headed for the trees where the breeze was running off the
dogwood scent. Others unshouldered their rifles and
struck positions. The first gunfire sounded soft, almost
harmless on the languorous yellow air. And then a Union
solider was struck in the chest and fell over backward like
an unhinged door and disappeared into the grass.

With flair and dash, the Confederates came on, hat
brims pinned up, beards rustling with the wind, eyes
aflame with excitement; one of the hell-bent riders with
a saber in one hand, a pistol in the other, and the reins
in his teeth. Rifle fire picked one from his saddle and he
dropped from his running horse and struck the ground
hard and bounced once and whirled over in the air and
then struck again and lay there and seemed to curl as if
trying to mold himself to the earth's contours.

A major in gray, with peacock feathers pinned to his
slouch hat, bore down upon a desperately reloading man
in blue and ran him through with a saber, withdrawing
the blade before the twisting, writhing man could fall. The
major wheeled his horse and sped with his smoking saber
held high. But a bullet from a crackling rifle struck him
before he could impale another victim. He struggled to
remain in the saddle, his gray-bearded face taking on age
as his life's allotment suddenly exceeded its brim and he
began weaving precariously, and the saber, forged for war
and later the honored place above the mantle, dropped
into the grass. His head fell heavily forward and his blouse
began filling with blood and the reins slipped from his
hand. An abrupt turn by his horse seemed to make his
suddenly rigid shoulders shudder and a moment later he
was dislodged and slid helplessly out of the saddle, struck
the ground in a face-bowed sitting position and then fell
over and passed to shades and ashes.

The remaining riders swept with slashing sabers and
cumbersome cavalry pistols into the Union soldiers. The
riders presented huge targets to the foot soldiers; they

looked like wild men, man and horse galvanized into single, mutually divining action, wheeling and twisting with consummate skill.

Ben swung his rifle upon one of the riders who had slowed his horse to wheel about; he fired, missed, and then without time to reload, cut across the grass and ran hard for the Confederate's blind side. Ben reached the horse just as it was turning and threw up his hands and hooked his fingers into the man's belt and dragged him from the saddle. Even as he was falling, the Confederate was reaching for a stiletto sheathed in his boot, and as he struck the ground, kicking his foot free of the stirrup, his hand had withdrawn it. Ben fell upon him and seized the lethal hand as they wrestled into the legs of the placidly standing horse, their contorting faces and glaring eyes inches apart, gasping through clenched teeth. Ben broke the other's grip on the stiletto and it fell free and he swept it up as the horse moved a black foreleg, and as the Confederate was rising, Ben, on his knees, whirled and drove the blade to its hilt into the midsection of its former owner. The Confederate's blue eyes flashed with shock in his bearded face and a soft suffering gasp fell from his lips and he sank back into the flattening grass, his shocked eyes gleaming like jewels.

Caught in cross fire from all sides of the field, the riders in gray were dwindling. It was hopeless now; nevertheless they continued to storm through the raging simultaneity of killing and dying, slashing with their sabers like men caught in an intractable undergrowth, possessed by a certain implacable momentum, a sense of fate or inevitability maybe that they had carried with them to the crest of the hill and which they had recognized when they saw that field and its windblown shadows and the blue soldiers and the flowered sunlight—fighting on and on, their faces filled with soft astonishment. One after another they felt rifle shots opening their vents of life and they fell headlong; one by one they were shot from their horses and

became untenanted bodies, their eyes glazing with everlasting night even as their bleeding, sweat-blackened uniforms bespoke furious teeming life. Finally the last of them
was thrown back on his reared horse, one hand clutching
the taut reins, the other aiming a pistol, posed for an instant like some sort of trick-shot artist. He pulled the trigger; the pistol was empty. A snapping of rifle fire tore him
from his saddle and suddenly it was done and over and
the immediate silence was so totally abrupt it was as though
the hand of God had swept over the field.

The acrid odor of combat was still faintly in his nostrils.
From where he was lying he could see a dead Confederate
trooper stretched across the beat-down grass where he had
been hurled, one eye gouged and blasted into a black crater
that glared accusingly across the warm earth at Ben. Ben
closed his own eyes softly and turned his head away.

"Whoever was hit was hit dead," a voice said. That was
Malloy, Ben recognized the faint Irish lilt. "I mean they
ain't no wounded."

"It was smart," another said. "Right smart."

"Say, round up those horses."

"I got me a saber, by God."

"You can scratch your arse with it."

He had seen an eye shot out at Fair Oaks Station and
the man go on fighting for several moments before turning
and sliding backward against a stone wall, the socket foaming blood down his cheek, some dripping into his gaping
mouth. *He drank of his own eye, saw his soul, and died.*

Not far, he thought. I can feel it murmurous in the
ground. McKinley dust, confined and vibrating. *No, no.
Don't think that. Just don't think that.*

"We're returning to camp, men." That was the lieutenant. "I think it would be advisable. We won a remarkable
victory here."

When he opened his eyes he saw Malloy standing over
him, watching him.

"By Jesus," Malloy said, "I was afraid you might be dead."

"No, old friend," Ben said, contriving a tone of feebleness. "But hit bad enough."

"Are you? You ain't bleedin'."

"Inside."

"By God! Lieutenant," Malloy shouted, wheeling around. "Come on h'year—Ben's bad off."

The lieutenant hurried through the grass, a look of consternation in his face. He bent over, placed his hands on his knees and looked at Ben.

"How is it, Ben?" he asked.

"Pretty bad, sir," Ben said.

"He's bleedin' inside," Malloy said.

"You had better get on, sir," Ben said.

"We can't leave you."

"Why?"

"We're a unit."

"I'll be all right. You go on."

"We'll throw you over a horse," the lieutenant said.

"I don't think I could take it."

"We can't just leave you here, man," the lieutenant said.

"Leave me a horse and I'll get back on my own, sir," Ben said. "You had better get on. There might be more rebs, more than you can handle."

The lieutenant swung around, hands still on knees, and looked at the skyline. He hadn't thought of another attack; Ben could see it in his face. He turned back.

"Can you manage all right?" he asked.

"Yes, sir."

"I hate to leave you."

"To do anything else would **be** unwise, under the circumstances."

"All right. You start traveling in when you're able." The lieutenant had risen to full height now. He stared out toward the hill, touching his chin with his fingertips.

"You'd better hurry, sir," Ben said.

"Yes," the lieutenant murmured. "I suspect this was only part of their force."

"Lieutenant," Malloy said as the officer began moving away. "Can I stay with Ben, to help him along when he feels fit to travel?"

The lieutenant stopped, looked back over his shoulder as if perplexed; his mind had clearly taken a quantum leap during these past few seconds. He paused, then irritably said, "All right. All right. But see to him," he added sternly. Then he hurried on, clapping his hands and shouting orders.

"Kind of you, Eamon," Ben said, looking up at him with a wryly amused smile.

"Just can't leave you here," Malloy said, not looking at him. "Anyway, you'd do the same for me, wouldn't you?" Now he looked at Ben. "Wouldn't you?"

"Yes, Eamon, I would."

"So," Malloy said, turning away again. "There."

"Can you ride a horse?"

"A little."

"Make sure they leave two," Ben said.

He rose to one elbow to watch them depart, some walking, some mounted. Malloy was standing off to a side, holding the reins of two horses. There were unpleasant odors on the wind. He could see some of the scattered dead. There were seven Confederate and two Union. They were going to lie here for a long time in the growing grass, under the sun and in the night. They would blacken and swell and burst and stink, souring the sweet wind, attended by the elegies of buzzing flies and ranks of maggots. The cold hard feeling he had was that there was no way he could have died there, not with what he had suddenly felt and known. It was a fate at once calculating and protective that had brought him there.

"Hey!" Malloy cried out to him, seeing Ben rising from the grass. "Should you be doing that?"

"Why not, Eamon?" Ben asked.

Malloy began walking toward him, followed by the two horses. "Jesus Christ, man, you're bleedin' inside."

"Who says?"

"You."

"Well, it just stopped."

"Ben," Malloy asked, advancing slowly, followed by the two horses, holding the reins over his shoulder in his fist. "Wot'n hell you talkin' about? By Jesus, you weren't hit a-tall. Wha'd you want to say that to the lieutenant for?"

"Eamon," Ben said as they drew together in the middle of the field, "were we ever here before?"

"No."

"Sure? We've been at it for two years now. Been in a lot of places. Are you sure?"

"We've never been here before," Malloy said with the stubborn, indignant certitude of one who knew little but who stuck to that paucity with a fervor approaching hostility.

Ben, who had been holding his forage cap in his hand, now placed it on his head, pulling it slightly askew.

"Why'd you want to stay behind?" Malloy asked.

"Eamon, the way I figure it, the army owes us some time. I want to take it now."

"Time?"

"Just a few days' worth. That's all. We'll get by with it."

"But to do what?"

"A little traveling," Ben said, casting a wide-ranging expression of interest around at the whole circular landscape.

"Off to where?"

"Not far, Eamon, not far."

"Christ," Malloy said, "and here I thought you was bleedin' inside."

Six

YOU SAY YOU'VE NEVER been here before, Malloy said. But yet you seem to know where you're going, where you're at.

Did I say I'd never been here? I said. Well, I thought, it was true and it was not true. So and not so. How can I say I was here before if I am not now who I was then, nor then who I am now? Here before? Who? The four-year-old, innocent and unshocked? Of what mind was he, what as-yet unspanned aspiration? What is he to me anyway—more ancestor than self. What point here anyway? To go back there and shout *I remember!* Not necessary, really, since Mr. Hook remembers for you, with all clarity and fine sense of nuance. Curiosity, that's what. Indistinct but trusted. And instinct, any poet's pure and faithful conveyor. More trustworthy surely than memory, in this matter anyway, since what memory was summoning could well be out of fertility more than what was once upon a time represented. I would be little more than a leaf of lettuce if I was this close and did not want to ride to see it. The only problem lies with expectations; but these can be handled. After all, they can have no logical reason for rising.

If memory is mute, what then ashes? Ashes cold these many years and long since wind-borne, dispersed, mere wisps of painted air. The dispersal final and complete, and perhaps I should not even be doing this, riding from without back into that charred past, that completed history of sad lost people from whose fire-dance of death I was literally pulled. Perhaps my mere shadow gliding this earth was impact enough to cause tremors in those sad lost souls; perhaps it was unwarranted intrusion upon the dead. But, after all, these intrusions were mutually exchanged, because they are of course my dead, as I am their life, all that remains to evidence the fact of their existence.

You don't have to come along, I said to Malloy. I don't give a damn if you do or don't.

Riding slowly on his appropriated horse with the CSA stitching on the worsted saddle blanket, one hand holding the slack reins, the other resting at his side, Malloy watched me, his tough pug-face filled with offended skepticism. Like most men of limited grasp, he resented what he could not understand.

Is that the same man talking? he asked. By God, it don't sound like the same man, the one who said Come along, I need a friend for this. Wot in the hell, I didn't ask any questions. That word— *friend*—carries weight with me.

This war, this crucible, certainly conjoined odd and inexplicable associations. Of everyone in the Army of the Potomac, why this one, this Eamon Malloy, who had volunteered out of a New York City slum because he thought he was needed to fight Indians, that it all somehow had to do with Indians, who had been reticent and solitary until I befriended him. I found him a perversely fascinating character, who in the beginning talked to no one but himself, of whom it was said there were little clappers in his head which occasionally set off little bells and turned him to acts of lunacy. Eamon Malloy shot a stray dog one day in camp and then tore the buttons from his blouse and proclaimed himself a great hunter. Silent for days on end, he would suddenly climb upon an inverted barrel and raise his arms high into the air and stand Y-shaped, declaiming senselessly until told to be still. But mostly he merely sat and gazed into some self-puzzling nothingness, obfuscated by what lay without, or condemned by what lay within; and at these times there was a softly meditating sadness, a deeply appealing aloneness that fell over him like a netting. Why was I friend to this self-measuring lunatic? Kill a reb every time the question was put, by myself and by others, and Lee's army would be thin gruel indeed. I simply appreciated the mad dogs that had been set loose in his head to run among the gnarled bramble that seemed to catch and tear apart his every thought at inception. His tent mate, I would study his sleeping face, countenance to moonlight that sometimes palely silvered and ennobled those apparently untroubled features, fascinated by the disarray that lay within, as if in repose some secret would be adumbrated. Sometimes he would be privileged a glimpse through the interstices of his wall and break into a detachment, and I would ask him about his provocations (this after many months of friendship, when there were enough shared experiences to cushion an indelicate question). Oh, it was always like that, he would say. He could remember as a boy people asking him why he had done this or that thing, and his answer: Done what? You mean, I asked, you did things that you couldn't remember later? Then the slow grin, the chuckle, not embarrassed, not self-conscious: that wonderful familiarity with himself, the acceptance, the unperturbed ease of it. Maybe somebody dropped a rock on my head when I was a baby, he said.

Then the regiment was bloodied for the first time. That was toward the end of May, 1862. We were at a place called Fair Oaks Station when we heard the rebs had hit our lines very hard on the south bank of the river and we were pulled out of reserve to help turn them back. First blood for most of us and by God the stink from boys retching and defecating in their pants when we got near enough to hear shot and then saw the wounded stumbling and staggering back from the front, slack and ashen-faced, some of them broken three-legged beasts using their muskets for canes or crutches; a stark, ghastly column of the unearthed, who seemed blasted beyond our understanding or our ability to communicate with them—not that we would have; there was no way we could have been coerced into speaking to or touching any of them. They were weaving along the road, most of them bitterly silent, others moaning; and some of them were wandering through the woods, looking as if they didn't know where they were, or maybe just wanting to be alone in their suffering. We were the blessed, filing passed the luckless. We, the unhurt, the unscathed, would of course do better, would stride in rank and go forward and plug those gaps left opened by these battered retiring strangers, engage, and then stride back, still unhurt, unscathed, because we were stronger, faster, smarter. The trick was to ignore the grim and minatory messages that had been gouged into those faces, that were screaming from those eyes; the trick was to believe that they had gone into battle the same way they were emerging—stumbling and broken and defeated.

I thought briefly about Malloy as we went in, that here was this patently unstable character, charging ahead into this unspeakable chaos called war combat death defeat triumph glory, into a carnage that from the time man first came running down from caves waving clubs no one has been able to convincingly explain; and for several minutes I was concerned about him, as though he might do something to needlessly endanger his life—this of course before I had seen any war for myself, knew what it was, the organized, orchestrated dementia of it. So for those few minutes I was worried about Malloy, and then of course I forgot about him, forgot almost everything and became a near-primitive thing functioning on instinct alone as the wounded continued drifting back, the horror in their faces fresher and the blood on their uniforms brighter; and the noise up ahead was growing louder. And then the lieutenant, his face suddenly distorting into a frenzy and his voice turning shrill as his responsibilities began to burgeon, telling us to move on the double, on the double. And now we no longer saw those wounded, those scare-mongering lepers, and we tried to ignore those inert bundles that lay here and there, and I was holding my rifle the way a desperate man holds to a spar in the ocean. And then more than anything else, the general frightened me. He came galloping toward us, diagonally across an open field, a half-dozen of his staff at his back. I had seen generals before, of course, watching us at drill and on parade, always sitting their horses with great dignity and aloofness, like grand masters studying their pawns. But now to see one of these top-ranked deities agitated and perspiring, galloping one of those horses that always seemed anatomically part of them and which you always had the feeling were better fed and bedded than you were, was an awesome thing. He swung his horse with consummate skill, and in that instant when he had stopped but was actually still moving, turning, shouted to the lieutenant to get the column the hell forward and to hurry, hurry. We ran than, ordered by the lieutenant and frightened by the agitated general and frightened even more by what was generating him; for if it was enough to steam a general and make him swing his horse so, then it was going to be pure hell for us.

The road lifted and as we went over the crest and then down the other side we could see the field, our line below and blurred huddles of men in the distance—the rebels—and the air around us quivering with the noise of rattling muskets and the roar of artillery, shells bursting in the sky as if roaring against invisible obstructions. We were fed into the line by our yammering lieutenant, who had drawn his sword now and was ordering us to get down. We didn't kneel or crouch but went bellies down, as close to the ground as we could get, glaring into the webs of smoke that were undulating over the field like morning mist. There was no cover, no trees or rocks, just some modest earthen mounds that previous men had built up. By God, a major yelled, now we'll hold 'em, and a soldier nearby muttered, We held 'em before, you son of a bitch. I brought up my rifle, got a rest on the pile of dirt, took aim into the distance—I was shooting at space, at smoke, at noise—and fired. The recoil snapped the stock against my shoulder and into me a sense of importance, of participating. I drew my ramrod, cleared my barrel and reloaded. We would hold, I thought. Yes, by God, we would hold.

I must have fired three or four bullets into the noisy haze, firing with great solemnity and resolve, as though history would take note of each shot. And though each shot was conscientiously dispatched, there was one problem: there were no clearly visible targets; it was as if we were trying to kill the air that the rebels were breathing, or to make so unendurable their side of the world that they would withdraw; or simply to show them that we had rifles and bullets too and could and would use both and therefore they had better leave us alone. When we were told to cease firing, I assumed we had accomplished some of that; and so there I was, mere minutes into combat and already a notable success, ready to have my name and deeds measured by the balladeers. I took off my forage cap and rolled over on my back and breathed deeply, with gratification. A bit of rest was all the reward a good soldier wanted.

But then the lieutenant was in a frenzy again, running back and forth with his sword in hand as if he had been grievously insulted. All of the officers, in fact, were yelling, and I heard the man nearest me begin cursing. They're coming back, he said. He muttered the words aloud but to himself, with a mingling of disgust and despair; others spoke them with fear and astonishment and excitement.

Coming back? I thought. Had they been here before? I rolled back over on my stomach, biting my cartridge and slamming my ramrod, then squinted into the smoke. They were gray out there, not just of uniform but colored by distance, indistinct behind the haze, gradually materializing from out of it, as strange as things risen from a foggy sea, advancing, not running but walking, their flags above them. In the smoke it was impossible to ascertain their number, how deep that flow. Our officers were behind us, telling us to be steady, to hold our fire. The face next to me was watching them with the detached, ironic amusement of a philosopher, as if the gods had already decided the question and all of this was an exercise in futility. The quivering question in my mind was, *How close do they come?* Were they really serious about this, or were they merely trying to scare or taunt us? Was this patch of ground with its little mounds of loose earth so important that they would keep coming? The flags told me yes; those regimental standards carried the blunt and brazen answer. Kill the flags, I thought, bring down their swollen and emblematic weight and the men would stop. I wanted to howl that insane message to the line: *Shoot the flags,* as if I were clinging to some ancient conviction, dream, so infantile and untested it seemed desperately true.

Gradually they were becoming distinct one from the other, not a mass of shapeless gray anymore, but a crowd of upright two-legged men marching across a field already consecrated by their own dead, whose inert bodies they passed and seemed to consume. The order to fire was reverberated up and down the line, each officer receiving and then delivering it, and God only knew from where it had originated; from that general probably, unless he was still riding and wheeling about like a madman with his staff obedient and imitative at his back. So we fired and then withdrew to reload while our second line moved into position and discharged their rifles, and then stepped back as we moved forward again, performing this deadly cotillion, until the Confederates blazed back, nasty little flashes erupting through the smoke like sparks from a whetstone. That broke the symmetry of the cotillion as some men were shot. The back-and-forth dance continued, but ragged now, broken, and the officers' shouts that we hold our ranks became more insistent, frantic.

The rebels paused to reload and then came on again, and now those flags were moving faster. Again and again we fired into them, opening gaps in their line, but they kept coming, faster, with a lethal noise now that was part yell, part cheer, something that seemed to gain momentum as they came nearer, as though it were a friction sound of their bodies moving through the close, hot, acrid air; a roar from out of the pine hills and the piedmont and the moist decadent forests and broiling cotton fields and from out of the Appalachians and Ozarks and the Blue Ridge peaks and valleys and from out of the torpor of motionless Southern nights. The noise, the yell, with its rising surflike plenitude, struck terror into my heart and then almost immediately provoked a reactive fury at my having been made afraid, a muscling indignation and resentment: I would not be unwound from my senses or chased from my obligations by a barbaric yell. They drew close—close enough for me to distinguish sizes and shapes now: tall men and short men, lean ones and round, beards and hats and a disparity of uniforms; the impersonal irregularity of any crowd. Some were falling, those in the front rank going down with what seemed terrible suddenness; but now the gaps were not being as quickly filled. A few of the onward-sailing flags whirled eccentrically and then tilted earthward, only to be swept up again as other hands took hold of the staffs. And then the rebels had stopped their forward movement—or maybe it was an illusion caused by the shimmering smoke or maybe even by what was rattling inside my head. I raised my head several inches with a spastic movement and squinted; yes, by Jesus, they had stopped, and in the gaps of musket fire I realized that the yelling had stopped too. They seemed to be wavering, and then they began to withdraw, slowly, some of them going off with half-turned bodies, faces toward the Union lines, as if to convey the message that this was a reluctant retreat, against both will and desire, and that they would be back.

What would have been an attitude monstrously presumptuous upon any other occasion—mourning for someone whom you assumed upon no evidence whatsoever was dead, and further, thinking with monumental arrogance that he was better off for being removed from this hugely complex and overbearing world—seemed perfectly natural that evening. It took some time for the regiment to regroup; men had a tendency to drift, especially those new to combat as ours were, to become part of other groups, to impact into them and then move with them and pass into still other groups, that concentration upon survival being so cold and total it blurred names and faces into distinctions of no importance; it was like being in the presence of the devil and all his surrogates, and all men were alike and naked in the heat, in the passion of prayer.

It was not until twilight that I rejoined the bulk of the regiment, laying eyes on those faces once again distinct and familiar, exchanging foolish, almost sheepish grins, and handshakes and warm fraternal backslaps, and then quickly sobered by the news of what had happened to so-and-so. The news of the dead and the wounded now carried different impact; unlike before, when it had to travel for days and weeks, over rivers and across miles to reach us, when we cursed and grieved and brooded, now it was received quietly, philosophically, with the bearing of veterans who understood precisely, who no longer raged blindly at the unknown. We had been baptized and had risen dripping, recreated by the sound of death, the sight of it, the terrifying nearness of it which seemed to have brutally sealed off certain spouts of sensibility which under other circumstances might have broken and unnerved us. These were nightmares of epic fertility we were filing away in the rafters of our minds, not eerie little candlelit-face-in-the-coffin memories to jog our sleep upon some uneventful night in the future. This was the real thing, veritable geysers of emotion shot to the very summits of our awareness, destined to spangle there forever the same as the piercing stars of the night; a nightmare so awful that in its first gripping there was exaltation: it was as though we had consummated some Faustian arrangement, mortgaged our souls into the future so as to be able to laugh now and grasp the hands and shoulders of our friends, even while other friends were still holding the line, forever holding the line, with nothing in their eyes, their unspent time beginning to molder into the dust even as the days of their lives would soon swirl into the melancholia of memory.

So when the regiment gradually drew itself together in the woods at twilight and I saw Malloy, I felt a burst of embarrassing elation at finding him alive. He of the clouded mind and uncertain judgment had survived. Apparently madness was not always an invitation to disaster (though its contemplation might be).

Supper was a different affair that night, though at the time I did not, could not, know just exactly how, or why. As ever, we ate by ourselves, my doppelgänger and I, around our own small fire (it was quiet around the campfires this night, the men with their grimed faces staring dreamily, mouths filled with half-chewed food). This had long been our routine, because of his strangeness, which no one else could abide and which had isolated him from the others, and which had drawn me to him in the first place as if I might glean from it some insight, revelation, some sense of expectation. Always it had been Malloy who stared vaguely into the fire or off into the night, the mutilated food showing in his hanging jaw, while I would watch him with almost impertinent scrutinization, with dreadful fascination, waiting for his eyes to finally move and set upon me with some sort of anointing. But tonight,

tonight it was Malloy who sat with his tin plate in his lap and ate briskly and steadily, cutting at his meat with his pocketknife, scraping up his beans with petulant alacrity, gulping his coffee, and then lighting his pipe and leaning back on his elbows and gazing into the firelight not with dull, vacuous mirrors but with the wistful expression of a lover, an asker of questions. This while I sat with my plate still two-thirds full, unable to lay food on a stomach still pained from constriction, listening to the murmurous quietude around me that was broken only by the reappearance of another of the regiment's missing, appropriately welcomed back from the dead. As I sat shivering in the night's mild chill, my plate of uneaten food on the ground before me, Malloy sighed and, turning to his blankets, said, Well, we come through the first one, didn't we?

We came through some others during the next few weeks, in what was to become known as the Peninsula Campaign, at loud and violent places called Mechanicsville, Gaines' Mill, Savage's Station. And then in September something so horrible that I truly believed I was commuting from alive to dead to alive to dead, that I was a sinned-against lamb running endlessly through an oval room walled with cracked and blood-splashed mirrors, circulating through dream and reality and nightmare and disbelief, thrown loose into a cornfield filled with barbarians manipulated by a hierarchy of satans, wheeling and pivoting through a drumbeat-steady racket of muskets, seeing dead bodies used as breastworks, seeing a dead body hanging over a rail fence hit by so many shots it finally fell apart like a rag doll. This was called Antietam, a place that made me dream of thumbs in my eyes and powerful hands trying to rip loose the top of my head.

We survived Antietam, after a fashion, and went on. I say we, meaning Eamon Malloy and myself. It was after Antietam, when along with my dreams of thumbs and hands I would suddenly find myself gasping for breath even while sitting still, my brain suffocating with images of death—after Antietam that I realized what was happening to Malloy. It was not that he was being ravished or captivated by war. It was more arcane than that. Everyone, after all, was being transformed or modified. The permutations were producing a splendid crop of killers and cynics. The sudden imposition of overnight maturity had come like a seizure, with scars and distortions planing off the bloom of youth even as we gazed upon and ached for what was still sentient, still tantalizingly visible but irretrievable; the moribund stirrings of our lost innocence, slashed and brutalized beyond repair or healing, were perilous to us now. But as the rest of us lunged and whirled through days of shot and nights of recoil, Eamon Malloy had slowly found a certain ordering of mind. The slack jaw was now firmly shut, the vacant eyes frequently bestirred by contemplation, the wild suppositions of mind replaced with thoughtful commentary about—things. What could be more ludicrous, I thought, than a man driven sane by war? Again, he was no bloodthirsty seeker of combat; he quaked the same as the rest of us, he dreaded as fearfully, he brooded at the sight of the dead and retched at the stink of their decay and the malodorous emanations of their fear-exploded bowels. He was commended for gallantry at Antietam, and I continued to watch him, march with him, eat with him, bunk with him. He became a quiet, ordered man. The rain of fire had decimated the regiment at Antietam, and Fredericksburg that December was even worse; so there were not many who had begun with Eamon Malloy the madman who were able to note the change in him, and few who cared. Just another man psychically sundered by the war and then come together again. Just another man blown out of his soul and dropped back in again in total re-creation. All very normal, given the abnormal context. And all unnoticed, unremarked, except by his vigilant auditor, his witness. And what in God's name was I to say to him—Eamon, you were crazy when we first met as recruits, and now you're whole-minded? How in God's name have you done it? They made him a corporal after Fredericksburg, and now Eamon Malloy no longer sat cross-legged in his blankets at night, but in a camp chair he had culled somewhere, socked feet near the stove, quietly polishing his boots with bacon rind, at peace with himself. And I wondered: Is the sanity of the madman more horrific than his aberrations?

Within the chaotic dislodgements of war, there had been a beguiling perfume, and Eamon Malloy had somewhere caught its scent, either in the rapt bowers of the night, in the spring muds of Virginia, or perhaps within the crucible itself, running upon the blood-slippery altars even as death was glaring upon him from out of the cold eyes of Alabama and Mississippi and South Carolina; the odds of something tumbling into place from out of the myriad constellations and convolutions of the brain and establishing a rational connection had to be astronomical, no less so than a pile of kicked sand falling to earth and spelling a name. Name? He still could not sign it. His mark was *X*, in itself suggestive and imponderable, a prostrate pyramid of a symbol now begun to gradually inflate itself into a structure of abstruse and unanswering mystery. But I told myself: All right now, Ben, consider it carefully. Of all the tens of thousands of men in the Army of the Potomac you might have be-friended, you have chosen the one who is going in the direction opposite to so many others—the ones who have been led away howling and gibbering under shock and phantasm; those most heart-rending casualties of all, de-tached from faculty and stripped of dignity, proud men reduced to baying hounds and squawking chickens and dead-eyed somnambulists. There were times when I waited for him to revert, to emotionally detonate, to either fly to heights of murderous rampage or fall to animallike grov-eling, as if the observable madness had all this time been gathering in a seething miasma, to erupt all at once, finally and definitively. But he did not. Not even after Fredericksburg, when we wept at the sounds of the crying wounded left behind on the field in the cold December night. Sobered and matured, he went on, Corporal Malloy now, duly proud of his rank, impeccably honoring his modest responsibilities. He put on weight, he raised a small spade-shaped beard which he would finger with pride and delight, infuriating me with sly winks of the eye. So this is your friend, I told myself. A symbol of light deep in the night, a positive transfiguration; or perhaps a metamorphosis of lunacy into a sphere of delusion so rarefied it had to have been sublimated a thousand times over; a man gone so far out of his mind as to have become no one, that what was to me reason was in him the unabating final stage of mental abdication.

So I was riding back into the opening jaws of memory in the company of none other than a redeemed madman—for irony, the perfect companion.

We rode along dirt roads that petered out, and through balsa-scented pine forests, and across fields where young pine stood staid and dignified amid brown grass and sassafras bushes. Much of the cleared land we passed was out of cultivation, overgrown with a stubborn reclamation of brier and bush and long, coarse grass, watched over by abandoned cabins.

The last stretch of road was unspeakably lonely; it made me feel reverential, humbled into childhood. I looked up into the old guardian oaks, wondering what voices had risen and died in those full-maned rafters, so strong and gathered that even the sun had to seep through in speckling splashes. There seemed to be clinging to these trees a mustiness, a catacomb air of time undeparted and in decay, unrefreshed by living memory.

We were following a beautiful carriage, with painted doors and upholstered interior, the liveried driver watching the road unspool between the nodding heads of Kentucky thoroughbreds. That carriage is not far ahead of us, Eamon, I said, kicking lightly at my horse's flanks, moving just a little faster through the shadows of the oaken world with its erratic sunlight designs. I don't want to get too close, I said. I just want to get in sight and then follow it in.

When the sound of the carriage ceased, I knew we were close to the house and my heart began to surge with a fullness of joy and rapture and vindication; all misgivings about making the trip, the pilgrimage, vanished. In the air ahead I perceived a brilliant, almost blinding sunburst of the most ravishing yellows and oranges and reds: warm fires and leaves in their glory, a father's pride and a mother's love, radiating in greeting and welcome out from the house and toward me and colliding softly with my own radiant furnace of emotion. I rode on toward the beckoning, seductive sunburst, on into the light, the warmth, the downy softness of patiently abiding love, feeling time and weight and even sound slipping by me on either side as though I had entered some Elysian corridor that was womblike in its languor and its assurance. The alchemy of desire—that true and unrelenting cutting edge of faith—had transmuted striving and yearning memory into belief, trust.

Liar Hook, I thought when I saw the house from the road, that beautiful white warm wonderful house with its immensely pillared portico, standing back from the drive that curved between the expanse of immaculate green lawn and the front steps. Liar Hook, who had concocted his malicious fable of fire and madness eating it to the ground. For there it stood as it had in the better panels of my imagination these past two years, in beckoning welcome and embrace. My home, uniquely my home, and waiting within my vigorous father and my perfumed mother. And within, too, my child-self, as preserved in the toyed and undisturbed room from which I had been carried by one madman and to which I was returning with another. Within, too, all the objects and possessions, ready to realign with memory and resume: the chairs, tables, high tester bedsteads; the china with the painted flowers, the heavy silver service, the delicate long-stemmed crystal; the solemnity of the library with my father's thousands of volumes burdening their polished mahogany shelves with the wonders of human knowledge; the damask and linen in the dining room; the glass-dripping chandeliers; hickory logs sizzling on the andirons in the living room hearth. All as I had left it that night when I had been lifted away and spirited into a darkness that had stifled all echoes and tried to cancel all remembering, that had gone on for years and years. The sigh and the fullness of returning.

By God, Eamon, I said, it's a glorious sight, isn't it?

Glorious? he muttered, breaking his silence, sitting next to me on his motionless horse. All I see is ashes, he said.

Hook loved my mother. My sojourn upon these ashes of antiquity began with that incantation. Hook loved my mother and therefore killed my father who may or may not have been mad, and then set fire to the house *and something had happened to my mother* and then took me in his arms, and in his passion or his devotion or his guilt carried me away and we left behind this sacred place, this mockery, this nothingness where I was now sitting, clinging to it, trying to find in the sacristy of my mind the ritual of resurrection, even as my reconstructed companion stood with his legs crossed and one hand against the only upright remnant—a shaft of fire-blackened chimney. I don't know why I'm here, Malloy said. Did you know why you were at Antietam and Fredericksburg? I asked him. No, he did not (and I could have told him: to be rushed once more through the crucible, that mean-souled heat that was remolding the inside of your head. Give me that same chance now, I could have told him, but didn't—for how could he have been brought to understand any of it, his side of it or mine?)

Yes, Hook had implied as much. It was there, in his voice, his eyes, when he spoke of her. Too much of the gentleman to say it outright. And if he loved my mother, then how could he have felt about my father—her husband, bedmate, the breaker of her body and slayer of her spirit? What did he really feel when he swung that ax into my father's neck? What were really in Mr. Hook's silences, when he would sidle his glance at me? Whose secret was he meditating, his or mine? (It was not the lack of an answer that tormented, but the persistence of the question.) Yes, it is highly reasonable to assume that there was nothing amiss here, that Allen Travis McKinley was a pillar of stability, upholder of distinguished lineage, a loving husband and father, in love and at ease, until his world was invaded by the taciturn stranger who came through this doorway with ruin and devastation at his back, who plundered and then killed and then carried off the child, the survivor, hoping through it to gain atonement and mercy; and then finally weaving the elaborate tale of generational madness and imputing it to my forebears in order to seal my lips. Is that it, Hook? Is that what these remindingly dolorous ashes are telling me? Is that what you have been secreting in your crepuscular soul these years? Forgive me, Mr. Hook, the trespass of my presumptions; but we must presume in order to know, finally, *something*, of ourselves, of others, or that which transpired out of our presence. There is no alternative to presumption, unless one considers desolate and barren darkness an alternative. There is no less truth in it than there is in the narratives of medieval tapestries. If the slander I heap upon you assures me my stability, you will understand, and accept it. Reasoning may be mad, but if done under lucid consciousness it must be given endorsement. After all, I do beguile myself with a pen, and when the pen is laid aside the small revolving wheel of my imagining does not necessarily cease its revolutions and God forgive what murky nooks and corners its candlelight turns upon. How else to explain why in these ashes I can clearly discern my father's pride of expression and my mother's shy beauty in a broad-faced bonnet? If they be faces without meaning, without history, then I myself must be as vacant and insubstantial as the last coil of black smoke that fled these ruins.

I walked the woods around the house, at all times accompanied by my circumspect companion, whose curiosity was beginning to get the better of his indifference. The ancestors of the robin red breasts and the grackle that you see now and then, I told him, were known to my ancestors. Does that answer it, Eamon? You mean to say your people lived here? he asked. Yes, I said. You mean you're Southern? he asked. Yes, I said, and then added with a harsh laugh, I own all this, showing with a sweep of my arm the woods where according to Hook my father howled like a dog one night, the dead leaves, the ashes, the chimney, and (most of all) the silence, the haunting. He watched me for several moments; the eyes of Eamon Malloy were wary, self-protective, still bruised and slightly calloused from the old hurts and blanketing confusions; and then he turned away and looked in another direction. He would not get involved. It was as if he were saying: I've been there. I have already emerged from this. If you go, you go alone. Because now I believed Hook. Of course I believed the old ne'er-do-well; by God, one of the few things I had, ever had, was belief in Hook, who always stood by, ready to play Damon to my Pythias. What trust I ever had was given to that man. And anyway, I *wanted* to believe him. Else why come here, for what other reason? If he had said, your father was a fine gentleman, quiet, well-spoken, prosaic but respectable; and your mother a nice little lady, reserved but lovable: together a charmingly hospitable pair—would I have wanted to come? Would that have been near as enticing as reiterative lunatic genes and a tale of lurid flames against the night and a house going down as if swarmed by avenging angels? The enticement spoke for itself. The son of Allen Travis McKinley, the lone survivor of all those frenetic and zealous generations, would return and regard the dust of old ashes as his summit, bringing darkness to Erebus.

Hook might have said: Believe but do not attempt to participate. But the improbable old sinner knew better, otherwise why conceal it for so long and then reveal it only under a certain duress? Because he knew my turn of mind. Telling me was like packing the gunpowder and pushing it near the heat. Or perhaps he was trying to arm me against myself, imparting a knowledge for conversion into vigilance. Beware, mistrust, gauge, hold on. Now you know its shape, its voice, the glint of its eyes; be at all times guarded, prepared to summon your strength and defend against it, for its manifestations can be subtle and deceitful, not necessarily the yammering of frothy lips or the rolling of frenzied eyes. Just think a moment of the highly cultivated brain of Allen Travis McKinley, what rushing convulsions it could suddenly be heir to; this by all accounts most charming and erudite gentleman could read his Pindar by day and bay at the moon by night, breathe his love and dream his destiny by day and by night run amok under the heavenly tiara. He could—did—love tenderly and destroy monstrously; and worse, he could, and did, perceive his madness, feel himself suddenly rudderless in all its scheming tides, twisting from lucidity to incoherence, from gentleness to violence. And worse yet, the worst of the worst, he could in his lucidity and his gentleness inspire love, with his own love disarm his vulnerable victim, sucking her into the perfumed morass of his derangement. The love had to be so unbearably genuine, otherwise the wreckage could not have been so unspeakably total. So not even love could be trusted, was white valance to the shroud; neither in the giving nor the receiving could it be trusted. Even love had to be shut away and forbidden, and for any who in their innocence doubted it, who thought love the inviolate redeemer, the salvation, there were only these surrounding ashes to contemplate. They incinerated here, my mother and my father, upon whatever altar it might be called. These ashes could be—all right, are—theirs, and by extension mine, who was already becoming echo to the voice. Each age has its own pestilence and hence its own curatives. But my forebears were their own singular procession, and now it was I who was the constant among the variables, grimly unique, a historical vessel in passage through circular waters, the oval waves taunting me with the grasping vortex somewhere near.

I knew everything of my father (to my satisfaction at least) except the desperation of his suffering, the barbed and mangling pit into which his woe and despair crushed him. That was for me to find out on my own, and how does one avoid one's own encasement? This was Hook again, talking to me, but again, the old sinner cannot teach me to differentiate between high spirits, raucous joy, idiosyncrasy, and what is dangerously something else. But there could be a perverse, even romantic, pleasure in succumbing to the idea of it. Admit it: It could be exhilarating in concept, provocative of fierce individuality, as though it were somehow anointing and sanctifying, as though I were living among primitives who regarded the bizarre and unconventional with awe, who were millennia away from understanding my mind's unique visitations. Think of the total dispensation, following every unfettered impulse to its tapered end without fear of reproach or condemnation; as if I had been chosen for glimpses of the most sublime regions, a privileged communicant, set free for inspiring journeys to the most exalted promontories.

At twilight I saw the shadows moving in the woods, where there was no wind, no life. Malloy, building the fire at the base of the chimney, did not see them, and I said nothing. I felt as if my potent germs had mixed with the ashes and breathed into them embers of shadow life. And anyway, would Malloy have been able to see them? No, they were mine; and barely so, for they seemed to move only when I was not directly looking at them. I did not think it strange; after all, I was back, wasn't I? It was hardly likely that I would return to no response or recognition, no matter how slight or deft. Nor did it have to be cosmic or majestic; simply the sign, and shadows at weave in the twilit woods was adequate, the same as one lucid syllable on the wind was.

Malloy raised his head for a moment, then turned slowly to me. Did you hear something? he asked. No, I said, astonished that he should ask it. Where in hell did he come in hearing anything? You want coffee? he asked. Leave me alone, I said. I felt churlish; he was getting in the way now, getting between them and me. If he had not been there, perhaps they would be presenting themselves more boldly, not be skulking spectrally in the woods. Naturally, after hovering in solitude for so many years, they would be timid in the presence of a stranger. It's getting chilly, he muttered, crouching over the fire, folding his arms and rubbing at his elbows. The fire was running antic shadows along the side of the chimney. The night was shading deeper now, dropping yet another stratum of darkness upon these strewn ashes. I stared off into the woods, where it was shadow unto shadow now, seamless and without definition. I could feel them watching me, their dead yearning eyes feasting upon me. Malloy must have sensed them too, for even though he was silent, his eyes kept sidling toward the woods with the shrewdness of a man on picket, as if feeling the disquiet of some nettling thing below the level of consciousness, and I thought: Is it through his old madness that he is hearing them, their vibrations coursing through the old indelible fissures in his head? Were we two zealots attuned to the same inaudible murmuring? Our horses, tethered nearby, were growing restless, shifting their weight and perking their ears. Malloy turned to me and watched me with grave, inquiring interest. He was breaking my concentration, the intrusive son of a bitch, violating the moment's tender, delicate equipoise. I smiled faintly at him, as if to say, you may hear them, but the communion is mine; whatever might emit from that everlasting finality is privately and exclusively mine.

And then madly my heart leaped with joy and astonishment because suddenly they had succeeded in tearing asunder whatever ghostly bonds had been inhibiting or restraining them and they were thrashing violently in the woods, not only physically in motion but with voice too, voices full and shrieking in the darkness, storming into materiality (the shrieking did not shock me, for how was I to know with what articulation the dead spoke?); too abrupt and chaotic to be miracle, with none of the solemn dignity or majesty of miracle; it was hot throbbing flesh flown upon the bones of the wish; and with the joy and astonishment there was also hatred, for Malloy, for his being there, for making a quartet of my sacred trinity. I could feel the hatred writhing inside me and I wished to God that Malloy would die or turn to stone or be sucked into the small fire he had so assiduously woven to life against the chimney wall. I wanted to scream at him to in the name of the almighty leave, leave me alone with they who had effected this tremendous upsurge from whatever earthen vaults they had been pressed, for who knew how many moments, how much air, they had been granted before dissolving back into a flutter of ashes?

Their motion was swift, violent—evident from the rapid snap of bramble—and their voices pitched even higher, to decibels approaching hysteria, and my shuddering mind reasoned that they were trying to frighten Malloy, this lunatic-cum-soldier who even at that instant was swinging one arm out with stiff grasping fingers for his rifle which lay nearby, with his other hand striking a blow against the knife sheathed at his hip, not drawing it but simply, intuitively assuring himself as to its presence, its placement—a movement and a gesture which stunned and outraged me, and then sent through me a shock of terror at the idea of this madman wanting to kill the dead who were howling from out of decades of patient, watchful muteness.

And even as the blood-hot thought of killing him began to throb through my mind, they began to bulk out of the darkness, nearing the fire's faint radius of light, and I wondered why my father, dead these nearly two decades, was wearing a torn butternut Confederate tunic, why his emerging eyes were glaring and murderous under the low-worn brim of his black woolen slouch hat, why those egregiously set eyes flashed the same white and storming malice at Malloy as at me, and why he was clutching a butcher knife so tenaciously it seemed additament to his arm, why he was raising that brute and incredible adjunct to his anatomy as he came rushing through the diminishing shadows. The second one—the one who was not my mother—the one who was doing the yelling, the shrieking—was just behind him, similarly abrupt and furious, likewise clutching a knife in a fist that was raised, poised, already gauging its aim and thrust; this one, the one not my mother, hatless but with a face blackened with beard and yelling with barbarous fury: the two of them of the night, as if hatched from stone by the crouching woodland blackness. And even as I saw Malloy, still on his knees alongside the fire, swinging his rifle upward, without time for shouldering, the stock at belt level, two distinct and unassociated sets of thought were roiling through my mind, the one chasing and shredding the other; the first in its scattering vestiges beseeching him not to shoot because they are—I almost said it even though I no longer believed it, as with the second, icy thought came clarity and comprehension, as I realized who they were and what they intended. Malloy of course had known immediately. Malloy, in his long interval of sanity—an interval carved by roar of cannon and crack of rifle—had moved more quickly and decisively than I, reaching for his rifle which he had had the wit to keep near (mine was tied across my pommel, useless to me) and was about to slaughter the first one—the one who was not my father—even as the spark that had never been turned cold and plummeted.

Malloy's shot took his charging assailant full in the breast and spun the man hurtling sideways, both feet off the ground for a moment, and as he spun an expression of convulsive shock filled his eyes and drained them of their murder. Shot dead in full flight, his momentum carried him for several steps and then all weight and cohesion seemed to leave his body as he plunged forward with broken, flopping emptiness. But the newly minted death had no time to register as the second one erupted toward me as if suffused by and maddened with the blood and the slain spirit of the first, as if some whirlwind baton-passing had occurred, for there was that other knife, raised and with a glint of firelight glancing from the blade. Halfway to my feet, I bobbed to one side as man and knife both came upon me, the knife barely missing my shoulder as the diving body struck me and we tumbled over together and rolled upon the ground, he gasping from his run, his effort. And then I saw Malloy, at full height now, his eyes fixed and white like two tiny moons set into his head, gripping his rifle midway along the barrel, the stock swung back over his right shoulder, giving him resemblance to some gigantic woodcutter; and then he was bringing it down in a savage arc, the edge of the stock smashing into the back of my antagonist's head with a barbarously blunt thud, knocking him instantly still. Malloy dropped the rifle, his right hand sweeping back and reappearing with his own knife now and in the same fluid motion he was on his knees straddling the man's back. With his left hand he seized a handful of hair, jerked the head up and back. I caught a glimpse of rotted teeth as the man's jaw fell open, and then a moment later Malloy's knife sawed against the throat's taut flesh and a thick looping arc of blood flashed several feet through the air and Malloy let the face drop back into the dust.

I got to my feet and hurried to my horse and untied my

rifle, fixed the bayonet into place and now stood armed against the night. Do you think there are any more? I asked. No, he said, moving toward his horse. He untethered and mounted. But just for good luck, he said, let's get to hell out of here. I don't like this place.

As we rode back into the night, he said, So that was the place you wanted to go to? By Jesus, I'll never know why. Still dazed, just beginning to assimilate it, I said nothing. No-good bastard bushwhackers, he said. Probably wanted for murder or desertion by their own. Did you see them? I wouldn't call them soldiers. By Jesus, if we had gone to sleep there it would have been a long one.

And of course that had been my intent, to sleep there; no, not sleep—dream. Dream it all into being again. Open my soul as snare to whatever ghost-energy yet pulsated within those hallowed ashes. Enter upon a doorstep that led to nowhere, to the vast emblematic nothingness that was the past, with its fertile and accommodating shapes, its pliant relinquishing and withholding. Architect the corridors and lay the carpeting and walk within, toward the voices. My God, I thought, what must have been the depth of the buried yearning, to have sprung so complete and intoxicating a delusion. What a deadly, pathetic spin it had been—but it had been, unquestionably had been, and how desperately I had held to it, even as the two rebels were coming to slice us to pieces, trying to transform them into the loving lost. My God, I thought, the power which that tightly coiled obsession had sucked from me into itself, to make me vulnerable to such feverish turns.

The wrong had been in taunting and disturbing my ghosts. The wrong had been in passionately embracing the evidence of ashes, in believing an obsession. The wrong had been in wanting to sit in the library where he had built his boat in which to navigate the Hellespont, in wanting to find the drop of poisoned blood which made him believe he was ancestor to genius and inject it into my own stream, in wanting to unearth and appropriate the lunacies which a merciful providence had seen fit to terminate, in wanting to sleep in the shadow of that upright chimney which once upon a time had streamed skyward the smoke of the fire that warmed me as I lay in my mother's cradling arms. Lunacy. My own. Slightly diluted by the thinning of one generation later. Attended by my own true-breathing madman who was himself the symbol of the restoration I had hoped to achieve by the light of my eye, the tone of my flesh, the murmur of my blood. I wanted to say to him: Watch me carefully, Eamon, for heaven knows there must be a thousand upright chimneys standing guard over a thousand turned-to-ashes houses in Virginia tonight. And there would be more. And there would be more. Would to God there was one less.

Seven

NO LONGER DID HE push to the front of the crowd of men standing around the mailbag waiting to hear the sound of their names. Too many disappointments—months of them now—had gradually removed him to the outer rim, where he stood looking at the backs of blue shirts crisscrossed with white or yellow suspenders, listening with diminished hope for his name to be read from an inked scrawl on the face of an envelope. He stood there now, upon this warm spring afternoon, sleeves rolled to the elbows, arms crossed, a cold pipe hanging from his clenched teeth, listening to the monotonous reading of names, watching with hostile envy the lucky ones come pushing out of the crowd, oblivious and smiling as they gazed upon their envelopes.

When it was over—and he would not move until the empty mailbag was picked up and carried away—he walked back along the aisle of tents and resat himself upon the inverted barrel in front of his own, while within, his tent-mates sprawled on their cots and read their letters in grave, insular privacy. How many months now? he asked himself. Three? Four? Five? There had been several letters just after Fredericksburg; he remembered lying in his blankets, up on one elbow, reading them by the light of a rusty oil lamp as a sleetstorm tore at the sides of the tent, remembered Susan's letter in particular, how it was reassurance of the ongoing existence of warmth and softness and stability, that the entire world had not degenerated into a pair of immense warring armies hurling themselves upon each other. She was praying for him, she wrote, and where once he would have chided her for it, now it seemed to have meaning. While he did not feel any closer to God, suddenly he felt God closer to him, because of what Susan could feel and say and he could not. So that was sometime not long after Fredericksburg, in December, and now it was May, and after returning from those ashes and that solitary chimney, he wanted more than ever to touch something that had been touched by Susan, or by Eva, or Hook or Ryler. Before, he had always chosen his isolation; but isolation by choice as opposed to imposition was of different character and quality. He felt unmoored, abandoned to tremendous impersonality. The mail was fickle and irregular, one of the officers told him. It was not uncommon for some imbecile to misdirect a packet. But no one else's mail call had been dry for so long as his. Even Malloy, an illiterate, received mail, which Ben read to him, and which Ben answered for him, taking in dictation Malloy's halt, self-conscious phrases, which Ben dressed for him without disturbing their sense.

Until a month ago he had continued his own letter writing, to each of them, questioning their silence. But the void only lengthened and finally silence engendered silence, and he stopped writing. One night he suddenly became desperate and even considered the possibility of stealing a horse from the corral and breaking away and riding north, back to Capstone, to seek an explanation. He saw himself making the trip in one furious leap through the night. The idea simmered and then subsided and collapsed into its own impracticality. And then the realist, that cool lurking stranger so strenuously resisted by the mind's surface, finally said: Yes, it's been a time and they can forget. Ryler certainly, and Eva with her quick passions and volatile flings, and even sweet Susan perhaps—either forgetting or else becoming bored with remembering; time rubbing memory into the dimmest of imprints. But old Hook? No, he would never change or defer or forget; his mind was too crammed with remembering to permit the least forgetting. *He better than any knows my mind's porcelain construction.* From Hook above all those letters should be coming, with their reserved, faintly cynical phrases muttered in their small, crabbed hand.

It was so maddeningly without plausible explanation. Those four were the most unlikely to be caught under the same roof, victims of a single calamity. The answer had to lie in darker logic. None would willingly and deliberately forget him: not Hook; not Ryler, his friend of a thousand carousals; not Susan, with her cup of love filled to the brim; not Eva, who had bitterly reproached him the night before he left. She hated him for it, she said. How dare you take yourself away from me? she demanded. I forbid it, I forbid it, I forbid it! God damn you for it and I hope a thousand bullets catch you. I hope you die. I hope they bury you under a cartload of manure and mark the place with a dead rat. All this while she was holding him tensely in her arms, her cheek laid against his breast, the sobs wracking her even as the invective poured from her lips. You'll die, I know you'll die, she said. I won't cry for you. I'll forget you. I'll forget you ever existed. I'll fill my head with a million things until there's no room left for you and you've been driven out. And then demanding: Why? Why was he going? What was so important about a damned war that could be fought by tens of thousands of imbeciles who had nothing better to do, and whom no one cared about anyway? You don't give a damn about the war, she said. The only thing you give a damn about is me. I can't understand why you're going away. It's an impulse, isn't it? That's all it is. You're going to be sorry in a week that you did it, aren't you? For once in his life, she implored, he ought to resist the impulse and not permit its consequences. And then she looked at him, her eyes burning through her bruising tears, and shaking her head slowly and disconsolately told him she loved him, repeating over and over those deceptively plain words. He had never heard them in declaration before, not even from Susan in whom their avowal had always been manifest, and their sound at once baffled and intrigued him and he frowned into her eyes as if trying to perceive what it really was she was saying. She held him more firmly and again rested her face against his beating heart and, emboldened by what she had said, by its pride and its will, said quietly, You'll stay the night.

The aloofness of her four-poster stood in anomalous contrast to her hot, almost feverishly urgent body. Under its canopy the bed looked cold and inviolable in the silver moonlight that chilled the window panes and lay upon the satin spread in polished revelation; not a moon mellowed by song or summer or softened by earth heat, but a remote globe of motionless rock that palely defined Capstone's trees and houses and meadows. In that mystic light he watched her raise her dress up over her head, unveiling her strong voluptuous body. Then she pulled down her pantaloons and stepped out of them, and a few moments later was stark naked, lifting both hands and pushing her hair back over her shoulders. Then she came at him and began tearing at his clothing. He seized her by the wrists and roughly pushed her back until she fell across the cold satin spread. She did not move, watching him intently as silently he stripped himself, their eyes locked upon each other with the pent, building passion of imminent duelists. And then he was upon her. Tossing her head from side to side as he plunged against her, the murmured words escaped from her teeming torrent of thoughts: You'll never leave me . . . I'm going to keep you here . . . forever, and then screaming without inhibition as their mutual friction unbound her and sent her pulsing and racing within herself, and when they were finished—the first time—he drew back and looked at her, at the passion still intact in her bright moon-fired eyes and asked, Where the hell is he anyway? She laughed, sounding the hysteria of a private, self-amusing joke. Only you, she said, only you would wait until later to ask, not before. God almighty, do you still want to go away from me? I'm not going away from you, he said; I'm simply going away. Well anyway, she said, he isn't here. He's at the Dooley House drinking rum and playing cards. But I wish he were here, so he could fill you with bullets. But a hundred wouldn't kill you, would it? Nothing can kill you. Only me. I'm the only one. She put her arms around his neck and drew him against her. You're not going anywhere, she said. The sun isn't coming up again, ever. You're going to stay here, with me, forever.

Standing at the window, he watched the magic of dawn, the renewal, the new day widening the sky with its first blushing heralds as the slowly empowering sun bulked just below the horizon. He heard the cocks crowing and the twinkling sounds of awakening birds. Sometime during the night he had listened to LeGrange return home, heavy boots rising unsteadily on the stairs, and then a door slamming along the hall. She turned in the tossed, twisted blankets and looked at him. He was fully dressed now, openthroated white shirt, jacket, trousers, boots. They stared at each other for several moments; her eyes were mild now, lonely. Now, she said, you have something to come back to. Let *her* give you a woolen muffler to take along. He smiled, until her eyes filled with tears. Then he came and sat on the edge of the bed and with his hand moved the hair away from her face. Will you write to me? she asked. He nodded. Everything? she asked. Everything that's in your heart? Nearly everything, he said. She laughed with soft self-mockery, and murmured his words back to him: Nearly everything. He brought his face close to hers and kissed her lightly on the cheek. Please leave very quietly, she said.

When he had gone, she got out of bed and stood at the window and watched him emerge from under the eaves. He paused for a moment, extended his arms outward, stretched languidly, then strode on. He did not look back, and the smile she had poised on her lips to pass to him slowly curled into an ironic meditation.

Eight

THE ARMY BEGAN TO *move again, uncoiling itself in the mid-June warmth and taking once more to the roads. Phlegmatic, unemotional, it marched, its nerve and its spirit having been tested many times over, marching with that cynical, stolidly enduring, mildly suspicious personality of armies since men had first formed into files and regiments and smeared blood on the altars of their manhood.*

The roads were filled with the swinging blue columns of infantry marching steadily through their own opaque dust clouds, now and then being crowded by galloping staff officers and couriers whose mounted haste offended the marchers. The June sun grew hot, and as always in hot weather, roadside springs and brooks grew scarce. Then they crossed the Potomac and headed into Maryland's green fields and blue-shaded mountains, welcomed by townspeople now who set tables of food by the roadside and offered pitchers of cold water. They passed shining white farmhouses and granaries. Fields of yellow grain blew and nodded in the warm breeze. And at twilight a solitary bird broke the emptiness of the sky and they watched it fly high over the road ahead, north toward Pennsylvania.

We quickened our pace. We were running toward the gunfire and away from last night and the field to where we had drifted from the road to sleep in peaceful moonlight. I think it was the most peaceful night sky I had ever seen; so peaceful I felt close to heaven, I believed in heaven, with the warm earth under me and the clean moon-heavened sky above, and in the night the continual, murmurous march of soldiers along the road, sounding not like soldiers but simply people, the world's legions passing along the road, going to their homes and their farms and their churches; all the world's legions going on about their business while we took our rest upon the moon-tipped grass. And I understood then, as I drifted between wakefulness and sleep, how Eva could believe in the endless night, that it simply became too myriad in its fullness to ever exhaust its vault of shadows and promises, that all of the yellow suns and all of the blue skies would have to wait, or find other worlds for their benedictions. Being lulled to sleep by the marching, the great passage of men into tomorrow. But sleep was not sweet this night, it was restive, whispery, it quivered like a lake in the wind; a tiring sleep, tense with unease, spiked with the nerves of intuition. I would have been better off awake, watching that steadfast and compassionate moon and listening to the strength of that marching army, than trying to sleep.

Dawn the next morning felt like anything but the day's infancy. There was no ease or rustling softness about. No lazy aromas of coffee or bacon, no speculative pipe-smoking, but a suddenness, an instantaneousness, as if to make immediate payment for the night's brief respite. Striking the road again, feeding the pillars of dust, a tension in the column now, a bracing, a hardening. A portentous red sun burned low in the east with the ominous promise of scorching heat, a steadily growing and permeating heat, as if the sun itself had determined to make its impact felt upon whatever amphitheater lay momentously ahead. It hardened the shadows in the valley and seemed to hammer into deeper isolation the farmhouses and their stone-and-timber barns. Everything would be participant this day, from the lordly sun itself down to the merest stone as we marched forward into that delirium of vapors which we knew as soldiers lay ahead, following a road now that no longer seemed innocent and endless, but of decisive termination, culmination.

Quickening our pace, running toward the gunfire, running toward that which any sane or reasoning man would divert from, running toward that which every rational human instinct would normally avoid; not even suppressing fear, because there was no fear, though there ought to have been, but going on because there the road led; with an army at our backs and with the surrounding fields of green serenity now closed to us, there was nowhere to go but ahead, on into the muttering preamble: again, not with fear, nor defiance, not duty or obligation either, but with an impacting sense of motion as inexorable and mysterious as the ancient waves themselves; shocked and impressed by what man himself had wrought, who had once more built and created an occasion so colossal and foreboding he had no choice but to unleash it and then endure it until the volcanic force had spent itself and man again could assume control and dismantle the seething provocations, his soul purged of one more Tophet: man gathering once more to show the root-snapping winds and the raging upsurge of the seas that he too had a will and a way.

Now we could hear the artillery unlimbering and blasting its metal with stentorian thunder—our prophets and our elders joining the fray. Couriers were galloping madly, carrying the voices of commanders from one part of the field to another. Flags were being uncased and raised, as if this ground had now been staked and measured, and somewhere beyond the growing racket of musket fire a fife-and-drum corps was playing. Clouds of black smoke were beginning to smudge the morning sky as we hurried up a ridge that commanded a modest view of the Pennsylvania farmland upon whose luckless and unoffending acres this thing had befallen. Our officers were shouting at us, but little attention was being paid to them because they were telling us to do what we were already doing. By God, Eamon Malloy said, this is going to be a hell of a one. Eamon Malloy, who was again climbing his incredible rungs, finding his own heightening levels of order amid the expanding disorder. I told you, Ben, he said. I told you. What he had told me? I could not remember anything he had ever told me. Suddenly I did not want him near me; suddenly he was like a mystagogue and a memento mori and I wanted to be away from him before his words seeped into my brain.

And then the canister blasts grew deafeningly loud and I saw why we were there—the battery was being menaced by a column of Confederate skirmishers moving through the rocks below. We fired, reloaded and fired again, and broke their ranks. They began to drift back. Our gunners gave us a cheer; they were bare-chested, shining with perspiration, their naked breasts giving them an aspect of gigantic heroism as if they had been standing on this ridge for a hundred years, defending our sleep, our liberty. And then an officer came pounding into our midst on a chestnut sorrel, ordering us to retire, that we were too far advanced. Where the gunners looked heroic, he looked crazed sitting his horse, pompous and vulnerable. An artillery shell struck the ridge above us, sending down a broken shower of dirt and rocks. Now the Confederates in the rocks below had regrouped and were advancing again, in those damned ragtag uniforms that had become the taunting apparel of my nightmares, those creeping figmented figures who haunted my sleep and then emerged by daylight to companion my most awful moments. There they were again, too spectral to hate, too numerous to kill, coming after me once more in their stolen and patched-together uniforms, human beings who functioned the same as I but who turned other-worldly when they came into view, as if they carried in their brains all the secrets of my blood that I was not privy to, because I had been born among them and then fled them and left behind my ancestral blood to soak their earth, an earth I could not return to without seeing ghosts and indeed seeing my father's face in the features of my would-be assassin. So again they were coming after me, running across the un-moved stones of the past, lambent upon the old intact and unstirring landscapes, pursuing me, to murder my body and drag my soul back to those ashes and that guardian chimney; they were the murderous clay of decomposed memories who had captured my letters and read aloud the sentiments to the high glee of snickering laughter.

We climbed to higher ground, away from those faceless eternal soldiers and up toward the sun which was suddenly dramatically risen now and spinning a sultry, hellish co-coon for us to fight within. Hey hey hey, a soldier said, was saying, to no one in particular, his voice cajoling, as though wanting to impart a confidence. In passing I glanced at him; he was sitting against a low rock wall, legs extended before him, a large splash of blood just above his belt line. His arm was extended, his fingers reaching out; and then the tension left his arm and it fell abruptly, like a signal, and his head bowed slowly forward.

And then one of those unnatural moments occurred, that were sinister and made me feel the subject of baleful contemplation: a lull in the battle, one of those inexplicable breath-gasping interludes that once upon a time could deceive us into believing in miracles. Put to work building earthen embankments, we began scratching at the difficult, rocky Pennsylvania ground with bayonets, knives, tin cups and plates, our eyes rising and falling to study the dust clouds off to the north where the Confederates were com-ing from, wondering how many men, how much weight. This is going to be a granddaddy, the man next to me said, looking at me for a moment as he hacked at the ground with his knife. Upon another ridge to our left a

half-dozen brass smoothbores appeared—devastating at
close range, a proud artilleryman once told me, at two
hundred yards their canister was irresistible; and they
seemed to be suggesting something now, these disdainful,
thunderously articulate killers, that there would be close
range in this place before the last mark was made, that
there would be not only the whites of their eyes but the
steam of their breath and the reek of their bodies, that all
would be called into play, from artillery to fingertips.

The smoothbores broke the silence—which hadn't been
very long, not more than a few minutes—recoiling upon
their carriages and emitting enormous mouthfuls of smoke
and flame. In the distance we could see the burning metal
gouging into Pennsylvania farmland; and from the distance the Confederate guns blazed back, deity answering
deity, vibrating the air over our heads. There was an outcry
from along our line as a general in dress uniform replete
with red sash appeared on horseback, screaming to the
officers, galvanized into livid fury. His horse executed a
demivolt and he galloped off as the officers shouted to us
to move, run, on the double. Leaving behind our barely
piled embankments, we hurried along the ridge toward a
rising frenzy of rifle fire. The Confederates were charging
toward an exposed flank, and into the gap we poured,
throwing down our line and firing into the hot noisy air.
From above us the smoothbores, depressed slightly now,
began raking those haunting columns of faceless shadows,
sending them spinning, falling, lunging; dismembering
and decapitating. Regimental banners swung through the
air as if their staffs were caught in sudden undertows; they
fell and rose, and fell and rose. The noise grew toward
crescendo, became one rushing unpunctuated burst until
its thunder split for a moment and the shadows were now
lost in smoke. On one knee, trying to get a sight on one
of those smoke-shrouded shadows, I felt myself in spiritual
flight from here, from myself: the better part of me was
no longer there but was in swift shrewd sensible departure

from this place, from this maelstrom of Biblical terror and vengeance. They could tear my body to pieces, I would not be there to feel it; I would return later and in the coolness of a sane twilight reenter and restore it. Nearby a deadly calm voice was saying, Smartly, men, smartly.

Again we were shifted, again into the breach. I passed a hatless man on all fours leaning forward on his arms, his life's blood pouring from his mouth. The dead were appearing now, crumpled, inert, with their twisted lolling heads; the wounded staggering and crawling and crying and moaning, eyes huge and shocked in smoke-blackened faces. Here and there wandered a riderless horse, free and unemotional, like visitors from some mythological past. And then they were coming again, that remorseless Confederate infantry, yelling now, a surge of them, an army of them, a world of them, broken loose from my every chimera-laced nightmare. And this time they were too many. Our line broke and we gave up our position. And now voices joined the fray, swimming into the thunder of the cannons and the staccato of the rifles, voices telling us where to go and what to do, and then the voices were gone, or if not gone then drowned, outshouted, as the Confederate artillery found our range and their shells began exploding amid us. This, it seemed, was the ultimate vengeance, the very earth itself erupting against us as showers of dirt and stone came flinging down upon us. And now in sharp sudden fragments of hallucination there were pieces of men, incredible legs and arms and booted feet strewn about and men in torn smoking clothing rolling over and over; the wheels were shot off a hurtling ambulance and an orderly in a white linen duster set into flight through the air, arms open wide as if to plead his innocence in the face of death. Half-crazed by the idea that those gray phantoms were a thousand generations of unearthed lunatic McKinley's coming to suck the soul from my caverns and carry it in a glass jar back to those ashes and that chimney, I ran as I never had, ready to drive a bayonet into any who would bar my way, be he of the North or of the South. The battle was not for this rise of Pennsylvania earth now, nor was it for the Union, but for my soul, for that which was eternal and immortal, and if there was a God in heaven I would not let them have it; I would not be plundered and carried back to that gallery of bloodline maniacs, back to those ashes where for all eternity I would be forced to lie before that black woodland of erupting assassins forever charging with butcher knives in their fists. No, by God: a blasphemous assault called for herculean ardor, and this I would give them. I would use my last bullet and after that I would dull the point of my bayonet in their bellies and then give them my fists and my feet and my teeth, because I knew that what awaited me was an eternal hell of madmen with Bibles on their heads and sea-going vessels in their libraries.

And then we had been turned around and by a miracle of cohesion (No, it was not a miracle; we were soldiers; we had done this before; we knew when to run, and we knew when to stop and turn around: if there be miracle in it, then that was it—the stopping and the turning around to face it again; those paradoxical human fibers and instincts which are capable of rejecting prickly self-preservation in the name of something which would be honor or destiny or even something else which has yet to be isolated and named: but no matter the name—as for us, we were soldiers: and it was more than that: we had come too far north, this was no longer Virginia, the South, their land, their roads, their trees, their grass, their water, but ours, and the land that bred us gave us strength and we were hewn together once more: we would not lose under our skies: they were the strangers now and they could not help but feel the enmity of our soil), we formed another line and poured into them a withering hail of fire, and they had come so far that now their dead lay in association with ours, blood running to blood in common saturation. From behind us we heard the command to stay, not another inch. And when the ghosts kept coming—close enough for us to hear their own officers nagging them on—we held. Not more than one hundred yards apart, we fired bullets into each other, and then they were fewer, and smaller, and further away.

Other troops came pouring in to secure the position and we were withdrawn, to slide into exhaustion on high ground behind the line. We were too shocked for speech. The sole luxury open to us besides resting was to close our eyes for several moments and unscrew our canteens and slake our clawing thirsts. That I was still intact of mind and body I could neither believe nor understand. My head felt as if clubs had been at it. Looking around me, I saw such faces as I never had before, some of them friends of long standing whom I barely recognized, into whose grimed lineaments age had insidiously incised, emptying their eyes and wedging around their mouths scars of undying fury. We glanced one upon the other with expressions devoid of trust or comradeship, with mutual bitterness for being men who had gone through what men had created; for if the whole was greater than any man, was inhuman and impossible to comprehend, then its component parts were still human blood and mortal flesh, and there had been an incomprehensible mangling of mercy and love and whatever other bright and visionary tendrils made us the flowers of the earth. And I felt encompassed by it now, within its bubbling cauldron, the madness which was everywhere, which I had gone to probe and discern and which now I had unleashed: amid those ashes I had raised the lid and let escape the pestilence, and now its fever was general, infecting every mind. My world was disintegrating and atom by atom I was dissolving into its smoke, making motion within its pestilent vapors, swirling into nothingness, to become another smudge among the ashes.

It seemed that even old Mars and Ares could grow weary of their sport, and by nightfall the shooting had worn down to sporadic, irascible rifle fire along the skirmish lines. Throughout the night we could hear pickets barking their challenges, and ominously, the steady, murmurous rumble of massive activity on the roads—more horses, more caissons, more guns.

We formed a battle line and remained in place. Looking out across the field, we could see the rebel campfires burning and it was almost beyond comprehension to think that they were as we were—exhausted men eating their food, drinking their coffee, lighting their pipes, nursing their wounded and mourning their dead, and seeing such unwinding heart-tugging visions as befall those who have survived the battle. And if they are as we are, then who were those ghosts chasing me? I remembered that fear, the irrationality of it, and with a mordant smile and shake of my head I thought of it as one might some foolish antic of the day's hilarity. Well, old Ben, I told myself, given the order of business, it might have been the most coherent thought you had. But, God, how finely strung were those silken threads that held it all together. The miraculous thing was that we were still intact as human beings, resilient enough to be humanly exhausted and humanly hungry. Nevertheless, if the day had seemed the very bowels of madness, the night seemed unctuously sinister for its quality of tranquility, as if the night had arrived like an unsoiled gentlemen in evening dress, unmindful of the bedlam horrors that had been transacted upon the very field it was now covering. The warm July moon hung high, though now in delivering its delicate lovers' pathway through the night, it seemed somber, chastened, as though its eye were fixed upon this field.

The homey, familiar aroma rising from the coffee boilers was like a stranger's kindness, and I inhaled it like a sweetly intoxicating drug. The faces around me were in shadow, but the brooding silence that hovered about told me that nothing had changed, that nothing had gone back, that those faces would reemerge with the same grimed and sullen unfamiliarity in the morning as I had left them in the smoky twilight.

Tired beyond belief, so tired that endurance was rising again from out of unappeased exhaustion, I took a wish to sleep with me that night, hoping it would catch the wings of a dream and shepherd me through realms of love and softness. I wished I could be unborn, cleansed of all stains and sins, emptied of all knowing, and returned a seedling to my mother's womb and there dissolved into a love that never was. I was that tired, and I was that frightened, of this and of all the dark places.

Whatever the dream was, if there was a dream for me that night, the church bells seemed part of it, greeting the birth of a new day with solemn tolling. When I opened my eyes and saw where I was the bells sounded incongruous, a pathetic innocence in their indestructible faith.

The water carriers were about, refilling our canteens. We boiled water and made our coffee and ate our hardtack, listening to a growing exchange of rifle fire rising somewhere south of us, or was it east, or west? We did not know; those divining needles inside our heads seemed to have been dulled by yesterday's pounding. No matter. As we sat and drank from our tin cups, there was general indifference to the shooting; we knew that in due time it would catch up to us, or we to it. There was no wind, and the air, already warming with a relentlessly climbing July sun, was yesterday's, still upon us, stale and rank with yesterday's fumes.

Little by little the regiment had pieced itself together during the night. Has anyone seen Eamon Malloy? I asked. And quite matter of factly, from a corporal touching a match to his pipe, He's dead. I waited as he drew several times on the pipe, and when he had it smoking to his satisfaction, he shook out the match, pulled the pipe from his teeth, holding it slightly aside his face, looked at me and said, I saw him. Saw him? I asked. He replaced the pipe and gazed steadily at me, like a guardian of wisdom about to deliver a kernel from his storehouse. What was left, he said, then looked away. All I could feel was a troubling sense of the mysterious. Conditions were not conducive to mourning or sorrow. Eamon, I thought, you have gone and left me uninformed: Eamon, who had been so enviably impervious to his own self, to his mosaic of fragments which had come shattering into place, with light shining through their arrangement.

By noon it had been aroused once more to its full fury, again under the sultry malevolent radiance of July sun which poured heat from its own mouthless cannons; by noon the guns were roaring and belching from their caissons, filling the air with grape and canister and cannonballs that would sometimes bounce with the earth-indenting strength and fury of the heaven-flung, bowling over men and horses before exploding and blowing them apart; filling the air with the barking rifles of divisions and regiments and brigades of men whose faces were shining and ghastly in the battle fires; filling the air with the hurrahs and the curses of the embattled, with the abrupt and incredulous outcries of the struck and with the screaming of the maimed and the bleeding. Like so many flying teeth, the bullets sawed fence rails in half and cut down trees. Entire wagons, with drivers and cargo and horses in their traces, were blown skyward by artillery shells. Riderless horses came suddenly plunging in senseless hysteria, empty stirrups flying, eyes rushing and teeth glaring, like the great beasts of painted nightmares. Noise: an enraged bedlam of it: every conceivable sound the air was capable of transmitting and vibrating: the sonorous, the shrill, the thundering, the rumbling, the hissing, the whistling: shrieks and howls and yells and mewling cries for God and for mother: all cascading in one gigantic assault of murder and lamentation. Men died: running, kneeling, crouching, waving, yelling, cursing, sobbing; defiant, angry, frightened, stunned and unknowing; slowly in agony or dropped suddenly into whatever soul-melting abyss received the smoking victims of the carnage. The bloodstorm swept back and forth, back and forth; tearing up by the roots, tearing down to the primeval, ripping away the veneer of civilization and scratching to the very marrow of instinct and flinging the species back into the mud, the ooze. All that remained upright and unbroken were the naked edicts: kill and survive, endure and outlive it, and turn these scars and these grotesque visions over to annealing time. Angle your flesh away from the screaming steel, and pray that God, whose face had surely turned aside from this bestial virtuosity, would not suddenly erupt and fling down and smite with His vengeance. We who once upon a time would have gazed with awe and stirring fear upon a man dead in the street or even in the peace of his winding sheets now rushed past the most awful mangled blood-drenched human wreckage imaginable with barely a human feeling, shocked into a world of smoke and dust and noise. Alien to what was human, we were allied to such steel and rock as would outlast us by a thousand years and be forever as if we had never existed, that would endure in mockery of our excited breath and our footprints.

Back and forth we surged, upon fields where two days before only the butterfly had disturbed the summer's gold. We were rushed to the south slope of a hill by an officer who was shouting, For the Union, boys, for the Union. Lord, said a tall soldier with a bloodied rag around his head, I'd love to drive a pitchfork into his ass. We went, for the Union, and for life and limb, swinging our ranks into line just as the Confederates were running their butternut formations along the valley floor. It began as a high, thin wail, then swelled into that yell which was as much a part of their weaponry as minié balls and canister; that mean wild yell behind which they charged, as if to paint the very air before them with their colors. They came rolling across the undulant ground, striking a hollow which hid them to their breasts and then rising again as if being hefted by the earth itself, driving their way through thickets and then smashing apart a rail fence by their sheer weight.

The signal to fire swept up and down our line, and from behind our boulders we poured lead into them. Their front ranks crumbled as a low cloud of smoke hung before us like an inert, poisonous fog. And again that madhouse vise seized me, and it seemed right and proper, for there was no other way to function in this frenzy of reek and noise; there was nothing of reality here; this was a convulsive departure from man's accustomed journey through this vale, a maniacal aberration suddenly imposed; man torn loose from every civilizing instinct except the most civilizing of all—that lethal obsession to live, to survive, to be able to withdraw into one more night's sleep, see one more day's break over the horizon; and we clanged ramrods into hot barrels and with blackened mouths bit cartridges, intent upon outliving the next minute and the next until extension was made into the sanity of succoring surcease.

Not more than a hundred feet from us the rebels stopped; they wavered there, taking our galling fire with uncertainty, at the very moment our cartridge cases were running to empty. As we began looking back to our officers, we heard words cried out which to me sounded like a zealot mustering his sect. Mistrusting the sound of those words, I sought out the speaker, needing to see the face behind them in order to establish in my mind their certainty. I could not find the order-giver, but a moment later there was a clatter of bayonet shanks on steel as we locked our knives into their sockets, gripping our rifles in both fists, stifling the barrel's heat with the firmness of our hands. A captain moved out in front of the line and, walking backward, sword in hand, said, Come on, boys. Step out, step out. Then he turned and began loping forward, waving his sword in the smoke, his empty scabbard oscillating at his side. With a yelp we followed, lowering our knife-tipped rifles before us, and charging. We came at them, a sudden spray of shining steel, heading through the acrid shroud of battle.

Some of the rebels ran; others remained to fight. Shouting up our courage, we plunged into them, killing in the most awful way possible. A Confederate officer—he had a gold embroidered major's star on the collar of his tunic—seemed to rise from the dead in front of me, one arm hanging shattered and useless in a torn away sleeve, the exposed flesh scorched black. In his other hand was a long-barreled pistol which he was shakily lifting and cocking at me, waving it though the smoke as he sought to sight me along the barrel, his face stern, as if under some profound concentration of thought. I ran at a right angle, compelling him to weave that gun as he remained intent upon me, his eyes never wavering above his tangle of black beard which had a bit of leaf clinging to its hairs. And then his body stiffened slightly and an angry consternation filled his face and I knew he had pulled the trigger and suffered a misfire; and now his eyes dilated and glowed like the last coals of a fire as he watched me bear down upon him and I wished to God he would turn and run, not just stand there like someone in proud and invincible martyrdom. It would have been better, easier, if he had done something—run, shouted, cursed, again tried his pistol—anything but just stand there as if lashed to a stake and take all of my bayonet through his tunic just under the heart. His face swung aside with stunned suddenness and he sank to his knees as I snatched back the smeared blade and went on.

The Confederates were running now, all of them. In their path lay a tangle of underbrush that had begun to burn and smoke, and through it they crashed and bounded. The smoke was thickening around us now, our colors swirling through it like lurid stains, and we began to withdraw. A soldier near me, his face utterly dazed, suddenly retched as he ran, splattering his chest with his own green and yellow bile.

As we returned to what had been our line, Confederate artillery began showering its metal upon us. Again the ground shuddered underfoot as screens of dirt and stone flew up around us and descended like so many melting hillsides. An officer of the Iron Brigade—on his head that unmistakable black felt Hardee hat with the left side turned up and the black plume on the right—was riding through the smoke on a magnificent bay, calling us back, and seeing his flowing white beard I suddenly had a twist of thought that he was some patriarch angel of deliverance, come to lay over us a patina of heavenly solace; and with that thought swirling my consciousness for an instant I lifted my hat to him, thinking, Yes, it was time, it was time; as if the resonance of our agony had finally reached the bowers of the mercies and widened their eyes.

The rebel artillery was pounding thickly around us, and through the dense smoke ahead there was an explosion and I saw a man climbing with outstretched arms an elevation I did not remember being there, until he pitched back to earth and fell draped over a cluster of rocks as if he had not a bone in his body. I stumbled, fell heavily, rose at full run, dirt sticking to my bloodied bayonet. Suddenly a cannonball tore through the Iron Brigade officer's horse at mid-flank and came out the other side, leaving behind a gaping hole that soon filled with pouring intestines and then the horse went over, taking with it my patriarch angel with his white beard and his solace and his mercy.

Somewhere in the din I could hear cheering, like people at a horse race. It carried through the smoke, an unnatural, hordelike chorus in celebration. We ran back beyond our original line, climbing over the bullet-chipped boulders and up along a rocky incline toward a sheltering ridge, where we were ordered to regroup around an artillery battery that was standing hub to hub. The cannoneers were loading their guns with canister to the very muzzles and firing, working with hypnotic fury, to the extent where I wondered the gun barrels didn't blow up in their faces.

In the distance the Confederates were in formation again. Long, low sheets of smoke hung in the small trees, featureless men darting through it like silhouettes. The sky seemed gone in a pall of sulphurous smoke, and what air there was to breathe was thick and choking. Far off in the distance there were small, hellish crescents of red fire. I saw things that were for memory alone, that were not for present awareness, that I was unable to register or reconcile or clarify from eye to comprehension. I was rooted to the spot, senseless and without purpose, watching it all from out of distance, time, as if the present had reached forward to the future and curved it around so that the future was now the present and I was recollecting it all in tranquility, secure from everything but the jarring of memory. My God, soldier, an officer cried at me, what are you waiting for? And to him I wanted to say: *Don't you see that it's long over now, that it isn't happening, that you yourself aren't here and that I'm only remembering you?* But I would hear him later, in actual memory, when there was that actual tranquility in which to assort and connect, because that thing which you cannot help but know about, and think about, and fear and dread and sometimes even anticipate even as you assure your fixed thoughts you are not thinking about it, because who can ever resist contemplating those at once peaceful and serrated incursions of the final, the irrevocable—that thing suddenly occurred in an unearthly explosion that lifted me into the air and floated me through the fuming smoke as though I were a leaf in a hurricane, turned me over so I was seeing the full hot face of the sun, and dropped me in discard back to earth as if I had been weighed and found wanting. Instinctively, as if to fight off a robed and grasping death, to sear it with my spark of life, I stumbled brokenly to my feet and flailed out with my arms like a drunkard fighting off the phantoms of his delirium. No! I shouted hoarsely. And then I felt the staggering weight of pain in my head and the giddy feeling of being loaded with smoking iron and about to be tipped into the gray caverns of the sea. I reached out toward a man, simply and desperately to touch him, to renew contact with life, and he screamed as my fingers pushed into the soft sticky ooze where his arm had hung, and as we fell away into the smoke I ran with my imbrued fingers reaching out ahead of me, desperate to touch another human being. And then I felt the dead weight of the pain sinking from my head and dropping through my body like leaden fire, and behind my left shoulder there was pain like hot white teeth chewing. I stumbled forward, my weighted legs no longer able to carry me, and with closing eyes crumbled to the troubled earth and sank into what a slowly circling thought told me was the sumptuous moment.

The ambulance's hard jostling brought him to. The rough, bounding ride tossed him back and forth upon the leather-covered bench. Above him the white canvas rattled on its bows. Across from him, stretched on the parallel bench built into the other side of the wagon, a man was struggling to hold his torn stomach together, screaming at the driver to go slower. Mother of God, oh oh God, the man said, looking at Ben with stricken eyes as though Ben possessed some authority or at least power of amelioration. The man bared his teeth for a moment, glaring inhumanly, then with a spastic movement rolled his head aside. Take that one first, Ben heard when the ambulance had come to a halt and the two orderlies were climbing in to lift him out. As he tried to interpret the significance of the preference, he heard, the other one's about done anyway. Ben was lifted out and placed upon a stretcher and then raised and carried toward the hospital tent, toward a terrifying and menacing raving of voices in scream, outcry, shriek, moan, appeal, with rending invocations of God and mother and mercy and water, with one thin childlike voice pleading to be shot and put to peace. Carried toward them, Ben saw their wild haggard faces, their vaguely supplicating arms, the twisted frenzies of pain and fear as they suffered beyond endurance, further from home and family and all of the old intangible consolations and velvet mercies than ever, parted from their known world by continental rifts of blind agony. The hating, animal terror grew in those who could see the accumulating heaps of arms and legs as within the tent the bare-armed surgeons in blood-drenched linen dusters and aprons sawed through sinew and bone, holding their knives between their teeth while they probed the flesh of the next patient who was lifted to the amputation bench and stretched full while an orderly held a cattle horn over the patient's mouth and from it applied the chloroform. Rattled with fear, Ben raised himself from his stretcher and under the furiously swimming eyes around him got up and stumbled toward the tent and peered in and watched them at work, the surgeon and his team of intent-faced orderlies gathered intently around a prone figure with bare feet and upright toes protruding under a ghastly white light streaming from an overhead lantern. He watched the surgeon's elbow angling in and out like a piston and heard the grating of the catling as it began to splinter bone, the sound quickly drowned out by the sudden shrieking of several wounded whose stretchers had been placed close by. What are you doing there, soldier? a sentry asked, scowling at him. Ben moved away, the pain in his head and the mauling white-hot teeth at his back deferring for a moment to desperate fear, to hatred of the sentry because the man was whole and erect and unsuffering, scornfully out of place among the ever-rising sea of lamentation around them; and as protectively he clutched his arms with his hands he could remember once being one of the hated himself, when after Antietam he had been detailed to help carry the wounded into a nearby white-pillared mansion where they were being placed upon thick blue carpeting beneath muraled ceilings and crystal chandeliers, windrows of poor devils who would never have otherwise seen such an interior, their being placed to die amid such alien splendor a further insult. Through parted French doors which gave into the dining room he saw the surgeons using the mahogany table for their grisly work and he wondered if someday a family would again gather around its polished contours for their dinners, stabbing their silver forks into the succulence of a truffled bird. Now he staggered away from the white fetid hell, the miasmic stench of its frail mortality impacting in his senses. *I've got to get out of here,* he told himself as, still holding his arms protectively, he dodged between arriving and departing ambulances, watched balefully by sets of sunken, red eyes. Get away from that slaughterhouse before they hauled him up to that table and put that horn on his face and cut away his arms and his legs. Draining the strength of his deepest reservoirs, he stumbled into the darkness. He passed a row of horses killed by artillery shells, the air reeking of their torn bellies, some of their heads twisted sickeningly up by the taut reins which still bound them to their rail fence. A squad of moving infantry opened their ranks to let him go blundering through, his flexed, sagging knees barely able to carry him. *Get away,* he murmured. *Get away.* And then a pounding of horse-drawn caissons came heading for him and he swerved aside, and with the last melting dregs of his strength threw himself upon an embankment, arms flung up ahead of him. He raised his head for a moment, gasping, his eyes unable to focus, turned his face to a side and let it sink to the warm earth as darkness upon darkness rushed over him and drowned the last spark of consciousness.

When he opened his eyes the first things he saw were raindrops splashing against the panes of glass. Beyond the window lay a dreary, rain-gray sky. Guardedly he moved his eyes and saw hanging on the yellow wall a pair of embroidered samplers with needlework that spelled out GOD BLESS OUR HOME and MY NAME IS JENNIE. Then his eyes shifted back to the window and its soft-hitting blur of raindrops. He lay tensely and self-consciously motionless for several moments, then took an accounting of his extremities, moving his toes and doubling his fists. Finding himself intact, he relaxed.

Where then? he wondered, and then remembered—in the head and behind the left shoulder, not shot but brought down by the indiscriminate shredding of an artillery shell. While there was little more than sullen nagging in his head, the other wound felt like a sheet of baked tin was being held to it. Lowering his eyes, he saw the heavy swathing of white bandage coming from behind and looping under his armpit.

He tried not to think about time, about how many hours or days had been consumed since that explosion had carried him out of the battle, since he had run from the surgeons and their dripping knives. He vaguely remembered a prolonged, momentous roaring, as if rock by rock the world had undergone dissolution and then re-creation, gouging its canyons and hanging its crags anew. Or had it merely been a thunderstorm, this soft rain its assuasive end? He believed he had wakened once and seen the glass in that window quivering in its frame, felt the floor vibrating under his pallet. He was, however, but mildly curious, was still luxuriating in his resurrection, in the miraculous restoration of peace and quiet. He had forgotten that inevitably it did come around again, as it always did, as it had after Antietam and Fredericksburg. Sometimes you might have thought otherwise, as sometimes you thought winter would never end or morning never arrive.

On the pallet to one side of him a man was sleeping, hands reversed upon chest like a corpse in arrangement, but Ben could seen the placid breaths rippling through the long dark beard. And on the pallet on his other side he was startled to see one of those butternut tunics open and spread across a bare chest, and this man, young and with curly yellow hair, also asleep. With wonder and curiosity, he gazed upon the Confederate, studying every feature of the sleeping face—the dirt-smudged forehead and the small round nose and the finely shaped mouth that seemed almost girlish in repose; and the tiny cuts with their congealed blood on one cheek, where a growth of golden stubble had begun to cover. The engine of death, the smoky silhouette, the ghost of relentless pursuit, was at rest, and at rest merely a man, no older than Ben, vulnerable and unthreatening, reaching deeply for his breaths and releasing them in long, gratifying suspirations as if trying to empty himself of some inner disquiet. There were dark stains on his torn-apart trouser legs; his boots were off and his stockings were worn away below the toes so that they resembled gaiters.

Across the small room, which had been cleared of all furniture except a table, lay several other pallets, unoccupied. Listening now, he could hear beyond the ticking of rain on glass the rumbling sound of endless wagons in passage, across cobblestones it seemed. There were voices in other parts of the house, occasionally a soft moaning.

A rather bulky young man with flourishing brown sidewhiskers entered the room. He was wearing a long, blood-smeared white smock and was carrying a pan of water which he put down on the table. He appeared to be avoiding looking at the men on the pallets.

"Hello, doctor," Ben said quietly.

"I'm not a doctor," the man said, eyes still averted, "and you ought to thank your stars for that. The doctors are seeing to the desperate cases."

"I'll bet there are a few of those."

"A few."

"You're a nurse?"

"Yes," the man said, glancing at Ben for the first time. "And I know how to dress a wound."

"I don't even know for sure what happened to me."

"Shell fragments," the nurse said. "Against your head—you were lucky there, my fellow—and into your back below your left shoulder."

"When was I brought in?"

"I can't say for sure. Early yesterday morning, I'd guess."

"Then I lay out there overnight."

"I should think you did," the nurse said, standing at the window and gazing out, hands in pockets.

"Unless I died, made a tour of the heavens and came back."

"Yes," the nurse said abstractedly, and as Ben was thinking the man was paying him no mind, the man said, "If it were so, then you were a damned fool for coming back," and turned from the window to Ben with a look that implied a superior indifference to whimsy.

"Where are we?"

"In a private home, in town," the nurse said, looking back outside at the rain again. "Everything has been commandeered—houses, churches, schools, wagon sheds, barns, hen coops. Everything," he said, speaking in a disinterested monotone. "In order to take care of you all." He spoke this last as if trying to establish a subtle distance between himself and what was happening.

"What are you seeing?" Ben asked.

"Caissons, ammunition wagons, commissary wagons, sutlers, horses, men. The army," the nurse said dryly. "On the roll again."

"In victory or defeat?"

"Oh, victory," the nurse said, a faint rise in his voice. "They said it was quite a sight. Quite a sight," he said thoughtfully, studying the caravan under the window.

From another part of the house there was a sudden shout of anguish, followed by an embittered stream of profanity.

"Private Smith has awakened to find himself short one leg," the nurse said, engrossed in his view; and then, just audibly, "We didn't shatter it, Mr. Smith; we merely saved your life."

"What was quite a sight?" Ben asked.

"The Confederate advance. I didn't see it, of course. But some people are quite lyrical about it. 'A flowing sea of gray'—that sort of thing. Catchpenny poetry. But it must have been quite a spectacle. They just lined up in formations, a wide mile of them, and then walked across the field, right toward the guns. A division's worth."

"A division?"

"At least fifteen thousand, it was said. Whatever it was, it was one hell of a lot more than walked back, I can tell you," the nurse said soberly, gazing through the rain-smeared window. "It must have been something to see. By God, I'll bet it was. It came soon after the artillery barrage. You didn't hear that? Lord, man, you must have been out to the depths of you. I think every field piece in both armies must have had its say. I'd wager they heard it in New York and Philadelphia. It seemed to me to have lasted for over an hour. I said to the surgeon, 'Well, doctor, when that's done there'll be little for us to do, because I don't think there will be two bones left hanging together.' "

"And when it was over, they charged."

"Walked, actually."

"We call it a charge," Ben said.

"I always thought a charge was a pell-mell onset upon something. Forgive me, but I'm still fresh to this. So across they came—your charge, my walk; be that as it may. In a way, I would liked to have seen it—the advance, that is, not what happened when the guns went off."

"What happened?" Ben asked.

The nurse passed him a look of skepticism, then turned back to the window. "How many engagements have you been in?" he asked.

"They belie my years and my sweetness of disposition," Ben said, flat irony in his voice.

"So you know what happened."

"Were our cannons still in operation?" Ben asked. "I mean, after that barrage . . . "

"From what I saw on that field this morning, I should say yes. The dead were lying in rows, some of them in almost perfect formation. And then there were the bits and pieces. Oh yes, our guns were in fine working order. The barrels got so hot, a sergeant of artillery told me before he died, that when you spat on them the spittle turned into a little ball and bounced right back up."

"So we turned them back."

"With some perspiration," the nurse said, a bit remotely, Ben thought.

"When you walked on the field, were you sick?"

The nurse turned and gazed inquiringly at Ben, whose face was watching him expressionlessly from the blanket roll which was his pillow. The nurse seemed to be per-plexed by some extraordinary thing.

"Yes," he said. "I'm not ashamed to say."

"Nor should you be. It speaks well of you."

The nurse's gaze lingered for several seconds, then he turned again to the window, though now his expression seemed studiously interior.

"Tales to tell into your old age," Ben said, his voice insinuating quietly. "You'll be the center of every Sunday tea. 'I was there. Ah yes,' " Ben said with faint mimicry. "You'll hone it to dramatic perfection, noting the envious eye and preening under it."

With concession, the nurse said, "Yes, I'll speak of it."

"You will find understatement most effective. Also most seemly. Graphic description can be offensive," Ben said. He turned toward the Confederate. "What do you think his version will be?"

The nurse looked from the window and studied the sleeping Confederate. "I suppose," he said, "since you have the victory, he'll lay claim to the glory."

"Was he badly hit?"

"He has some modest wounds in his legs. But he was

lucky after all; they found him lying in the midst of a lot of his fellows who looked to have died by every device known to man—the cannon, the rifle, the rifle butt, the bayonet, and God knows maybe even bare hands. He was found right up front where it was thickest. I don't know how he got that far; they say the field pieces were depressed to almost point-blank range. He's been unconscious since he was brought in."

"Doesn't know he's alive, does he?" Ben said. "Here's a fellow lying there thinks he's dead. What's he dreaming of, do you think? Angels swimming through white clouds? Beautiful ladies at their lyres? Poor fellow. What's his dish when he wakes up—this stinking place and then a prison camp and watered-down gruel." Ben smiled coolly at the nurse, whose face, framed between its vainglorious whiskers, was contemplating him thoughtfully. "My best friend was killed," Ben said. "Eamon Malloy. Ah, Eamon." He chuckled. "He was one for the jars in your medical school."

"How did you know—?"

"I could tell."

"I've a long way to go," the nurse muttered.

"Eamon was progressing so nicely through it all. A beautiful sample of the powers of warfare. Unique man. I think the gods must have been appalled by him and decided they had better pull him in. He was running against the grain of all intention."

Ben sighed and closed his eyes. The discomfort in his head, soft, like long-deferred sleep, was expanding against him again.

"What's your trade, anyway?" the nurse asked.

"Poet," Ben said with a pleasant half-smile. "But like you, a long way to go."

After a few moments of silence, the nurse said, "You can ask him now."

Ben opened his eyes. The nurse was staring at the Confederate, whose eyes had opened into a wide, shining gaze.

"What he was dreaming," the nurse said laconically.

The Confederate's eyes worked from side to side for a moment, lit with bright, wondrous curiosity, and then a deep, almost beatific calm filled his face. He began making some effort, as if to rise, but Ben rose to one elbow and reached out and put a hand on the man's smooth, hairless chest and settled him. The man's lips parted across his small white teeth in a weak smile, his eyes remaining like bits of polished glass. Again he made an effort to rise and again Ben's hand went lightly but firmly upon his chest.

"Where do you think you're going, man?" Ben asked.

"Home," the Confederate said quickly, with simple, almost protesting logic.

"And where would that be?"

"Prince Edward County, Virginia," the Confederate said possessively, with pride. "It isn't far." He lay motionless on his pallet, his shining eyes gazing upward, the vague half-smile upon his lips. "I'll be there by sundown. Ma and Pa and Rebecca and Tully and Tom St. George are waiting for me out on the front gallery."

"He's off his chump," the nurse said.

"No he's not," Ben said, sitting up, contemplating the Confederate's calm, untroubled face, the eyes with their fervent, consecrating glitter. "Where were you?" Ben asked.

"A bedlam place," the Confederate said softly, without inflection. He touched his underlip with the tip of his tongue. "Like chickens squawking at a tomcat. Like squealing shoats looking for their sow. But louder. I've seen that a thousand times in our barnyard. I wasn't afraid. Not really. But after all, it was a wolf and it had killed our Gordon setter. Tore out its belly. Pa said we were going to hunt it down, once and for all. I said, 'Pa, I'm afraid,' but he said, 'Bobby, you're twelve years old and that's man enough to go after a wolf.' We walked across the pasture real slow and the rifle felt too big for my hand. Thunder, too. But no rain. Not even black clouds; just thunder. You'd swear it was making furrows in the sky."

The Confederate fell silent, wet his underlip again, like moistening a finger to turn a page, his eyes still fixed upon the ceiling, though narrowing now as if trying to adjust his focus.

"Oh, it was a long walk," he said, his voice soft, slow, with a downy, dreamlike quality in its drawl. "Ma said don't take him; he's too young. But Pa said it was all right. We marched into the valley behind our colors. Tully was up ahead. I was watching him; the back of his shirt was black with perspiration and there was a piece of straw hanging to it from where we'd been lying in tree shade. He was holding his rifle at angle in front of him as he walked with his big steps. General Garnett was killed. We saw him ride into the fire and smoke, and his horse came back empty, running wild-eyed and streaming blood. But Tully and Tom St. George will wait for me. They're on the front gallery now, watching the road. Tully was marching right in front of me and once he looked back at me and smiled, like to say, 'It's all right, Robby.' He was the only one who called me that. He was one fine brother, Tully was. He won't be in the tent tonight. Tully was the strongest man I ever knew. One year older and ten years stronger, Pa once said. Tully was always the favored. Why, I saw him lift a young heifer clear from the ground so you could see daylight under all four hoofs. Why, Tully took a ball in the shoulder at Sharpsburg and he only smiled and said, 'Don't tell Ma, Robby.' But even Tully was screaming, lying there and looking at his own insides streaming out of his belly, and men on all fours around him yelling and choking on the smoke and groping like blind men. Even Tully was in pain and he was afraid, too. But I didn't stop."

"How far did you get?" Ben asked.

"Only to the stile at the far end of the pasture. Pa said, 'Come on, Bobby, climb over.' But I couldn't. Not with that wolf out there. I started to cry and Pa said, 'All right, go on back home. That's what your Ma wants anyway.' Pa came back at dusk and said the wolf was dead, and he looked at me and I turned away. But it never rained. That thunder went clear to God's gates, but it never rained. Colonel Buhler and his horse went straight up into the air like a statue when the ground blew up under them, and the horse's legs looked like they were trying to ride up into the sky, and then it all came apart. The forelegs kept going and Colonel Buhler flew out of the saddle and the horse was rolling away while its forelegs kept flying. But this time I climbed over the stile, only it was a rail fence, and the racket was the devil's chatter. I was afraid, but I went. You could see the red flashes in the smoke like snake tongues trying to get at you.

"Ma said, 'Don't go out, boys, it's going to rain.' But Tully winked at me and we slipped out when she went to the shed to get some wood. Tom St. George came by and we went into the yard to burn some leaves. We stepped over dead horses and dead men and pieces of dead men, and when we passed the cannoneers they shouted to us and waved their hats, and there were places where the holes in the ground were still smoking. We walked in the longest line you ever did see. It was like a thousand Sundays, so quiet you could hear all the feet—until the Yanks opened up on us. It was fierce, oh; it was hailstones, coming at us straight along instead of from up above. And I said, 'Pa, I'm going over now.' I wanted him to watch me, to see me doing it, that I wasn't afraid. And I did go over, because I knew Pa would like it. There was an awful noise of men roaring at each other. It kept getting louder. It was a riot. A mob rioting. Crazy people. Clubbing and stabbing. The canister tore into us point-blank. I could see the cannons recoiling. Tom St. George's hair was burning and Ma was yelling to us to put out that fire and come back, and when Tom whammed his hands into his burning hair and looked at me with his bleeding face, I said he had better put out that fire or else Ma would give him what-for and he was crying my name, but it was Ma's voice coming out of his mouth.

"Then we heeded Ma and headed back and I saw Tully lying where he'd fallen, dead asleep he was, and he looked like the wolf had chewed on him, he was all red and raw in the middle. 'Come on back,' Ma was yelling, 'it's going to rain.' Finally, after all that thunder, I thought. 'You boys,' Ma said sternly. We're for it now, I thought, because Tom St. George had made the fire and caught his hair in it and the wolf had got Tully. But Tully and me didn't run because we liked to feel the rain on us and the wet ground under our feet, so we straggled back to the house and we all looked as if we had stepped far ahead into time and taken our years of a sudden because we resembled old men when we got back. I lost my hat, too. With Rebecca's letter in it. Lord, I'd better find it. And off near the trees I saw Lee, sitting his horse in his plain gray uniform, talking to some of the men. 'There he is,' I said. But Ma didn't care and Tully didn't hear and where in God's name Tom St. George had gone off to I didn't know. Then I just stood there shivering in the heat, waiting for Pa to come up and put his arm around me and say, 'Ah, Bobby, you showed them the way, didn't you?' "

Abruptly the Confederate stopped talking, his lips coming together and not parting again. In the slowly expanding quiet which of itself seemed like a breathing in the room, the nurse stared at him from the window, Ben from his risen position on the adjoining pallet. The Confederate's eyes remained fixed upon some mysterious vision overhead, then began to falter as an expression of deep unease slowly filled and confused them, and then they closed as the corners of his mouth sank with mute, unutterable pain.

"So," Ben said. "His version."

"Clear off his chump," the nurse said.

"Twice wounded, you may say."

"One of which we can see to."

"And the other?" Ben asked, musing upon the broken fortunes in the face next to him.

Yes, she replied shyly to my question. I am the Jennie of the sampler. She had made it when she was nine years old and now she was sixteen, a beautiful young lady with tightly brushed-back and beribboned russet hair and attentive black eyes like warm licorice set in an oval face and a pursed, most concerned little mouth. She was a wellspring of compassion and when she came into the room to dab my forehead with a cool wet rag I told her I had all my life dreamed of such a lady coming to soothe the simmering coals of my pain and that I would surely fall in love with her, and she smiled, as well-bred young ladies will at a man's leathery banter. No you shan't, she said, her smile the more winning for its concealments. I asked her if she had a sweetheart and she said yes, that he had enlisted last winter to fight for what she solemnly called the cause. She had not heard from him for a time, she said, but I told her not to worry, that letters sometimes went astray and were a long time in catching up. I was an authority on the subject, I assured her. She sighed to the depths of her devotion, sighed to the very edge of prayer.

She kneeled over me and dabbed my forehead with the wet cloth which she drew from the pan of water at her side. And asked if I had a sweetheart. Two, I said. She studied me for a moment, then through dissolving skepticism smiled at me as though I were a veritable sunshine of lovable mischief. *Two* sweethearts! Lands, to be so popular! Well, she hoped *her* sweetheart didn't have twins in his heart. Well, I told her, let him beware in any event, since I had fallen in love with her. She studied me wonderingly, then smiled into herself, a pleased little headshake of a smile, one of those ineffable, sweetly maddening woman smiles that makes you feel helplessly the child no matter how old you are nor how young they; one of those smiles of wisdom ancient and innate with which they flatter our strengths and reassure our weaknesses. Then she went on with the cloth again, so cool upon my brow, shutting away for the moment that unpleasant outside world of rainy skies and interminably passing wagons along the town's cobblestones. Well, she said, I suppose you'll be off to the hospital soon and then home again, to your two sweethearts. What are their names? she asked. Susan and Eva, I said. And now the smile was but faintly present. And which do you prefer? she asked. Well, I'm hard put by that, I said, since one is the sun and the other the moon. She looked aside to rinse the cloth and freshen it in the cool water. Oh, go on with you, she said quietly.

Nine

AS THE FERRY NEARED the river's eastern shore, Ben rose from the bench in the gas-lit interior and, with his paper-wrapped parcel under his arm, went out on deck to watch the Queens shoreline approach from out of the darkness. The cool September wind sounded like the fluttering of pennants and he could hear the strong East River currents dashing against the large side-wheel vessel. The ferry houses with their red and yellow lights were now distinct, and beyond he could see a further scattering of lights in the distance. Dispassionately he gazed far beyond those lights, out into the unmooned and unstarred night toward the small backbone of hills, toward the meadows and pastures he had not seen for nearly two years now, separated from them not only by time but also by those smoldering abysses called Antietam, Fredericksburg, and Gettysburg. As he sought the night sky over Capstone, his attitude was moodily self-protective, as if coating himself against some emotional assault, some disfiguring differences that might have to be encountered, some jarring displacements effected upon old familiar landscape; he had no idea what awaited and he would not allow himself a sense of gratitude at his return lest it turn euphoric and make him vulnerable.

An elderly produce farmer returning with his empty wagon from the Manhattan markets offered him a ride up to Capstone, through which the farmer passed on his way back to Long Island. "I'd consider it an honor," the farmer said, regarding Ben with the deference that people, older people especially, showed soldiers in wartime.

If the farmer was hoping for conversation during the slow, clattering ride, he was disappointed. His companion showed no inclination for talking or, the farmer soon began to realize, for listening either. From large conversational gambits like the war the farmer worked his way down to the turmoil and congestion of New York City and then finally to the weather, before giving up. So they sat side by side, the farmer holding the reins loosely in hand, Ben leaning forward, hands clasped between his knees, the soft brim of his gray felt slouch hat pulled down so that it nearly covered his eyes, the parcel containing his personal belongings between his feet. The horses kept them slowly, steadily in motion as the wagon wheels turned and ground and bumped along the deep ruts that had been carved by back-and-forth traffic for generations. They worked their way inland from the river, covering the ground where the first Dutch settlements had stood, two hundred years ago now since the Dutchmen had first crossed the river in their boats and strode here in their knee breeches and fat-buckled suits and high-crowned hats, with their blunderbusses and their deeds and their hopes and dreams. Some of their farmhouses still stood, cowled in frail and secretive dilapidation behind low rail fences. The Dutch had not ventured too far inland, choosing to huddle protectively together, near the river, in deference to the unpredictable Mespatche and Merrikoke tribes that prowled the hills and forests beyond.

Ben knew, when the team began to work just a little harder, that the long, gradual upgrade into Capstone had begun and for the first time felt a sharpening awareness of things around him, of landmarks, of familiar white clapboard houses behind their lawns, of clustered oaks and maples, and then the feed and grain store, the stable, the smithy, all as he had left them, rooted as if in mockery of the fear he had had of returning to find all things different.

As they approached the lights of the Capstone Inn burning under its low flat roof, the farmer sighed and announced he had decided to lay over for the night. They dismounted before the low wooden porch and the farmer looped the reins around the post.

"I reckon you're not too far off now," he said.

"Not at all," Ben said. He extended his hand. "I thank you, sir," he said.

"You're most welcome, sir," the farmer said, eyeing him curiously.

They clasped hands lightly for a moment, then Ben turned and walked off, clutching his parcel under one arm. The farmer watched him until Ben left the fan of light thrown by the inn and was gone into the darkness, listened for a moment to the young soldier's boots striding methodically on the road, then shook his head and turned and climbed the porch steps and entered the inn.

He walked steadily, with long, slow, steady strides, along the side of the wide thoroughfare called Grant Avenue. When the constant upgrade began at last to level, he saw the lights in the Dooley House, Capstone's premiere hotel, dining room, bar; not elegant but comfortable and receptive and central; in the summertime its high front porch was a senate and judiciary of staring, gossiping, chewing, spitting, smoking witnesses and arbiters. Above the tall front porch were piled three stories of rooms, and behind the white clapboard structure a stable and corral. He passed the hotel on the far side of the road, seen but undefined by the few porch-sitters.

He went on, back into the darkness, seeing no one, continuing his methodical unbroken strides, shifting the lightweight but cumbersome parcel from one arm to the other. Cutting away from the avenue, he crossed a pasture, making his way toward the narrow lane where the dairy farmers drove their herds. Despite a growing sense of urgency now, a tension beginning to constrict his insides, he continued his methodical, almost monotonous pace, as if marking off his distance in accordance with a nodding pendulum. Here and there a house bulked out of the night, darkened windows obscuring all dimensions. He cut away from the lane, went through a grove of trees, following unerringly the old, known path in the dark, memory and not eye guiding his footsteps. Emerging from the trees, he followed another lane, getting closer now to where he had been brought those years ago, extirpated from his generations—or so he had always thought, though now he knew that was not so, that he had been carrying and would always carry those generations, an unwilled inheritance that was vastly more than physiognomy.

He stopped when he reached the front gate, pausing there to gaze at the house, at the light in the downstairs window, and finally he allowed himself to feel the sense of relief he had been suppressing since disembarking from the ferry, as he realized he had been afraid the house would not be there, that plague or fire or wind might have dismantled or eaten of it, leaving behind another scattering of ashes and another gaunt column of bricks. The old son of a bitch is in there, he thought. No one else in Capstone stayed with the night as long as that old man did, sitting near the lamp with his books or simply sitting, with God knew what thoughts. With wry affection he smiled, swelling now with the delectable surprise he was about to spring. I'm going to shake him back and forth as hard as I can, he thought. You old bastard. Got arthritis in your fingers or something? Misplace your pen? Run out of paper? Forget how to spell? Suddenly lose the language you're so conceited about knowing and shaping? Or maybe you figured I'd be so headstrong and lunatic I'd let them get me, that the McKinley in me would have me charge their formations with the jawbone of an ass? Well, I'll tell you: not two with butcher knives nor a hundred thousand with muskets and artillery could do it. A bit of hot metal in the back, that was the best they could do though they took ten thousand shots at me.

He opened the gate, entered, then shut it behind him with a deliberately loud click. Those cat's ears would perk at that; he heard everything, that old man, from the wind coming up off the river to the touch of starshine upon the grassroots. He'll be pulling off his spectacles now and putting down his book and turning in his chair, those brigand's instincts worked down to the quick. By the time my boot strikes the porch he'll be behind that door wondering from what unremembered transgression this shade of the past has emerged.

He did not have to knock; the door opened as if from the pressure, the faint thud of his boot heel on the porch; it edged back by degrees until it revealed the man in his height and width, the parlor light falling into the entrance passage behind him. To Ben he looked smaller, older, but nonetheless sturdy, impervious, carapaced in that strength and those secrets that seemed to feed one upon the other; as ever in his stillness he looked as charged as a statue carved in simulated animation. They stood silently for several moments, divided by the threshold. Hook's eyes, always so warily restive in his impassive face, seemed to be trying to puzzle something out in his mind.

"Ben?" he said, asked, his voice a breath above a whisper, as if inquiring of a passing breeze, a nothingness.

Ben pulled the slouch hat from his head, smiling affectionately as he did so. Hook lifted his hand and with it touched absently at his short, neatly trimmed beard, then let it fall, and continued to stand motionless, in continuing scrutiny.

"Ben," Hook said again, this time in recognition, as if suddenly successful in piercing a disguise.

Ben's smile faded, the affection remaining in his eyes, softly and clearly. He felt the sensation of being studied and scrutinized, of being put together feature by feature under the old man's gaze.

"Yes," Hook whispered, his voice distant, detached from this moment, this time, as if informing or responding to moments and time past, adding the final, culminant word, the affirmation. "It's you. By all the graces . . . it is you." He took Ben's hand in his own, though not so much in greeting or embrace but as if to establish through physical contact the indisputable and irrevocable fact of the arrival, the presence.

"It's been a long way, Mr. Hook," Ben said. "Do I need an invitation for the last step?"

We sat alone in the house, in the parlor downstairs, in chairs on opposite sides of the table upon which stood our whiskey glasses and bottle and upon which lay my book and spectacles and upon which stood the lamp with its slow, mellow light seemingly intent on showing the time and the wear which had occurred to his face; he had never really been a boy, not in that sense of gaiety and innocence and disbelief in time; not with that taut, wary face, that fixity of eye, which now had added to it something even more indelible, that seemed not so much to have been instilled or engraved as to have risen from within, furthering and making even more permanent whatever had set that face to begin with. Trying to sense what lay behind those eyes had been as futile as trying to wash water; but at least now I saw something comprehensible, responsive: he stared at the tears which formed in my own eyes as I gazed at him (now that I had accepted his presence, the astonishment and the incredulity were settling upon me, and not with the joy which should have been natural, but with a certain philosophical melancholia). He acknowledged the tears with a look of warmth, an embarrassed smile. My own emotion I could not identify. My God, I thought, I had shed no tears when I believed him dead, but merely sat, alone and bereft, with a density of feeling that swelled and hurt but which would relinquish nothing; had sat night after night, thinking, *He's at rest, found elsewhere what was not to be given him here.* Accepted it, buried him; thinking, *Now it's finished, the last nail in the wood, the last stone in the wall.* Philosophical, yes, because I accepted it as something that had always been inevitable, that I would live to see; and if there was any comfort at all to be taken, it was that at least he had spun out with a measure of dignity—killed in battle—and not as the consequence of some tragic destiny. That much at least, I thought, he had wrested from the bitter foredooming. Crying now as might the skeptic who suddenly is confronted by the deity he had so long disdained and defied; crying because of the sheer overwhelming weight of it.

He sipped some whiskey, then put the glass down. I was wounded, you know, he said. At Gettysburg. Some Confederate metal burned a hole in my back, as well as gave me a knock on the head. In the hospital a long time. They've given me a few months to leather myself up. But I was one of the lucky ones. That was a hellish place, Mr. Hook, that Gettysburg. They seemed to be getting worse, one after the other. After Fair Oaks and Mechanicsville, I thought, Well, now I've seen it all; Hell can't compare. But those places were Sunday afternoon rabbit hunts compared to Antietam. I swear the sun streamed blood that day. It got so that for a while the dead were gazed upon with a certain envy. But then Fredericksburg. That was worse because we never had a chance. It was almost like our officers had decided to punish us; or maybe they just weren't paying attention. The rebels had a position at the top of that hill that was just impregnable; a battalion of schoolgirls could have stood us off from behind that stone wall. And it was so cold. Jesus Holy Christ, some of the boys said, December ain't no time of the year to be fighting a war. It's a bit much, bleeding to death and catching the pneumonia at the same time. Well, when we came away from Fredericksburg, the consolation was that we'd seen the worst and that now things had to get better. We were held in reserve at Chancellorsville and saw little of it, and all I'll tell you about Gettysburg is that it was the worst of all: forget the horror and there was a nobility about it, an aura. I tell you, the very stars pierced the blue at high noon to come out and watch. Something died there and only time will tell what. But there was something else, between Fredericksburg and Gettysburg, and that was for me alone.

His voice had ceased and he was regarding me with an expression of lofty, almost supercilious satisfaction, as though he had performed and got away with some exceptional piece of mischief. Yes, there had been something else, between Fredericksburg and Gettysburg, something peculiar and unrelated to the war, something which had obviously seared itself into his consciousness more vividly and more dramatically than even those twin hells of our time. This was in the spring, he said, some weeks before Chancellorsville. After the winter's inactivity the rustling of spring had been inviting and he had volunteered for wood-cutting details. They rode out of the encampment by mornings with their empty, clattering wagons to cut down trees. Because the wintering army had been cutting away the wood in the area for many months, they had to go wandering for miles around to find fresh timber for their blades. After some days of this, he said, something began nagging at him. It was slowly dawning on him that he had seen some of these places before—these roads and pastures and configurations of rock and earth, these cross-roads of ramshackle structures—that from out of the pent, hermitic hoardings of memory, scraps were being released into the flotation of active thought. And then there had been an action—small—and the familiarity became so intense and demanding he had felt compelled to follow its lead.

I knew immediately what he was talking about; I knew he was not remembering a place or places he had marched a year before with the army; I had too much respect for him, for his mind, and too much knowledge of the torments and the experiences that had been drained from the night, the air, the wind, and stored away. I never expected him to forget them, as I never expected him to reencounter their landscape. Soon he knew he was being led, he said, and not by anything supernatural or fantastic, but by the hard remembering, by recognition. It was Biblical, he said, for a little child—the himself I once was, he said—was leading him. And then he was upon *that* road, and though the air was still and unsparked, the cascade of memories was golden and radiant. As he spoke I began to wonder: To what did he go back? How far? By how much tortuous dissembling was he subject, and how much did he believe?

All right, I said. And arrived where? There, he said. There? What did *there* mean? Well, he said with gravity, to my own satisfaction I saw the house standing intact, with hospitable smoke rising from the chimney, with a carriage as fine as a Dresden piece standing in front. And I saw—again to my satisfaction—my mother and my father. He did seem a bit intense, Mr. Hook, but strong and interesting. She, of course, was spun in all loveliness, so beautiful and vulnerable, with such unhappy eyes. I could see why you loved her. You did love her, didn't you? He was watching me carefully now, not without a certain sardonic whimsy. God almighty, I thought, he has come on tiptoe to my innermost place. I could feel a rising of ghosts and the dragging weight of old futile longings. I could barely remember her face, but the sound of her voice and the gossamer of her presence had never for a moment left me.

And he knows it, I warned myself. This boy knows his mother lives within me, that I am the last place on this earth where any part of her still endures. And my God, I thought, given his bent of mind, what is to stop him from separating me bone by bone to look for her? There we sat, he looking for his mother in my eyes, and I for his father in his, for there had been something quite pronounced in the face of his father, so that if you had been addressing an assemblage and McKinley was among them, you would sooner or later note him and thereafter be unable to move your eyes from him. It had been my intention when finally telling him the story of his antecedents to place in his hands the weapon of vigilance, but now I could see that he had taken to romanticizing it, that he had given dispensation to the wind to talk to him and for the night to sire his chimeras. What I saw now in his face was either the romance or the reality, neither of which was a comfort, and the fact that he had risen from the dead made him all the more strange and unlikely. Or maybe, I told myself, it was merely the besetting visions of the fields of Fredericksburg and Gettysburg I was seeing, since the abominations of battle must surely flood higher in the young than the old. But he wanted his answer.

Yes, I said. I don't think the man ever breathed who would not have gone in love with her, even given that she sat an invalid. She was simply the most angelic of creatures, and the most sensible, accepting her homage with dignity and tact. He nodded, wetting his lips, and said (as I knew he would; I had long ago realized that life would be much more tolerable if I made an effort to understand and anticipate that mind), Then when you swung that ax it was— To save you, I said sternly. With an intensity of gaze he read deeply of me for several moments. Ah, I thought, this was as close to it as he would ever get; he was now at the furthest limit, the very lip of the abyss; never would a moment ripen just this way again, nor quest and willingness this way juxtapose, nor pride and reticence. Then you did it for her, he said. Would you have done differently, Ben? I asked. Well, he had no answer for that. The ensuing silence seemed to draw him to a crest, but quickly a kind of recession appeared to take place, as the tension began leaving him and he sat back in the chair. A slow smile of rakish self-mockery crossed his face. A pile of ashes, he said. That's what I found. Burned down to the ground and scrambled by the wind. Nothing there but ashes and the one chimney. By God, Hook, he said, I don't even know that I was at the right place; these open air sepulchers are all alike. It makes no difference, I said; the widows of sea captains go and with no demeaning of honor weep at engraved stones placed in memory of men who are at the bottom of the ocean. But everything I felt, he said, told me that was the place. All of my feelings, he said, and all of my imaginings. His imaginings? I shuddered at what those might have been.

Then he rose and paced slowly around the room, in and out of the cast shadows. He gazed inquiringly at things as he moved, as if reacquainting himself with each piece of furniture. His boot heels rapped quietly on the floor. He looked to have matured physically, seemed broader through the chest and shoulders and more manly in his carriage. He was wearing his hair longer, thickly down the collar of his blue shirt. As he moved in and out of the light, I caught glimpses of his face in various degrees of profile and believed now I was seeing more of his mother in it than his father, though I feared it was the father who was more commandingly behind those strong, fine and troubled features. He paused several times to gaze out the window, and it was from this stance, his back to me, that he spoke again. You all stopped writing to me, he said. The four of you, simultaneously. I can tell you, there is no more acute way of hurting a man at war than through such silence. On my part, I kept incessantly at my writing board, until the futility of it all finally overwhelmed me. So I stopped. If you were trying to tinker with my mind, you did an excellent job. Sometimes when I got my hands on a little whiskey, I found myself entertaining some vivid questions: Do they exist? I asked myself. Is there really a Susan and an Eva, a Ryler, a Mr. Hook? I had to take your old letters out of my box and look at them again, to reassure myself you all weren't just figments. All right, I told myself: Ryler would stop writing after a time, and Eva too. But Susan? And you? Now he turned from the window and stared at me, a stolidly accusing figure in the darkness across the room. You, Mr. Hook? he asked.

Better measure this carefully, I told myself. Your toes are right against it now. He's going to have to hear this. And I found myself thinking: His father would have been grimly amused, would have reveled in it, would have given it instant interpretation, accepted it not as part of the human turmoil but as another signal of the cosmic favoritism in which he walked. Not only that, but would soon enough subscribe to the truth of it and, effusive with self-persuasion, would go on: *Yes, yes, of course it's so. But now I'm back, soul and all, and wouldn't you like to know what I learned?* That was the father, the reins on his lucidity carrying very little slack, inciting those sudden, horrifying departures of mind even while he sat before you man-of-the-castle, legs crossed, sherry in hand, smiling while he opined about last night's lucubrations, and then unwarningly usurped in mid-sentence by that degrading shade that hung inside him like a rattling gibbet, and for a while he could be quite urbane and intricately charming as his mind followed its slippery descent into disorder. But that was the father, who would eventually restore himself and be remorseful, trembling with expiation, loathing the indignity he had been helpless to resist. And this was the son, product of the same long, murky caravan, but different enough. He meant to control his derivations and master his displacements of mind, though not for the sake of caution but for use, for carefully applied service, as an instrument, to sublimate at his will an action of celestial folly and make it subservient to him. That thing running on leash within the borders of that capacious July-blaze of an imagination was frightening to contemplate.

You wrote letters? I asked. Until when? April or May I should think, he said. By then you all had stopped writing for months and months. I tell you, Hook, you put me through it. Your letters, I said, never arrived here; not after December. He returned to his chair and sat down, frowning across the table at me. Never arrived? he said. Weren't you curious? Didn't you make some inquiry? Ben, I said, this is painful, but it is best that you hear it from me. To whom were we to write? You had been marked dead. He gazed at me with a growing intensity of disbelief, of almost hostile incredulity. Then, in a whisper: Dead? After Fredericksburg, I said. What kind of grotesque joke is this? he asked. Joke? I said. My God, boy, you were mourned with the very deviltry of grief. By whom? he wanted to know, speaking out of that odd quirk of mind. Primarily myself and your two ladies, I said. They came here, one by morning and one by evening and sat with me, each holding her face and crying into her hands. Good Lord, he said quietly, as if feeling a twinge of pained responsibility for that grief. And then he began a senseless, mirthless laughter, shaking his head at the macabre humor he found in this. I must say this is a damned odd feeling, Hook, he said. I'm glad I didn't know about it when I was in the field fighting for my life. To have one side trying to kill you and the other believing you're already dead, well, it doesn't leave you much, does it? Sort of disembodied, a shadow running around in a uniform. Dead at Fredericksburg? he asked. Well, nearly, Mr. Hook. Damned close. At Antietam, too, and still closer at Gettysburg; in fact at Gettysburg I think I even heard the heavenly choir. What would they have told you if I had fallen there—sent you a message that I had been killed yet again? That would have turned you around. There's my Ben, you would have chortled; no Nathan Hale regrets for my Ben. He laughed again, shaking his head. Then he looked at me quite soberly and said, Forgive me, but I was never killed, not even once. Tell me, Hook—did you believe it? I don't know, I said, taking several seconds. But you must have, he said, and I don't mean by the evidence of the War Department. I know you too well: everything must be part of the grand design; everything must be part of the majestic tidal flow, as perceived by Henry Hook. Forgive me; it isn't said in derision. But you sat here alone in front of the fire and thought, Well, it's all over now. Done. Finished. The last of them gone now, packed into the earth with not a root or seed left behind in contamination; the infection healed by the only medicine there was for it. I say this because you are the sort of person who believes he will live to see the end of every story of which he has heard the beginning. You see yourself standing on the mountaintop someday watching the rush of the last sunset, the furling of the last purples and scarlets. Then he turned away and muttered, This is absolutely the most damned odd feeling. Then he reached across the table and covered my hand with his for a moment, smiling at me. God, he said, I must have given you a shock.

He withdrew his hand and sipped some whiskey. And how are my ladies? he asked. How is Eva? She's in high dissipation with your friend Ryler, I said. Eva and Ryler? he said with a spark of interest. And added, with worldly irony, Well, friends ought to stick together. Her father's dead you know, I said. He laughed: Are you sure, Hook? How can you be sure anyone is dead? Did you hold a feather in front of his lips? Oh, he's dead all right, I said. He was cuckolding a farmer named Madison up here in Little Village, until one night Mr. Madison found them desecrating his sheets and dispatched LeGrange into the next world with a rifle. LeGrange is dead all right and since that time—it's about a year now—there have been no restraints upon his daughter. As if there were any to begin with, he said. At least there had been a modicum of discretion, I said. But now that house is hers, and all of that money. She can be controlled, he said. Not by Ryler Stevenson, I said. They're at cards every night in the Dooley House, he playing and losing, she sitting there egging him along. You know this? he asked. He seemed troubled by it. How long has this been going on? he asked. It began early in July, I said. The way I understand it, she decided she had to celebrate the victory of Gettysburg and chose Ryler as her co-celebrant. They've been celebrating ever since. They ride about in her carriage like a couple of jehus and heaven help anyone who gets in their way. He's in and out of that house periodically, anywhere from a day to a week at a time. I imagine she's supplying his pocket, since he was thrown out of his job. Since I'm not a moralist I won't say anymore. No, you shouldn't, Mr. Hook. After all, he added dryly, they're my good friends. And then he looked at me in wry amusement and said, They began by celebrating the victory at Gettysburg? (The way he dwelled on ironies, I knew he would not miss this one.) Well then, he said, I helped set the table and groom the bedsheets for them, didn't I? Sometimes we don't know how much we're *really* fighting for, do we, Hook?

He amused himself with the thought for several moments, though I must acknowledge the expression in his face was more ironical than mirthful. All right, I thought, now he was going to have to hear the rest of it, the more serious part, the part that would not be so easily revoked. But before I could begin, he turned to me with a look that was most quizzical. Something I don't understand, he said. I can understand why I wasn't getting your letters—you weren't writing them anymore because you all thought I was dead. But I kept writing to you for at least four months after Fredericksburg, into April at least. It was winter, the weather was hellish, the army was inactive, and there was nothing to do but write. I must have sent dozens of letters to you and Ryler and the women. Do you mean to say that not a single one came through? I shook my head, as curious

about it as he was. And then I began to remember who
it was I used to see lounging with his arms crossed in the
doorway of the postal shack whenever I walked through
town, and I remembered once even thinking, *They're both
employed by the government—Ben somewhere in Virginia and
this smirking son of a bitch right here.* All letters in and out
had to be posted there, pass through his hands. And then
the rest of it came boiling to mind and in my anger I gave
voice to the middle of my thoughts: And not only that, I
said, but he was the one responsible for posting the casualty
rolls on the bulletin board. Who? Ben asked. What are you
talking about? That no-account son of a bitch friend of
yours, I said heatedly. I tell you, he's got the soul of a
lizard. Look at it: everything had to pass through his
hands—your letters, our letters, the casualty rolls—Who
are you talking about? he asked sternly. Ryler, I said. He
was in charge of the postal shack; he took the job when
Stetterson joined up. Ryler? he asked incredulously. Why
in God's name would he want to commit me to the dead?
Two reasons, I said, and both wear petticoats. He tried to
spark with each of them but they kept their furnace doors
closed to him. All he heard from them was your name. I
should think it became a clangor in his ears and a bone
in his throat, until the wily little bastard got his idea.

Oh, but my anger and resentment were storming: the
first flush of realization had done that. And then I saw
that perhaps I had left discretion too unattended, for the
heat was in his eyes now, which were glaring intensely at
me, and I knew that the steel which was now coursing
through his veins was aimed not at me but at the good
friend who had marked him dead and then gone off to
sordid minuets with his women. Look now, Benjamin, I
said, there is no real evidence here, only speculation. But
he knew it was true, as did I, and that I was merely trying
to fan off some of the heat I had caused. That boy, he
said, was always a trickster. He wasn't my friend until I
showed him I could whip him. Of course it's true, and not

just because he had the opportunity and the reason, but because he is *capable* of doing it. You listen to me, I said. How many poor wretched bastards have been hanged merely because they were adjudged *capable* of doing something? Don't worry, Hook, he said. I don't mean to hang anyone. Right now the ranks of the dead are swollen with too many choice young men; I wouldn't want to stain their dignity by pitching him into them. Good, I said. You stick to that. Bear in mind that your mere appearance will be blow enough to him. When he sees you his heart will sink like a stone in a lake. What he did was stupid and despicable and had inevitably to unveil itself. No, he said. Not inevitably so. There was always the chance of a bit of Confederate lead marking me paid and making him a prophet. And I can tell you, Mr. Hook, the difference between it happening and not happening was so slight as to be virtually no difference at all.

He got to his feet, put on his coat and then reached for his hat. Where are you going? I asked. To perform a miracle, he said. I suggest you keep away from him, I said, until you've calmed. I'm calm, he said. Tonight I'm back from the dead and I feel godlike and indestructible, much too eminent to soil myself with the likes of him. I may even forgive him. What do you think of that? What are you peering at? For God's sake, Hook, stop looking for my father.

I was still peering, hours after he had gone, my eyes focused upon the darkness at the window where he had stood, my mind an agony of should have and should have not: I should not have told him so much, I should have stopped him from leaving. And I should have told him more, the rest of it, rather than let him find it out abruptly and without leavening. But God forgive me, for once some of the sense had left me—and understandably, after seeing him standing at the door like that, the weight of that shock. He was right, of course, for I had believed it and in believing accepted it as the calculated and purposeful will of some higher being, the verdict of some merciful providence which had finally grown tired of the unrelieved torment and stilled forever this lineage of disquiet. But no. It had not happened. And not only was he back, but it was to walk the night a dead man.

Ten

RYLER'S IRRITATION WAS GROWING. It was not bad enough that he had not pulled in a pot for several hours and was at the moment trying to wish jacks over into a winning hand with five competitors at the table, but she had suddenly begun to smile at him, and not with encouragement or rueful hope but with faint mockery, as if discreetly sharing in some joke at his expense. She was sitting in that chair across the room, wearing a buckskin-fringed jacket, her riding breeches tucked into her boots. Her legs were crossed. She was watching him. He could see her between the shoulders of two of his across-the-table opponents. There was something behind that smile, he told himself; it was oblique, barely perceptible, but nevertheless relentlessly communicating. They conducted a momentary contest of wills—his frown versus her smile—and then he was compelled to lower his eyes back to the table, thinking sullenly, All right, it's her money and her pleasure, so I suppose she has the right to smile or not, though I don't see anything funny about being a few hundred down and trying to bluff out five bastards with jacks over. Again he read the open cards around him, trying to focus upon their import, but could not. There was something distinctly pointed in that smile, and his inability to fathom it disturbed him. With conscious effort he kept his eyes down, reducing his visual horizon to the green-clothed table and the sets of open cards and the still, pondering hands next to them, and the pile of coins at the center, listening to his companions breathing softly, patiently, the cigar smoke in a motionless cloud around the kerosene lamp which hung above them. The bet had come around to him and they were waiting for him to call, or raise, or fold.

She was sitting in the dark green upholstered chair that Dooley had placed there for her when it became apparent that their—hers and Ryler's—presence in the inner room was going to occur on an almost nightly basis. No other woman had ever so much as set foot in that room. When Dooley told her that, Eva said, You mean none has ever asked to. And Dooley, with his white horseshoe mustache and short leather apron, had sighed and said, Miss LeGrange, you haven't asked either. You're already in here. She was not alone—Ryler was with her, though it was she who was doing the talking. Dooley knew what it was all about, and he knew, too, that there was no point in telling her that the gentlemen played high-stake poker in here, since she had at her command more money than any of them. Ryler had been coming around for weeks trying to get a chair at this table, in this room which was at the rear of the hotel's first floor and which was implicitly off bounds to all but the invited, who were Capstone's serious card players, the stoic and unmuttering and well-heeled. Nevertheless Dooley wanted to make her say it, so he could hear it for himself. Women aren't allowed to play cards in my establishment, he said. I know that, she said, going along with the formality. It's Mr. Stevenson who wants to enter the game. They looked at Ryler then, Dooley and the men. Ryler was by at least twenty-five years younger than any of them, slight of build, with a full crop of drooping mustache now which seemed incongruous against his still-boyish face. They all knew him, of course, and still could not accept the fact that he was a man, at least by legal definition if not social acknowledgment, that he had just too recently been one of the town's more conspicuous young hellions. And now here he was, replete with mustache, not just wanting admission to their inner sanctum but being proposed to it by this young woman who, by viture of her pride and arrogance and sensuality, had never been in their eyes a girl, the same way that Ryler in their eyes was not a man. There was no way that Dooley was going to say no to her, for the simple reason that none before him had been able to successfully put that utterance to her; it was too late. She never even considered the possibility of anyone, man or woman, saying no to her and that was ninetenths of the effort she put forward in getting her way.

That was several months ago, and by now Ryler's presence at the table was accepted, though not yet his stature as a man, an equal, despite his mustache and his manly decorum, and despite his supply of double eagles (which they all knew came from the young woman who sat in the upholstered chair on the other side of the room sipping brandy, who seemed to take a perverse pleasure in being there, who seemed indifferent to whether he won or lost).

He was becoming more and more distracted by that smile, unable to keep his eyes from it. He scowled at her, his mouth pouting under the extravagant mustache. One of the men spoke to him, and he studied his cards for a moment longer and then, petulantly, turned them over and withdrew from the hand. He sat back in his chair and picked up the glass which was standing next to his drawstring purse and sipped some whiskey, staring coolly over the rim at Eva. She for the moment was concentrating her gaze just over his head, at something or someone behind him, so intently as to make him frown and want to turn around. He resisted the impulse, annoyed in equal parts by her quixotic nature and his own curiosity. No one else around the table appeared to be seeing anything, either that or their concentration upon their cards was too complete. When again she looked at him her smile was fixed, icily sardonic.

Poor Ryler. Poor, poor Ryler. Startled as I was, I think that was the first thing I thought. No, the first thing I thought was, *Who is that? It looks like Ben.* So initially I was startled by what I deemed a resemblance, and then a moment later I realized it was he standing there in the corridor looking into the room (the door had been left ajar by the waiter who had gone out to get a tray of drinks). How I maintained my composure in the face of such a shock, I'll never know. The desire, the need to shout out all but gave me a physical shaking. What held me in check was, I think, understanding what had happened even before I knew that I did, even before I knew that any understanding was possible or relevant. Because I saw that he—the apparition materialized—knew something, from the way those malevolently leaden eyes stared at the back of his old friend's head, and not without a certain quality of sadness, as if they had been drawn against their will into this expression, this experience. It took only a moment for the paralysis to leave my faculties and by the time our eyes were matched I was smiling at him, not a smile of welcome or relief or amazement, but the best expression I could muster that I was at one with his thoughts, that he was not there to see me or to announce his homecoming or his resurrection; his face was too profoundly grave for any of that. When I looked at Ryler I thought, *Oh, you ass, you poor dumb stupid ass.* It was all water in a sieve for him now. His uncomprehending face under that heroic mustache suddenly looked so forlorn and desperate as perhaps he began to sense that his evening's ill luck was not going to be confined to this table, that an unseen hand had begun tolling for him a black midnight of bells.

Back from the dead. My God, wasn't that just like him? Not the first time, either. Once before he had been assumed dead, and then reappeared. Only that time I had refused to believe it. I had refused to believe it for a while this time, too, but that was only because I did not want to, and it took weeks before my stubbornness or my resentment or my faith or whatever it was finally began to give in. The irony of being the last to accept it, the last to capitulate to grief, was that it was Susan, ahead of me in grieving and therefore closer to God, who consoled me. It was she who walked with me through the woods and talked to me, who pointed out to me those places where they had played as children, all of it January-still, snow-covered, like an open-air mausoleum for youth's slain enchantments. I found her sentimentality maudlin and inappropriate; those sort of memories could be mourned at any time, they hardly needed tragedy to call them up. I knew she was trying to be kind, but there were moments when I wanted to laugh at her and say, *Children's games. Well, I had something more.* But even so, I envied and resented all the time she had spent with him, all the things she knew about him that I did not, and I even resented the feelings she had inside her that fueled her grief, her poignant sense of loss. I couldn't tell whether she was being melancholy and trying to relive those times or was trying to help me by sharing some of them with me. As she gazed around at the icy, winter-dead mockeries of unspooled and irretrievable time, her eyes reddened, and she said, as if urging me, that crying sometimes helped. It was a sentiment I found bombastic in its triteness. I felt like shouting at her. Did she goddamned think I was incapable of it, that I had laughed my father into his grave, that I could receive a blow such as this without tears? Tears, yes; but I did not spend them for public display.

I asked her if she had been in love with him. She narrowed her eyes and smiled wistfully, as though the question were ingenuous. An answer was unnecessary, but came forth nevertheless. She could not, she said, remember a time when she had not been in love with him. She could not remember, she said, falling in love with him. It had always been, almost as if she had loved him even before she saw him. She made it sound as if her love had existed as a pulse beat in thin air and upon her approach toward it he had materialized. I believed her, even though it was something I myself could not understand. But, frankly, I had never known a woman whose love was comprehensible to me; it always seemed naïve or misdirected or self-destructive or incomplete or merely hopeful. I considered my next question as we walked. The air was cold, very clear, windless. The tree limbs were snow-streaked, the thickets white-powdered. We followed the main path through the inhospitable woods, where the snow was packed underfoot. We each had raised our shawls to cover our heads. And did he love you? I asked. The question did not seem to take her by surprise; I would imagine she had been pondering it all her life, never once putting it where it should have been put, so familiar was she with his sardonic turns. The question evoked another smile, suggestive of the charm of mystery. Her answer surprised me completely. It was one word: *Yes.*

We became friends. It was true that there was but the single link—Ben—but it seemed enough. Oddly, we seldom talked about him. When she did refer to him, it was because he happened to be part of some larger memory, some episode which had included other children as well (her references to him were almost invariably in the framework of childhood). For my part, I would not talk about him, and as a matter of fact almost *could* not, since by saying he had loved her she had staked her claim to him, in a very firm, proprietary way. She never asked about my relationship with him; I felt it was uninterest rather than discretion, and I would think, *You wouldn't be so goddamned sure of yourself if he were alive.* I wanted to say to her: Did he ever take you to bed? Did you ever feel his body stretched naked upon yours, feel him hot and ripe inside of you? Sometimes I wanted to say to her: You remember him as a mother would—as a boy, dreamless and antic, as someone with whom you sparred away the springtime upon which you still meditate, watching the petals drop one by one from memory. Maybe he had loved her; but again, there were those varieties of it; his love for her could have been mere sentiment, sweet and incombustible, part of the lush romance that I know flooded his soul, part of the poetry that swirled up from it: he was a poet and poets had always to be in love, whether that love burned or merely simmered.

She seemed uncomfortable about coming to the house, seemed particularly embarrassed by the servants, not knowing how to react to them, thanking them profusely for putting down a cup and saucer for her. When I caught her eyes wandering furtively around the room, I studied her, wondering what it was that had attracted him. She was pretty enough, with a beautiful complexion, dark thoughtful eyes, a small nose, a smile I could imagine disarming a man. She was no delicate flower either—I knew that much about her—having been raised motherless by her saloon-keeper father, pushing a mop through the place as a child, washing glasses in the back room. And in spite of it all still emerging something of the lady, having through the years defended and maintained her pride and her self-respect, accepting her destiny without relinquishing anything vital to it. She asked if I became lonely, living as I did in this large house, alone. I told her that I was not often alone, told her quite directly that I enjoyed the companionship of males. I'm sure she knew that anyway, since there were few secrets in this town and certainly none to the daughter of a saloon keeper who sooner or later heard every bit of gossip, scandal and rumor. She studied me thoughtfully for a moment, and I knew exactly what it was she was thinking: Had *he* ever been here. Well, let her wonder.

But I did miss my father, I told her. She nodded, said nothing. She hadn't liked him; that I knew. I cursed the son of a bitch farmer who had shot him. Do you know what happened? I asked. Just how ludicrous and treacherous are the threads that bind us to life? Her face never changed expression. Every Saturday night that son of a bitch farmer took his wagon and went down to the Dooley House to play cards. He never came home before midnight, not once, ever. That was when my father rode up there. That woman had him in her blood, you see. I knew everything my father did, where he went and what he did. And as far as I'm concerned, he never did anything wrong, because he was a man, the same way Ben was a man (Let her chew on that, I thought.) But do you know what happened? She said nothing, just sat there motionless, her hands in her lap, watching me. That night, I said, that son of a bitch farmer sat down at the table and on his first hand drew four sixes. The imbecile went wild and started betting his whole purse. But goddammit, one of the other men drew four kings in the same hand. Now, how many times will that happen? Well, the son of a bitch kept seeing and then counterraising until he was clean, and when the other man turned over that fourth king, he simply got up and walked out. So he was already in a rage when he began heading home. When he got there, he found my father's horse tied up outside, and maybe he already had his suspicions in place because he slipped in quietly, took his rifle off its nails and tiptoed upstairs. You know the rest. Yes, she said softly. And then, I said, every sanctimonious bastard in Capstone said he had done the right thing, that he had only been defending the sanctity of his home. I'd like to look at the records of some of those bastards, just to see how holy *they* are. They made a virtue out of hypocrisy. So the son of a bitch was acquitted and to this day is living there and still lying in the very same bed with the very same woman. What you're saying, she said, is he should have shot his wife. It would have made more sense, don't you think? I asked. I should think so, she said, adding, But men don't think that way. That's because they don't

have to think, I said. Because they've made the rules. All
the rules have been made by men. But even then, I said,
if some beerswilling son of a bitch hadn't gone and pulled
four kings, my father would be alive today. It just seems
to be a bad time, she said. It's a very bad time, I said.

Forgive me for telling you all of that, I said. But I loved
my father very much and sometimes feel the need to talk
about him. I know he had faults, that he could be quick
and unfeeling. Oh, he could be abrupt with people all
right, I said with a shake of my head. But that was his
nature, you see. There may have been a want of tact and
discretion, but never of integrity, personal integrity. I
know that not many people liked him, but everyone re-
spected him, and that was what mattered to him. He maintained that someone who was liked by everyone had to be
basically weak and untrustworthy, because under what circumstances could that person have ever proven his strength
and reliability, if he was so widely liked: and he maintained
that someone who was feared by everyone was either ruth-
less or bestial, and a total failure as a human being. The
thing he emphasized was respect, and he had it. He had
it from those who knew him and from those who did not,
because of his bearing and his dignity. She had been listening very quietly, and suddenly surprised me by saying,
He demanded it. How do you mean? I asked. Because, she
said, he felt hard toward those who didn't give it to him.
I knew whom she was talking about and it nettled me,
because it was always she who brought him into the conversation, who felt secure and comfortable in doing so. I
let it pass. It was so ironic; that which had brought us
together in the first place was the one thing I could not
talk about with her. Well, I said, he was a good father to
me. I suppose in many ways I'm very much like him. She
smiled at that, and said, that's why you say you can't see
him as having done anything wrong. She said it with just
the right note of whimsy and I had to laugh. Do you mean
to say, I asked, I've been sitting here trying to explain away

myself? You make it sound like that, she said. Oh, Susan, I said, you're a fox all right. I was then going to say that all that fuss about us being rivals and antagonists had been so much nonsense, that we should have been friends all along, was about to say it when I caught myself up and realized it would only cause an evincement of that reticent self-assurance again, that she would not understand talk of rivalry when in her mind there had been none, that while there may have been occasions for jealousy and irritation, she had in her heart never doubted the inevitability of his return to her, that whatever links had been forged long ago were secure and unbreakable.

I suppose one of the reasons—perhaps the only—I wanted to be her friend was because of that very thing, that palpable possession she had of him, which for reasons of my own pride I yearned to wrest from her. Nevertheless, I grew to like her. She seemed sincere, without guile. It was always in my house that we sat down together, and though I sensed she was ill at ease there, she seldom refused an invitation. On those dark, heartless winter nights we sat before a fire, companions more than conversationalists. When we talked, it was about some business in Capstone, or about the war, which had begun to take on an endless, inconclusive character (and for which we shared a sharp, unspoken resentment, for what it had taken from us). The armies had gone into winter quarters after Fredericksburg and the only assurance for spring was more fighting. God's logic, she described it, since nothing about the war made any sense to either of us; the whole thing seemed so vast and out of control that it no longer had anything to do with reality, with anything that we could understand. Exciting at first, with parades and drums and flags and fervent oratory, it had come to run on like a river and become a bore. It seemed to me that a war that took so long to end should not have been fought in the first place. I had taken an interest in it only because of Ben; reading about the war, and talking about it and listening to talk about it, was as close as I could come to sharing his experiences and claiming a part of him. And of course his letters were vivid; he possessed that magical quality to weave words into pictures more graphic than those the front-line artists were sending back. The power he had over the written word had become the communicating voice of the man who had so often been so brooding and taciturn and inward; the silence and the solitude had therefore been more than sullenness and unsociability; it had been the poet's aura; the sharp, bitter phrases had been the tips of the fire. I treasured his letters not for their sentiments (there were few; the gift seemed not honed for intimate disclosure) but for the esthetically structured storms they conveyed—the glimpses of battle, the sound of shot, the damp fears, the portrait of the soldier on his inconceivable journey into nightmares of incredible truth and reality; and the sound of rain, and a river in the moonlight, and the eyes of foxes gleaming in the woods. I wondered what he could have written to her. It had to be different, I knew. Perhaps there was where the tenderness was directed. To her the man spoke, to me the poet. If that were true—and I sensed it was—then I took conceit from it, for finally the poet would be greater than the man.

To say I was enamored of his gift would be saying it lightly. I think it was when I began hearing Ryler rolling smooth provocative phrases that I became interested in him. Ryler's had always been a nimble wit, clear and winning but of little polish or substance. Now when we met his conversation was flavored with phrases and observations so well turned that they caught my ear. I had never given him much thought; he had always been merely the friend of Ben, a cool-eyed, rogue-smiled companion destined for some dim-witted farm girl who would adore him. But all of a sudden he seemed capable of dropping into his talk comments on the war, on people, on nature, that were jeweled in their phrasing, bold in their wit, acute in their insight; not many, not often, but enough to pique my curiosity. As I got to know him better, I realized that here was a totally emancipated spirit, bound by no man's rules; not the thoroughbred Ben was, but a runaway quarter horse who would burn the track until his breath gave out. Without conscience or scruple, he was consequently without misgivings. Of course he lacked the character that repudiation would have enriched him with, since he had no principle to repudiate, no doctrine to exorcise. Vulgar one moment, poetic the next, there was a certain perverse charm about him. Part of the charm lay, I don't doubt, in the fact of the initial delight I took in "discovering" this scoundrel who had been there all the time, faithful satellite to the moon of my heavens.

So was I despicable when finally I took her Ryler from her? I don't believe she ever truly loved him; he was merely the second apple on the bough, desirable only because a little of Ben burned in him. And why did Ryler want her anyway—because Ben had loved her? They had been so intertwined, those three, their emotions so interchangeable, that none of it seemed real; all emotional frontiers had been dissolved in childhood and they had been crossing back and forth for so long that all that was fatal or lethal had long ago been rubbed away. Ryler, for his part, seemed willing enough, with no compunctions. What does she say about it? I asked him. She doesn't know, he said. That couldn't be true, I knew. He was anything but subtle, this unbroken offspring of the wind, who rode up one night at two o'clock in the morning and blew a bugle under my window until I let him in. The truth was she would not fight for him, as she would have scratched and clawed for Ben. This fact was lost upon him; he assumed—if indeed he assumed anything—that it was simply a demonstration of his dominance, that he had not broken a compact because none had been morally established, because neither compact nor moral code were within his purview.

Because he was entertaining and because he was perpetual, he could also occasionally be a bore, most particularly when he had lain too long on the sofa drinking whiskey. Then, incongruously, he was capable of weeping for his poor friend Ben, his companion of myriad night-cloaked gambols, who had been slain. He would weep and curse the Confederate who had put his friend to earth, and sometimes turn to me and say, Can you believe it? Can you believe it's so? That he's dead? I was deeply affected, not merely for the melancholy anguish he was expressing, but as well for its correspondence to my own feelings. And then abruptly his lamentations would cease, followed by a stupified gazing into space, as if he had been horribly astonished. A few more whiskeys would send him into incoherence and then silence. With his vivacity drowned and his raucous spirit stilled, he looked foolish, in his sprawling drunken sleep. He seemed small and fraudulent. There were moments, looking at him, that I wanted to go to her and tell her to get him the hell out of my house, to tie him up and keep him away from me. But I didn't, because there were those other times, when he dazzled with his animation and charmed with his recklessness. He was impulsive, spontaneous, and sometimes curious in his responses. Once when we were spending the moonlight atop one of the town's higher hills, he became wantonly amorous and began tearing at my clothes. He would not stop until I took my crop in hand and slashed him across the face with it. He fell back into the grass, stunned for a moment, the blood running from the side of his face; and then he began giggling foolishly, rubbing at the wound with the back of his hand. Watching him, I shuddered at the thought of what the other one might have done had I ever struck him so.

Capstone's patent disapproval of the affair was a factor in its continuance. If there was one thing we shared, even thrived upon, it was disdain for public opinion. Where we differed was in attitude—he saw himself as the renegade, the deliberate provocateur; while I deemed the opinions of others as beneath my consideration. For him, riding side by side on horseback along Grant Avenue was a calculated act of contempt and defiance; for me it was simply a matter of doing what I wanted with whomsoever I chose to do it. He began becoming rather casual about his job at the postal shack. Three mornings a week the mail bag came in, and after he had seen to its sorting and waited for it to be picked up, he closed down. If by early afternoon there were still some letters remaining, he carried them across the street to the Dooley House and left them with the bartender. Soon word got around that the bar at the Dooley House had become the unofficial adjunct to the postal shack. On days when no mail bags were due, he simply did not appear. Why don't you just give up the wretched job? I asked him. At the rate you're going you'll be thrown out soon enough. They'd better not, he said quickly, a quick, nervous look in his face. I can't lose that job, not for a while anyway. Then you had better pay more attention to it, I said. We were at lunch in the Dooley House one afternoon when he heard that some new casualty lists had arrived, that the messenger was standing outside of the closed postal shack. In the middle of his meal he rushed out. When I walked across the street I found him inside poring over the lists. Whose name he might have been looking for, I could not imagine; it was true that there were a number of Capstone men who had signed up, but I had never heard him express concern for any of them. Finally, late in the summer, grumbling about irregularities at the postal shack became so loud he was thrown out of the job. When that happened he began spending more and more time with me, though with increased moodiness and restlessness. When he began stretching his stays through the night, and sometimes two nights, I wondered what she might be thinking, what she might be trying to decide. My impression of her was that she must eventually appear to claim him. But she never did. I tried to avoid her when I was in town, but it proved not to be necessary, for she turned away whenever she saw me. I felt sorry for her, but at the same time could not help taking a kind of perverse satisfaction: while she had been so content and secure in her possession of the dead, she had let slip away the living.

And then one night, he said, I'm beginning to feel uncomfortable about this. About a lot of things. We were in my bedroom, windows thrown open to the mild September night, the entering breezes dissipating the sultry ardor we had so recently raised. I was lying under the covers, he was slumped in a chair, a robe hanging slackly over his nakedness. A lamp burned on the nearby table. I asked him what he was feeling uncomfortable about. He would not say. About Susan? I asked. He shifted to me a glance that was sullen and self-defensive. I think, I said, you're afraid she will no longer have you back. That isn't true, he said with some irritation. I think, I said, you're staying here not because you want to, but because you're afraid to do anything else. I can go back to her anytime I want to, he said. Then go tonight, I said. He watched me, his anger subsiding into uncertainty. My displeasure with him was evident, and rising. You think I can't? he muttered. I have every expectation that you might, I said. And as a matter of fact we can leave now. Yes, we. I'll ride along with you—take you in the carriage, if you like—I would want her to see and know my breadth of character as I return her man to her. Return? he asked. Yes, I said. I think she should know that I decided I'd had enough of you and was returning you to her custody. What she decides to do about it is her business. He was watching me uncertainly, trying to get a clear picture of my meanings; and then he began trying on reactions for size: the menacing scowl, the smirking smile, the probing eye—none of which he delivered with very much commitment of feeling. Churlishly, lowering his eyes, he said, I didn't say I wanted to go back to her. Then what is it? I asked, and before he could answer, added, Oh, to hell with it, I don't care.

My God, I thought later that night when he had come

back to bed and was sleeping next to me, his face serene and composed under that mustache, which never seemed less than ill-fitting and ill-advised. My God, I thought, what a terrible and pathetic illusion there is about all of this. Something was going to have to be done, symbolic if nothing else, and the sooner the better. So the next morning, leaving him asleep, I put on my cloak and walked across the fields to that modest farmhouse, which was anything but farmhouse these days, since the land around it was no longer worked and probably would not be again until that old man died, if such a thing were possible—there was a quality of eternity about him, about the way he sat, so magisterially motionless and enduring; and the way he walked, as if he were measuring off the centuries with his short, precise strides; and the way he set his eyes upon things, as if in his time he had watched the wind collect grains into mountains.

I found him sitting on the porch, almost a caricature of my imagined portrait, with his feet flat on the planks, one arm at ease on the chair's rest, his other hand holding his pipe in his mouth. He was dressed in a suit of black broadcloth, replete with vest. His inevitable black derby was in place. This man had established for himself a level of dignity that was infernal and impenetrable and beyond compromise. He disliked me; that he always made quite plain, for while much about Mr. Hook was elusive and unfathomable, what he wanted you to know, he let you know. And you knew that a man so sparing with his words would be fulfilling of his promises and direct in his actions. (I could remember my father coming home one day, soon after he had sent those men out to give Ben a tumbling, and saying, Do you know what that fellow Hook said to me? Why, he came up to me at the bar and very gently laid his stick across my shoulder and said, I tell you, sir, if ever again any inconvenience comes to that boy through your auspices, I shall personally unwind you from your soul. And I said to my father, that man is strange. Very, he murmured.)

This was my second visit to this house, this man. The first time had been to share grief, and he had received me warmly, with understanding and compassion. Oddly, I had felt comfortable with him on that occasion, even though I doubted that we exchanged more than a dozen words, for I believed if there was anything the strange Mr. Hook knew about, it was the fervency of feeling; what else could make him appear so stolidly impervious to it? This time, however, those sharp little eyes were of different weather. He watched me come through the gate and approach until I was at the foot of the steps. Since I knew he was impatient with pleasantries, and since I knew my pertinacity was a match for his, I came quickly to the point. He listened impassively. When I was done he removed the pipe from his mouth and those unreceptive little eyes grew hot. Tombstone? he said, sounding as if he were ridding his tongue of something sour. And what, madame, he asked, do you propose to carve on it? Do you know when and where he was born? Do you know when and where he ceased? Then I'll do it without you, I said. You will not, he said evenly. Why do you oppose it? I asked, to which he responded, Why do you propose it? As a memorial, I said. Can't you trust your heart to be that? he asked. Feeling the heat rising in my cheeks, I turned around and walked away. I slammed shut the iron gate and when I had gone a few paces along the road my anger stood me still and I turned to him, and there he was, watching me, the caricature again, bolted in place by time, set there, as if to await clouds of messiahs and the coronations of kings yet unborn. You miserable little bastard, I shouted at him. His response? It was to reach up and tip his derby.

Eleven

"I DON'T KNOW WHAT the hell your hurry was tonight," Ryler said as they went down the front steps of the Dooley House. "You didn't give me a chance to win it back. My luck was about to swing."

She hooked her arm into his as they walked along the raised wooden sidewalk that ran the length of the hotel's frontage. In her boots she was nearly his height, an equity he found annoying, causing him to square his shoulders and walk at his full height.

"When it goes against you like that for two solid hours," he said, "you just know it's going to swing pretty soon. I lost that last hand with two pair. To me, that's a sign of my luck starting to turn sweet. I know my patterns in a poker game."

They left the sidewalk and crossed the hard dirt ground to the next stretch of elevated boards. Mounting it, they went past a row of stores, all dark except for a saloon. The stores on the other side of Grant Avenue were dark too, except for the lamp in the smithy, where the iron sounds of a hammer meeting an anvil rang methodically out to the mild September night. Soon they were away from the cluster of buildings, from the light, the hollow sidewalks, walking under the thick, sky-reaching old elms and maples that had grown to patriarchal dignity as first the Indians and then the Dutch and then the English had beat and widened and established the path which became Grant Avenue.

He rambled on, preoccupied and inattentive, in the manner of a man describing and rationalizing his defeats. Her head was turned aside as she listened, her eyes roaming the quiet, deepening darkness. Ben was out there somewhere, she knew, watching them, or was perhaps waiting up ahead, in the lane where he knew they would turn. As if trying to communicate privately with him, she smiled into the night with malicious pleasure, responding to the intensity she knew was possessing him, defiantly amused by it. It had been a fullness of gall that she had seen in his eyes, quite befitting a man back from the dead finding his world gone asunder. He surely knew some of it, she thought. Why else had he come to that doorway in silence, in silence remain and in silence leave? For confirmation surely, not discovery. Well, she thought, let him see what he would see. He had been dead, hadn't he? What did he expect— a rush to solitude and celibacy on the part of those left behind?

Suddenly she put pressure on Ryler's arm and stopped walking. When he paused she spun him into her arms and, embracing him, pressed a long, passionate kiss upon his mouth, moving herself erotically against him. When she drew her head back she was panting. He studied her for a moment, then grinned.

"Got the urge, huh?" he said.

"You have no idea," she whispered.

"Yes I do."

"No you don't."

"By God, I can feel it running through you," he said, tightening his fingers upon her.

"Yes, but you don't know for sure what it is."

"Something knows," he said. "Something knows for damned sure." He took her hand and pushed it down between his legs.

"Oh, Ryler is up," she said loudly, with a harsh and unruly laugh. "Ryler is up and ready."

"Ready enough," he said. "The most ready man in Capstone right now. You look out, bitch, or I'll pull your pants down and ram you right here."

"Dear child," she said with antic seriousness, placing a condescending hand upon his cheek. Annoyed, he jerked his head aside, scowling "Right here in the grass, Ryler?" she asked. "By the side of the road?"

"It wouldn't be the first time you showed it to the crickets, would it?"

"Kiss me, Ryler," she said quietly. "Long and deep and hard."

"Long and deep and hard better describes something other than a kiss."

"Oh, but you're wicked tonight," she said. "But without a wicked beginning no saintly thing can ever occur, can it?"

"Leave off the saintly talk," he said, "and I'm with you."

"Now kiss me again," she said almost primly. "Make it a beautiful one. The secret of a kiss is to make each one as if it were going to be the last. Because," she said, placing her finger lightly on his lips, "eventually one of them *is* going to be just that."

He stared curiously at her. "You're a bit peculiar tonight," he said.

"This is going to be a very peculiar night."

"How so?" he asked, turning his head and sidling at her a wary look.

"I just know," she whispered, embracing him tightly.

As they stood in the middle of the lane in firm mutual embrace, his eyes suddenly shifted sharply, catching a movement in the darkness. He withdrew his arms from around her.

"What is it?" she asked softly with a malign curl of smile, noting the shrewd inquiry in his eyes.

"Someone's standing over there."

Her eyes dilated for a moment, then she spun around and faced into the night. "Where?" she asked anxiously.

"Right up there, just inside the trees at the bend. I'll bet the son of a bitch has been standing there the whole time listening."

"I don't see anything," she said, peering intently, knotting together her fingers.

"Oh he's there all right. I know the look of these woods by day and by night."

She began walking slowly, Ryler following her. A moment later she was able to distinguish someone standing where he had indicated, a shape anomalous to the trees, poised, tentative, if possible more motionless; sinister and menacing for the inaudible draw and release of its breaths. Several steps ahead of Ryler, warily but with scintillant anticipation, she neared the uncannily still person in the trees. With her tongue she wet the expectant smile now on her lips. When the person moved she stopped, Ryler behind her. Quietly the shadow detached itself from the other shadows and came through the brush into the road. She recognized first the slouch hat, then his size, the outlines of his shoulders.

"Who is that?" Ryler demanded. He waited for the shadow to come closer, to assume its own free and unfettered independence of the portrait-still darkness from which it had stepped. Had he had the least inkling, he, too, might have recognized the familiar and guessed at it. He felt a certain unease at the confidence with which the person moved in the dark, with at once belonging and detachment, suffusing the night with menace so that he, Ryler, suddenly felt alien and uncomfortable in an element he had always campaigned through with recklessness and bravado. To his astonishment she went forward, opening her arms, and a moment later threw them around the person who in turn embraced and then released her.

"Ben?" Ryler said softly.

Eva removed the slouch hat, as if to formally present him.

"Hello, Ryler," Ben said as Eva stepped aside. To Ryler's steady, calculating staring, he said, "You don't seem surprised."

"Surprise is too slight a word for the occasion," Ryler murmured.

"Oh?"

"They told us you were dead."

"Did they?" Ben said, icily polite.

"And now we see you're not."

Eva laughed mirthlessly and said, faintly mocking of Ryler, "And now we see he's not."

"You're glad to see me, aren't you, Ryler?" Ben asked.

Ryler smiled cryptically for a moment. "Of course I am, Ben," he said. And then, with an exaggerated enthusiasm building in his voice, "Back from the dead. Just like you. By God, whoever gives you up for dead had better not take any bets on it. And I'll tell you something—I for one never believed it. No damned rebel is good enough to kill Ben. That's what I told myself. I knew somehow . . . somehow . . . you'd be back. Why, you said it yourself—I'm not surprised. Why should I have been, when I never really believed it?" He could not stop talking, as though a torrent of words was the only response he could make to Ben's steady wordless skeptical staring. He felt he must continue talking, lest some nuance of his own silence betray him. He went on, talking, laughing, gesturing; carried along by currents of apprehension and necessity. Finally he ceased, leaving a foolish grin fixed upon his face. He glanced uneasily from Ben to Eva, then back to Ben. "Listen," he said, "you must come up to the house. This is no small occasion; we'd be remiss if we didn't drench it with whiskey."

"To whose house are you inviting me, Ryler?" Ben asked.
"To mine," Eva said. She clasped one hand into Ben's, then reached out with the other, leaving it extended until a hesitant Ryler took it. "I just wish," she said as they began walking, she in the middle holding onto them, "that every woman's eye in Capstone could see me now. Has ever a woman been in such delectable danger?"

Only I didn't think it was so delectable. Seeing Ben come out of the darkness like that had made me afraid (and made me quickly regret the taunting nonsense I had contrived with poor Ryler for Ben to see), but after all, how could I have not brought them to the house? Something was going to happen; that much was so inevitable I could feel its aura being cast. And I wanted to be part of it, had to, because it was going to involve me, have impact upon me, in one way or another. I had a very strong sense of each of them knowing something—something antagonistic, that had put each on his guard against the other—that I did not and that it was this thing outside my knowledge which would be thrashed out. As we walked and as the silence of each lengthened, I realized it was no small matter that was at hand. There were even moments when you could nearly believe he *had* come back from the dead; there was something so grim and somber about him that it almost made you feel he had either bargained hard with the devil or else done what no man had done before—kick off the ghost and reclaim his soul and come back to life, to earth, to Capstone, because there was something so compelling for him to do that he could never rest until he had accomplished it; and you could almost believe that his restiveness and his rancor could be so unsettling that heaven itself could not be heaven until it had granted him an extension of his allotted time. Now and then as we walked I squeezed his hand, lovingly, not suggestive, simply to communicate to him the simple inexpressible joy I was feeling. But there was no response; and it was as if, just back from the dead, just up from subterranean caverns or down from celestial corridors, he had not yet begun to feel again, was still insentient, that the miracle was still in a state of incompletion. And then I thought what a damned shame it was I was not a religious person, a sender of prayers, because then I could say, Hallelujah, the Almighty heard me and answered my most heartfelt wish; I could say that Eva LeGrange talked to God and that God listened. Except I was overlooking one fact: He had not been killed, he had never been dead, and that I had better forget about miracles and begin getting ready to find out what they knew and I didn't.

Now and then I swung my head to glance at them in the dark (neither one spoke a word from the moment I took their hands and we started walking, remaining utterly and antagonistically silent until we were inside the house), at Ben, whose unchanging face suggested an imperviousness to frivolity, not just now, tonight, but forever; and at Ryler, whose clever smile and sly eyes had always seemed unable to recognize anything but the frivolous, but whose face now was uncharacteristically sober, struggling with the necessity of unfamiliar thoughts. It was so frighteningly typical, so pathetically human, all of it: man's most avid dream and delusion suddenly fulfilled—the return from the dead, the specter suddenly in appearance, full-fleshed and breathing and warm and reasoning, in possession of the most awesome knowledge; surely this epitome of human aspiration would be joyously received everywhere. But here he was, his restoration met by one person's exultation and another's furious apprehension and displeasure. And then again I had to remind myself that he had not been dead, that it all was so prosaically human, so wretchedly mundane—someone's unremarkable error—as to be little more than a macabre anecdote with which to spice future conversations. There was nothing here with which to captivate and mesmerize the imagination, except that it was this person, this Benjamin

McKinley, who if anyone could give tone and shadow to the unremarkable error it was he, who if he had not literally returned from the dead certainly suggested that if anyone ever could, would, it was he; no one was ever better equipped of eye and demeanor for it, who seemed not just intent upon restoring his presence but also to reclaiming the time that had been lost.

We gathered in what my father had always called the fire room, because of the two enormous fireplaces that faced each other across the room's forty-foot width. When raised on wintry nights, the fires stood like two seething Hadean palisades, casting shimmering heat back and forth beneath the beamed ceiling. This downstairs room had been my father's favorite. Furnished with gilt rosewood sofas, padded chairs, and Boston rockers, it reflected his eclectic tastes and impulsive buying habits. A Gothic bookcase stood against one of the papered walls, a mahogany French-style desk against another. The room was softly lit by silver wall lamps. The entire house was furnished in this style, expensively but without symmetry of taste or design, a sometimes jarring mix of Federal, Empire, Early Victorian, the gracefully proportioned and lightly constructed standing side by side with the ponderous and the ornate.

When they were settled side by side on one of the sofas and I went to the liquor cabinet above the desk, I thought, Don't preen yourself, girl; it wasn't you he came looking for, it was he, Ryler, his old boon companion he came back from the dead to see. Back from the dead? I kept thinking that; the idea seemed too enticing to resist, and anyway was not without a certain force of its own, since death was so wholly abstruse and unanswering, what validity it had was that which was conceived and bestowed by each individual mind, imagination, and which, like notions of God, carried their own individual faith and conviction; a case of truth in all its varieties and guises. If my notion of God was no less presumptuous than any bishop's, then my notion of death was as indisputable as that of any self-styled Azrael's, and it was from out of that notion, that sarcophagus of twilit memories, that he had returned, and the shock to me was no less than if he had truly been blown to pieces and then restored by pitchforks of lightning and coils of man-shaped smoke. In my mind he had been dead; I had even imagined him lying on the field, stretched full, in his blue uniform, his face turned slightly to a side, his eyes closed, his lips softly together, so in repose, so at peace, as I had never been able to know him in life. And then he disappeared from that field (Fredericksburg, they said it was) and my inward eye never saw him there again, but moved him to the knowledge of a grave somewhere, hasty and unmarked, but a patch of soil haunted and haunting in its dreadful solitude; and then resurrected him into ghostly flights of memory, of blurred definitions, selective and idealized: all of it, the death and the burial, carefully and lovingly ceremonial, complete and satiate down to the last emotional detail, so that as far as I was concerned, he had been dead, and he had been mourned, as much as a person could be.

I was apprehensive about having them enter the house. I even thought for a moment about going upstairs and getting my father's pistol and strapping it to my leg in the event they became unmanageable or in the event that whatever erupted did so with such ferocity as to threaten me. But I didn't get the pistol, because I was unwilling to leave them alone for even those few moments; their silence, the glances with which they studiously avoided looking at one another, were too ominous, too broodingly interior. I let Sir Walter, my gray-black shepherd, into the room, securing him with a chain that I hooked into the steel ring embedded in one of the fireplaces, the one where we were sitting. He settled there, coat damp from the night air, front paws out, head up, tail sweeping restively as his wet dark eyes watched my men.

And then they were talking. Ben was saying what he

knew, and then what he suspected, and then he was talking as if what he knew and what he suspected were one and the same thing. Ryler was sitting in one corner of the sofa, arms crossed, watching Ben with the most impassive expression, looking somewhat bored by it all, or maybe that was just a ploy, to try and diminish it, the significance of it, because Ben was very intense, sitting forward in the center of the sofa and turned to Ryler, his face severe, his voice steady, controlled. By bits and pieces I began to understand it, at least what had happened if not why it had happened. As Ben sat and described what he suspected and as it gradually blended into what he knew, or anyway believed, the smirk appeared on Ryler's face, a smirk not just of nondenial but of listless amusement, as if listening to the recitation of some stale old episode. Little by little the fear (or maybe it had been uncertainty) was leaving him, replaced by something more assured and familiar and trusted; and here was his mistake, which he did not realize but I did: Ryler had not changed; nothing had ever happened to him; he was for all intents and purposes—in spite of the mustache—still twelve years old racing through a great wild game which as far as he was concerned was perpetual and self-renewing. He did not realize that somewhere along the way the curtain had to come down and that if you were on the wrong side when it did, and remained there, the game became not just less humorous and inconsequential but serious and even dangerous. But there he was, still playing, caught at another prank, trying to work his way out of it with the smirk, that old infallible device for eliciting forgiveness and laughter. But that was his mistake, and I could see it growing before my eyes; because someone who has not changed thinks that others have not, or will not, or should not. But the two years that he had spent deferring his maturity, in ceaseless gamboling through the saloons and beds of Capstone, had been spent differently by his good friend. For Ben the two years had been measured not by consumed whiskey or seduced farm girls but by Antietam, Fredericksburg, Gettysburg, the barbarous implications of which could only be guessed at. So either Ryler was too inveterate and incorrigible a maker of mischief to lie about it, or else he simply thought it too extravagant a stunt to remain unacknowledged.

"Why?" Ben asked him. "What in God's name did you want to do that for?"

Ryler shrugged. I had been moving about the room, wanting to listen, to know, and at the same time not. Twice Ryler had called for whiskey and each time I ignored him; he could become surly with it, and as the conversation went on, the revelations made, I determined to keep him and whiskey separated. When he asked a third time, as finally I drew up a rocker and sat near them, I told him no. He frowned; Ben seemed to remember that I was there and half-turned to glance at me over his shoulder, then went on.

"You thought it was a good joke, did you?" he said to Ryler.

"Look," Ryler said, "it was always a hellish time, posting those lists. The whole goddamned town came running to see. The whole goddamned street was filled with horses and wagons and carriages. One day George Adamson's name was on there and you should have heard the screaming and wailing. His mother fainted dead away, hit her head on a railing and lay there bleeding. Listen, I'm sure it was pure hell for you fellows, killing each other down there in Virginia, but we were the ones who had to endure the reactions up here. Wait till the next lists go up and you'll see for yourself."

"All right," Ben said, "Go on."

"So when I knew the lists had to go up I said to myself, 'The hell with this, I can't take it anymore.' So I fortified myself. I kept a bottle in the drawer and when it came time I took it out and drank it straight down, right from the bottle, from top to bottom. That was the only way I could face it. Jesus Christ, can you imagine what all those faces look like? All those scared faces coming closer to read the names, with prayers on their lips and the fear of God almighty in their eyes? So one day I got good and varnished and said to myself, 'I can't take this anymore, I got to do something just for the hell of it.' I figured I'd play a good one on old Ben—hell, if we'd been switched around and you'd thought of it, you would've done the same."

"The hell I would," Ben said.

"All right, so maybe you wouldn't. But I did. I marked you in there, made it look just like it was printed. So I did it. When I sobered up it struck me. I said to myself, 'Now shit, boy, look what you did.' "

"You could've undone it," Ben said. His eyes were like ice crystals, fixed upon Ryler, coldly expectant. Good Christ in heaven, I thought, he doesn't know the rest of it. Whatever that old man told him tonight, it wasn't all of it. Even Hook, who was the only one ever capable of holding this boy still, the only one ever able to summon a will fierce and intractable enough to match his, had had to move carefully with him.

"You could have," Ben said.

"I could have," Ryler said, still sitting with his arms crossed, stubborn, becoming resentful now. "But the longer it went on . . . and anyway, what the hell was I going to do—walk up to that old man and tell him it was all a joke, that I had marked you dead, that it wasn't true? After him having grieved on it? He would've killed me, Ben. You know he would've."

"So the only hope you had was for a rebel bullet to make you a prophet. Friend or no friend, you had to walk around with that, didn't you?"

Ryler didn't answer, continuing to sit with his arms crossed, glaring, as if hardening his resolve, irascibly fatalistic. Through last winter, since Fredericksburg, since Chancellorsville, since Gettysburg, through winter and spring and summer and now fall, he had not known what to expect, what to anticipate, probably not even what to want; and so he was totally unprepared, and he was hating—doubtless with equal fervor Ben and the rebel soldier who had never become providential and squeezed the trigger accurately on what would have been the solution. His anger made him seem smaller, childlike, raging helplessly in foredoomed isolation; while Ben's cold self-command made him that much more menacing, unpredictable.

"That old man would've killed me," Ryler said, reiterating it, as if hoping it would touch some as yet unstruck chord and bring forth some understanding response, a softening of the eyes at least, a nod of the head, something.

"You marked me dead after Fredericksburg," Ben said quietly. "That was in December. So everyone knew—except me. You should have informed me about it. It would have been information gratefully received, especially at Gettysburg, where I went through three days of the most ravaging terror trying to prevent myself from being killed. It would have been most charitable to have let me know that I was already dead, because I don't know how many years of my life I spent during those three days trying to stay alive. All right. That was in December. And everyone knew except me. No one so foolish and futile and incongruous as the man who doesn't know he's dead. Because otherwise I wouldn't have sat in a goddamned Sibley tent with a blanket around my shoulders in December and January and February and written all those letters until my fingers were too numb to hold the pencil. What did you think when you saw them coming in? Didn't it occur to you that you had to do something, or were you still holding your breath until spring, when you knew the armies would be moving again and maybe your rebel would finally get in his shot? You could have saved your prayers during Chancellorsville; the regiment was kept in reserve throughout most of it. But by God, you almost got through at Gettysburg, you almost made yourself heard there, because it came close to happening; if I had been turned around just a half-step more, that metal would have taken me in the front and been enough to make you a prophet."

"You were hit?" I asked, realizing suddenly what he was saying. But he did not answer. He didn't hear me. I wasn't there. It was he and Ryler, the two of them, alone, face to face upon the burning of friendship, upon the repudiation and burial of all that had gone before in unity and camaraderie. He was determined to burn it all tonight, to leave nothing behind that might rise and betray him again.

"What did you do with them?" he asked. "I mean the letters. You read them all, didn't you, you son of a bitch? Have you any idea what it's like to be sitting down there wondering what in God's name, what plague, what disaster, had overtaken you all? Writing letters and wondering where the hell they were going. You read them, didn't you? And then burned them."

My God, I thought, so that was where he got those fine little phrases. Not only read them but then went about easing them into his conversation. Oh, Ryler, you bastard, I thought, trying to catch his eye. No wonder. No wonder. Speaking to me in Ben's voice. No wonder. Declaring a man dead and then plagiarizing his ongoing voice. Good Christ in heaven, he must have sat up nights memorizing those pages. Ben, I wanted to say, Ben, you're not just a poet but were a playwright too, writing your best for this scheming little intellectual thief, this strolling player of unparalleled mendacity who mouthed it with such ease, such conviction. A quick little glance from Ryler told me he knew exactly what I was thinking, as if to tell me, *Now you've learned something, haven't you?* but not in self-reproach, not rueful or embarrassed, impenitent, even defiant, his face hardening with his own anger and resentment now, unused to being cornered, brought to the bar like this, his eyes narrowing not like the accused but like the guilty accused who are incensed by the vision or the description of their misdoing, by the discomfort it is causing them.

"You offended me," he said suddenly to Ben, unfolding his arms, flattening his hands on his knees and leaning forward. "Going away like that was pure insult. It was galling. What did you think I was going to do—sit under a tree and swill beer until you got back? Well, you made a mistake when you left her here with me, Ben. You showed contempt for me, and I resented that."

He'll wait now, I thought, watching Ben. He won't say anything. He won't ask, just let it come to him, word by word until there were enough, until there were too many. That iron, enabling control kept him sitting absolutely still, silent, bearing him through these excruciating minutes. Incredibly, Ryler went on, not seeing in that deadly stillness what I was. I could have said something then, and I should have, because all of a sudden I had a clear sense of what was going to happen, the sheer inevitablity of it; and maybe it was that—the inevitability—which stilled my tongue, because no matter how awful a thing you feel is taking shape, that pride of perception subordinates the impartiality of common sense and you want it to go on, to prove you right. I could feel the future already in breath and beginning to coat with damnation. Ben's intent face was a formidable mask of dispassion. I could not keep my eyes from him. I don't think I ever loved him more than at that moment, when I knew he was about to be sharply hurt, because I knew he was powerful in his pride and unambiguous in his passions.

"Well, I proved you wrong," Ryler said. "Maybe I needed that little stunt at the postal shack to help it along, but I don't doubt for a minute I could have got her anyway, because maybe she was just a bit sweeter on me than you thought, or were willing to think. You always had her confused out of her wits so that she never knew what to think. Well, once you were gone, then she knew, then we both knew. She was scared when you went away, and lonely; and then she was neither, because I was there, and she realized I cared more for her than for a uniform and glory or whatever ruck it was that made you sign up. I know what you're thinking—what kind of husband is he? Well, that doesn't concern you. None of it concerns you."

"Husband?" Ben asked softly, then turned to me, an expression of wild astonishment in his eyes, wild and questing.

"He married her, Ben," I said from out of my suddenly odd, blatant situation. As he glared at me, I had to consciously urge upon myself the thought: *The content of those eyes is for Ryler; they just happen to be looking at me this moment,* for there was in them a look I had never seen before in a human being nor ever want to again. Then he turned back to Ryler.

"You married Susan?" he asked.

Now for the first time Ryler realized he had been giving not explanation but information, realized that this and not sometime before was the moment of impact. That the realization was accompanied by profound alarm was clearly in his face, and I understood it because I knew what he was looking at, what was boring into him. Dear God but it was all suddenly so primitive, reduced to such mindless surging fury, in its fear and in its anger and even, dear God, in its passivity: because there are things that stun and root you because of the foam they pound into your blood, because as a woman you're not permitted by custom or society to do them yourself and because anyway they're better done by men; there are things which separate the sexes and by their fascination define the separation, the difference. Ben McKinley in the fullness of his temper was a passage of experience at once irreversible and irresistible, capable of unleashing the most wild and violent responses. That turbulent friction rubbed passion bleeding raw. No man I had ever known could empty one vessel so totally and then so quickly fill another; whether it was blindness of rage or fidelity to instinct, it was sudden enough and total enough so that you knew that thought and reason had been pressed and suffocated.

He uttered a sound, little more than a gasp, then got to his feet and hurled himself upon the startled Ryler and with monstrous strength pulled him from the couch, raised him so that Ryler's boots dangled inches above the floor and then whirled and threw him down heavily in front of the fireplace. The violence, its abruptness, startled the shepherd to his feet and he lunged against his chain until its tautness jerked him to his hind legs, his forelegs stabbing at the air, and he began a loud furious barking which never relented throughout the struggle which was not more than a foot or two under those raised air-stabbing forelegs. Several times he retreated and made another lunge forward, snapping the chain taut again, twisting about on his hind legs, straining at his implacable restriction, forelegs clawing at the air, neck writhing and twisting to be free of the collar, tongue extended, teeth shining and watery.

Ryler's head had struck hard upon the flat slate-gray fieldstone in front of the fireplace and immediately a dazedness swam into his eyes, whether from the shock of the blow or the blunt fury of the attack or from the awesome despairing knowledge of what was going to happen, I would never know. Always aglitter with laughter or with the shrewd needlepoints of sardonic watchfulness, those eyes filled not with terror or the anger of resistance but with heavy pained dullness, seemed detached from the effort of his arms, which raised feebly and futilely against the massed muscularity of Ben's arms and shoulders. Or maybe the blow on the head had been merciful, deadening the senses to the reality of what was happening, about to happen, and maybe the raised resistant arms were merely reflexive. They were so wildly opposite—the one astraddle the other with surging violent hatred, with incensed life-strangling fingers inches deep into the other's throat; while the other lay almost inert except for the vague, almost casual attempt to free himself. And I, dear God, I never moved a muscle or uttered a sound, unable to do anything but sit transfixed, paralyzed by something I dared not analyze or question, my eyes wide open and my mouth too probably, watching it, watching those hands working at that throat. Once Ryler's eyes rolled toward me, gazed dully in my direction, without fear or appeal or even recognition seemingly, and then seemed to dim away like an expiring candle. And all the while the dog kept hurling its weight against the chain, backing up and taking leaps with such ferocity it's a wonder he didn't break his own neck, barking with greater and greater anger and frustration, the lamplight aflame in his storming, liquid eyes.

And then suddenly those hands were withdrawn, with the same shocked suddenness as though they had accidentally thrust themselves into fire. With the same abrupt movement, Ben got to his feet and stepped back, trembling, hands rolled tightly into fists as if to suppress and contain their fury. At Ben's rise the dog ceased his leaping and at last allowed some slack in the chain, drawing back on all fours, the barking becoming intermittent until subsiding into a low, sullen growling. Ben stepped slowly away, gazing down at Ryler, face utterly empty of expression—or maybe it was still the rage and the fury that I was seeing, cold and quiet and pent now, fixed upon the planes of that coldly handsome face which could burn it away at any time with a smile or with the heat of that perversely eccentric intelligence. Ryler was still flat on his back, emitting faint, broken gasps. Then he tried to raise himself, head and shoulders leaving the floor, like someone coming sleepily awake in the middle of the night at some dreamed or undreamed sound, his eyes filled with a puzzled, hopelessly questioning look. His head was not up from the hearthstone for more than a few seconds, but long enough for me to see the pool of blood on the stone. Then, again like that person who had come awake in bed and reckons it was a dreamed sound, his eyes closed and his head fell back upon the stone, and a moment later the pool of blood had increased so that I could see its slow, surreptitious margins advancing out from under his head.

I stood up and went and kneeled over Ryler. He was motionless, silent. His face was white. For a minute, or maybe two minutes, I studied him, tensely aware of Ben standing over me in what was increasingly becoming massive, menacing quietness. Ryler's repose did not suggest loss of consciousness; it was deeper than that, more profound, at once serene and mysteriously distant. So different a Ryler, so transformed; in fact not Ryler anymore, not anyone at all. Only a white face with a broad foolish mustache, and an insidiously creeping arc of blood under him. I looked at the dog; his soft panting was the only sound in the room.

And then Ben was gone. I heard him going across the carpeting, barely making a sound. And then I heard the front door close, not loudly, not softly, but normally, as if nothing had happened.

Twelve

LORD GOD OF MIRACLES, how do you explain such a thing? At first I thought that old man was of unsound mind, coming to the house and telling me such a thing. First off, to see him standing on the outside step in the darkness, as ever all preened up with his derby and his walking stick. What in God's name would he want? I asked myself when I opened the door and saw him. He had never come to my house before. Through all the years, how many words had he ever spoken to me? And the only pair of eyes in Capstone that could set right on you and give you the feeling you were pure air, that they were looking at whatever it was your body was blocking. He's not crazy, my father always said. He might want you to think he is, so you'll let him alone. Or maybe it's just a game he wants to play—to get you to think what he wants you to, so then he knows that he knows what you're thinking. God, girl, don't ask me *why* Henry Hook does what he does; it's enough I know what little I do about him. They had been boys together, my father and Mr. Hook. I would say: I can't imagine him ever being a boy. He was, my father would say. Just barely; but he was. And second off, to hear him actually talking to me, standing out there in the dark, addressing me as Susan (not that I was called by any other name, but by him never, not by any name; and it tells something of the quality of the man that I was surprised and flattered to be called by my only name by a man who had known me for more than fifteen years), and then speaking quietly and kindly, with a tenderness he did not often show, not referring to anyone specifically, not having to, because I suddenly realized he knew more about me than I gave him credit for, that there was a bond between us so thick and so beyond violation there was never any need for its discussion. Not the name, only *He. He is alive.* And then: *He came home tonight.* The shock was mitigated by the realization that Hook had come to both inform and forewarn me, as though handing out a piece of equipment for me to defend myself with. How can such a thing be? I asked. Such a thing is, he said, beginning to encase himself in the old, familiar, conspicuously taciturn Mr. Hook again. I didn't tell him about you, he said, but I suspect that by the time he shows up here he'll know.

That was all. He went away then, and I closed my door. I had been getting ready for bed, had in fact gone to the door with my robe covering my nightdress. But now I went into the bedroom and poked the fire back to life and fed another small log into it. Then I sat down in the rocker. My first thoughts were angry ones, anger at the unforgivable mistake someone somewhere had made. Couldn't they tell the difference between a dead man and a live one? But then I told myself I had better not think about those things, that that part of it was over and done with. And anyway, who was I to go condemning someone for having made a mistake, after the one I had committed and was enduring? *How long are you going to take this? her father had asked just a few days ago. You don't believe that nonsense about him being a professional gambler in partnership with her, do you? I don't care if he does give you some of the money now and then; the boys at the table say he puts it into his pocket on the sly.* But for God's sake, you don't like to give up on a marriage in less than a year. If you marry somebody you've known all your life, you just don't throw it in so quickly, or else who was it you knew or thought you knew all those years? And if you were so wrong about him, how can you be sure you'll ever be right about anything else, most of all about a decision to throw it in so quickly? And anyway maybe the fault is part mine, because he loved me more than I him, and I allowed that. I always saw him as being part of Ben; God, they were always together, weren't they? We just knew each other too well, that was the problem, and now those fractions that were missing or did not wholly cohere in the beginning, instead of healing or becoming less important have widened into gulfs. It wasn't that he was simply stepping out on me; he was also trying to prove something—something he of course had no need of proving. Yes. You know each other so well that finally there is no room for growth, for discovery, the magic melding glow of a marriage; it all blurs, back and forth, past into present, present into past, until there is nothing except the continuing re-creation of the child relationship, until I never know whether I am remembering or experiencing, except that now there is more consequence and less charm in irresponsibility.

I waited, sitting in the bedroom on the rocker that had been my mother's favorite, or so my father told me, and which he would sit on when he wanted to close his eyes and think about her, remember her. He had urged me to take the chair with me when I moved out and set up my own home with Ryler, saying, Take it, take it; I can always come by and sit in it when I need it. When he needed it? Needed it for what? She was dead nearly twenty years now. It frightened me. Did love and death (in their conjunction) create that kind of grip on a person? How soon before I walked across the meadows to Ben's house and asked old Hook for a chair to sit on or a sock to wear or a book to hold when I "needed" Ben? I told myself I had better

establish, and quickly, the lines dividing what was senti
mental and what was morbid. She helped me. It had neve
been easy living in the same town with Eva LeGrange
being a woman, the same age, being just as pretty or maybe
even prettier. Being just the same made all the inequitie
the less tolerable. She had all the accouterments of money
and I don't mean just the big house and the fine clothin;
and the carriage and horses, but the self-confidence and
the command and the arrogance; that was one of the grea
advantages to being rich, as far as I could tell—that ever
when all things were equal, they always held the high
ground, because they were capable of assumptions tha
were incomprehensible to the rest of us. But grief and
death were the water's edge, that was where it all stopped
that was where the mountains leveled. So unaccustomed
was she to losing anything that she still would not let go
even though he was dead. Did I love him? Did he love me.
Oh, those questions. They were impertinent, because
knew what she was looking for—me to relinquish, she to
possess. A ghost. But I wasn't going to fool with her. I told
her the truth, and there was nothing harsh or petty abou
it. And did her a favor in it, too, because heaven only
knows what flights of fancy she would otherwise have al
lowed into her head.

Without knowing, without caring, she helped me. It wa
in her that I saw the sad potential of romantic mourn
ing—the gray sunshine, the mildewed memories, the pres
ervation of cobwebs. My God, I thought, I could love and
remember him without any of that. What had his loving
untamed spirit to do with the maudlin? He was better and
more honestly remembered in full stride, loved but un
possessed, rather than supine and candelit across some
catafalque of decayed memory. If my reasons for marrying
Ryler had been imprecise, well, he was still my Ryler and
I still had stronger cause with him than she did. It was ir
outrage toward her grief that she took him; it was nothing
against me. *She's just like her old man was, her father said. Hi*

soul's rotting on a mound of scorpions somewhere, and she'll end up the same way, mark my words. Same thing's going to happen to her. She'll get caught in the act some night and . . . Only it's doubtful she'll be shot in the back, she said.

Ah, I thought as I watched the fire burning down to so many jumpy red cat's ears on the log, if only I hadn't hurried into marriage (it had been done quickly enough so that I was still getting furtive glances from people who were wondering why I hadn't shown yet). The thought tempered the yearning I felt for Ben. More than elation now, I felt resentment for the irony, uncertainty about the predicament. I got up and by the shadowy firelight stood in front of the small oval wall mirror and combed my hair. I had to hold bunches of hair in my fist while I drove the comb through the knots. Lord, I thought, how long had those knots been in there? When I finally put the comb down I leaned forward and peered at my face in the mirror; in the weak light it looked gravely backstaring, as though the real person was inside the glass, contemplating the other. Then I took a poker and knelt before the fire and stirred the logs about, raising a bit more flame and heat. *Yes, Ben,* I would tell him. *I heard you were home, that it was all a mistake. How glad I am. It's good to have you back. Won't you come in and sit for a while? Have a glass of sherry. Wait till Ryler hears about it; he'll be so excited. We ought to have a party to celebrate. Where is he at this hour? Oh, he's just . . . he's just. He'll be back soon. You just sit right down and wait. Can you imagine, they marked you dead? Isn't that the silliest thing? It all happens to you, doesn't it? And here I am, a married woman now.* I threw the poker into the fire with such force it struck the rear wall and bounded right back out past me and clattered on the planks. Damn, I didn't feel married any longer. I didn't *want* to be married. I *wouldn't* be married.

And then I heard him outside. I knew who it was; not that there was any particular pattern or impact to his step. It was my Ben outside in the darkness, and suddenly the whole thing was eerie, and unnerving; it was as though it were at this moment that he was returning from the dead, at this very moment being embodied in the shadows and coming toward the light. I got to my feet before he knocked and left the bedroom, going toward the door. He was on the other side of the door now, still in the shadows, but imminent, ready to begin breathing and seeing and feeling again the moment my eyes separated him from the night and gave him definition. I didn't wait for him to knock, lifting the latch and opening the door. He was standing there, hatless, gazing down at me. He seemed surprised—that I had opened the door before his knock, and surprised that I was not surprised. Then you know, he said. Hook was here, I said. May I come in? he asked. I extended my hand to him and he took it with a suddenness that startled and a strength that hurt; it was a gesture of terrible urgency. He held my hand for a long moment, then pulled me toward him and embraced me and held me against him. He did not kiss me, merely held me to him, wordless, motionless; it was almost as if I were the one being reclaimed from the dead. I had never known this feeling from him, this need, this unrestrained giving. It was strange and beautiful. I had heard new mothers tell of the first few hours of holding their newborn babes, of the perfect, unstirring serenity of the child, and then how that was gone, irretrievably, once the child began reacting to the vast new world around it. This was how I felt with Ben those first moments of his return; I knew that this exquisite balance of time would soon end and never again occur in just that sweet breathless way. But while it lasted I closed my eyes to it and let it suffuse me with a fragrance that sank to the bottom of my soul, storing it for future need. And then he raised my face to his and kissed me softly on the lips, luring my eyes with his, and with a gentle dreamy ease ran his hand through my hair.

When we went into the bedroom the fire was little more than a faint orange nimbus, like the last of a January sunset. How I missed you, I whispered (the whispering was so strange; there was no one else about, no one to hear; but yet we whispered, both of us, as though afraid that undue sounds might provoke some malign intervention upon our happiness). I missed you every day, I said. Every hour of every day and every minute of every hour. We sat together on the edge of the big brass bed. A chill had advanced upon the room, seeping into the fire's receding warmth. Through the mist of white curtains, I could see a quarter moon like the blade of a sickle afloat upon the high darkness. Oh, Ben, I said as he undid my robe and pushed it back from my shoulders. It's all right, he said. He won't be home tonight. He stared at me rather strangely when he said it, as if waiting for me to say something, as if hoping I might. For a moment his eyes held a look of plaintive appeal. Then he leaned forward and embraced me and put his face against my breasts. I held him close to me. It was different now from a few moments before; the serenity was gone, in its stead a warm gradually more urgent pulsing. I murmured his name, lowering my face, kissing his hair. He eased me gently onto my back and then I felt him raising my nightdress and when he bent and pressed his warm lips into the soft flesh of my middle I felt a sudden gathering of tension throughout my body. Oh my Ben, I thought, after all these years, finally. How often did you think of it? How deeply? And in what way? There were times when you wanted to; I knew it; but you would not, because you were in your heart—at least that part of your heart reserved for me—always the gentleman; in spite of what you seemed to be and seemed to want others to think of you, with me you were the gentleman. Only I knew that, and I loved you because you let me know it and you loved me because you allowed me to know it.

He lay beside me under the cover, and again he said it: *He won't be home tonight,* and again seemed waiting for me to say something. For a long time he held me in his arms,

close against him. There were moments when I felt he was
strangely remote, adrift in the distance upon some unmoored thought; and he might well have been, too, for
he would start kissing me, warmly, lovingly, as though each
time were another return, another homecoming. Yes, I
did think of Ryler, but only briefly, with such brief passage
that he was neither threat nor reality. I was sure—oh, from
what pit was I able to muster such certainty?—that he
would not be home tonight, as Ben said, kept saying. Some
deity ordained to dispense occasional happiness would see
to that, would give me undisturbed enchantment with my
Ben on this long, strange night. And then he was inside
me, with full, gentle force, loving me, needing me. As I
had dreamed of him, so he was: strong and perfect, uniting
me with him. We alone. Riding our solitary speck through
the darkness. My Ben and me. Together at last, exchanging the moisture of our fervid bodies. In the hearth the
fire had bowed into extinction and the dark room—the
dark world—above our blankets had turned chill, had
edged into the silent, impersonal emptiness of night; but
we were together in my bed, my Ben and me, beautifully
and perfectly together; it was for this, I thought, that night
deepened and sound fled into silence, to shape just such
cradling moments as these. When his strong power erupted
and poured into me, I clasped my hands around his neck
and with my thighs and muscles thrust my body up into
his, into his torrid buffeting.

Later, I lay on my side, watching his profiled face. His
hands were folded behind his head. Don't leave, I said. He
gave me a soft, mocking laugh. Stay, I said. Until he comes
home. We'll tell him. We'll explain it. He'll understand.
He will, Ben. Now he turned his face on the pillow to me.
Explain it to him? he asked. You would do that? How?
How is it to be explained? Through lack of guilt, I said.
Anything can be explained, if you don't feel guilty about
it. If he walked in now, I wouldn't skip a breath. I would
take his hands in mine and sit him down and talk to him.

He *knows* how I feel about you. Ben, he would *understand.* For a long moment he gazed at me with what seemed pity, then turned away. Did he talk about me very much, Susan? he asked. Not so very much, I said. Was he upset when I was marked dead? Yes, of course, I said. But why do you ask such things? My God, after so many years we three were like one person. Now he glanced at me again, briefly, sharply, as if he had taken offense. No, he said. One person can be three, but never three one. You thought you knew your Ryler; you think you know your Ben. But what is it that you really know, and how does it stand against what you think you know? Your husband sees another woman and his best friend is abed with his wife. We three have grown up and answered the years, haven't we, Susan? I know he's with another woman, I said, and I say to hell with her. Why are you saying such things? I demanded, becoming angry with him. Bitterly, he said, Tonight I can say what I damn please.

He threw off the covers and sat on the edge of the bed, his back to me. Ben, I said, what is wrong? What is *wrong* with you? He shook his head slowly from side to side. Then he reached down and began retrieving the clothing he had so hastily discarded. He dressed in the darkness, slowly, methodically, putting back upon his body that uniform which seemed so alien without its parades and its drums and its flags, that had seemed almost a third person in the house until he had removed it. I don't want you to go, I said. It would be wrong for you to go before he comes. Would it? he muttered, tucking his blouse into his trousers and then buckling his belt. Then he raised his hands to the sides of his head and pressed back his hair. I want to talk to you, he said, but I can't. Not now, he said, then repeated in a whisper, not now. You will have to understand on faith alone. Will you always love me? Can I take that with me? Take it with you? I asked. As ever, his departure was strange; his departures were forever strange. I was always left emptily with the feeling I might not ever see him again, or at best for a long time. He always seemed aimed for some place he could not quite reach. I asked him if he would come back tomorrow, but he didn't answer. When he had put on his boots and his coat, he sat on the edge of the bed. He put out his hand and I took it and pressed it between my face and the pillow. I've hurt you so many times, he said. You have never hurt me, I said. Hesitantly he spoke my name, then lapsed into silence. After several moments I said, What is it, Ben? What is it you want to say? Studying me with a sternly unwavering look, he said, Would you forgive me . . . anything? I forgive you, I said. Anything. Then I sat up and threw my arms around his neck and began crying. He embraced me for a moment, held me against him, then gently pushed down my arms and got up and left.

Thirteen

HE WENT QUICKLY AND with uncanny quiet through the night, purposeful, but at the same time filled with a vexing frustration. He had gone to her with the express purpose of telling her what had happened; with the words on his lips and the anguish in his heart. But he had never come even close to the telling. The warmth and the sweetness and the serenity presented to him had been too precious to disturb. But now the force of the unspoken was coming back at him like so many cyclic ghosts. He felt the night at his back as he walked, filling his footsteps and obliterating his existence as surely as time removes mortal evidence and the waves flood the tracks of ships. *The irony,* he thought, *the irony is head-pounding: returning from the dead and sending my spurious executioner in replacement. So now Ryler is me and I am Ryler, in more ways than one, except that I am guiltier than he ever dreamed of being. And so it moves in its natural way, full capacities under full throttle.*

He hurried along a narrow road bordered on either side by trees. The last few minutes with her had been agonizing. He felt his head would explode if he did not get away, and now that same need, that same fervent urgency was driving him into the night. For a moment he yearned for those ashes and that chimney with its heat-impacted memories of untroubled peace and security, those sanctified ashes with their promise of release and cessation, which at this very moment lay scattered under this same solemn sky, within this same cowl of darkness. Then he cursed the thought. *There is nothing there. I saw it. I saw it. Nothing.* Don't think those things, he told himself. Think of rational things. And he amused himself with a grim litany: Antietam Fredericksburg Gettysburg: the fume of smoke and the rush of bayonets, the sky-breaching artillery, unnecked heads, the yips and yowls of charging Confederate infantry. Now that, he thought savagely, *that* made great sense.

He cut away from the road and entered the woods. In spite of the deeper darkness here, his way was unerring as he followed the path, listening to the mild sibilance of a whippoorwill. He tracked on through the woods for a quarter-mile and emerged into the bordering sedge where in yellow days of remembrance he and Ryler had come to pick wild strawberries. Going on, he strode through the knee-high meadow grasses. Crossing the meadow, he reached another road and followed it to Eva's house, walking on the mound between the wagon-wheel ruts.

The downstairs lights were still burning. What in God's name was she doing in there? He did not know what he had expected to see, but surely not a scene of unruffled stillness. It seemed almost offensive. Scowling at the light, he walked a long arc around the house, eyeing it warily as he ran the back of his hand across his mouth. He climbed over the low rail fence, pushed through a crowd of forsythia and approached the stable. *He's dead,* he thought. He had seen too many dying men these past two years not to be able to recognize it; it got so that all it took was a glance to know. No question about it. The only question was, *What is she doing in there?* He paused for a moment, stood poised in the stillness, turning his head slightly in an attempt to pick up any sound. Then he moved again, quickly now. As he neared the stable, the dog began barking. He ran to the door, pushed up the latch, then stepped back and swung the doors out. He entered the horse-smelling darkness, aware that the barking was coming from another direction now, that she was hurrying the shepherd toward the front door. He opened the first stall on his left and a large sorrel tossed its head and rose slowly from its spread of straw. He threw a blanket across the horse, then lifted a saddle from the wall and heaved it into place and tightened the cinch, aware of the horse sucking in its breath. Then the barking was outside, loud and indignant, its constancy implying a note of frustration. She's still got him on the leash, he thought. "Who's there?" she called. "Who's in there?" He inserted the bit into the horse's mouth, slipped the bridle over its head and fastened the throatlatch. Then, as the barking came nearer, he tightened the cinch once again, took hold of the pommel and swung himself astride. "Come out of there," she called, and a moment later he heard the barking bearing down on him and knew the dog was loose. Leaning forward and lowering his head and shoulders to gain clearance through the doorway, he kicked at the horse's flanks and rode out past the excited shepherd, who leaped to its hind legs for a moment and then swirled around and began chasing the horse, with barking so constant it seemed to be chopping out on a single breath. "Ben?" Eva called, her voice inquiring, uncertain. Then, defining his crouched figure in the darkness, she cried, "You fool! Don't go! Come back!" Gaining speed with every folding and unfolding stride, he swept away, soon outdistancing the shepherd, and a few moments later was out in the road, galloping into the night.

Ryler laughs no more, he thought. Little Ryler, who with quip and laugh companioned me through the briers and the bowers of youth, is now no more feeling than the pounded road underfoot. It came upon him like a flood, whirled up by the speed and the motion, by the lonely race across the empty road, the inrush of wind, the fleeting threats of leaf and rock on either side. Little Ryler, so boon and genuine a friend through all those garish and unfettered years, shareholders of myriad precious memories, holds now not memory or breath or laughter anymore, only the endless capacity to haunt and hound. Oh sweet goddess Mnemosyne, the time we saw fat Old Mr. Fox sitting asleep in a chair outside the general store and went up to him on the sly and snipped off one half of his drooping white mustache and he never knew it until he had walked around town for half the day growing more and more belligerent at the giggles directed at him, never knew it until his sister came along and hissed at him and called him a fool. No, no one else, only he. Why do I think *little* Ryler? Why *young* Ryler? Why the boy who lived so gaily and not the man who betrayed? This was the most telling form of self-punishment, he thought as he galloped on, this idea of having slain all that was good and irreplaceable because it was infected by some rank weed of impurity. A dead Ryler could not split time with him in the future and call up escapades of joy and light—the only one who could have, too, for there had been no other friend of such standing, of such trust and intimacy, because there was, could be, only one friend for the first inebriating overdose of whiskey, the first sickening cigar, the first woman (yes, they had shared that too, at the foot of Billy Goat Hill with Mamie Pollard, and then ran a quarter-mile toward town until they realized that in their exultation they were carrying their trousers in their hands). Why did I hack down the only green enduring thing in the morass? We had poured life together in such uncaring abundance as to be able to warm all the winters ahead merely on the glow of remembering. And now by Jesus Christ how was he going to quench the aridity that lay inevitably in life's outreach? It was too late to add to it; there were no blank leaves left at the end of that particular book. It had all been frozen into preservation by the war: he knew after the first gunfire and the first blood that youth was now complete and no supplements were possible; so what was gone was the more precious, and now with one murderous, unreasoning act he had turned it all into a desert of bones and dust where yearning memory could never graze. In taking life the murderer not only plundered but relinquished, gave up not just serenity of soul and conscience forever, but in this instance saw the victim in departure seize from the murderer the most irretrievable of assets.

And worse, worse than anything, was what he had done to Susan. He had contrived and left behind the most fraudulent dreams and hopes. Ryler had at least betrayed him; all she had ever done was offer unswerving and unremitting devotion. I should have told her, he thought with cold self-contempt. By not walking in and telling her, he had destroyed his last hope. His deception was brutal and unforgivable. At the very least he should have stayed until morning and with sunlight filling the room—there are some things, he could have said, that cannot be told at night—told her. Shared tears were more permeating and more enabling than those dropped in solitude. Instead of imagining mindless rage (which she will when she hears about it, he thought; and not only rage but callousness, too—how could he have spent a night of tenderness and love coming fresh from murder?), she would have seen grief and anguish in their most profound expression. Even now she was abed, surely unable to sleep, her mind a typhooned sea of wrestling currents, reveling in what she did not know was her curse—her love of him. Even now as she was abed, savoring the miracle of his return and breathing deeply into their moments of locked passion, she would be thinking about Ryler and what she would say to him when he returned. His sweet Susan was lying abed at this moment trying with all her heart and soul to shape the words she would speak to a man who was dead, for whom she would wait anxiously through the night and the morning and afternoon and on into evening, with her

gathered love and her despairing fortitude. She will forgive anything, he thought, except this one thing—the not
telling. The starkness of it will be incomprehensible and
then barbaric to her—killing the man and then going to
his house and making love to his wife and then departing
with sealed lips. What will that seem like in contemplation?
To be called callous and contemptuous would under the
circumstances be flattery. Even forgiveness, should it be
forthcoming, would not be enough. There would have to
be understanding of near-saintly quality. But understanding of what? Explain to her? With what beginning. *For
fifteen years you have loved someone who is mad, whose forebears
have left an unbroken and traceable stain of the most bizarre and
grotesque anomalies. I am not who or what you think, therefore
you must reconceive me in your mind: consequently I am a
stranger, and if you continue in your love it must be under the
awesome knowledge that any sleep might be your last or that the
stranger may at any moment unfold into a further stranger, tilting
into another world, beyond the loving touch of your Christian
forgiveness.*

There was no way in which to justify himself . . . no way
except to call in witness those unruly ancestors, to take
salvation in what he most dreaded. He was possessed by
past selves whose unbound wills and whims were savagely
unknown to him, who came searing at him from out of
festering and concealed places. Like all tyrants, they preferred rule above justice, guile above truth. He could only
say: I am not they, but they are me, with their chortling
laughter, their merry slits of eyes, their incoherence; subject to their vagaries and their abberations, tempted by the
rattling of their bones; his brain within the clamp of their
jaws, forever prey to their spectral control. All he was was
the most recent container for their abysmal convulsions,
carrying seeds of indestructible destruction that had survived every crucible. He could not fight legions that pulsed
in sultry impulses, that could attack without provocation
while remaining immune to retaliation; untamable hordes

of previous incarnations and insatiable furies; storming from out of unhealing time to cry, *Maintain, descendant.* Christ's blood, what walls and ceilings does it have? Any? What doors and windows? It could lie coiled anywhere, even in laughter and in light, started equally by whip or caress. Spring's own renewal could be rife with it, and summer's peace. Is there a trigger for it, or does it strike from the void? Can it be forewarning, detected in the word, the gesture, the impulse? How does it verge and diverge from what is natural to others but unnatural to me? When is the fateful pause before its eruption?

Marked dead, tonight he was his own ghost, grim, omniscient, and insubstantial. I need sane meditation, he thought, as the horse carried him past black trees and silent fields and dark houses with tranquil souls in enviously untroubled sleep. Good God, he cried in his heart, was there no such thing as a man of stainless inauguration, free of taint, primary in direction? or are we all simply the continuance of those unruly ancestors mixed in our blood in such defective composition as to make us hopeless in our strivings?; are all of us in procession set loose upon the earth as sport for the bygone? They cry "run" when I want to walk, "walk" when I want to sit, "scowl" when I want to smile, "withhold" when I want to give, "seethe" when I want to reason. Contrary to the pattern of most men, the past reveals me and the future enshrouds. Or am I annihilating myself with my own delusions? *Re-create thyself. Did not the whited sepulcher Ryler show you your channel? Leave past Ben buried, the old boundaries demarcated forever. Resurge anew, up from the dead. Muster your virtues and marshal your strength. Be master, not slave. Seek other suns, other moons, other stars and other heavens to guide by; cast out your blood to its last drop, outlast its hellish tracking; light your own candle and live by its glow and its warmth, defend it against the wind, defend the frail light with might and vigilance. Hurl the corpse of your dead friend upon them and let him be their feast, let their*

jaws snap at him—"Here is your sacrifice; I am free"—while you
break the crucifixion though the nails tear out your flesh.

After miles and miles of ceaseless riding, he finally
slowed to a walk, panting, the reins coiled loosely around
his wrist. Turning the horse, he left the road and entered
a field. Reaching an elm grove, he dismounted. He tethered the horse and then let himself down on the grass,
cradling his head in the crook of his arm. He closed his
eyes, feeling consumed with aloneness. A whispery breeze
was redolent with fragrant wildflowers. He sighed. Thoughts
as neighborly but as unmeeting as the eyes in his head
were racking his brain. The unresolvable and the irre-
ducible shot through him in currents. Was he the dreamer,
of delicate conscience; or like the viper, that could die of
its own bite, its poison capable of wholly dispassionate
death? Whom had he killed—the friend of a thousand
uproarious occasions, or the man who had betrayed him?

Answer me, he whispered before falling into exhausted
sleep.

Fourteen

"BY JESUS," ONE OF the loungers on the Dooley House porch said as their slow, monosyllabic conversation ceased.

"Then it's true," another whispered, feeling the need to lower his voice. "He's back."

The sorrel moved slowly along Grant Avenue and then stopped in front of the Dooley House. The men on the porch, motionless on their arrested rockers, stared silently back at the face that was turned toward them with a malicious half-smile as if he were depository of their gaudiest secrets. As long as he sat there, the rider held them transfixed, not just with his enigmatic smile but as well with the palpable strangeness of his bearing, as if through some remote act of homeopathic magic he had scratched their flesh. Then the sorrel began moving again, with almost calculated deliberation, the rider still watching them, mocking them into a sense of unease with what seemed a hypnosis of inanimate motion. They watched him with shrewd mistrust, as if he had invaded their dreams the night before. As he moved further along the road, he finally turned his face from them, then kicked his sorrel into a trot.

"Son of a bitch is back all right," one of the men said.

"He is, by Jesus."

"Thought he was gone and done for."

"War Department made a mistake, I reckon."

"You mean the rebels did," one said, and they all guffawed and resumed their slow rocking.

Because she was listening for a certain sound, Eva heard it before she would ordinarily have. She reached for a towel, dried her hands, then left the kitchen. When she opened the front door, he was sitting the sorrel in front of the portico, looking stubbornly unrepentant in the clean, bright sunshine.

"You're wearing an apron?" he asked.

Self-consciously she brushed some strands of hair away from her face.

"I let the servants go," she said.

"Are they talkative?"

"When they know something," She paused. "But they don't know anything."

"I see. Then you are the only one who knows anything."

"*We,*" she said pointedly, "are the only ones who know anything." Then, brusquely, "See to the horse and come inside."

A few minutes later he climbed the portico steps and walked through the open door. He stopped, surveyed the vaulted entranceway for a moment, then shouted, "*Ryler!*"

She came running from the kitchen, incensed. "What the hell do you think you're doing?" she demanded, barely able to contain her fury.

He shrugged. They stared intently at each other for a moment, then she drew her mouth back into a tight line and went to him. He put his arms around her.

"Where the hell have you been for two days?" she asked quietly.

"Ask the horse. He knows better than I."

"Where have you been?" she asked, impatiently now.

"Nowhere. Just riding. Twenty-four hours in one direction, twenty-four in another."

"What did you do?"

"I rode and I slept, and I drank and I ate; but my primary occupation was warding off my thoughts."

"I was angry with you," she said, "Very angry." And, as he waited expectantly, she said, "For running off like that."

"I'm sorry I offended you," he said with irony so lambent it slipped by unheard.

She took his hand and, with an odd smile on her lips, led him through the entranceway into the room with the large opposing fireplaces. When he realized where they were going, he hung back for a moment, and then under her gentle urging relented and followed. As they went deeper into the large sunlit room, the site of his rage came into view. He approached it with tense uncertainty, wondering what he might see there, dreading it, as if that hearthstone were capable of excreting some physical threat or accusation. Still holding his hand, she glanced back at him, as if anticipating praise. She led him to the sofa where he had sat two nights ago, and together they sat down, she in a corner, watching him with cool, inquiring interest. He was sitting away from her, patently ill at ease, his brooding eyes fixed upon the hearthstone.

"You look exhausted," she said. "You'll have a hot bath, a good meal, then get some rest." She studied his profiled face. "Did you think of me very much these past few days?"

He moved his head from side to side. His coat collar was raised, the lapel hiding part of his golden-stubbled face.

"I thought of you incessantly," she said. "I knew you'd be back. It was just a matter of when."

"Then you knew more than I did."

"Where else?" she asked.

"Who have you seen?"

"No one."

"You didn't go to see Hook?"

"No," she said. "Why should I?"

"I might have gone there."

"I never considered it," she said, "because you never considered it. I know you better than you think I do."

"That would be interesting," he said vaguely, "if you did."

"I realize it calls for a large effort, Ben. I've never slighted it."

His eyes still fixed upon the hearthstone, he asked, "What did you do with him?"

"Don't worry about it," she said.

"No?" he asked skeptically, glancing at her for a moment.

"Everything has been seen to."

"By whom?"

"By me. Alone."

"You—?"

"I don't want to talk about it," she said. "It was neither easy nor pleasant, but it was done; it had to be done."

"How did I seem to you?"

"Angry," she said. "Frightfully angry. But no one could blame you; you had been provoked beyond endurance."

"Yes," he murmured, "of course."

"I don't want you to think about it. Everything has been seen to."

"One thing remains," he said.

"What is that?"

"The ghost."

"Yes. A bit of quicksilver in your conscience. That's why I knew you would come back. You'll need help with that."

"Above that particular fray, are you?"

"Far above."

"I'm glad you're callous about it," he said.

"I'm not being callous."

"But I would prefer that you were. If you felt as I do, then it would be impossible."

After several thoughtful moments, she said, "Is that why you came here instead of to her?"

"I've been trying not to think of her."

"She's better off without him."

"There's my callous lady," he said with a wry smile. "Yes, perhaps she is. But she doesn't know that. She doesn't know anything."

"His absence will grow on her, and grow to fit her well."

"It's cruel," he said quietly, returning his gaze to the hearthstone, watching with the stillness of a person maintaining a vigil.

"You're going to have to resist the temptation of telling her. And believe me, it will be a powerful temptation at times. One day you'll have the grand idea that you'll be able to unburden yourself by going there and telling her. I don't want you to do that. I don't want you to go there, to see her. It's most important; I'm asking you to rely on my judgment in this matter. Everything has changed, Ben."

Late that afternoon, after an exhausted Ben had gone upstairs to sleep, Eva hitched up her chaise and rode to see Hook. When he admitted her to the house and asked her to join him in the parlor, she realized he had been drinking, that he was in fact slightly inebriated. It was a shock to her; it was the first time she had ever seen the slightest fissure in this puzzling old man's austere facade. His small eyes were reddened slightly; there was an unsteadiness to his walk. His white shirt was open at the throat, his vest unbuttoned—seeming disarray for one who always appeared so formal in public.

When he sat down in the parlor, it was next to a table that held a nearly empty whiskey bottle and a glass. Her evident surprise at him evoked from him a look of cool amusement.

"Ben is moving in with me," she said when she had seated herself in a chair opposite him at the table.

Hook nodded, smiling listlessly. "Well," he said, "it's a big enough house." Absently, with slow, unsteady fingers, he buttoned his vest. "Actually," he said, "I considered that he might. I trust you'll see to his care."

"He's not a child, Mr. Hook."

"Is not," Hook muttered. "and never was."

He emptied the bottle into the glass, making great show of suspending the upended bottle over the glass as if to coax out the final drop.

"I have two requests to make of you," Eva said, watching him sip from the glass. Upon saying that she saw those two small reddened eyes sharpen upon her with a piercing inquiry that not only dispelled all notions of intoxication but was also more than mere sobriety. "I would prefer you not come to visit," she said, matching him eye for eye.

"Why?" he asked, holding the glass before his lips, his hand steady as a rock.

"I don't want him upset."

"Then something is troubling him?" he asked with what sounded to her like mock innocence.

"He's been rather unsettled from what he experienced in the war. He needs rest, quiet, solitude."

"All of which you can supply in abundance."

"Among other things," she said dryly.

"I don't doubt your myriad capacities, Miss LeGrange," he said, drinking, then putting the glass down.

"I'm very serious about this, Mr. Hook."

"I'm familiar with your seriousness, Miss LeGrange. I've always associated it with a lack of humor. Now, as far as Ben is concerned, is he free to visit me if he likes, or do you intend to keep him confined?"

"Confine him?" she asked, arching an eyebrow. She smiled knowledgeably; he responded with a hearty laugh, a raucous noise culled from deep in his powerful chest.

"We know our Ben, don't we?" he said.

"I'm not afraid of you, Mr. Hook," she said.

"You have no reason to be."

"My father was. You were the only man he ever feared."

"He had reason to."

"My father was a very brave man," she said, offended.

"That looks very good on paper, but it's a foolishness. If he had feared the man who shot him, he would be alive today. Forgive me; but you're going to have to be educated in some unpleasant realities if you're to get along with that boy. Do you want a word of advice?"

She remained silent, unwilling to give him the benefit of her curiosity. He understood.

"Don't ever feel you have power over him," he said. "Nor ever try to seek it."

"I understand him."

"Well then," he said expansively, "you have no problem."

"You resent him wanting to stay with me."

Again he leveled upon her a gaze of piercing acuity, and, coming forward in his chair, in a low, terse voice said, "I do not, have never, nor ever will resent anything he does, says, or feels. And I counsel you to do the same."

His intensity of manner struck a momentary disquiet into her. Now he sat back and in a relaxed, almost cordial voice, said, "You referred to two requests."

"I would like to take back with me some of his personal belongings."

"There isn't much," Hook said. "Unfortunately much of it was disposed of. You can have that though," he said pointing to the paper-wrapped parcel Ben had brought home with him, still resting untouched on the floor. "I don't know what he's got in it, but that's what came home with him and I assume he'd like to have it."

When she returned home, Ben was still asleep. After seeing to the dinner preparations, she went into the living room, built a fire and then sat down with the parcel. For some time she simply sat and stared at it, as one might at some mute thing of intriguing history. Then she cut the string that bound it and began parting the folds of rough brown paper. Among the neatly pressed and folded articles of clothing, she found several books—Blake, Cowper,

Tennyson; each volume was worn, dog-eared, as though the eye had been trying to clean the words from certain pages. She smiled knowingly at the books, caressing their water-stained covers with her fingers. Yes, Mr? Hook, she thought, I know him, I understand him, more than you think.

Also in the parcel were a half-dozen thickly crammed envelopes, tied around with a piece of string. Undoing the string and rotating the envelopes through her hands, she saw that each was addressed to him—she recognized her own handwriting on the face of one. How sentimental—and revealing—she thought, this preservation of letters. Upon emptying the envelopes, however (and she had no reservations about doing this, did not even consider that it might be an intrusion upon his, or someone's else's, privacy), she found they contained not letters from herself or anyone else, but neatly written stanzas of poetry. If in the books she had sensed his heart, here she discovered his soul. Here at last was the inner man, probed and risen, free of that self-protective shroud of secrecy and torment.

The poems—some thirty-five of them—were written in pencil on an incongruous assortment of pages, some of which were fine paper adorned with patriotic emblems and mottoes, others were lined pages torn from notebooks, and some of the poems were written on the backs of envelopes. In each case the page had been carefully, meticulously, folded, before being tucked into an envelope; none seemed to have been handled very much, as if after having been put away they had not been taken out again.

She had known that he wrote poetry. Once, a year or so before the war, while horseback riding together, he had fallen into a rare mood of high spirits and begun quoting some of the English poets, pointing out appropriate places upon which to orally inscribe the lines—flowers, trees, a stream. Most of the lines she could identify, by both poet and poem. She heard Keats and Byron, Tennyson and Wordsworth. They played the game back and forth for several moments, until she heard him speak a particularly beautiful, sharp-edged phrase which was unfamiliar to her. Who is that? she asked. Whom are you quoting? He passed her a sly look, saying nothing. Not until she asked again for the author did he say, Do you like it? Very much, she said, and then, with intuition shoving impulse, asked, Can you recite more of this fellow? He laughed cavalierly and said, I should think his whole wretched collection. I would like to read it, she said. He looked away and said, Someday, perhaps.

That he possessed a lyric gift had been evident from his letters. When they were read carefully, she could sense it beginning to take possession of him, as his perfunctory descriptions of the banalities of camp life began to change into beautifully observed scenes of what was going on around him, his view of the woods or whatever landscape was to eye. She could feel herself, as recipient of the letter, melting from his consciousness as he wrote, as he was carried forward by the sound and the feel of words locking together and sentences flowing through his mind. Under this mysterious transmutation the handwriting would suddenly appear hurried—the *t's* crossed with flying little dashes—as his hand ran to keep pace with the flow and the sentences became almost metrical.

She was, however, still unprepared for the elegance of his premeditated poetical writing. With Pierian beauty he wrote of marching armies, of war and death, of the juxtaposition of wildflowers and gleaming bayonets, of campfires, loneliness, the heart's brimming fullness, of nature in all its manifestations of mood and array. He wrote with spirited hope, with vision, with poignance. All of it in controlled, measured lines at once simple and luminous. In the silence of the many-roomed house, she sat and read them.

When she had finished reading, she was surprised to look up to see that night had long since fallen, that a veil of moonlight hung over the window. She went upstairs to where he was still asleep. For a long time she stood quietly in the moonlit room, hands clasped gently to her breast, gazing with longing and with anguished love, studying his sleeping face in the pale light as one might an *objet d'art* long ago suffused with sinister and enduring beauty. Then she removed her clothing and, without disturbing him, got into the bed and lay next to him under the covers.

Fifteen

"YOU HAD NO BUSINESS reading them," he said. There was no anger in his voice, no resentment; merely a note of what sounded like formal protest.

"I opened the parcel to see if any of the clothing needed to be cleaned or mended." To his look of amused skepticism, she added, "Yes, I know how to do those things. In any event I have no choice, now that the servants have been discharged. So I opened the parcel with all good intentions, and when I saw those papers I naturally was curious and wanted to see what they were. I read them, and I won't apologize for it, because the moment you write something of that quality you lose all right of exclusive possession. Writing like that is not yours to hoard alone."

He stared curiously at her. He brought his wine glass to his lips. They were sitting at opposite ends of the long dining room table, just finishing dinner, though it was past midnight now. She had set the table with her best silver service, finest china, heavy white linen napkins, a parade of glowing candelabra down the table's center. Making a mockery of these formalities, however, were his bare chest and her robe, under which she was naked.

"When you've written some more," she said, "I'll see to it they're brought between covers."

"We'll call it 'Ben's Nosegay,' " he said.

"I seem to be taking them more seriously than you."

"Which is as it should be," he said, emptying his glass and then twirling its stem in his fingers.

"How do they come to be written?"

"Oh," he said casually, "one line draws up the next."

"One of my deep desires is to get Mr. Tennyson in a chair before me and press him with the question, 'How do you do it?' "

" 'Why' would be more interesting."

"Is that where it lies—in why?"

"The best of it, yes. The tone and the coloration and the grace come from 'how.' The feeling and the music and the special words . . . "

"Come from 'why.' "

" 'Why' makes the difference between noise and music, between noise and silence."

"Silence?"

"Don't you sometimes feel it inside you when you're reading a really good poem—a silence? Sometimes sweet, sometimes sad?"

"I haven't felt that yet in your work."

"Well," he said, examining the wine glass with great studiousness, "knowing the poet can be a certain disadvantage. It's like sitting in the kitchen and watching the cook concoct a fine dinner—it can spoil the taste later on. Or going backstage and seeing King Lear sitting in his underwear."

"You've never shown them to anyone, have you? Not even to Hook."

"Ah, that old man," he said smiling with fond disparagement. "He thinks poetry stopped with Virgil. Though if you cajole him enough he'll admit there's a bit of dash to Shakespeare."

"Well," she said, "I think there's more than a bit of dash to Ben McKinley."

"Ben McKinley is a murderer," he said softly.

She stared through the candles at him, at his face behind the decorous and ceremonial points of fire.

"Are you afraid of it?" she asked.

"I'm a reasonable man. Shouldn't I be?"

"Not until you've very carefully measured the act against the victim."

"I knew the victim too well for that kind of trick," he said.

"But you didn't, Ben. You saw what he did to you. Was that the man you knew? Maybe you haven't given thought to its fullest implications. He marked you dead and after that had no choice but to hope it would come true. From remote distance, he was trying to kill you."

"But what about the good that was in him? Can't I mourn that?"

"He had very little good in him," she said, gazing steadily through the burning candles at him. "So stop lacerating yourself. In any event, you never intended it. It was an accident. Regard it as a religionist might. The fortuitous is the will of God; you were merely the agent."

"A new religion, this?" he asked with a cynical smile. "Accidentalism?"

She laughed, then rested her face in her hand and regarded him with bemused affection. "Yes," she said. "And begun as any good religion should—with the shedding of blood."

The following afternoon they walked together through the fields behind the house in a slow, misty rain, he bareheaded, coat collar turned up; she in a long gray cloak, her face deep in a capacious hood.

"Sometimes," he said, "when you start thinking these things, you just have to get out of doors and walk; get away from walls and ceilings, back out to earth and sky.

Maybe feel some wind on your face . . . some freedom."
He spoke quickly, in a highly animated, almost agitated
voice.

"What things?" she asked.

"It's just impossible for me to stay indoors right now,"
he said, ignoring her question, looking up into the soft
rain for a moment.

"Why?"

"When I rode out of here the other night, well, the first
day was all right. I avoided people. I stayed to the back
roads. Didn't eat anything at all; wasn't hungry for it,
either. As a matter of fact, I felt fine. Those keen little
teeth of hunger going round and round at my insides felt
just right. A man has no right having an appetite so soon
after killing his best friend, does he?" He forced a short
grunt of false laughter. "Then the next day, the next day,
you see, I was good and hungry. I had slept under the
stars for a second night in a row and I was good and
hungry. Virtuously hungry, you might say, having served
a certain amount of penance. The empty stomach, you see,
countervails the lowering conscience. The empty stomach
is a most potent pouch—greater and more pious in its
commands than any juridical edict or Biblical injunction."

"What are you talking about?" she asked.

"Let me talk, please," he said quickly, without change
of tone, raising his hand. "I have to talk when I feel this
thing. So I rose from my bed of grass and swung myself
upon the horse and said aloud, 'By God, I'm going to stuff
myself with food and then ply myself with whiskey until
I swoon off.' That's what I decided—to get heroically
drunk and then profoundly asleep and let the decision be
made in my absence. You can feel it, you know, when some
critical decision is being made about you, when the gods
are about to give your wheel another spin. It's best not to
sweat through it minute by minute, but to wake up to it
and get about the job of obeying. So I rode into a town
out on the island and some little boys playing in the road

stopped their activity and stared at me just as impertinently as only little boys know how, with all of their innocent indifference—or is it sophisticated contempt?—to civil behavior. My God, I thought, how do they know? I wondered if maybe there was blood on my face—I hadn't seen my face for quite awhile. Little boys are menacingly sensitive creatures, you know; untried in the world, they're still so finely attuned that they can pick up the scent of danger the way a deer can. It's a pity those senses become eroded and jaded as life goes on. Think what a pleasurable world it would be if only we were all capable of picking up the scent of danger and able to sidestep it.

"So I wondered what it was these boys were perceiving of me. The little bastards never took their eyes off me as I dismounted in front of the restaurant. They *can't* know anything about me, I told myself; but they *can* scent the danger. For a moment I actually stood there with the reins in my hand, debating whether to tie up and go inside and eat, or mount up and ride away. All this on what I imagined they were thinking. Then I began seeing accusing eyes becoming avenging eyes, and it so infuriated me that I spun around and gave them a look so withering it made them draw back. Then I took my empty stomach into the restaurant.

"I gorged myself. Eggs, bacon, a slice of ham, corn bread, hot coffee. The proprietor sized me up with a single look and after serving me went behind the counter and leaned there and watched me, never saying a word. Then I heard from outside—boy-voices, very excited—'He's in there. That's his horse.' All right, I thought. Something, somebody, is coming through that door. I'll tell you something about raw conscience—it puts you under the conviction that your life is subject to radical change every ten minutes. You simply can't help believing in portents and figments; you mistrust noise and absolutely mistrust silence.

"Do you know what came through that door? Thump-

thump-thump. A one-legged man, with a crutch. A soldier. In his uniform, forage cap and all. I turned around in my chair, put my arm up on the back, and looked at him. Then I looked down at myself, at my own uniform, which I'd forgotten I was wearing. *Ah!* So *that's* what the little boys had seen—not anything but a soldier; not so frequent a sight, I suppose, in this community. So they'd run and told the other soldier in town, and he'd come bounding along on his crutch, along with that swinging stump which had made him for the time being the town hero and celebrity. He was no older than I, though he looked ten years my senior—pain leaves behind a rugged landscape on the human face. But when he sat down and stood that crutch upright and tilted against the chair, what boy there was left in him became illuminated, because, you see, he had a peer to adventure with, just like Ryler and me could have always been boys again unto and beyond wrinkles and white hair and doddering steps just by the magic of a finger-snap, because we had shared it, you see, passed the elixir back and forth until we'd drenched some patch of soul with it forever—forever, forever, no matter how arid we turned. So here was this boy now, with his one leg, exulting because he'd found himself a kindred spirit, somebody else encased in that uniform he himself had worn through peaceable afternoons and bloody battles, as if the uniform of itself made us all of the same stock and subjects of the same ritual. He'd been at Antietam, he said. His last stop, he said; that's where he lost his leg. So we spoke of Antietam. Remember the cornfield and the Dunker church and the sunken road? Did I ever, I said. Oh yes. What a frolic, I said. What a frolic, said he with a forced little laugh. Frolic indeed. By God. His eyes fairly glowed at the memory. We told our tales. Competing back and forth, while those little boys stood in a silent semicircle, at an awestruck and respectful distance of course, each one doubtless damning the ill fortune that had so far cursed them with two legs and unshed blood. He was the grand winner, naturally, because he had lost his leg, while all I could call forth was a rebel shell at Gettysburg that had split its bowels too close to me. I tried to counter the impossible glory of his lost leg with sumptuous descriptions of places the poor fellow had never been privileged to visit—like Fredericksburg and Gettysburg. But he would not be outmatched, this fellow. Had I been at Brannon Station? No, I said. By God, then I'd missed something, he said. I had really and truly missed something. Had I at least heard about Brannon Station? he asked. No, I said. Well, he said, it was a fair stand-up fight, with us on one side of the field and the rebs on the other. Just shooting away at each other like gentlemen, with some artillery mouthing off from behind the lines. Then a shell flew on an errant course and blew out one wall of this big white building that was off to a side. Did I know what that building was? No, I said. A lunatic asylum, he said. A lunatic asylum? I asked. By Jesus, he said, did they come pouring right out of it. A hundred of them at least, yelling and screaming and cackling like chickens and gobbling like turkeys, wearing these long white gowns, he said. Running in every conceivable direction, with their unearthly noises, with their fingers jammed into their mouths, with their hair flying, with their eyes aglitter like mica in the moonlight. Some of them ran into the woods, and some were so bereft of their senses that they ran right across a field where two formations of infantry were dueling away at each other, and you should have seen some of the bedlamites get shot and go flying. Some were not so mad, of course; these, he said, got down on their knees and clasped their hands and prayed, or fell down and covered their heads. And there were two, he said, who locked hands and began dancing round and round, their nightshirts flying and flashing over their bony legs. A lot of them, he said, came running straight into the lines of infantry, absolutely maddened—made even worse, he said—by the firing, their faces glaring with terror, shouting for God and Jesus

Christ, although, as my one-legged friend said, those worthies had been being beseeched by the wounded all afternoon and not yet made an appearance. He was more afraid of the bedlamites, he said, than ever of any reb, because they put the chill on his blood as the rebs never could. He didn't know human beings could be like that, and seeing them mixing in with the everyday good fellow was a purely terrifying experience. He said he was more of a mind to shoot them, because he was so scared of them, rather than the rebels. He said he'd rather give up his other leg than go through another such experience, and that by God for the next seven nights he was afraid to go to sleep because he'd find himself dreaming of spiders and lizards and snakes and worms and all manner of foul and disgusting things, dreams incurred by the sight of what was more than animal but less than human. You never heard about it? he asked. No sir, I said, I never heard of an asylum wall being blown open and all those shrieking lunatics running out in their nightshirts with their fingers in their mouths and their eyes glittering. And he sweared to God that a lot of the boys were shooting at the bedlamites and swatting them with rifle butts because they were more terrified of them than of the rebs."

They stopped walking when they reached the woods. He turned to her and she put her arms around him.

"Why do you talk about it so?" she asked. "You weren't there to see it."

"It haunts me."

"Then write it," she said.

"Write it?"

"It wants to be written, if it's crowding you so."

He stared moodily at her for several moments, then they walked again through the softly swirling rain, back toward the house now, carefully over the gray-splashed field rocks.

"Were you badly wounded?" she asked.

"It wasn't too bad. A piece of shrapnel took me in the back, and another struck me in the head. Since that time though," he said, lowering his voice, "I've had some strange feelings . . . headaches, nightmares . . . things like that. From the shock of that blow, you see. But nothing to worry about, of course."

"I understand," she said. And then, in a quiet, insistent voice, "Write it, Ben. That's what it wants."

"Maybe so. Maybe that's all it wants."

"If you have the power to write, and don't, then what recourse does it have but to continue swirling through your head and blurring everything else? Write it," she said, "and you'll lift it away."

I suppose she's not the one to be afraid of it, he thought. She seemed capable of coping with anything, except perhaps not getting her way. She had a lot of her son of a bitch father in her all right, an awful lot of man poured into that hard-thighed strong-breasted woman's body. She gauged him carefully—it had taken him just a few days to take note of that. When he was angry, she was contrite; when he was turbulent, she was tranquil; when he was unsure, she became decisive; when he brooded, she was observant. He knew her strength and her vigor, and so he marveled at how deftly she could manipulate herself in deference to him. But he should not have been surprised; after all, this was a woman tough enough to witness a murder and then by herself dispose of the body (he dared not ask how, where), with what seemed complete efficiency, and then appear to seal off the episode from further thought.

Write it. That was her unvarying uncompromising prescription for whatever disturbed him. She thinks every knock inside my head and every sheet of turmoil is a poem trying to get free. As if madness was that; as if poetry was that. *Write it.* And often when he did he was able to make some sense of the chaos, divert its distortions into lines of metric beauty, and he would feel the tension that had been building begin to ease. Maybe there was some logic to it after all, he thought. If the ferment and convulsion of battle could bring order to the mind of Malloy, why not the probing, unveiling subtleties of poetry for his own? Looking back, those poems had been a source of consolation and tranquility during some bad times, each one a transporting experience that had lifted him high enough above the crowns of trees to enable his aspirations to soar without limit. Thunder for Malloy; for me, this. To each man his own God, and to each the solvent of his own distress.

The view from his upstairs writing room (so arranged and so designated by Eva) was the fields behind the house, out to the ring of trees that defined the limits of the LeGrange property. He could sit for days and not see another soul. Beyond the trees lay the woodland where he and Ryler and Susan had spun to life their innocent enchantments; he would gaze out toward it as wistful as though it were a picture on the flat page, dimensionless and inaccessible. But when at last he picked up his quill and lowered his head and wrote, it all dissolved—fields, and trees and woodland and even the bittersweet queries of held memories—as he cocooned himself in rhythmic discovery and the lines began reaching across the page. When he looked up again it might be all gone, the autumnal browning gone under night's cover, and a slow, throbbing headache beginning, striking at his brain in iambic pulse beats which grew to feel like tiny silver hammers tapping upon bone. He would knot together his fingers and raise his clasped hands and slowly bring them down upon his head as if to press into stillness those ancestral echoes *Leave me alone I'm not doing anything,* but most of the time unable to, imagining slow, chortling figures performing grotesque quadrilles around and around his head, bumping at the walls of his skull, trying to get out and seize his arms and legs and put their fingers in his mouth and spin him and spin him madly about until he became helplessly part of the dance, his nightshirt twisting around his fetid body, and now and then in the whirling, smoking background Malloy's shouting face would appear among the gun flashes, calling him to come over there among the bayonets and the artillery and the blood and the legless torsos, where it was safe; but then Malloy was spinning too, round and round in the same place, as if being whirled about on a smoking spit, and then abruptly he was still, *Killed by his own salvation:* and then one afternoon as he was watching the roof-shadow press the sunlight back across the brown grass like an advancing waterline, the spear came at him, shattering the glass and throwing him out of his chair to the floor, and he heard her running up the stairs. A spear flew at me through the window, he told her, crouched now, pressing himself protectively against the desk. A spear? she asked incredulously, looking at the window. From out of the Crusades, he said. It came all the way from the twelfth century and would have hit me between the eyes if they hadn't swung my shoulders around and saved me. They? she asked. He looked around the room. The stillness suddenly became oppressive. Oh, he murmured. I see.

Sixteen

AT THE END OF October Eva told him there were now enough poems to make a collection. He showed little interest in the project.

"I approve of your attitude," she said; "let the enthusiasm come from others."

"It's not a pose, I assure you," he said. "They've tired me out and I don't want to think about them anymore."

"I don't want you to either. I want you to think ahead to others."

"Others?" he asked quizzically.

"Of course," she said. "You've only just begun, Ben."

The following day they rode in her chaise down to the ferry. She planned to be in Manhattan for two days, and though she would be spending most of her time shopping, the primary reason for her trip was delivery of his manuscript to a publisher. When he chided her about its acceptability, she told him that she had weeks ago made copies of a dozen of the poems and sent them to the publisher for an opinion. The response, she told him rather smugly, had been high praise and a request to see more, with a view toward book publication. Are you pleased? she asked. I suppose I am, he conceded. You may even become famous, she said with a teasing laugh. Certainly the crudest form of dissection, he said.

As the side-wheeled ferry began to roil the waters in preparation for departure, she asked him again if he would not accompany her.

"No," he said, glancing across the river at the spires of New York.

"All right," she said. "I want you to relax for the next two days. Give your mind some ease."

He kissed her, helped her aboard the ferry, then returned to the chaise and headed back to Capstone.

"How do I look to you, Hook?" Ben asked. "What do you see?"

"Some weariness, more tension," Hook said.

They were sitting in rocking chairs, facing a low fire, each puffing at his pipe.

"How long will she be gone did you say?" Hook asked.

"Two days. And I'll tell you, I can't stay in that house alone."

"Lonely?"

"Uncomfortable."

"Is it any better with her in it?"

Ben pondered for a moment. "Everything is given a different quality," he said.

"Hers."

"Mostly."

"That's quite a choice carving of woman, isn't it? Or am I thought beyond such considerations?" Hook asked with a note of whimsy.

"I think you should be above them, Mr. Hook."

"Don't be impertinent, boy. But I'll tell you a secret: when I was younger, that was my kind of woman. Arrogant and haughty. You have to admire them. Nothing intimidates them. I can see her equally letting a drop of perfume into her bodice or sitting behind a gatling gun. A marble pillar in the wind. But not designed to be the comfort of any man's old age. But by God, I'll bet she's a spur to manhood."

Ben looked at him with amused curiosity. "Details, Mr. Hook?" he asked, feigned archness in his voice.

"Hardly, boy, hardly. I've catalogued too many to believe in the possibility of fresh news." The older man removed his pipe and jabbed the stem toward the low, quietly burning fire. "As you see, the fires of late autumn burn very close to the bone. But Eva LeGrange now," he said with a malevolent grunt. "If I had a handful of gunpowder I could show you what I mean."

"You know, when I think of you sitting here alone, it's a portrait of a man pondering the classics."

Hook turned to him with a most genial smile. "You see you've been right all along," he said.

They looked at each other and exchanged a pair of shoulder-shaking chuckles.

"And so," Ben said, "the enigmatic Mr. Hook emerges from behind the falling of yet another veil."

"Listen, don't ever get into the trap of forgetting that an old man was once just as young as yourself. That's a valuable piece of advice I'm giving you. Give an old man respect and nothing else and you're insulting him. Particularly when it comes to considerations of the enjoyment of women. Why do you think I stayed away from here for so many years?"

"You were having too good a time to come back."

"Now you have it," Hook said with satisfaction. "Or part of it, anyway. When I read about those young Pony Express riders they had out West, I said to myself, 'That's it—one fast rider for many fast horses.' "

"I see," Ben said with a smile. "All right. From now on I'll treat you as an equal."

He got up and stoked the fire, then added two small logs. For several moments he remained crouched in front of the fire, feeling its murmurous warmth upon his face.

"I had a most unique experience recently," he said, opening his hands to the fire. "A spear came at me, hurled from out of the Crusades. It shattered a window that remained intact and caused me to fall to the floor. Quite a throw, eh, Mr. Hook—to keep it in flight for six or seven hundred years? Whenever something like that happens, she says, 'Write it. Write it, Ben, take command of it, refine it, purify it, impale it with your quill and hold it in place forever.' "

"She says this to you?" Hook asked, holding his pipe in his mouth, watching Ben crouched before the fire.

"Enough times to be carrying a sheaf of poems with her to New York, to hand to a publisher."

"You've been at poetry?"

"Very steadily," Ben said, turning away from the fire and resuming his seat in the rocker. He struck a match and relit his pipe. "This woman," he said waving out the match, "seems to want to harness every energy to poetry. In some ways it's been helpful, but in other ways it seems to provoke certain things and compel their protraction and vividness. 'Write it,' she says. Well, lady, in order to write it you have to make it stand still in your head for hours and hours, keep looking at it, keep feeling it."

"That isn't good, Ben," Hook said quietly.

"Sometimes I'm unable to differentiate between what may be rhapsody and what may be . . . a disturbance."

"Like spears flying out of the Crusades?"

"That was pure terror," Ben said. "Even as I watched it come rushing toward me, one corner of my mind knew better."

"Keep that corner uncluttered," Hook murmured. "Listen, this woman may have an awful lot of determination to do what she thinks is right, but she may in good faith be cultivating and sanctioning things that are best let alone."

"It's strange, Hook, very strange. Sometimes, in the writing, I have such a soothing sense of depth and distance.

I catch currents that may move fast and turbulently, but at least are clear and symmetrical. Others, however, may begin that way and then suddenly dive into a vortex. But how in hell do you tell the difference between gusts of imagination and gabbling chaos? By trying to gratify one you make yourself vulnerable to the other."

"Promethean fires or the devil's furnace," Hook said. "Heat is heat. You may be indulging the very thing you ought to be standing vigilant against. Your father fancied himself a poet, you know."

"He did?" Ben asked, jarred by mention of his father.

"He showed me some of his poems one night. Each was a complete muddle, but within each was an occasional line or phrase of such luminosity as to be startling. I don't know what he was experiencing when he wrote them. Knowing him, he probably tried to write them when he was disturbed. Leave it to him to try and make spiritual wisdom out of his abyss. He told me once that it was when men were at their most abject that the opportunity for ennoblement was ripest. That's utter nonsense, of course—unless you believe it. Goddamn, once you believe something, you've manufactured a slice of truth, yours or somebody else's. God knows how far it goes, how it modifies, how it ever stops being truth."

"Do you think I should put a stop to the writing?"

"I don't know, Ben," Hook said. "How can I answer that? How strong is the urge, how independent the impulse? The only reason I told you anything in the first place was to put you on your guard, to enhance your powers of mind, not diminish or confuse them."

"I daresay the telling had a dual reason; you wouldn't have imparted any of it if you hadn't seen something that caused you concern."

"Not entirely," Hook said. "It was more that you were entitled to the telling. Unquestionably it was going to be unsettling; but if I didn't think you could cope, I would have remained silent."

"And now?"

"Well, now you have this woman stirring the brew. God knows what sediment she might bring to the surface. Is she the type to accept resistance? I don't think so. It seems to me there are too many conflicts and too much strength there. I don't like it."

They sat quietly for several minutes, rocking soundlessly back and forth, smoking, watching the fire. And then, from out of a very profound depth, Hook said, "All right. Where is he?"

"He's dead," Ben said.

Hook stopped rocking. "The night you came home?"

"Yes," Ben said, not missing a beat in his chair. "It was unintentional."

"Who knows about it?"

"Only those who were there—Eva and me."

"She was there? Jesus, along with your other virtues she smells blood on you. She'll never let you go, boy."

Seventeen

AS I HAD BEEN doing for several weeks now, I got out of bed immediately upon opening my eyes, put on my robe and went outside. Each morning it was the same—the compulsion to get into daylight as quickly as I could and see if anyone had been there during the night. Why anyone should have been, or what I expected to find if they had—what note, what carving, what symbol—I couldn't say. So again this morning I got out of bed, put on my robe, walked through the chilly house and unlatched the door. I stepped outside, closing the robe at my throat against the cold, and walked along the crushed-rock path that Ryler had imbedded during the summer. I went as far as the front gate and then turned around and looked at the house. It was as unchanged as ever, with its pitched roof, white curtains over the four-squared windows, the hawthorn bushes quivering in the cold wind.

I turned at the sound of an approaching wagon. It was a farmer, with a load of hay. He removed his pipe from his mouth and said, "Morning, Miss Gibson." I smiled at him. Here I was, Mrs. Ryler Stevenson for so many months and still seen as Miss Gibson by my neighbors. Well, I thought, he was probably closer to the mark than I wanted to admit.

A strong north wind was blowing, throwing the dead leaves against the sky in sudden, gusty scatterings and sweeping them out of the woods and up against the stone wall on the other side of the road. Summer was long gone now, and gone too was that special brightness that sharpened the colors of autumn, replaced by a gray-feeling harbinger chill.

I was about to return to the house when a final look along the curving road showed me Ben. He was walking slowly. He was hatless, head bent, shoulders pressed forward into the wind, hands in the pockets of his coat. He was coming here; he knew the roads too well to pass my house in an idle walk. Yet again, I thought. Yet again. God, how many times had my heart rushed at the sight of him? Those arrivals, those departures; so often abrupt, troubled, mysterious. And here he was again, swung in this direction once more.

He raised his head and when he saw me he paused for a moment, some several hundred feet away. Then he surprised me by calling out my name and waving, as if he thought perhaps I had not recognized him. When he began walking again, it was quickly.

I stood at the front gate, one hand still at my throat holding shut the robe.

"It's as if you've been waiting for me," he said as he came up.

"Yes, Ben," I said. "I've been standing here for five weeks."

He seemed a bit dismayed by the coolness in my voice. He stopped on the other side of the gate, looking at me, as if unsure what to do.

"She's let you out, has she?" I said.

He didn't respond to that either. For a moment I thought—without conviction, admittedly—of not allowing him any further. It was a very sensible impulse, I felt: if

I continued to make it easy for him, he would never cease making it difficult for me. But even if I had been firm about it, I couldn't have done it, because this time I sensed in him a fairly palpable need, an appeal, almost a submissiveness.

"I would like to talk to you," he said. And a moment later, without giving me a chance to respond, he said, looking directly at me, "Ryler is dead."

I suddenly realized that I had known it even before he said it, that sometime during the past few weeks what had been a lingering suspicion had gradually come in out of the dark, that I had been acknowledging my unsummoned intuitions of fear and dread. Hearing it spoken, though, hearing the pronouncement, was horrible, another component of death's cold ceremony, adjunct to illness and suffering and burial and grieving. The abrupt numbing enabled us to take the sharpest shocks without a quiver. Or maybe because it was Ben who was saying it to me, because of that instinctive solicitude which will not permit a display of grief before those we dearly love, for fear of adding to their unhappiness.

We went inside and sat at the kitchen table, across from each other. His face was filled with forewarning. *Notice of this death,* I thought, *is only a half-told tale.* He was now grappling with the rest of it. I wondered what I could do to make it easy for him; and then I realized that that would have to come later; right now he wanted and needed the pain, the suffering, that he had fervent need to relinquish a burden and that part of the subsequent alleviation was this grueling passage. I had to keep my hands folded tightly in my lap to keep from reaching out to him. As he continued staring at me, his face grew very pale and I began to feel as though through my silence I was causing him deeper distress, that I had at my command the power to help but was withholding it. And then as the terror began mounting in my heart, I realized it was for my own sake that I had to say something, that adding his measure of suffering to my own full share was becoming unbearable.

"Talk about it," I said, "I want to know."

"It was an accident," he said quietly. with difficulty. "So many things happened at once. It was all moving so fast . . . with so much agitation. And then he told me he had married you. That was why he marked me dead . . . because he loved you."

For that last I was totally unprepared. What small defenses I had been building—Ryler had been unfaithful, had been contemptuous, he had been this and he had been that—suddenly crumbled. *Because he loved you.* At first I thought how cruel it was to be told that, and then I realized how badly he needed to say it, and say it first, before anything else, that he had to be brutally unsparing, diminishing nothing, asking for nothing, accepting everything in its most awful and glaring light. He would *not* spare himself, nor would he allow me any false props with which to do it.

He got to his feet. Fearing it might be his intention to leave, I rose also and went to him. Again I found myself suppressing impulses—this time to throw my arms around him; he was in too deep a state of suffering; it was so clearly etched in his face. I stood near him, then followed him as he walked to the window and stared out into the distance as intensely as though trying to wish himself far away, into some fresh and unremembering realm. Finally the pain in his face grew too much for me to bear and I threw my arms around him. He looked at me strangely.

"I don't think you understand," he said.

"I do," I said. "More than you think."

"Did you hear everything I said?"

"Yes."

"And you know what I did?"

"I heard what you said, and I say, no, no, you couldn't have done it."

"What do you mean?" he demanded, fro.ming.

"I mean it couldn't have been *you*."

"No? Who then?" he asked, as if disturbed by some cutting inference.

"You said it was an accident . . . you didn't want it to happen . . . you didn't do it."

"Who else then?" he asked, seemingly caught up by something, demanding an answer. "Why are you saying that?"

"Because it wasn't in your heart to do it. Because . . . I don't know . . . I don't know," I whispered, beginning to cry, beginning to feel a terrible helplessness.

He put his arms around me, one hand resting gently at my nape.

"Will you help me?" he asked.

"Stay here. Don't ever leave again. Promise me."

"But will you help me?"

"Why do you ask foolish questions?"

"But you don't understand everything."

"People don't have to understand everything," I said, counting on the love I felt, the years of it, the depths of it; counting on its might, its endurance, the way some people draw strength from their piety, their faith, who live inside the compensations of their devotion. What I did not understand I would love, and what I loved I would understand.

"I killed Ryler," he said.

"Why do you keep saying it? Why are you torturing yourself?"

"Did you love him?"

"Ben, please . . . "

"Did you?"

"I tried to help him, Ben. He was trying to be so many things he couldn't. After you left he just didn't know what to do with himself. He wasn't bad. He really wasn't. You know that."

"I know that."

"We'll go away from here," I said. "I've got some money

wrapped up in the quilt. We'll take it and go wherever we want. We don't have to stay here."

He looked at me with a condescending smile. "Won't you be afraid?" he asked.

"No," I said. "I won't be afraid."

"Maybe I'm not in the mood for traveling just now."

"But . . . "

"How can I stay here after what's happened?" he asked, giving voice to my thought. "Well, as you say, it couldn't have been me. And if that's so, then no amount of running, no distance, is going to set it right."

I didn't know what he meant, nor did I care. He was there, our arms were around each other, and that was all that mattered.

He stayed for four days, days that were for me a mix of the most pathetic joy and the most ineffable tension. Much of the time he was very quiet. I tried to be as circumspect as possible, moving about as softly as I could. Now and then I stole a glance and found him watching me, a sad smile on his face. Then he would look away again, at the window or into the fire or just nowhere, into thin air, and I would continue watching him for as long as the smile remained, which was never very long, just a few seconds, before it was replaced by a poignant sadness. I made a few attempts at conversation, only to hear my words trailing off into nothingness as he made no effort to reply; in fact, I couldn't be sure he had even heard me.

In the afternoon we would lie in bed together. His bursts of passion were sudden, fitful, soon begun and soon completed. The nights were the worst for me; I was afraid to sleep, lest I waken in the morning and find him gone. The first night he would not lie in bed with me, preferring to sit in a chair. I lay awake for as long as I could, watching him, his merest gesture frightening me into thinking he was about to get up and leave. The second night he got into bed with me and I fell asleep in his arms, but when

I opened my eyes in the morning he was sitting in the chair, fully dressed, smoking his pipe, staring dreamily into space.

On the third day he began taking full meals—hitherto he had only been nibbling now and then. Again we talked about going away. Though he was not very responsive, I could tell he was thinking about it, at least considering the possibility. I guess he was trying to come together with his conscience. He knew he couldn't run away from it, but at least he could get away from all those old familiar places that could so readily and unexpectedly trigger it. There was hardly a square foot anywhere in Capstone that didn't have something to do with Ryler. I felt all I had to do was wait, that he would soon come to the conclusion that remaining in Capstone was impossible.

My father came by that afternoon and they sat and talked for a little while. My father started talking about Ryler and I watched Ben's face to see how he might react, but he never moved a muscle. "Nobody's seen the son of a bitch for weeks and weeks," my father said. "The talk is he's joined up." Ben nodded. "Yes," he said mildly, "I should think that's what he's done." "A little taste of it might square him out," my father said; "but you'd of thought he'd at least tell his wife." "That's right," Ben said. "Frankly," my father said with a glance at me, "I don't care if the son of a bitch never shows up."

It was on the third night that we heard the horse. It began at about eleven o'clock. We were sitting in front of the fire. I was worn out from fighting off sleep—I just didn't feel comfortable going to bed before he did, and Lord, I was getting to believe he never slept. He was slouched in his chair, legs straight out in front of him, hands folded in his lap, his eyes fixed upon that fire as though the flames were painting a portrait. Suddenly we heard a horse come galloping along the road at great speed, its hoofs pounding like so many cloth-covered hammers. At that hour it was a strange and unnerving sound.

A little while later we heard it coming back, a swift, rhythmic sound, racing across the stillness. We listened to it pass the front gate and go off into the night. His eyes shifted to me, but he said nothing. About fifteen minutes later it came again—we could hear it approaching in the distance, soft and eerie, listened to it grow louder and louder until it passed again with that strange, unreasoning speed, and again we listened to the hoofbeats go cluttering off into silence. It came once more, some minutes later, and this last time the galloping seemed faster and more frenzied. As it faded with hurried diminishing softness, he said, "She's going to wear that horse out." "Who?" I said. "Who is it?" "It's her," he said.

The following afternoon, the fourth day, he left the house for the first time. He didn't go far, just out into the open field adjacent to the house, where the tall grass had turned a sickly-looking brown. I watched him from the bedroom window for several minutes, then threw a shawl around my shoulders and followed him.

There was a long, upward tilt to the ground here, to where it crested in an almost straight line against the sky, treeless, the symmetry broken only by a few swellings of rock. He looked quite solitary as he walked through the knee-high grass. Then he stopped midway in the field and took what seemed a deeply absorbing look around. Some forty or fifty feet behind, I stopped also—it was as though we were both animated by the same gears—and watched him. He was turned in profile to me, so profoundly in thought he didn't appear to be aware of me. So I saw it first, the slow looming of rider and horse coming over the crest from the other side of the field, rising with a motionlessness that suggested levitation. They kept rising until they had assumed enormous size (to my eye, anyway) and portent against the pale, empty sky. She was wearing a long gray cloak, the hood thrown back. She remained there for perhaps a full minute, absolutely still, her head slightly raised, staring imperiously at him like some imminent conqueror. He for the moment did not see her, was probably not seeing anything beyond what the pained constrictions of his thoughts and feelings would allow. Then she moved her head slightly to look at me; I stared back as resolutely as I could, even as I felt my resolve eroding under a growing sense of powerlessness, of irresistible threat. I began feeling smaller and smaller standing there opposed by the high ground and the broad backdrop of sky, each of which she seemed to have taken command of. And then with a quick, wrathful gesture she swung her horse about. The motion caught Ben's eye and he looked around and saw her. She glanced over her shoulder at him as the horse began moving down the other side of the crest. I saw her lift her hand and with her crop strike the horse as she disappeared from view.

That night there was no moon and a strong wind was blowing in willfull, intermittent surges, occasionally throwing a dead leaf against the window. It sounded like a trumpeting of the changing season, of winter's white stormy prodigality beginning to labor into being. Vivid autumn was passing into the same shades as caressing summer, driven by the gathering robes of that wind.

It was after ten o'clock and I began urging him to go to sleep. It was more for myself than for him that I was pressing; these nights of restless and sporadic sleeping were beginning to drain me

"Please, Ben," I said.

"Soon," he said.

He was fixed in his by now accustomed place, in a chair before the fire, his eyes watching the animate flames with lethargic disinterest. He had spoken very little since seeing Eva that afternoon. By the time we returned to the house, my sense of fear had been kindled into anger. What was she doing there? I demanded. He shrugged. I wouldn't have it, I told him, wouldn't have her around. If she came near again I would take a rifle to her. He smiled weakly at that, with a kind of indulgence that made me even angrier. I banged the pots and pans about at dinner, then went into my own sulky silence. Now and then I caught him looking at me with a searching interest that made me uneasy and caused me to turn away. It was hard, so hard, to be consumed by so many burning things and unable to release them into conversation. I wanted to know what he was thinking, what he was feeling—about Ryler, about Eva, about us, about the route that lay ahead and the decisions that had to be made. All I knew was my Ben, that unfathomable well of dark unreflecting water; instead of being clarified by my love, he was becoming less and less evident to me.

"Come to bed," I said.

"Soon," he murmured.

I was about to rise and go to the kitchen when a strong gust of wind rose up from out of the night and cast some leaf or other object against the window and caused a faint scratching noise. He suddenly whirled around to the window; his eyes dilated for a moment and then opened widely and he uttered a ghastly cry that sounded as though it were strangling him. He leaped to his feet with such violence the chair tumbled over behind him. He remained poised for a moment, arms partially raised, glaring at the window, motionless but so alive with seething turbulence that I was terrified.

"What is it?" I asked, watching him, appalled by the glitter in his eyes. "Ben, what is it?" I asked, in a sudden grip of fright and bewilderment; but even as the words fell from my lips he was in sudden frenzied motion across the room, toward the window. Violently he heaved it open and leaned outside as the wind tossed the curtains around him.

"Ryler!" he yelled outside.

"Ryler?" I asked, getting to my feet, feeling an emotion against my face like a shock wave.

Then he was running from the window, his hands doubling into fists, an expression in his face of enraged fear.

Never had I seen him so possessed; reasonlessly, sense-lessly, he had erupted and in this one mighty upheaval gone beyond the flood mark of all previous passion. He ran to the front door, threw it open and rushed outside. A moment later I heard him calling the name again—the name of one supposedly dead, being beseeched with full expectation of response by his confessed killer. I looked at the open window and the blowing curtains, then at the open door—two sudden dark windy gaps in my house. *Dear God,* I thought as I forced myself toward the door, *what is it?* I went with an almost overwhelming feeling of despair, as though beginning some interminable and hope-less journey.

"Ben!" I yelled, going out into the dark, noisy night. The wind was throwing the forsythia against the front windows.

He came running from around the side of the house, his face utterly distraught. He came up to me; his lips parted and I thought he was going to speak. I clasped my hands against my mouth, dreading what he might say . . . but he didn't say anything, or couldn't. He only stared at me with wildly excited eyes, then turned around and began running again, to the front gate which he threw back with a reckless gesture, and then into the road. I ran to the gate and leaned on it with both hands and cried after him, sending his name off into the flying, twisting winds.

Eighteen

FOR THAT FIRST SPLIT second he had been startled because he thought it was the moon dropped from the sky and hanging at the window and in spite of its astonishing nearness still no larger than a skull; but then he realized it was not a phenomenally fallen moon but a human face in phosphorescent glow, with merry eyes and lugubrious smile, the features taking shape slowly and familiarly as if rising from under fathoms of clearing water.

So now he would find out, once and for all. That cold apparition or hallucination or actual physical presence or whatever it had been had thrust upon him the sudden opportunity for discovery, revelation; enabling him to at last take hold of his yearning soul and perceive clearly the quality of its nature. *This will tell me,* he thought as he continued to run with full speed along the dark road, with determined, conscious effort holding in mind Ryler's floating white face as vividly as he could, maintaining it in focus with near reverence for its evidential significance, for its every bizarre detail. If he is not dead, he thought, then she's tricked me and has been trying to snatch up my reason for whatever her cause; and if he is dead . . . if he is dead . . . then I had better throw a silken yoke of prudence and control about my neck and seek a hand and a light to lead me through my days: because it would mean that all of his sires were alive in him, feeding upon every drawn breath, mingling at the center of every thought, part of the weight which guided direction.

Nearing her house, he stopped to gasp for breath, falling to one knee in the middle of the road and covering his eyes with his hand, looking for a moment like a man exhausted from passionate supplication. *Endure your suffering nobly and you'll free at last all secrets, unmask all deceptions, disarm all untruths.* Soon, he told himself. Within the frame of this night. He found the prospect not intimidating but bitterly pleasing; he had wrenched free of alien control something that was rightfully his. He got to his feet and began moving, walking now, rapidly, lifting his face to the casting wind which was swift across the dark meadows and pastures and softly active in the woods.

Dark, he thought when he saw the house looming out of the night. Unaccountably, this seemed to confirm something in his teeming mind. It was likely that they were in there, somewhere in those dark rooms among the incongruous mix of elegant and execrable furniture, crouched in a corner or stretched upon a bed, laughing at him, chortling at this devilish new trick with which they had victimized him: *first mark him dead, then steal his woman, then pretend you're dead; see what he does, watch him run, watch him come flying out of the side of the building with his fingers in his mouth.* But it's all right, he thought. It's all right. All I want is one brief glimpse of him, only that, and they will have stolen nothing from me but given me more than they can ever imagine. If he's there, Ben thought, then I'll bless him for it, not for being alive but for being not dead. That's all I'll want to know, and then they can run their track all the way to hell's mercy.

He went up onto the portico and tried the door. It was locked. He ran back down the steps and picked up a rock.

Moving toward a downstairs window, he reached back and hurled the rock through the glass. Then he hurried forward, reached inside and turned the lock just as the dog began to bark—the noise, begun and maintained at loud, harsh, angry pitch, seemed to be coming from every corner of the house. He raised the window and climbed inside, sliding from the sill and landing on the grinding shards of glass. *"Who is it?"* he heard her call from upstairs as the barking came nearer, became more concentrated, direct; a moment later he heard the running paws flicking on the entranceway's marble floor. Familiar with the room, he rushed to the fireplace, fumbled in the dark for a moment until he touched and then wrapped his fingers around a poker, just as the dog came running into the room with furious, outraged barking. In the darkness he saw it come soaring over the back of a sofa, an opaline light flashing through its eyes. He set his legs and swung the poker back over his shoulder with both hands, remained poised for a moment, waited for the dog to strike the floor, waited for it to come up again on the bound and then whipped the lightweight poker through the air and made solid contact on the dog's skull; a split second later the dog's flying weight hurled into him with snapping teeth and reeking breath, knocking him back against the wall. Staggered, he regained his balance as the dog dropped to the floor. He moved away from the wall, gripping the poker. The dog growled sullenly, then he heard it thrashing on the floor and he knew it was up again. He backed away, raising the poker, not as far back now, holding it almost vertically, prepared for a tighter arc of descent. The dog made its second leap, this time with failing strength. He brought the poker down with all his might, not so much in fear or anger as with irritability, wanting to be done with it. He felt the iron make full shocking impact against bone and again the dog collapsed, this time without touching him. The animal lay still, uttering whimpering noises. He dropped the poker clanging on the hearthstone and ran from the room, toward the stairs. He could see a pale light along the upper wall and he heard her again—she had probably been saying it the whole time—*"Who is it? Who is it?"* Not a thread of fear in her voice, he thought as he ran up the stairs two at a time, but imperious anger and indignation. When he reached the head of the stairs and spun around into the corridor, he saw her standing there behind the pale yellow lamp, in her nightgown, her long hair braided, and again not fear in her palely lighted face but that regal anger inherent to arrogance and command. She was holding a pistol, pointing it at him.

"Where is he?" he demanded, coming toward her.

"What do you want?" she asked coldly. "What are you talking about?"

"I want to see him," he said, stopping a few feet from her. He was panting.

"Want to see whom?"

"Ryler. Where is he?"

She stared incredulously at him. She was not unfamiliar with the tempests within him, with their passionate, head-long rush. But this she found incomprehensible. The pistol seemed to mean nothing—if he had even noticed it.

"Ryler is dead," she said.

"Where is he?"

"He is dead," she said icily, enunciating each word as if with the ends of her teeth.

"No," he said shaking his head. "I saw him tonight, as clearly as I see you now."

"You saw him—?"

"Where is he?"

She said nothing, remained severely composed, holding steady the bell-shaped lamp with its thin, ghostly light, and the pistol which he still had not seen or else did not care about.

He took a step forward, and when he spoke his voice was pent, unappeasable. "I saw him."

"You could not have," she said, then caught several short, tense breaths, watching him uncertainly.

Now he came forward again, reached out and took hold of her arm, passing his fingers over the hand that held the pistol to do so, so that the weapon was now pointing not six inches from his heart, and still he ignored it.

"Where is he?" he asked quietly. "Show him to me."

"You want to see him?"

"Yes."

"Ryler!" she yelled. "Come out!" Then she stared into his eyes, at once sardonic and defiant, even as she felt his fingers tightening upon her arm. He waited, staring back into her eyes with the fullness of the tempest. They waited, motionless, the light rising between them. And then he thought he heard the echo of her voice, the shouted name, coming faintly back at him from all parts of the house; the name of his best friend, whom he had killed or not killed, seen or not seen; the name breathing back at him in soft derision, taunting, reverberate. His eyes moved, began roaming through the dark as if trying to hunt down the echo, as if trying to attune his ears to a sound or to some soundless motion, trying to see or to perceive an expelled breath or the blink of an eye.

A slow, malicious smile curved her lips. "There is no Ryler," she whispered.

He looked back to her with puzzled mistrust, his tightening fingers putting more pressure on her arm.

"Show me there is no Ryler," he said. And then, to her cold insinuations, *Show me!* Angrily he shook her. She pulled away and drew back, and now for the first time he seemed to take notice of the pistol. He looked at it as though it were some ludicrous adjunct to her arm, then stepped forward and contemptuously slapped it from her hand, sending it to the carpeting. "Show me there is no Ryler," he said again.

"What do you want me to show you?"

"Where is he?"

"I buried him, goddammit!" she cried. "For *you!*"

"Then retrieve him," he said bitterly. "For me."

Then they were sitting in her chaise, riding through the night along the empty wind-swept road, past the dark outlying houses, rolling toward the perimeters of Capstone where the woods thickened and went deepest. In the carriage along with its two severely wordless occupants were a kerosene lamp and a shovel, each taken from the shed behind the stable. She was wearing riding breeches and a flannel shirt and the hooded gray cloak she had worn that afternoon when she had appeared on horseback. He was still coatless, hatless, facing into the wind with blowing hair. They rode for nearly a half-hour and then she raised her hand and pointed to a place where the road forked, became less than a road and more than a path, a route into the woods he knew to be narrow, seldom-traveled, that he had taken countless times in **and** out of the timber as a boy. It ran for less than a quarter-mile of irregular ground and then came to a sudden halt, as if whoever had pressed it out in the first place had grown tired or changed his mind, or as if the woods had finally massed against the encroachment and simply risen intractably in the face of its advance and stopped it.

"Here?" he asked, reining in the horse.

"Why are you doing this?" she asked, speaking for the first time since leaving the house.

"Here?" he asked again. "Out here?"

"Ben, I want to go back. Please, let's go back."

He put down the reins and climbed out of the chaise, then reached in behind the seat and pulled out the shovel.

"Light the lamp," he said. Then he turned around and walked a few feet toward the woods, hefting the shovel in one hand. He looked around in the darkness at the small clearing that distended outward from the end of the narrow passage.

"Where?" he asked.

"Will you tell me why you're doing this?" she asked, walking toward him with the lighted lamp.

"Where?" he asked again, peremptorily, not looking at her.

"Ben," she said sharply, "I must know why you're doing this. I want to know what's *happening*."

When he did not answer, merely stood stolid and adamant, she put the lamp and its quivering pale orange light down on the ground and retreated several paces and folded her arms, assuming a stance, an attitude, of her own. "I'm not staying," she said petulantly. But she knew better; she would stay, and not just because he wouldn't care if she did not, not because it was alien to her nature to yield an inch of ground, but because of the near-hypnotic influence of his inflexible resolve to go on with this thing that was at once so outlandish and so infuriating. The wind came up again, running a sound like dissolving foam through the trees, and she felt it as though it were pouring into her a ruthlessness that began hardening her against what it was he had to do and why he had to do it. She continued to watch him standing there in the orange-filtered darkness, the lamp at his feet, the shovel in his hand. She wet her lips, pressing her folded arms more firmly into herself.

"You're standing on him," she said coldly.

His shoulders swung as he looked at her, then swung again as he looked down at the ground. A moment later—and it was to her amazement; she suddenly realized that she had not at bottom been expecting him to actually do it—he stepped back and it seemed almost vengefully thrust the shovel into the ground, drove the scoop down with his foot and then threw aside the first upcast. In utter disbelief she watched as he began working in an increasingly compelled rhythm, driving the shovel into the ground with full weight on the crossbar, dislodging and removing one scoopful of dirt after the other. As she watched she began feeling a torrent of appalling horror as the nightmare of her own macabre hours at this place returned to her.

"Stop it," she said in a hoarse whisper. "What in God's name do you think you're doing? Stop it. I beg you."

He ignored her. He was working at the ground with a smooth, curved-back, rhythmic symmetry that appeared almost self-mesmerizing: the thrust, the bite, the lifting, the hissing of the emptying shovel; and then again, unvaried, imperative. In the thin light she could see the tautly set muscles in his face, the fixed baring of his white teeth.

"What are you going to do?" she demanded. *"Answer me!"* she cried. She went to him and took hold of his arm, breaking for a moment the relentless symmetry. With a gesture more of annoyance than anything else, he threw her off and returned to the digging, to the scrape and the rasp, faster now, frenetic, as if something precious had been lost in the interruption.

"Hold the lamp up," he said.

"Go to hell."

He paused for a moment to catch his breath, panting. He looked out into the surrounding darkness. "In these woods," he murmured.

She put one hand to the side of her head as if to placate a hard throbbing. "Stop it, Ben," she said.

"When I know," he said, looking at her.

"Know what?"

"What's here," he said, lifting the shovel in one hand and striking it against the troubled earth.

"I can *tell* you what's there!"

"No," he said, shaking his head resolutely. "You can tell me if there's a God . . . or why the stars are . . . or the color of the wind."

"What's making you do this? I want to know. I demand you tell me. What did she say to you? What? What went on there? Why did you go back to her? What made you do that?"

He began digging again, making no answer. For a few

moments she watched the rise and fall of the shovel, again with its metronomic rhythms, listening to the spill and fall of dirt.

"She's making you do this, isn't she?" Eva said. "She can't help you, Ben. Look . . . see what she's doing to you . . . " She went to him and again took his arm; this time his off-throwing motion was more forceful, and he turned to her for a moment, the threat, the warning, clearly apparent in his face. Then he turned back and dipped his shoulder again, and again drove down on the crossbar and lifted and threw aside another scoop of dirt.

"Ben!" she cried from out of her infuriating helplessness. "What in God's name are you *doing?*"

"I have matters of thought," he muttered.

"Stop it! Stop this!"

She turned away, turning her back on the relentless and unstoppable digging. The horse shifted patiently in the dark.

"Are you going to stay with her?" she asked.

He made no answer. She spun around.

"Are you?" she demanded.

"Raise the lamp," he said.

"I want to know what you're going to do. I want to know if you're going to throw away everything. Ben, there's still time. Put down that shovel and come home with me. I'm begging you."

He went on, grim, wordless, constant, separating earth from earth. The wind blew some dead leaves across the path of his shovel.

"Talk to me," she said.

"I can't."

"Why?"

"I have matters of thought."

With an expression of sickening realization, she looked down at the uneven opening he was making in the ground. He did not have much further to go, she knew. She pressed her palms together and raised her mated fingertips to her mouth, gazing raptly at the ground, her eyes filling with irresolute terror.

"He's wrapped in a coarse brown blanket," she said vacuously, as if in some idle way trying to help him. She continued to watch for several moments, unable to shift her eyes from the remorseless black scoop. Then she turned away again, impulsively. "You're destroying everything," she said quietly, almost wistfully.

"Raise the lamp," he said, gasping now, feeling the toll of hard, constant effort.

Her back to him, she closed her eyes for a moment, lacerated by a taunting inability to forget: What remained most vividly of that night? Out of all the violence, the horror, one thing continued brutally clear and immutable: it was upon learning that Ryler had married Susan that Ben became enraged and launched into that murderous volcanic fury; that was the thing he had been unable to abide. That, she knew, was the immovable and irrefutable cornerstone, and nothing would diminish or obscure it. Trace the ultimate source of passion so foamed and heightened and one found the most nestling tenderness. She shook her head, smiling ruefully for a moment, then opened her eyes as he said again, "Raise the lamp."

She turned around and picked up the lamp, casting the light upon him. She looked at his face, at the obsession.

"Higher," he muttered.

"Higher, higher," she said senselessly, raising the lamp up in both hands until it was over her head, and then hurled it into the underbrush. Then she turned and ran toward the chaise and climbed up into it and seized the reins. "Go to hell!" she cried. "I don't need you! I don't *want* you!" She snapped the reins and forced the horse into the woods, where it made a slow, laborious half-circle, dragging the chaise through the splitting brush, one wheel running high along a rock and then dropping back down as the chaise shuddered and swung around, facing away. She snapped the reins again, viciously, and began riding out as the wind came swirling through the darkness at her, lifting the dead leaves and swaying the tops of the trees.

He knew what she had done, was doing, but did not care, never missing a stroke of his steady muscle-aching digging. The ground was becoming softer now, yielding more easily. Soon, he thought. Soon soon soon soon. Done and enough and all. Soon he would know what he saw at the window, what he had seen and heard and felt among the ashes in the shadow of that solitary sky-pointing chimney which had become symbol and torment. I'll find myself, he thought as he continued to bend furiously at his work. Myself, not Ryler; it will be me, discovered in discovery or nondiscovery. The secret is not in the glittering grandeur of the stars ... not in the wind ... not in the laboring sands ... not in seeded springtime ... not at the ocean's weighty pit ... but here under this patch of relinquishing, upflying dirt. Soon, he thought. Soon. Soon. And at first he saw the light as a symbol of the impending revelation, permeating the unsealing earth with a soft reddish glow that was the uttering blood of the apocalypse. Now he could see the clods and the stones more clearly under the rasping shovel, and the deeper he dug the stronger became the light, and its heat. He looked up for a moment at the steadily growing fire in the brush, the edges of curling smoke, then down again as he continued digging. The flying wind whipped the fire like an overseer's lash, carrying it through the underbrush, in savage ribbons at first and then like so many crackling bright veins running up and across and converging and rising.

Soon he stood bathed in the burning light, still relentlessly attacking the earth, digging with the rushing excitement of his imminent discovery, beginning to feel the murmurous heat now, the perspiration shining on his face. The wind blew wrestling black shadows across his ceaseless arms and shoulders. He looked up again and the sight of the fire's weaving expansion impelled him to dig faster, not with fear but excitement, as though the burning woods in their stark autumn desiccation were at once stimulus and dispensation.

When at last he struck something solid below him, he threw the shovel aside and fell to his knees and began clawing at the last thinned layer of dirt with his fingers, digging at it like a child in a sandpile as the shadows writhed and flared over him. When his fingers clawed into the blanket's rough material he suddenly stopped, arrested by some violently compelling realization. He withdrew his hands and curled his fingertips into his palms for a moment, staring at the lumpy dirt-clinging measure of blanket. Then he reached out and tore at the blanket and in the firelight touched and saw a head covered with dried withered hair, and then the face, only a glimpse of it in profile in the lurid glare, the bones pointing through the dead withdrawing skin, several teeth bared in a grimace; only a glimpse, but enough, enough to throw him back on his haunches with a terrified outcry. His mind seethed with searing crosscurrents as he looked up at the fire, and then around him. Using his heels and hands he scrabbled backwards, then leaped to his feet. For several moments he stood gazing into the fire, one arm raised as if to ward off the strong gusts of heat that were coming at him, and then taking one swift final glance at the thing uncovered by the blanket, before leaving, before moving quickly away, back into the cold wind and the dark.

Nineteen

HE SAT CROSS-LEGGED ON a hilltop, watching the fire, the lusty bright glow upon the night, watching with detached interest, as if it had nothing to do with him. The sun crashed there, he thought.

The cold wind was blowing easterly, in from Long Island, rising to traverse this hilltop and then crossing the river into Manhattan to wander through the maze of those many streets. He lay down upon the short, rough grass and gazed with sullen curiosity at the stars. Once upon a time you may have amazed me, he thought. But no more. With my loops of mind I can lasso any one of you and store you in my brain. You only think you are clothed in mystery; to us recondite and enigmatic. But what must we be to you—we who cleave together and press our bodies eye to eye and procreate giants from out of pulsing spores? What do you make of the chafing erosion that lies between our precocity and our senility? Even as we smash ourselves to pieces we know everything and you nothing. We are all of us ripe with our singular antecedents, our ranks of grace and nobility and divinity. And the unique. The very special. The chosen. There was nothing fortuitous about it, he thought. There had been profoundly gifted artisans for this, with particularly powerful hands and fingers, because they had had to hew and carve mightily in their quest to achieve permanence, since it was ongoing, transitional from one generation to the next, with no telltale lines to show where the one left off and the other began. It had to be designed to endure not only time but the dilution of extrinsic genetic permeation, to resist all attempts at yoke and harness, remain splendidly free. It called for features carved in stone, with prescient vision broodingly rigid and unassailable, for it needed to cause, and endure, much. Rock. Monolith. Singular unto anomalism. Proud container of unconforming ravers and moon-strikers, of unwonted annointing, of divine obsessions and infatuations. Created separate in the untimed pre-Genesis protoplasm, under the din of cosmic roaring, remembering that sound forever, its vibrations locked to every thought and passion. Raised monolithic over the receding waters and under the fading lightning bolts. The first thin spear of time-light unveiling the granite face that had seen everything and which broke the first virgin winds and sent them scattering to eternal wandering; the first light-revealed face of masonry impassivity reflecting for all time the soul of the sire of the legions of the damned. This rock, this monolith, waiting for glacial masses and volcanic furies to shape the continents and curve the mountain peaks and sound the oceans; waiting to begin its stride into the pristine procession of centuries; waiting for the first man-made fire to lift reddening shadows against its impervious face and thus stir it to life. There before time and waiting for the end of time before executing its own maniacal dissolution.

He did not know for how long he slept, but when he opened his eyes the stars were still up, watching him with their sparkling amazement. He was shivering now from the cold. He sat up and wrapped his arms around himself and hunched his shoulders. The woodland fire was still burning, noiseless in the distance. He watched it with vague disinterest.

"One, two, three, four, five, six, seven, eight, nine, ten." He paused, giving consideration to the order. It seemed correct. "My name is Benjamin McKinley. It is November, 1863. I know the difference between right and wrong."

Hugging himself, rocking back and forth in the cold wind, he considered what he had spoken. It seemed in order, it seemed correct. He was ready to swear to it. He looked down the slopes and across the dark fields at the fire and thought, *Yes, just as you were ready a few hours ago to swear you had seen his face at the window.* How many more windows lay ahead? When did the face begin to come closer? Did it ever speak?

Hook is standing at the upstairs window, staring at the glow of the fire. I know he is, Ben thought. He's wondering about it. No, not wondering: he knows. He has always known. And now we both know. Shareholders in something that is not iniquitous but sad. There was no point in going to that old man and telling him something he already knew. All Hook would do was gather him up and run: Hook always did that when there was a fire. *And anyway I didn't do anything Ryler killed Ryler through his own low and provocative actions including bringing his dead face to the window and so I had to kill him a second time and kill the woods too because that's where he'd be every time I went in there the young Ryler the boy climbing the trees and hiding in the brush and holding his arms out stiffly behind him and bending at the waist and kissing Susan on the cheek even while she smiled with her lips and looked at me and even then he was planning his deceit waiting to mark me dead and what difference did it make anyway which one of us climbed the trellis to heaven since we were the same loving the same little girl woman who loved us both not Ryler less but me more and now Ryler's had his comeuppance a sound knock on the head and a good roast right in the middle of the place where he is still a little boy spinning through yellow spheres of sunlight which would always have been ours secretly to evoke if only he hadn't done it not just tried to make me dead with the tip of a pen but then gone and taken her and by that snapped the chain with which I had secured them and let them come pouring out through the hole in the wall not knowing or caring where they were or what was happening feeling free not to obey or disobey but simply to do special things unique and hated and feared by God because aberrantly attuned to God's voice and the angelic hymns because God in his heaven is mad too and because of His unrelenting error we know it too and will never be forgiven for it for knowing the sun's agony and the sere leaf's creaking pain and for knowing that the stars do not know and that the springtime seed is afraid and for remembering the recessive oceans and when dawn was black and knowing that such knowledge was meant to be sanctified and so brought damnation and striving for salvation through incoherence and derangement but not water enough across the earth to wash it free nor silken petals enough in a thousand forests to sweeten the odor and the dead of dust-laden milleniums and the suckling child both are struck with fear and fascination yellow galaxies of motes swirling in sunshafts seeking to find some settling arrangement for an eternity of stillness sighing waifs of melody discoursing in tears and never will that face be rubbed from the window the dream is shut the caverns of the mind slowly flood.*

He got up and walked down the far side of the hill, feeling like a maypole in the midst of the cold, reveling winds. At the base of the hill, he began a long, circuitous walk back to the center of town, following the long, gradual decline of Fresh Lake Road to its intersect with Grant Avenue. No matter at what point he was, however, he could still see the glow in the sky, a faint quivering nimbus like an echo of light.

The scattering of houses on either side of the avenue, some of them with modestly pillared front porches, were dark, with not so much as the eye of a candle to be seen. The wind continued, vigorous and antic, spinning dead leaves across the dirt road. Then he saw the Dooley House up ahead, with men in nightshirts standing at the lighted upstairs windows watching the fire. The lights in the hotel seemed like beacons of calm and stability opposed to the wild inferno in the woods.

He moved away from the avenue before reaching the hotel, cutting through the alley between the smith's and the hardware store. He followed a wagon road down a slight incline, then veered and cut across a field toward Susan's house. The closer he got the more he hurried and at the last quarter-mile became almost desperate, as if afraid that because he so badly needed her, she would like some precious essence vanish. She was the only one now, the only one on earth with sufficient radiant calm and love at her center to help him, the only one who would not try to probe or incite him, who would prompt his strengths by tempering his weakness. He was avoiding looking at the soft flush of light over the woods now, as if to disavow his involvement with it.

Approaching the house from the side, he felt a leap of excitement at seeing a lamp burning in the kitchen. The sight of that light was like a validation of hope; she had left it there for him, in expectation of his return. She knew I would be back, he thought; she had known it before he himself did; even as he was suffering shocks and vivid horrors, she had been sitting quietly and enduringly with her indomitable faith. She knows my heart better than I, and why not? he asked himself with a sudden surge of wild and romantic fancy— Haven't I given it to her? That simple, almost banal declaration brought a smile to his face as he hurried across the grass toward the house. He was at once amused and solemnly impressed by the purity and the banality of what he was thinking. Yes, he thought, back to where my heart lies hidden. He had made that deliverance a long time ago, with the foresight to make his life coextensive with hers—one of the few sane things he had ever done, and it had been kept pure by the very banality which had blinded him to its sweet harmony.

Then he was running toward the window, as if the weight of the night were gathered at his back. The wind was flowing through the grass with a hiss. I'll get inside that house, he told himself, and lock the door and bar it. The roof will be sturdy enough and those walls will hold, and if his face returns to the window I'll simply let it hang there and say that it is no face but merely a composite of corrupt chemicals painted by my seething bequeathers; I'll be able to do it by taking her hand and letting her currents wing to mine. Together we can scorn the tormentor and mock the mocker. As he neared the house, he resolved to tell her everything, that she would have to learn to watch his eye with care and listen for the warp in his voice, to be at all times prepared for that deviation, to cope with it, and to be unafraid.

Drawn by the light, he hurried to the window and peered in. She was sitting in the kitchen, her head resting on the table, cradled in her arm. She was asleep. The lamp burned nearby. He raised his hand and was about to tap on the window with his fingertips, then desisted. He did not want to startle her. He lowered his hand, staring at her with tenderness so fine it seemed dreamlike. Around him the wind beat tirelessly at the forsythia and seemed to be sharpening the bare branches of the hawthorn. Pensively, he continued to gaze at her. He felt himself being suffused with something undeniable, submitting by degrees to a poignant reality: she seemed so peaceful, as if afloat on the mildest dream. *What face is this now at her window? What will it look to her if she wakens?* He did not want to startle her: his mind carried the thought higher and higher until it was at the crown of his soul, in incandescent admonition. He felt estranged by her sleeping serenity, by the faithful lamp with which she had waited. *Allow her. Do not.* He turned for a moment into the nagging wind, regarded the thronging, solid darkness: his companions; to him their cry seemed reasonable. He turned back. How dearly she slept, unmindful of—ill-equipped for—a face at her window. He did not want to startle her, and if not this mere disturbance, intrusion, how then would others a thousand times worse be permissible? *What right? Mother. Father.* He lifted his hand and lightly placed his fingertips on the glass, as close to touching her as he dared come. With the fullness of his love in a soft, bittersweet smile, he lowered his hand and began withdrawing, watching her, moving from framed shadow back into the cold, rustling night. *Sleep, sleep, dear Susan; the sweetest blessings are the unseen.*

He roamed with the wind for the rest of the night, ever turning his eyes from the burning woodland. With the first muted hush of dawn, he slipped into a grove of trees and lay down upon the curled brown leaves, cold and shivering. Typically, he thought, I go to rest as the new day hoists its round shoulders into the sky, as all around me come to life. Sweet Jesus, he thought wearily, there's one other who follows the same cycle, and she'll be waiting for me.

It was past noon when he wakened, his eyes opening to November trees standing starkly against a cool blue sky. He sat up slowly, dead leaves clinging to his shirt. His back felt stiff, and he was hungry, and last night's chill was still in his bones. A lot of last night was still in his bones and he wondered how much of it was nightmare, how much reality. It was all too sumptuous for a single night, he believed; at least some of it had to be product of the mind's brutal embroidery. But what was which, and when did one cease being itself and become part of the other? Or did they commingle without distinction? Like my parents starting out of the darkness toward me with love and warmth and then turning into two cutthroats with butcher knives, but still believing until the last instant that they would revert again, and if not for Malloy . . . yes, Malloy . . . the mad saving the mad. Malloy: my symbolic ancestor, calmed and comforted by drumbeat and cannon fire, lured vibration by vibration into clarity, shown the golden thing itself (which by all the holy ironies is possessed by unlettered farm boys and ignorant merchants and even thieves and murderers and swindlers and forgers and fools and numbskulls), and then ran full force with absolute faith into its open arms and found clawing death. I might even ask: Did Malloy actually save my life or merely slaughter my figments? *Do you want to go back there too and look for it again, the ashes, the chimney, the two dead bodies, the knives; sit down there and say to yourself, I was mad here once, and the fact that I have come back and sit here saying it proves that I am not?*

He sat gazing at the dead leaves, the thorny bramble, the stolid, winter-awaiting trees. From out of this stillness came the sensation of time in abeyance, in spite of the sunlight; it had all happened outside of clock time, and Susan was still asleep at the kitchen table, unaware of how close she had come to being impaled upon his shadows. Yes, he thought, if he had done any sane and decent thing at all in last night's fiery windy darkness, it had been to silently withdraw and leave her sleep unbroken. Not her, he thought; she would try too hard, she would lose herself in trying, and her gathering confusion and unhappiness would only worsen his. Going to her would not only have been reprehensible and unfair, but almost a blasphemous act of challenge and defiance; it would have been a rewinding of those leering ghosts, and some night, inevitably, brought another Mr. Hook rushing to salvation with an ax. Only tempest could match tempest; only Eva had the teeming darkness to match his own; only she could bring equal strength to the combat. Only with her would it not be imposition, for when considering the damnation of our destinies, it was worth considering also that sometimes others saw themselves concommitant with us, willfully and fervently.

Later he emerged into the full sunlight, feeling, he thought wryly, the very sane need for a meal and a hot bath and a soft bed with Eva beside him; to lie in that bed all day and all night with the feel of her body next to his and her arms around him, close and interactive, exchanging and shoring up those energies and those desires that they would be calling on and depending upon when the lowering clouds came to blot the sun. Not love: more than that and less: need, dependence; emotional ropes and pulleys and latches to hold and lift and secure against July's icy blasts and December's sultry incursions, against midnight's phosphorescent faces and noontime's vulturous wingspreads.

Twenty

SHE WOULDN'T TAKE A thing with her, Eva thought as she prowled the unlighted house, out of familiarity finding her way easily through doorways and up and down stairs. She would turn loose the horses and then simply leave, just let it stand empty and unechoed until it collapsed under the weight of its own vacancy. What alternative was there? To sit here and hear stories of his days and months and years with Susan, to perhaps accept an occasional visit, start another Ryler-like affair, with the intolerable irony of having him risen from the same bed, the same wife? No, she could never abide that. Nor could she satisfy herself with these muscled farm boys with their unquesting minds and their dung-smelling boots. Leave, she told herself as she moved restlessly from dark room to dark room, hearing the wind outside tossing the treetops. Leave before the advent of loneliness, that product of abused self-assurance; leave before the further commission of mistakes and the inevitable self-revulsion.

There was no reason for staying, nor would there be regrets at leaving. She had never liked this town anyway. She knew how she was spoken of here: spoiled, arrogant, demanding. She and her father had always been tapestries for small-minded interests. Capstone had sated its petty envy upon the occupants of this house, reveling in the swords that fell upon it, knowing little of the shadows within the dreams of those occupants. She would be leaving behind nothing, because she had always felt the outcast anyway, from the earliest, when her parents had dressed her in silks and velvets, imbued her with a sense of sovereignty, frowned upon her mingling with other children, educated her with private tutors.

She had misjudged Ben. Beneath that facade of lordly self-possession lay just another small-minded provincial, slightly more glib and interesting than the average, but little more than that. The poetry? She could explain that: it was a freakish thing. An aberration. The product of a natural unrefined talent that had been subjected to an extraordinary compression of emotion, so that what might have come trickling out over a lifetime was given sudden blazing eruption. With that single exhaustive effort he had doubtless drained himself. Poet, she thought contemptuously. *Without me there would have been nothing. Without me . . .*

Listen to that wind, she thought. It was tearing at the night, sweeping the name of her deceitful lover who was somewhere out there, who seemed the very cause of the airy commotion, as if no night could merge peacefully with him abroad in it. Downstairs, the wind blew in through the smashed window, rippling the dead shepherd's short gray hairs. *Tired of burying his handiwork.* Damn him, he would soon see that Susan was not woman enough for him—not for all the varieties he required. He'll want to come back. Let him. Let him break every window and climb in and out a thousand times. Let him walk about in here until the dead rise. I'll be across the river indulging polite society.

Stop thinking about him—she found herself in sudden self-admonishment. *Put your thoughts instead on the insult.* But the insult did not exist in solitary; it was hammer and anvil together. Goddamn him. Some men—most—could with little effort be detached from whatever vine they were clinging to and brought hither; but not this one, and true to human nature, this was the one she wanted. But where had he gone?—to *her,* who had simply sat and waited with her impermeable and unquestioning fidelity, who had remained bovinelike in her acceptance of unremitting indignities; who, unlike Dido, waited for the winds to arch over and bring the vessels back to shore.

She continued ceaselessly, restlessly through the house, moving about in the darkness with unerring familiarity, knowing that here was the chair in which he sat, the desk at which he wrote, the table at which he ate, the bed in which he slept—all of them imbued with something of his presence, and not just an aura either; more, almost physical. She turned sharply at the faint metallic sounds carried on the wind, pausing, clasping her hands together, her eyes darting. Then she relaxed, with a knowing beyond mere identification: someone in town was beating at the fire gong with an iron pipe, and she knew that now they were rising from their beds, swinging up their suspenders and hustling into their coats, and rushing from all directions. Harnessing horsepower to their engine and chasing it out to the fire. The bustling red engine with its steel rods and brass supports bounding importantly over the dirt roads to confront the flaming woods.

To hell with them all, she thought, and I hope he's still in there, incinerating with his dear friend whom he hated enough to kill and loved enough to mourn.

She was wakened at noon by a steady knocking on the door. She came immediately awake, sitting bolt upright on the bed, befuddled for a moment by the flurry of a departing dream. She was fully clothed, even to the boots which she had been too tired to remove when finally at dawn she had thrown herself upon the bed. The knocking persisted. *Damn him,* she thought. *Goddamn him.* She pushed her hair away from her face and looked around at the bright sunshine that was flooding the room, then turned her head, scowling at the open bedroom door and the expanse of carpeted hallway beyond. She got off the bed and hurried downstairs, impelled by the anger and resentment which seemed not to have diminished during her hours of sleep.

When she opened the door she was surprised to see not Ben, but Capstone's sheriff, John Rice, a tall, red-mustached man wearing an overcoat and a slouch hat. At the sight of Eva he quickly slipped his smoking cheroot from his mouth and held it in his hand, out of sight. Then he took a moment's opportunity to study her, as though he were still himself unseen. She looked harried, drawn, older, as though she had reached ahead into time and pulled unfallen years over her.

"It's Sheriff Rice, Miss LeGrange," he said, his voice unaccountably lowered for discretion. "May I speak to you?"

"You already are, Mr. Rice."

"I'll be to the point. A fire broke out in the woods last night just east of town. You were seen coming away from there in your shay just after it commenced. I was wondering if you might be able to tell us something about it."

"You want to know how it started?"

"Well, yes, that would be helpful. If you could."

"It was started by me."

"Ah," he said, nodding. "Unintentionally, I'm sure."

"No. It was quite intentional."

Damn her, he thought. She tells me that and then stands there looking me in the eye like I'm supposed to apologize, bow and go away.

"Why?" he asked.

"There was something out there I wanted to burn."

"Well, now, Miss LeGrange," the sheriff said, shifting his weight from one hip to the other, "it could have spread and done a lot of damage, what with the high wind and all."

"I'm sorry," she said quietly, her voice falling somewhere between impertinence and contrition.

"The boys had the devil's work beating it down. You caused quite a bit of trouble, Miss LeGrange," the sheriff said with an edge of reproach.

"I'm sorry, Mr. Rice. But it is the first trouble I've caused around here. Others have done far worse, I'm sure."

"That's poor reasoning, Miss LeGrange, and you know it."

"There will be no more fires from me, Mr. Rice. There will be no more trouble of any sort around here from me, ever."

The sheriff nodded, staring inquiringly at her.

"You all right, Miss LeGrange?" he asked quietly.

"I have a headache."

"Ah. Sorry to hear that."

She remained poised, watching him, waiting for him to leave.

"Just what was it you wanted to burn out there?" he asked.

"Something personal."

"I see. Well, I'll have to consider whether there are to be any repercussions."

"I understand."

"So I'll be saying good afternoon," the sheriff said. He touched his forefinger to the brim of his hat, then turned and walked down the portico steps toward his horse, which he had secured to one of the columns.

She watched him for a moment, then clasped her hands and raised them to her breast. "Wait," she said, stepping outside.

He turned at the foot of the steps and looked up at her, the cheroot back in his mouth now, his eyes squinting in the trail of smoke across his face.

"Yes?" he said.

"Do I have your understanding?"

"Ma'am?" he asked uncertainly.

"I'll need your understanding," she said. "It concerns Ryler Stevenson. I should have spoken out long before this. Six weeks ago, to be precise. I suppose there are legal penalties for maintaining silence in such a situation. But there were circumstances, and I was terrified. You look surprised, Mr. Rice—that there was something or someone capable of putting fear in me? Maybe you haven't known me as well as you thought you have, all these years. Why shouldn't I have been afraid—after what happened to my father. I live alone here. My life for these past six weeks has been one long, uninterrupted hell.

"You want to know about the fire. The fire was the end, the culmination of something that began here six weeks ago. It was the night Ben came home. The three of us were here—Ben, myself, and Ryler."

Now she was speaking to a deeply intent face from which the cheroot was not only not removed but had begun to puff as the eyes squinted more and more narrowly, first warily, then gradually with guarded belief. Her voice almost droned in its mild, calm divulging, with neither hesitation nor inflection; but more than her voice, it was her eyes that held him in thrall, fixed upon him with the condescension of one who expected to be believed, without question or doubt.

"Suddenly there was some mild disagreement, and he—Ben—exploded with unbelievable violence. He went into an absolute frenzy, attacked Ryler and with a blow on the head killed him. Right in front of me. I think I must have fallen into what I can only describe as a paralysis of fear. How else to explain it? One thing I've learned these past six weeks is how relentless fear can be, how it can crawl into your bones and become like a frozen prayer of self-preservation. But the worst of it, Mr. Rice, the thing that was more terrifying than anything else, was that there was not the slightest flicker of remorse from him. You would have thought he had done nothing more than drop a glass on the hearthstone.

"He warned me against speaking of it to anyone—a warning couched in very explicit terms, I might add—then he removed the body and went away. I lived in such terror the next few days that the thought of going to you never occurred to me; it was almost as if I believed he was inside my head, reading my thoughts. A few days later he returned and asked if he could stay here. I said he could. Why? Because he was a different person now. Now he was racked with guilt and grief; I found myself confronted by an entirely different person, and I felt sorry for him. He told me he had experienced the most terrible things in the war and was not to be held responsible for what he had done. He said he had momentarily been deprived of his senses and that what he had done had left him shattered. I had always been fond of Ben and now I suppose a rush of compassion dominated my better judgment, or maybe it was still the terror, the fear of saying no. In any event, I permitted him to stay.

"There was a passage of time, during which he was quite subdued, obviously suffering deep remorse. Then I had to go to Manhattan for a few days. I worked up my courage and told him to please not be here when I returned, that I had done all I could for him. He agreed, and when I returned he was gone. You can imagine my relief. But then late last night he came back. He broke into the house while I was upstairs asleep. He killed my shepherd. Then he forced me to accompany him into the woods, where he disinterred the body and started the fire. For what reason he was doing any of it, God only knows. In the midst of it I ran away; I couldn't stand it anymore. I don't want to stand it anymore. I refuse. He's not a rational person, Mr. Rice, and I fear for my life."

The sheriff removed the cheroot. "Where has he gone?"

"I have no idea," she said.

The sheriff pondered for several moments, then said, "You'll give evidence to this?"

"Yes."

"He was always a headstrong sort, wasn't he?" the sheriff murmured.

"He killed his best friend, for no apparent reason."

"And you saw it?"

"I've been seeing it every hour of the day, for six weeks," she said. "I don't want to see it anymore."

"All right, Miss LeGrange," the sheriff said, turning away. "I'll most likely be back later. Will you be able to show us the place in the woods?"

"Yes. You follow the wagon path that bends out from the road on into the woods. It's just beyond that."

The sheriff glanced back at her and nodded, smiling briefly, unpleasantly. "Yes," he said. "That's just about where we found him."

She watched him ride away. He rode slowly, as if under the impact of what he had just been told. She remained standing there even after he was gone from sight, staring at the sullen November trees, the brown lifeless grass. If there was a preferred time of year for this sort of business, she felt, then it was now. Winter was coming, with its unyielding sweep, its ice-borne indifference, coming to hide yesterday's world under mounds of snow.

Now, she told herself, don't think about it. Don't you think about it at all. You've done it and now put it out of your mind. Now you can truly leave this place. Now you'll be able to reorder your life for other times and other places without always having some stubborn coil of curiosity left dangling, trying to picture him, what he is doing, thinking. Let the law deal with him; it would take something cold and impersonal to deal with him—no human being could, no one who felt and breathed and loved and yearned ever could. I'm not going to worry at all. It's in their hands now. Yes, I'll give evidence, she thought, and then he'll see his mistake, in not recognizing a will equal to his own, in not willing to yield an iota of himself in order to conjoin for the sake of his own well-being. He'll see that some mistakes—some insults—the ones that take root and cause the deepest pain, are irredeemable and unforgivable. He'll learn that—*learn what? see what? for how long and to what purpose? they'll hang him as soon as they can seat a judge and swear a jury.* Damn him anyway—always this restless enigma, this thing in her blood. She had already once endured and survived the mourning of him; she could do so again. And then belong to herself once more, unencumbered by romantic vulnerability.

She went back into the house. She remembered the dog. She paused for a moment, irritated, then left the house and went to the barn. Pushing aside the door of an empty stall, she found a blanket on the straw. She picked it up and began folding it into a manageable shape, then stopped. The idea of going into the house and covering and then lifting the dead animal made her uncomfortable. I'll hire somebody to come in and do it, she thought, but immediately upon this thought was another, a realization: Alone, without fear or qualm, she had bundled and dragged and lifted and transported and finally buried a human being in the woods in the dead of night. The paradox disturbed her. And then, angrily, she threw the blanket back down on the straw. She stood there gazing at it, her eyes widening by fractions. Then she wheeled around and closed her eyes, covering them for a moment with her hand, listening to her father's voice in the encompassing horse-smelling stillness: *Don't cry. You can do without that. Tears are the white flags of human emotions.* And she had suffered almost physical agony at her mother's funeral, trying not to cry, suppressing those tears, damming them, fighting them with stiffened nostrils and pursed lips, and succeeding. *Be strong. Take hold of yourself.* Yes, father dear, but why did you rush to disappear behind your locked door the moment we arrived back home? Why wouldn't you let me see you for hours and hours? What were *you* doing in there all the time, and why did I with such delicate discretion place myself at the other end of the house so as not to hear in the event you were giving vent to that which was forbidden me? Because I can barely remember her today. My mother. It is as if without tears her memory quickly dried and withered and curled into dust.

Slowly she sank to her knees, softly into the straw. She closed her eyes and sighed. She had never been taught when to stop becoming strong, until even pride had been corrupted into hauteur and happiness became a calculation. All of that accumulated strength had turned into a freezing dictatorial power, a tundra of unreleased feeling. She opened her eyes and lay her hand on the blanket. It was so salutary, she thought, to be unable to simply march in there and wrap up a dead shepherd and dispose of it. The sense of apprehension was pleasing. *Tonight I may even be able to cry,* as once before she had allowed herself to cry, at Ben's reported death; but those tears had been slow and pensive and heatless, more like the tears provoked by a cinder in the eye than gusts of emotion. This time she would cry for herself, begin the process of watering down that relentless unforgiving strength; and before giving up Capstone she would visit her parents' grave and allow herself the outpouring she had so rigidly withheld from public scrutiny when that melancholy earth was being turned over.

When she left the barn, she was exhausted. She walked slowly back to the house, entered and closed the door behind her. She leaned against it and folded her arms and with flat, almost sightless eyes took the measure of the house, the silence. Already she had begun to feel alien here, disturbed by the wrathful stranger who had so furiously paced these floors the night before, who had delivered the statement to the sheriff not many minutes ago.

So exhausted was she, so emptied of response, that when he stepped from the living room she could summon no feeling, not fear or surprise or elation. She simply gazed at him as though he were materializing atom by atom, a gently evolving specter, wan and tentative and unthreatening, an expression of appeal in his face that went to the very pit of her soul before beginning a slow spiral to awareness.

"Last night . . . " he said.

"Why are you here?" she whispered.

The question seemed unexpected, to take him by surprise.

"There is nowhere else," he said. He was standing utterly still, almost self-consciously so, as if with this express immobility to reassure her, convey. Now he shook his head and repeated it: "There is nowhere else."

"You'll stay?" she asked softly, her voice barely carrying to him.

She began feeling an uncanny sense of security from the smooth oaken door against which she was leaning, which was shut to the world with what suddenly seemed airtightness, and from the silence which felt stealthy with renewal; she felt again the flow of her strength, but this time not as an icy torrent rushing to command and dominate, but the fierce warmth of regeneration.

She walked across the entranceway toward him. He remained motionless, watching her, still as if to reassure through immobility. She put her arms around him; he hesitated for a moment, then embraced her.

"Last night," he said, "Was too close to hell, closer than I ever want to be."

"I know; I could feel it."

"I can explain some of it."

"Not now. There'll be time for that."

"But you'll have to know all of it," he said.

"In time."

"I'm bringing you a heavier burden than you think."

She looked up at him with deeply measuring eyes. "Last night," she said, "I thought you'd never come back. It wasn't just that I thought you'd go back to her, or that maybe you would never come out of that fire alive, or that you would go away and this time stay; it was that I felt something had torn loose inside you and gone so completely asunder that you would never be able to know who you were or who you wanted to be, not ever again."

"You must have been terrified."

"No. Angry."

"Only that?" he asked.

"Only?"

"Is that why you ran away?"

"Ben, you'll never go back to her."

"I can't."

"I know," she said softly. "What do you want now? Food? Love? Rest? Tell me."

"Warmth," he said. "I want to be warm."

They went upstairs, to her room. He removed his boots and, fully clothed, got under the blankets. His breathing was deep, weary, as though each expelled breath was draining him. "You would think," he said quietly, vaguely, "that time—enough of it—could finally have some effect. What good is time, if it can't change anything? Is aging us the only thing it can do? You would think that it would now and then allow some interval for a wisp of change to slip in, to allow things to be just a little better."

"It's going to be better now, my darling," she said. She had been standing at the foot of the bed, watching him. Now she sat on the edge of the bed, slipped off her boots and joined him under the covers, lying close to him, and then a moment later gathered in his embrace.

"Maybe it can be," he said. "Maybe I just never believed in it."

"We'll go away from here," she said. "And just be together."

"I'm going to make myself believe that it can be better."

"We'll go away, and we'll forget about all the old things."

"Where, Eva?" he asked. "Where can you go to forget?"

"If we want to find such a place, we will."

"Let's not allow the wind to decide, or the tides. *We* have to decide; we have to decide everything, very firmly. We have to say, '*This* is what we want, *this* is the way it's going to be.'"

"Yes, that's just what we're going to do. We'll decide exactly what we want, and then we'll do it."

"We'll own some land," he said, his voice running with animation now, as though some interior vision was clarifying itself. "Land that no one ever lived on before. That nobody has ever despoiled or corrupted." He turned his head and looked at her with a faint, whimsical smile. "But we mustn't ever look upon it as running away, but as a new beginning. Running away is foolish and impossible; but a new beginning is praiseworthy. It's going to be a metamorphosis . . . that's what it's going to be. Because, you see, if you understand everything that's gone before . . . if you've experienced it in totality, if it's rubbed you raw . . . then you can rightfully say you're done with it, that you're no longer vulnerable. God almighty, don't the mists evaporate every morning in the sunlight?"

He fell asleep, peacefully, breathing evenly. She lay next to him, gazing at him, at the short rough stubble that had overnight risen upon his cheeks and along his jawline, gazing lovingly and piteously. They'll be looking for him, she thought. On every lane and path, and in the woods, and probably at that pestilent swamp too; they'll all be looking for him, every son of a bitch who never liked him because of that tempestuous freedom he's got inside him and who smirked when they thought he was dead. But I have him here, next to me, needing me. It took the full glare of whatever vision of hell he had to have for him to realize it, but he knows now he belongs to me. But he won't want to leave by night, he won't lie under a cover in the back of a buckboard or sit in a carriage with the curtains drawn; he won't want to leave furtively or like a fugitive, because that was running not leaving, and he would never be at rest for it. He wants to leave in full sail, like a clipper in high wind, in the sunlight, without so much as his shadow following.

It was just before dusk when she heard the soft rhythms of hoofbeats on the road. She stared up at the darkening air and held her breath. The sounds came nearer, filling the silence with an ominous softness. They would not pass, she knew. She rose from the bed and went to the window. They were swinging in from the road now, six of them, approaching the house, led by the sheriff; six brute figures on horseback, in hats and coats, with pistols and rifles.

She hurried from the window to the bed and gently took hold of his shoulders and shook him awake, whispering his name with breathless urgency. His eyes opened, found her and stared at her with puzzlement.

"You've got to get up," she said. When he did not move, she repeated it, with deeper urgency.

"What's wrong?" he asked, still submerged in the languorous stupor of broken sleep.

"Please get up," she said.

There was pounding on the front door and his eyes darted to a side, filling with something mistrustful and dreadfully alert, something feverishly self-protective.

"Who is that?" he asked.

"They know," she said. "You have to get up, now," she said, and found herself unable to add, *You have to hide;* unable to say it because she knew he would not hear it, not now, not anymore. "Oh, Ben, I didn't think you were coming back. I thought . . . "

But it was the pounding on the door he was listening to, hearing, his eyes filling with consternation. "Do you hear it?" he whispered, his averted eyes returning to her face.

"What are you going to do?" she asked.

"Do you hear it?"

"Yes, I hear it. Ben, what are you going to do? Please get up."

Then the pounding stopped and she knew they were inside. A moment later she heard her name being called, anxiously, questioningly.

"Who is that?" he asked. He pushed her away, threw back the covers, swung his feet to the floor and stood up.

"I'll tell them you're not here," she said.

Again from below came the calling of her name, anxious and insistent, too, now. There was a thronging together of voices and she heard one cry out that he had found a dead dog.

Standing near the doorway, Ben turned to her, fully awake now but still puzzled. "Who is that and what do they want?" he asked.

"Don't go out there," she said. "Ben . . . they'll be upstairs in a minute. I'll tell them you're not here. They'll have to believe me."

"Why are they here?"

She began sobbing. She sat on the edge of the bed and closed her eyes and lowered her head. "I didn't think you were coming back," she said.

"What have you done?" he asked quietly, his voice not demanding, not accusing, but mild, almost compassionately curious.

She raised her head and opened her eyes and stared at him with shining fierceness. She heard them on the stairs now, still calling her name. Quickly she got to her feet, went to the bureau, lifted the shawl that lay there and uncovered the small pistol she had carried into the corridor the night before. She picked it up and pointed it at him. He stared quizzically at it, and then at her, running his underlip along the edges of his teeth. He was about to speak when another shout—from the corridor now—made him snap his head aside, and as he did she fired, hitting him high in the left side of the chest.

Twenty-one

IT WAS EIGHT O'CLOCK at night when Hook heard the buckboard come to a halt outside. When he went to the window, he saw in the moonlight the minister getting carefully down from the seat, too carefully perhaps, as if feeling a need to be laden with the church's dignity. Reaching the ground, the minister straightened his back, seemed to arrange his features into an austerity of expression, then groomed the front of his frock coat with his hands, adjusted his flat-crowned black hat, and headed for the front door. Jesus, Hook thought, what now? He's not coming to pass the time of day. What's happened now? First, this afternoon, the sheriff poking around with asinine questions and ambiguous glances, and now this one.

He got to the door before the minister did and when he opened it found himself confronted by a most solemn face. They studied each other for a moment, and then the minister said gently, "Well, I guess you'd better come along, Henry."

Hook withdrew to get his jacket, coat and derby. Then he went outside and climbed up onto the buckboard and sat next to the minister, who already had the reins up.

"Under whose auspices is this?" Hook asked.

"Sheriff Rice," the clergyman said, clicking his tongue at his horse as the wagon began to move. "He asked me to come out for you."

"And so you have, Mr. Lloyd."

"They brought Ben in a little while ago."

Hook waited. The minister sat quietly, watching the slow narrow moonlit road coming forward just above the horse's nodding head.

"Is he in trouble?" Hook asked.

"No, Henry," the minister said, eyes remaining fixed upon the road, "God help him, he's dead."

When they reached the sheriff's office, they found a knot of men milling about in the street outside. There was a self-conscious absence of conversation among them, even an apparent reluctance for eye meeting eye. With the minister, Hook dismounted and walked through the men to the office, ignoring the curious, sidelong glances. Entering, they found the sheriff just turning away from a rolltop desk, pen in hand. There was no one else in the small, cramped office, which was lit by a pair of gas lamps. The minister stood at the door, his hands clasped behind him.

"Henry," the sheriff said, rising. He walked toward Hook and gravely they shook hands. "I'm sorry about this, damned sorry."

"I'm sure you are, John," Hook said. "But I wish you would tell me just what it is you're sorry about."

"The whole thing. I'm sorry about the whole god-damned thing. I tell you, there's times when there's not money enough in the whole world to make this job worth it. She shot him, Henry. He was threatening her life. That's the plain, naked side of it. What more there is, or was, if anything, we'll never know. And if there is any more, then maybe I don't want to hear about it. Hellfire, maybe she could've waited another ten seconds   me and the boys were right there—but she was terrified. He'd invaded her house, so I suppose she was within her rights."

"Miss LeGrange?" Hook said.

"That's right. He'd threatened her before, you see, and now he was back there and—How'd you know it was her?"

"He was threatening her life," Hook said, unmoving in the flaring light, eyes stolidly upon the sheriff, his voice almost grim with skepticism. "Was he armed?"

"Henry—"

"She was armed and he was not? Is that what you're telling me?"

"Henry—"

"How was he threatening her life when she was holding a gun on him?"

"Henry, he killed Ryler. Six weeks ago."

"I see," Hook said. His gaze did not falter, nor did the strength of his demeanor. "She told you this?"

"She saw it, then was too scared—scared of Ben—to say anything, until today. He dragged her out to the woods last night to dig up the body—don't ask me to explain this, Henry—and then the fire broke out, and she ran away. We found Ryler, just where she said he was. He was done to a turn, but it was Ryler all right. So I'd say she had a little bit to be worried about when Ben came back, everything considered. Would you like a whiskey, Henry?"

"Not just now," Hook said. "Where is he?"

"In the back."

"May I?" Hook asked.

The sheriff nodded.

From his position at the door, the minister asked, "Do you want me to accompany you, Henry?"

Hook shook his head. Alone, he walked past the two empty cells that comprised Capstone's jail and went into the back room. Closing the door behind him, he stood there, letting his eyes become accustomed to the moon-watered darkness. He stared dully at the draped white sheet on the table, at the stockinged feet protruding, each lolled to a side as if come to rest after idle oscillation.

He closed his eyes. Dear boy, he thought, you started the race with such weights on your back. I pray there is a place for the ill-starred of this world; if there be such a place, it must be the most verdant of heavenly vales. He opened his eyes, unable to remember when last he had felt tears in them. He stared at the covered body. The shroud at last had come down from the rainbow. What earthen crypt would ever hold this dust without quivering under the sweetness of dawn and the passion of sunset? Dear boy, he thought, shaking his head at his stabbing sense of guilt. It wasn't from want of love. So many people loved you, to the tops of their hearts. But to what end: even as I carried you from your burning home, I could see ahead to one form or another of . . . this.

He went to the table and lifted one corner of the sheet and let moonlight upon the strong young face laid to a side in repose. How many times had he seen it so, but asleep? Ah, he thought, what to give to make this but sleep now.

"I'll ride you back, Henry," the minister said when Hook returned.

"Thank you, Mr. Lloyd," Hook said. "But I think I'll take to the road alone." Turning to the sheriff, he said quietly, "I'll see to the arrangements, John."

I'm one with the season now, he thought as he walked alone through the quiet moonlight, following the dirt road away from town. He buttoned his coat against a chill he hadn't felt earlier. Going into my own winter now. Soon I'll have the wheeze. Phlegm on the chest. Lightness of mind, heaviness of foot. What a wretched one-way lane it all is. Time, that creeping infidel, here all at once. What had the sustenance been—a runoff of the boy's own vigor, his mother's color in his eyes, or the tension of that unceasing vigilance? It's a damned chill wind. I don't like it. Lord, that boy took more than his own oaken frame with him into the winding sheet. But death, the slowly pacing Hook thought, was always a rapacious snatcher; it went whirling like a vortex, and woe to them who stood too near the last cascade. How could I have stopped him from opening his arms and beginning his final gyration? Stopping him, holding him firm, would only have set the ground to spinning beneath him. I would have had better luck trying to throw a blanket over the sun. But you knew all that a long time ago, from the moment you measured the depth of his father's eye. You allowed it to be tempered by your own silent love, which after the passage of so many years became—had to become—little more than incantatory memory. So you knew what you knew, and went on, trying your damnedest, for everyone, yourself not least. So let us not talk of destiny; such talk diminishes the will of man and the divinity of God both. This ending—this weathered bucket, this empty well—so absolute in its conclusion, speaks for itself.

He would leave now, Hook thought. There was no longer any point in staying. The land was good and the house was sturdy; they would fetch a price. There were simply too many memories gathered in the corners of that house now, too many dead promises, too many fallen shadows. Although he would not be able to empty his mind or appease his heart, at least other walls and other landscapes would be free of sudden echoes and unexpected visions. But where? he asked himself as he walked. Surely not South again, for too many reasons; and the West seemed intended for builders and seekers, not one looking toward a sanctuary for meditation. New England perhaps, with those wild winters so hospitable for introspection. Well, he thought, he would probably do what he always did—move on and trust to chance and instinct and never guess at alternatives. But this time he would be taking his years with him, the road traveled much longer than the way ahead. Properly contemplated, however, the willful Mr. Hook thought, even so terminal a prospect could prove interesting.

Twenty-two

IT WASN'T UNTIL THE following summer that Susan could bring herself to return to the woods, to what was left, had been spared by the fire. She was saddened by the charred desolation she found. The flames had consumed more than leaf and bough; time, also, had been voraciously devoured, leaving behind a sinister vacuum, unrecognizable and uncommunicative. The revels of youth were not only past but now as if they had never been. No longer could the unchanged woodland with its sweetly redolent shadows freshen and replenish.

It was worse than she had expected; it had been a total assault upon the very heart of their treasured playland, from where out of the bright crystals of time so many memories had been shaped. Once she could have come here and by standing still in some mote-swirled shaft of sunlight—itself like the incarnation of a blessing—hear again those child-voices deep in the woods, coming from all directions at once through the lavish foliage. But now it was gone, generations of trees and a lifetime of memory, replaced by scorched and sullen gloom. Today the silence was empty, unechoed, lost. The shyly returned flowers and the shade and the untouched trees that remained were not hers, but vales and bowers awaiting other gamboling feet and other wind-borne voices, chrysalis for other begetters of memories who would be unmindful of the dethroned children of the fallen paradise.

The past had died; the future remained, still a wide and untried expanse rolling with limitless fertility and welcome, waiting to be filled with those shouts of fearless and striving joy which the shouters always feel are so unique and compelling but which are as old as time, as they seize their chance to leap into the tidal currents of unreckoning ambition. For them the woods would renew and lift fresh flowers and raise new towers of leaf and branch; or maybe for them it would be vastly different, as already the ring of the ax was being heard around the woodland margins as more and more people were appearing in Capstone to till and cultivate, and more houses, and more stores, and talk of a new, larger school, and—paradoxically—less and less to till and cultivate. And that new phrase, which she was hearing with increasing frequency, as though in it lay some panacea, some magical spring into the future: "When the war is over": as if the war in its unspeakable horror and frenzy had mixed into its blood some ingredient powerfully creative and buoyant. There was a kind of desperation in the phrase, men saying, in effect, "if something forward-marching and better doesn't come of this madness, if we can't beat those swords into not just plowshares but engines and machines, then it'll be damnation of another kind."

She walked slowly through the burned-down woods, past blackened rocks and scorched trunks, toward where the fire had finally become tired of hissing and tossing and begun to thin its waves. Tiring, she sat upon the trunk of a fallen tree. She closed her eyes and lowered her head. She missed her Ben. She wondered if this sense of emptiness would continue always, if it was possible for pain to finally curl into nostalgia. She missed him in all weathers and in all seasons. She missed him now, amid the barrenness of vanished idylls, and she had missed him most of all during his re-creation, those thirty-six hours of unremitting, laborious fear and agony, missed his strong hand and the communication of its love and its strength. *Lord God*, the midwife said, with her spartan's eyes for pain. *Push, push, girl. Push!* Lying on the soaked and twisted sheets, watching that incredible woman finally reach down and lift the foot of the bed from the floor and drop it, lift it and drop it, lift it and drop it. But still not yet. Still more crushing pain and whatever release piercing screaming allowed. A night, a day, another night of it. And that woman watching her, by sunlight and by lamplight, with features etched into cracked parchment, like a face awaiting the immortality of its daguerreotype, as if gazing into all of oncoming time, proud and defiant before all of those unborn strangers who might look upon her face centuries after she was dead. Finally Susan hated that face and concentrated the wrath of her constricting agony upon it and drove herself into deliverance, pumping those corded abdominal muscles with gritted determination. *Lord God*, the midwife said, wrapping the bawling small-fisted infant in a coverlet, *it's almost like he didn't want to be born, like he was fighting it.* And she lay there panting and sobbing, face glistening with tears and perspiration, surviving now solely upon the savagery of pride.

She rose from the tree trunk and walked again, further into the woods, where the fire had not been, where the overarching trees allowed cool shade and shadowed silence. She paused for a moment, lacing together her fingers. Closing her eyes, she transcended the stillness, and through a deep, deep savoring of memory heard faintly the lilt of crystalline voices and tumbling laughter etching golden afternoons.

Her princes, her cavaliers. Deep, deep unto memory: her boys, her knaves, her men.